The Russian Library

GENERAL EDITOR

ROBERT PAYNE

TITLES IN PRINT, FALL, 1967

IN PREPARATION

THE TALE OF THE
Unextinguished Moon
AND
OTHER STORIES

THE TALE OF THE
Unextinguished
Moon
AND OTHER STORIES

by Boris Pilnyak *[handwritten: pseud. of Boris Andreevich Vogau]*

TRANSLATED BY

Beatrice Scott

WITH AN INTRODUCTION BY

Robert Payne

WSP

WASHINGTON SQUARE PRESS, INC. • NEW YORK • 1967

CONTENTS

vii

BORIS PILNYAK

It sometimes happens in a time of great upheaval that a writer emerges who possesses exactly those qualities necessary for recording his chaotic age. Such men seem to have spent their early lives in training for the catastrophes they will live through, and they have steeled themselves to be calm amid calamities which drive other men out of their minds. They are schooled in sciences not taught in schools, and they know things that are dangerous to know. Prepared to pit themselves against an all-encompassing anarchy, they calmly survey the ground to find the vantage point from which the anarchy can be best observed. They know the escape routes and the rare places of shelter, and they know better than most what is at stake. They have studied the seismographs and they can calculate exactly when and where the earthquake will take place. When the earthquake finally erupts, they walk through the ravaged land with an enviable self-assurance.

Such men are rare, for it is not in the general nature of men to be detached in the midst of holocausts, and there are few men who are completely without illusions. Some very special qualities are demanded from these men: a proper heredity, much knowledge in many cultures, a hunter's eye. One could imagine such a man in the years shortly before the Russian revolution. He would be perhaps the son of a provincial doctor, brought up in many different regions of Russia, of mixed blood, with an Oriental strain in him, learned in many languages, much traveled, undistinguished in appearance, able to lose himself in the crowd. He would see himself always as a foreigner in his own land, and he would wear his detachment like a garment. He would regard all sciences as his proper field, and he would prepare himself methodically for the coming cataclysm, regarding it with no more emotion than a scientist observing the fall of an avalanche. Only one overwhelming passion would master him: the need to understand. Only one fate would be reserved for him: he too would perish in the cataclysm.

Such a man was Boris Pilnyak, who wrote about the years of the Russian revolution with superb artistry and died in Stalin's prison.

His real name was Boris Andreyevich Vogau. He was born on September 29, 1894, the son of a veterinary surgeon descended from German colonists who settled on the Volga in the reign of Catherine the Great. His mother came from an old merchant family in Saratov. On his father's side there was German and a trace of Jewish blood; his mother was partly Slav and Tartar. When he was born the family was living in Mozhaisk, some seventy miles from Moscow. Mozhaisk was as old as Moscow, saturated with ancient history, and the battle of Borodino had been fought near a small village on the outskirts of the town. There he grew up, and on one winter day at the age of nine, watching the icy wind driving people helter-skelter down the street outside the window, he wrote his first poem. It was not a very satisfactory or memorable poem, but it described the rage of the elements outside and the quietness within the house. For the rest of his life he was to study the raging elements from the quietness of his intellectual house.

He was about ten when his wandering life began, for his father was continually on the move. For a while they lived in Bogorodsk, another small provincial town in Moscow province. Shortly afterward they moved to Kolomna, which was even more ancient than Mozhaisk, with its crumbling fortress and medieval towers. Suddenly, when he was about thirteen, the family moved to Saratov on the Volga, where the boy went to high school. It was his first visit to the Volga region, and he was intoxicated by the wide-open spaces of the steppe and the small villages clustered along the banks of the river. He was beginning to learn languages, which he collected as other boys collect postage stamps.

It was a happy family, the father intense and methodical, the mother kindly and expansive. The doctor read widely, and had accumulated a large library. Both parents were sympathetic to the popular movements of the eighties and nineties, and endlessly discussed the politics of the time. In St. Petersburg and Moscow the Populist movement had come to a dead end, but it survived in the provinces, being especially prevalent along the Volga. Boris thought of becoming a doctor or a scientist, two occupations especially favored by the Populists, but the urge for travel led him to study modern languages almost exclusively, and in 1913 he graduated from the Nizhni Novgorod Academy of Modern Languages. Two years earlier he had already published his first short story.

He was still unformed, still searching for a way of life. He was convinced he would become a philosopher, a writer, a traveler. He was living in Kolomna when he read Andrey Biely's novel *St. Petersburg,* which had been first published in 1911. In that experimental novel Biely deliberately strained all the resources of the Russian language, changed the shapes of sentences, accelerated the rhythms, and gave it a new and more exciting tempo. By a prodigal display of virtuosity he was able to invent a new kind of speech—harsh, sardonic, brilliantly colored, more in keeping with the violence of the times. Like a magician Biely had released unsuspected forces hidden within the language; for the first time it was provided with a jagged cutting edge.

Although Biely's experiments were largely based on his study of music, and the self-conscious virtuoso was always getting in the way of the novelist, the experiment was so successful that it spawned a generation of imitators. Biely's mind moved among ideas, and he had difficulty in depicting people. *St. Petersburg,* for all its brilliance, was a closed circle, and the ideas, however wonderfully expressed, never escaped into real life. The theme of the novel was the assassination of Senator Apollon Ableukhov by his own son Nikolay; the time was 1905, the year of revolutionary violence; the instrument of the assassination was a bomb concealed in a sardine can. Biely had devised a language more powerful than his theme, and he could not prevent the novel from soaring at intervals into farce. What if that many-colored, rich, abrupt and menacing language were used to depict not some imaginary and improbable assassination but the lives of the Russian people?

Pilnyak did not imitate Biely's style; he humanized it, gave it weight and substance, a stronger music. He showed that abrupt changes of mood, accelerating rhythms, staccato conversations, and the deliberate creation of extended poetic images to convey the inner life of a character could be used

even more effectively to describe peasants and railroad workers, landlords and foresters, birds and beasts. He had a special
sympathy for animals, and he enjoyed setting them to music
in his prose. He was a provincial, rooted in the countryside,
with a lingering distrust of city dwellers. Where Biely aimed
for virtuosity, Pilnyak aimed for urgency, the naked impact of
life.

In his own day Biely was a giant, for he not only revolu-
tionized the Russian language, but he also acted as the
supreme instigator of talent. He performed an immense service
to Russian literature, which has never been adequately recognized. But he had his weaknesses. He was a follower of
Rudolf Steiner, the Austrian mystical writer. Pilnyak chose a
sterner master. It was said of him that he carried throughout
his life a dog-eared copy of the surviving works of Heraclitus,
who dreamed of worlds in flames and spoke of "the thunderbolt which drives all things in their course." Steiner played
with ideas; Heraclitus took them by the throat. Pilnyak saw
the world through the eyes of the long-dead Greek philosopher.

By 1915 Pilnyak was already showing that he had mastered
the new language. In that year he published "Above the
Ravine," a short story about an eagle living in its eyrie high
above a desolate ravine. It is a remarkable work for a man of
twenty-one, for he was able to penetrate into the eagle's
mind, seeing the world through the eagle's eyes. The torment
and violence of its brief existence were expressed in a prose
which mirrored the sound of the wind rippling through its
feathers, the sudden spaces of the sky. His eagle lives and
breathes. Grown old and weary, the eagle at last dies and
falls to the bottom of the ravine, where it is devoured by
wolves. It is a pitiless story told with sympathy and uncanny
insight. In much the same way he would describe a few years
later the lives of the Russian people caught up in their terrible catastrophe.

For Pilnyak the Russian revolution was never anything so
simple as a war between the Bolsheviks and the rest. He saw
it as a sudden release of primitive energy; vast ancestral forces
were at work; and all Russian history, and all the ancient
customs of the Russian people, were implicated. It was an
upheaval which had little enough to do with Lenin and his

leather-jacketed Chekists. Old traditions had broken beneath the weight of history, and what was left was a surging mass of desperate people searching for a new way of life, a new understanding. Cities died overnight. Whole provinces were decimated by famine. Russia had abandoned history altogether and entered into legend.

Such an attitude gave him a greater insight into the character of the revolution. The Bolsheviks despised the peasants with whom Pilnyak sympathized. He could see the world as the peasants saw it, observing how in the midst of civil war they still followed the rituals of the seasons and worshiped their ancient gods.

Bells tolled above the spring earth. Typhus, hunger and death walked the villages and huts. The blind huts stood as before, their rotten thatch waving in the wind as it had waved five hundred years ago when it was removed each spring and carried deeper into the forest, toward the east. There was death in each hut. In all of them someone in high fever under the icons was yielding up his soul to God in the same way that he had lived his life—quietly, cruelly, wisely. There was hunger in each hut. Each hut was lit with torches in the evenings, and they made fire by striking flints as they had done five hundred years before. The living carried the dead to church, and the spring bells tolled. The living in their confusion walked the fields in procession behind the Cross, and they went round the villages, sprinkling them with holy water and blessing the hedgerows; they prayed for the corn, and that they might be spared from death, and the sound of the bells broke on the spring air. At twilight the songs of the young women still rang out: at this hour they came to the barrow in their bright homespun garments and sang old songs, since spring was coming and the time was ripe for childbirth. The young men had left for the cruel war; now they were stationed near the Urals near Ufa, near Archangel. This spring the old men would come out to plow the earth.

So he wrote in 1919, in a short story called "A Thousand Years." The story describes the breakup of the feudal estate of Prince Vilyashev, whose title was a thousand years old. Pilnyak half sympathises with the Prince, for he too is a part of Russian history and belongs to the Russian earth. The princely family was predatory and ruthless; now the tables are turned, and the people have taken possession of his property, becoming more predatory and ruthless than the princes had ever been. Prince Vilyashev bows to the inevitable and wanders away from the estate with the air of a man who knows there is a debt to be paid.

It is a theme which constantly returns in Pilnyak's stories. We meet it again in "The Bielkonsky Estate," written in 1918, and in "The Old House," written in 1924, and it is the central theme of the novel *The Naked Year,* which appeared in 1922.

With *The Naked Year* Pilnyak showed himself to be the supreme master of his craft. It was as though all his life, all his experiences, all his travels during the years of revolution and civil war, were a preparation for that work of superb artistry and chaotic violence. His canvas was all of Russia. There are no heroes, no protagonists: only the living body of Russia. There is the sense of vast spaces, of elemental winds pouring out of the frozen north and reducing the country to a state of stupor. A train winds through the steppe with its cargo of human squalor; no one knows where he is going; the wolves are waiting at the bottom of the ravine. Then, quite suddenly and very briefly, Pilnyak presents us with vivid portraits seen obliquely in the harsh light of a wintry dawn or in the high noon of summer. The faces pass. Some will return again. He is not concerned to tell a story so much as to build an elaborate musical form which will portray the voice of Russia in its agony.

The prodigious achievement of *The Naked Year* lies in the fact that he captures the living voice of his time: the sighs, the groans, the cries of the newborn, the mutterings of the dying, the clatter of machines, the humming of telegraph wires, the chugging of locomotives as they sweep across the Russian plains at night. He conveys the precise accents of the aristocrats, the barking orders of the men in leather jackets, the interminable garrulous monologues of peasants. At the same time he was able to suggest the totality of an experience which for most men was limited and parochial. He had the eagle's eye. He saw Russia in its immensity, and sometimes the eagle would swoop down and see some detail which gave depth and significance to the whole.

The Bolshevik critics were less than pleased with *The Naked Year*. They objected that the novel was fashioned out of a multitude of short stories, that it scarcely mentioned the Bolsheviks, and that it was concerned with life in the provinces. Trotsky, the commander in chief of the Red Army, objected that the Red Army was never mentioned, and he observed that whenever Pilnyak introduces a Bolshevik, he is treated with respect, a little coldly, as though he were a foreigner who had strayed into the novel by accident. What did Pilnyak know about "the industrial proletariat," who had brought the revolution into existence? "Pilnyak has robbed the city of its glory," he announced, and went on to demand an apology.

Pilnyak remained impenitent. He had welcomed the revolution, although his reasons were diametrically opposed to Trotsky's. He regarded Lenin and Trotsky as barbarians who had let loose the age-old forces of anarchy upon the country. The flood tide had come, and the old order had been drowned in it. When the flood subsided, there would be a new and altogether different Russia, which would have nothing in common with the blueprints of the communists. Like Heraclitus he saw the world given over to perpetual flux. Meanwhile his task was not to shore up the Bolshevik ruin, but simply to describe Russia as she was, as she had been in the remote past, as she would be in the future. He had created a symphonic panorama: his theme was Russia, not the Bolsheviks.

The Naked Year became deservedly famous and went into many editions. He was recognized as a writer of formidable power, whose work would survive long after him. Even the Bolsheviks came to recognize his authority; and in a long essay devoted to the novel, Trotsky saluted him for his realism and sharpness of vision, while maintaining that he had got everything wrong.

In 1923 Pilnyak published his collected works in three volumes. He wrote in the preface:

I have collected here everything I have written from the beginning of my working life as an author, and I consider this the wisest course because I shall now never need to return to these books again. They are now being published as I wish them to remain permanently. I have failed my readers. My stories and tales have been published in such a haphazard way: extracts from the short stories became chapters in the longer tales or the tales became scattered into stories. There are many reasons. The principal reason is our Russian flood tide, and then too every day things had to be contrived afresh, a hut and flour exchanged for a desk, the desk for hay-making dawns, the pen for a spade. Manuscripts were lost, or were mixed up. It was impossible to tell where they were, when they would be published, and, when published, whether they would reach the reader. And then it would be necessary to change everything.

But the flood tide is now over. As I collected my manuscripts, sorted and reread them, I realized two things very clearly: I realized that everything I have written and collected here is already past history, and I realized too that the hero of these three books is always one and the same person—myself, my life, my thoughts and actions. And if in some thirty or forty years someone in a new generation reads these books and thinks about them, he will experience the very life blood of a man who lived through those wonderful years of Russian storm and flood tide and will smile at my delirium and excuse my romanticism, the romanticism of "a blithe spirit" visiting the world "in a fateful hour." This justifies my efforts and these three books, to which I will return again in this way.

I dedicate these books to my wife, Marya Alexeyevna Sokholov-Vogau, and to my children, Natalya and Andrey—to my wife because without her I would not have written them, and to my children because they are to read them in the future, and I, like all Russia, live only for the future.

The preface has been quoted in full, because it is one of the rare passages in which Pilnyak speaks of his personal life and hints at his motives. There is a sense in which these words were his swan song. Rarely again would he write as well as he wrote in those three volumes. When the civil war was over, he seemed to be a man in search of a theme. The urgency had gone out of him. He would write brilliantly, cogently, in that jagged prose which is the despair of his translators, but something had died in him. He traveled abroad, visited England, France, the United States, China and Japan, wrote *reportages,* short stories and novels, and generally hewed to the party line. He was a man accustomed to walking tightropes, and he could usually convey his real feelings in the spaces between the lines.

Sometimes he was bolder. In "The Tale of the Unextinguished Moon," the story which has been printed first in this book because it was an act of extraordinary human courage, and also because it possesses a remarkable intensity, he attacked Stalin. In December, 1925, Stalin had given orders that Mikhail Frunze, Trotsky's successor as Commissar of War, should submit to an operation in the Kremlin Hospital. It was widely believed that Frunze's death on the operating table was not due to the carelessness of the surgeons but to the direct intervention of Stalin, who feared Frunze's rising popularity. Pilnyak decided to tell the story in fictional form. He would tell it very simply, without orchestration. He would enter quietly into the minds of Frunze and Stalin, and attempt to show how the murder came about.

In the story Stalin is never identified by name; he becomes "the man who never stoops," ruling Russia from a room with an English fireplace and a desk covered with a red cloth. There are three telephones and a holder for the red and blue pencils which the dictator liked to use. The Army commander Nikolay Gavrilov is seen first on a gray autumn morning when his special train is shunted into a siding; he has been summoned to the capital, but has no idea why he has been summoned until he is shown the newspapers, which announce that he has been ordered to submit to an operation for a gastric ulcer. We see Gavrilov talking to "the man who never stoops," to his closest friend, and to the doctors who must perform the operation. In House No. 1, "the man who never stoops" waits calmly for the inevitable report from the operating theater, and then makes his way to the hospital to pay his final respects to the man he has murdered. He seizes Gavrilov's hand and murmurs, "Farewell, comrade! Farewell, brother!" and orders a state funeral.

Pilnyak describes these events so quietly and convincingly that we are scarcely aware of the formidable artistry which has gone into the story. We are made to understand how such a murder could take place, and how it was inevitable that such murders should take place. Although "the man who never stoops" is seen only briefly, his menacing presence remains long after the story has been read.

"The Tale of the Unextinguished Moon" was written in the early months of 1927, when the memory of Frunze's death was still fresh. With a dedication to the Marxist critic Alexander Voronsky, it was published in the May issue of *Novy Mir* and in 1927 appeared in a collection by that name in Germany. The police confiscated all the copies they could lay their hands on, but many copies had already reached subscribers through the mails. The June issue of *Novy Mir* contained Voronsky's protest. "The story has been dedicated to me," he wrote. "I regard this dedication as the greatest possible insult to me as a Communist, and I fear it will cast a shadow on my reputation as a Party member. I indignantly reject the dedication."

Surprisingly, Pilnyak went unpunished. He continued to write and to publish his works, and from time to time he would travel abroad. At last in 1937, during the great purges, the thunderbolt which drives all things in their course caught up with him. Stalin, who never forgave or forgot, ordered him to be shot. It was the year when hundreds of thousands of Russians were being shot, and there were no obituaries.

THE TALE OF THE
Unextinguished Moon
AND
OTHER STORIES

The
Tale of the
Unextinguished Moon

At daybreak factory sirens hooted all over the town. The gray murk of mists, of night and frost, pushed its way through the alleys, indicating that the dawn too would be gloomy, gray and frozen. It was the hour when the rotary machines were releasing the latest editions of newspapers in the printing works and soon boys would come running from the dispatch office and scatter in all directions with bundles of papers. Clearing his throat, first one and then another would begin to shout at empty crossroads the phrase he was to go on shouting all day long:

"Revolution in China! Commander Gavrilov's arrival! Illness of Gavrilov!"

At this moment a train arrived in the station where trains arrive from the south. This was a special train and at its end a dark-blue salon compartment gleamed silently, guards at the footboard and drawn curtains over the mirror-like windows. The train had emerged from a dark night and fields which had run through the splendors of summer and become wintry, having been raided in the summer harvests so that they might age in winter. The train passed slowly and silently under the station roof and came to a halt in a siding. The platform was deserted. Reinforcements of militiamen with green stripes stood in the doorways as if by chance. Three

military men with diamond-shaped insignia on their sleeves
entered the salon. Salutes were being exchanged there. The
three stood on the footboard, the guard whispered something
to someone inside and then the three went up and disappeared behind the curtains. The electric light went on in the
carriage. Two military electricians were working by the carriage and getting a telephone connection fitted up from
below the station roof. Another man approached the carriage.
He wore an old between-seasons coat and an unseasonable fur
hat with ear flaps. This man saluted no one and no one
saluted him. He said:

"Tell Nikolay Ivanovich that Popov has arrived."

The Red Army man examined Popov slowly, noticed his
unpolished shoes and answered slowly:

"T' e comrade commander is not up yet."

Popov gave the soldier a friendly smile, and then for some
reason switched over to the less formal mode of address and
said in a friendly way:

"Go along, my dear chap, go along and tell him that Popov
has arrived."

The Red Army man went and returned. Then Popov
climbed up into the compartment. Because the curtains were
drawn and the electric light was on, it still seemed to be night
in the salon. On a table beside a lamp lay an open book and
near it a plate with some unfinished semolina pudding; behind
that, there lay an open Colt holster with a leather strap like
a small snake. At the other end of the table stood some
opened bottles. The three military men with diamond-shaped
insignia sat in leather armchairs, away from the table, along
the wall, very modestly, at attention, with briefcases in their
hands. Popov pushed by to the other side of the table, took
off his coat and hat, put them down beside him, picked up the
open book and had a look at it. An attendant, quite uncon-
cerned about anything, came in to clear the table. He put
the bottles aside somewhere, swept the pomegranate skins up
onto a tray, spread a cloth, put a solitary glass in a holder
there, a plate with some stale bread, an egg cup, and fetched
two eggs on a saucer, salt and some medicine bottles. He held
up a corner of the curtain, examined the morning, opened
the curtains, the drawstrings hissing sadly, and put out the

electric light; a gray, frosty, autumnal morning crept into the salon. Everyone's face looked yellow in this dull morning light—a weak, watery light like the ichor of the gods. An orderly took up his position next to the attendant by the door. The office in the field was already at work and a telephone rang out.

Then the commander entered the salon from his sleeping compartment. He was not very tall, broad-shouldered, fair, and his long hair was brushed back. His battle jacket, which had four diamonds on the sleeve and was made of the same green material as those of soldiers, did not fit neatly and was creased. The boots with spurs had been assiduously polished but their worn heels showed they had been long in use. This was a man whose name reflected the heroism of the whole civil war, the thousands upon thousands of people that had stood behind him, the thousands and thousands of deaths, the suffering, crippling, cold, the freezing and heat of the march, the roar of guns, the whistling of bullets, storms in the night, campfires, marches, victories, flights and again death. This was a man who commanded armies of thousands of men, who held sway over people, victory, death, with powder, smoke, broken bones, torn flesh, held sway over those victories which stormed on the home front with hundreds of red standards and enormous crowds, news of which was sent by radio round the whole world, those victories which were followed by the digging of deep pits in sandy-soiled Russian fields, pits for the corpses, into which thousands of human bodies were flung together. This was a man whose name was a military legend for valor in leadership, endless bravery, daring and steadfastness. This was a man who had the authority and power to send people out to kill those who were like themselves and to die.

A broad-shouldered, not very tall man entered the salon, with the kindly and slightly weary expression of a student. His gait was brisk and simultaneously reflected the cavalry officer and also the civilian with nothing military about him. The three staff officers stood to attention. The commander paused and made a gesture which allowed them to stand at ease, but did not shake hands. Each in turn stepped forward, stood to attention and made his report: "as entrusted to me," "in the

service of the revolution." The commander shook hands with
each man in turn, apparently paying no attention to their
reports. Then he sat down in front of the solitary glass, and
the attendant appeared to pour out some tea from a shining
teapot. The commander took an egg.

"How are things going?" he asked simply, ignoring the
reports.

One of the three told him the latest news and then asked
in his turn:

"How are you yourself, Comrade Gavrilov?"

The commander's expression was momentarily aloof and
he answered unwillingly:

"I've been to the Caucasus to have treatment. Now I'm
better." He was silent for a moment. "Now I'm quite well."
Silence again. "Give orders—no ceremonies, no guards of
honor." Silence. "You are free to go, comrades."

The three staff officers got up to take their leave. The
commander did not get up, but shooks hands with each one,
and they left the salon quietly. When the commander had
come in, Popov had not greeted him, but had picked up the
book and turned aside, thumbing through the book. The
commander glanced at him, but refrained from greeting him,
as if he had not noticed him. When the staff officers had left,
the commander asked Popov, as if they had met the night
before and there was no need for a greeting:

"Would you like some tea, Aleshka, or some wine?"

But Popov did not have time to reply, as the orderly
stepped forward to make a report. He said the car had been
removed from the platform, documents had arrived in the
office, one secret document had been brought by a secretary
from House No. 1, a flat had been prepared in the staff headquarters and a pile of telegrams and letters of congratulation
had arrived. The commander dismissed the orderly and said he
would remain on the train. The attendant did not wait for
Popov's reply, and placed a tea glass and a wineglass before
him. Popov clambered out of his corner and sat next to the
commander.

"How are you, Nikolasha?" asked Popov in the concerned way one would ask one's own brother.

"I'm quite all right now. Things have improved, I'm well

again, but for all I know you'll have to stand in the guard of honor by my coffin," Gavrilov answered, half joking, half serious, or at least in a joking way which hid his sadness.

These two, Popov and Gavrilov, were bound by an old friendship, had struggled together in the underground movement, had worked together in a factory, long ago in their youth, when they had begun as weavers. Then they had served a prison sentence together and later followed the life of typical professional revolutionaries—exile, escape, underground work, deportation, exile, escape, emigration, Paris, Vienna, Chicago. And after the storms in 1914 came Brindisi, Salonika, Roumania, Kiev, Moscow, Petersburg and finally, after the thunder of October, 1917, the roar of guns over the Moscow Kremlin, one became chief of staff of the Red cavalry regiment in Rostov on the Don and the other became a leader of the proletarian nobility, as Rykov puts it, in Tula, so that for one there were wars, victories, command over guns, people, death, and for the other, provincial committees, executive committees, conferences, meetings, reports. Both concentrated all their lives and thoughts on the greatest revolution in the world, the greatest cause of justice and truth. But they always remained to one another simply Nikolasha, Alexey, Aleshka, and always comrades, weavers, without ranks or formalities.

"Tell me about your health, Nikolasha," asked Popov.

"Well, you see, I had, and perhaps still have, a gastric ulcer. You know how it is—pain, vomiting with blood, frightful heartburn, a filthy business." The commander spoke quietly, leaning over toward Alexey. "I was sent to the Caucasus for treatment. The pain went, I returned to work, worked for six months and then the vomiting and pain began again, and again I went to the Caucasus. Now the pain has stopped and I even drank a bottle of wine to check." The commander interrupted himself. "Aleshka, perhaps you'd like some wine. I brought you a whole case; it's over there under the bench. Open up a bottle!"

Popov sat, propping up his head on his hand, and answered:

"No, I don't drink in the morning. Go on with what you were saying."

"Well, my health is in good order." The commander was silent a moment. "Aleshka, do you know why they have sent for me?"

"I don't know."

"I had instructions to come here, straight from the Caucasus. I haven't even been to see my wife." The commander was silent again. "The devil only knows what it's all about. Everything is in order as regards the Army, there aren't any congresses, nothing."

The commander probably did not notice that when he began to talk about the Army, he stopped being a weaver and became an Army leader, a Red general of the Red Army. And when he spoke about their days at Orgkhuvo, he probably did not notice that he became a weaver again, the same weaver who fell in love with a schoolteacher, for love of whom he polished his boots and went barefoot as far as the school, only putting on his boots in the woods close to the school so that the boots should not get dusty, the teacher for whose sake he bought a fancy suit and a hat à la devil-knows-what, yet they never got beyond discussing books; there was no romance, the schoolteacher rejected him. The weaver-commander was a good, friendly man who knew how to joke and had a sense of humor. He joked with his friend and only occasionally became the commander again and showed signs of anxiety. When he remembered the inexplicable summons, he began to move clumsily and then the healthy weaver discussed the sick commander: "I'm a field marshal, a well-known senator, but I can't eat buckwheat! Fate plays with a man and you can't get rid of the words in an old song."

"Nikolasha, tell me sensibly, what do you suspect?" said Popov. "What were you babbling about when you spoke of a guard of honor?"

The commander did not answer at once, then said slowly:

"I met Potap in Rostov"—he gave the Party name of one of the chief revolutionaries of the famous group in 1918—"and, well, he said, he tried to convince me that I must have an operation, cut the ulcer out or stitch it up or something —tried to convince me in a very suspicious way! I feel I'm quite well and my whole being resists the idea of an operation, I don't want it—I'll get better without it. I haven't any more pain, I've put on weight and—damn it—I'm a grown-up man, an old man already, a senator, and here I go gazing at my belly! I feel ashamed." The commander was silent and picked up the open book. "I'm reading the old man, Tolstoy— *Childhood and Youth*. The old man wrote well and he had a feeling for life and life's blood. . . . I've seen a good deal of blood in my time but—an operation! I'm as scared of that as a little boy, I don't want it, they'll butcher me! The old man really understood about human blood."

An orderly came in, stood to attention, made a report: a messenger had come from Staff Headquarters to say a car had been sent to take the commander to House No. 1, where he was expected, new telegrams had arrived, someone had called for a parcel from the south. The orderly put a batch of newspapers on the table. The commander dismissed him and gave orders to have his army coat ready. He opened a newspaper. In the column where the most important events of the day were listed there was the heading: "COMMANDER GAVRILOV'S ARRIVAL," and on the third page it said: "Commander Gavrilov is to arrive today. He has temporarily left the Army in order to undergo an operation for a gastric ulcer." This same statement continued: "Comrade Gavrilov's health gives rise to some concern, but the specialists guarantee that the operation has the best prognosis."

This old soldier of the revolution, a commander, a military leader, who had sent thousands to their death, in the service of the machinery of war which predestines killing, dying, conquering by bloodshed, Gavrilov, leaned back against his chair, wiped his brow with his hand, looked fixedly at Popov and said:

"Do you hear that, Aleshka? That's serious! Well, what am I to do?" and he shouted, "Orderly, my coat!"

II

A house with columns stood behind a railing at the crossroads of two major streets where cars, people, dray horses passed in an endless procession. There was no sign to indicate the importance of this house. Two guards in steel helmets stood by the gates, surmounted with griffins. People flowed past the house, the hooting of cars, a crowd, human time elapsed, a gray day flowing past, news vendors, men with briefcases, women with skirts to the knee and stockings that deceived the eye into thinking they were bare-legged—but beyond the griffins at the gates, time was in abeyance, time stood still. And another house stood at the other end of the town, with the same classical architecture, also with railings and columns, with its wings and the terrifying visages of mythological gargoyles on its bas-reliefs. This house had double gates, where fauns grimaced, and two sentry boxes with benches, and there guards sat in protective great coats, in boots, and with copper name plates on their great coats. A closed black car stood by the gates, with red crosses and the label "FIRST AID."

The leading article in the main newspaper that day spoke about "a three-year plan for the gold standard," showing that a solid currency could exist only "when the whole economic life of the country is established on a firm basis, a firm economic basis. If the national economy exceeds its budget, a solid financial system will inevitably suffer." Headlines proclaimed "CHINA'S STRUGGLE AGAINST IMPERIALISM." A side column contained telegrams from England, France, Germany, Czechoslovakia, Latvia and America. Lower down there was a long article headed: "THE PROBLEM OF REVOLUTIONARY VIOLENCE." Two pages were devoted to advertisements and held the statement in large print: "SYPHILIS IS A FACT OF LIFE." A new book by S. Broide was reviewed: *In a Lunatic Asylum*.

At noon, a Rolls-Royce drew up by House No. 1, the house where time slowed down. The watchman opened the door and the commander got out of the limousine.

In the farthest corner of the house there was a study, its windows half-curtained, and a street ran past the windows. A fire was burning in the study. On the red baize of the desk there were three telephones, which emphasized the silence and the crackling of the logs on the fire. These were three city arteries which held sway over the town in the silence, held information about everything in the town and about its entire circulation. On the desk there was a massive bronze writing set with about a dozen red and blue pencils stuck into the penholder. Behind the desk there was fixed to the wall of the study a radio with two earphones as well as a row of bells, from the bell ringing in the antechamber to the bell sounding the general alarm. Behind the desk on a wooden chair in this study sat the man who never stoops. The curtains were half-drawn, the electric light was burning behind the green shade of the reading lamp and the face of this man could not be distinguished in the shadows.

The commander crossed the carpet and sat down in the leather armchair.

Then the man who never stoops said:

"Gavrilov, it's not the moment to discuss the millstone of the revolution. The wheel of history, unfortunately, as I think, moves largely by the force of death and blood—especially the wheel of revolution. It's not for us to discuss death and blood. Do you remember how together we led the naked Red Army men to attack Ekaterinov? You had a rifle, and so did I. Your horse was blown to pieces and you went ahead on foot. One man began to run and you shot that man so that the rest would not panic. You were the commander and you would have shot me too, if I had turned coward, and, I believe, you would have been right."

Then, the commander said:

"Goodness, what a setup you have here, quite the minister. Do you allow smoking? I don't see any cigarette butts."

"Don't smoke. It's not good for your health. I don't smoke either."

Gavrilov said quickly and sternly:

"Talk straight! Why have you brought me here? Don't let's have any diplomacy. Out with it!"

The man who never stoops said:

"I called you here because it is necessary for you to undergo an operation. You are essential to the revolution. I've summoned the specialists and they say that you'll be on your feet again within a month. The revolution demands this. The specialists are waiting to examine you and they know all about it. I have already given the order. There's even a German specialist."

Gavrilov said:

"You can do as you please, but I shall smoke all the same.

My doctors have told me that I don't need an operation and everything will heal by itself. I feel perfectly well, an operation is unnecessary and I don't want to have one."

The man who never stoops pushed a button on the wall behind him and a secretary entered silently. "Is anyone waiting for an interview?" The secretary said yes. There was no reply and the secretary was dismissed.

The man who never stoops said:

"Comrade Commander, do you remember the time when we discussed whether we should send four thousand men to certain death? You gave the order to send them. You did right. You'll be on your feet again in three weeks. Forgive me, but I have already given the order."

The telephone rang, an internal telephone which had only some thirty or forty lines—not the city telephone. He took up the receiver, listened, asked a question, said, "A memorandum to the French government? Of course, an official one, as we decided yesterday. You remember, don't you: it's like fishing for trout—the French are slippery customers. What? Yes, just invent something."

He said:

"Forgive me, but there's nothing further to discuss, Comrade Gavrilov."

The commander finished his cigarette, pushed the stub among the red and blue pencils, got up.

"Good-bye."

"Good-bye, for now."

The commander walked over the red carpets and left the building. At the gate the Rolls-Royce carried him into the noise of the streets. The man who never stoops remained in the study. No one else came to see him. Upright, he sat over his papers with a thick red pencil in his hand. He rang for the secretary and said, "Tell someone to remove the stub from this tray here!"

And then again he fell silent over his papers, the red pencil in his hand. An hour passed and then another, and he remained at work. Once the telephone rang, he listened and said, "Two million rubles in galoshes and manufactured goods for Turkestan to close a trade gap? Yes, go ahead!

Good-bye!" An attendant came in quietly and put a tray on a little table by the window, with a glass of tea and a slice of cold meat covered with a napkin, and went out again. Then the man who never stoops again rang for the secretary and asked, "Is the secret summary ready?" and when the secretary replied that it was, asked him to bring it. And again the man sat silent for a long time over a lengthy list with important matters from the People's Commissariat for Foreign Affairs, the political and economic departments of the OGPU, the Commissariats for Finance, Foreign Trade and Labor. Then a man and another man came into the room—the others of the triumvirate.

At four o'clock, several cars drew up in front of House No. 2. The house was wrapped in mist as if the mist could warm its rancid damp. Two militiamen took up their positions at the gates beside the guards in their great coats and boots. Two others stood by the front door. Kraskom, with two Orders of the Red Banner, supple as a whip, accompanied by two Red Army men, entered. A man in a white coat met Kraskom and the two men in the hall. "Yes, yes, you know . . ." The room was empty and large. A table covered in white oilcloth stood in the middle and there were chairs with high backs, such as you see in railway stations, standing all around the table. A couch covered with oilcloth, a wooden stool beside it, was arranged by the wall. In a corner over the washbasin there was a glass shelf with various bottles bearing different names, a great bottle of mercury bichloride, a tin of green soap, and yellow, unbleached towels hung nearby. The first cars brought the professors, the specialists, therapists and surgeons.

People came in, exchanged greetings, and a tall, bearded, kind-faced, bald man acted as host.

Professor Lozovsky came up to him, a man of about thirty-five, wearing pince-nez with a straight nosepiece, his eyes staring from the corners of the lenses:

"Yes, yes, you know . . ."

The close-shaven man handed the bearded one an open envelope stamped with sealing wax. The latter took out a sheet of paper, adjusted his spectacles and began reading.

Then he touched his spectacles again and in some perplexity passed the paper to a third man.

The close-shaven man said pompously:

"As you see, a secret document, almost an order. I received it this morning. You understand?"

A first, a second, a third, fragments of discussion, quiet, hurried.

"What is the consultation for?"

"I received a special summons. The telegram was addressed to the Rector of the University."

"Commander Gavrilov, you know, the one who—"

"Yes, yes, you know, a revolution, the commander in chief, a formula and, if you please—"

"A consultation."

The electric light cast sharply defined shadows. One man took another by the button on the breast pocket of his white coat and a second put his hand under someone's arm to step past. . . .

Then Red Army men's rifles thundered in the doorway, their heels stamped and they were again frozen into immobility. A tall, wiry youth with the Order of the Red Banner on his chest stood to attention by the door, and then the commander quickly entered, pushing his hair back with his hand, adjusting the collar of his battle jacket, and saying:

"Good day, comrades! Would you like me to get undressed?"

Then the professors slowly sat down on the oilcloth-covered chairs around the table, put their elbows on the table, stretched their fingers, adjusted their spectacles and pince-nez and asked the patient to sit down.

The one in pince-nez who had handed over the letter said to the bearded man:

"Pavel Ivanovich, as *primus inter pares,* I imagine you will not refuse to take the chair?"

"Do you want me to undress?" asked the commander and his hand went to his collar.

The chairman, Pavel Ivanovich, appeared not to hear this question and he said slowly, as he took the chairman's place:

"I think we will ask the patient when his illness first came on and what pathological symptoms showed him he was ill. Later, we will make an examination."

A piece of paper covered in illegible professorial hand-writing resulted from this conference.

REPORT ON THE CONSULTATION IN WHICH PROFESSOR SUCH-AND-SUCH, SUCH-AND-SUCH [naming seven] TOOK PART:

The patient, Citizen Nikolay Ivanovich Gavrilov, presented with pain in the upper abdomen, vomiting and indigestion. He became ill gradually about two years ago. He has always received ambulatory treatment and has been to spas—without effect. At the request of the patient a conference was held consisting of the above-mentioned specialists.

Status praesens: The patient's general condition is satisfactory. Lungs—NAD. A slight dilation of the heart was remarked and an increased pulse rate. There is a mild neurasthenia. Nothing pathological was discovered as regards any other organs except the stomach. It was established that the patient apparently has an *ulcus ventriculi* and that an operation is essential.

The conference proposes that the operation should be carried out by Professor Anatoly Kosmich Lozovsky. Professor Pavel Ivanovich Kokosov has agreed to assist at the operation.

The name of the town, the date and the signatures of seven professors followed.

Subsequently, when the operation was over, it was established in private conversations that not a single specialist actually had considered that an operation was essential, but felt rather that the illness was taking its proper course and an operation was unnecessary. However, this was not discussed during the conference. Only the rather silent German suggested that an operation was unnecessary, but he did not insist after hearing the opinions of his colleagues. People also said that after the conference, when Professor Kokosov—the one whose eyes were clouded with hate—was getting into the car to drive to the Academy with Professor Lozovsky, he remarked, "Well, if a brother of mine had this trouble, I wouldn't start operating." To which Lozovsky answered, "No, of course not, but, after all, the operation isn't dangerous." The car revved up and moved off.

The man who never stoops was still sitting in his study
at House No. 1. The windows were heavily curtained. The
fire was burning as before. The house was wrapped in a
silence which seemed to have collected over the centuries. The
man sat in his wooden chair. Now he had large volumes
written in German and English open in front of him, and
he was writing in Russian, in ink, in a straight, clear hand.
The books spread out were on government, law and power.
Light fell from the ceiling and now the man's face was visible.
It was a very ordinary face, perhaps just a little harsh, but
certainly full of concentration and without a trace of tired-
ness. He sat over his books and notes for a long time. Then
he rang and a stenographer came in. He began to dictate. The
themes he discussed were the USSR, America, England; the
world and the USSR, English pounds sterling and Russian
tons of wheat, American heavy industry and Chinese labor.
The man spoke in a loud, firm voice and each of his phrases
was like a formula.

The moon shone over the town.

At this moment, the commander was with Popov in the
room of a hotel exclusively reserved for communists. There
were three of them. Gavrilov sat at the table and Natasha
jumped up and down on his knee. Gavrilov lighted matches.
Natasha gazed at the light in wonder, the wonder of a child
confronted with mystery. Natasha gazed at the light, made a
little pipe of her lips and began to blow, but she did not have
enough breath to blow the match out immediately and it took
some time. And then Natasha's blue eyes showed so much amazement, delight and fear when confronted with this wonder that
it was impossible not to submit also to the wonder that lay
in her. Then Gavrilov put Natasha to bed, sat down by her
bed and said, "Shut your eyes and I'll sing you a song," and
he began to sing, although he did not know how to sing, did
not know any songs, and just made it up as he went along:

> *A goat came in and said,*
> *"You sleep and sleep and sleep . . ."*

He smiled, looked at Natasha and Popov with a wily expression, and sang the first thing that came into his head to
rhyme with "sleep":

> *A goat came in and said,*
> *"You sleep and sleep and sleep . . .*
> *But not a peep, a peep, a peep. . . ."*

Natasha opened her eyes and smiled. Gavrilov went on singing the last two lines (he really had no voice at all) until she fell asleep.

Then Gavrilov and Popov drank tea together.

Popov said:

"Should I make you some semolina pudding, Nikolka?"

They sat opposite one another, spoke quietly and slowly, did not hurry, drank a good deal of tea, which Gavrilov sipped from the saucer, his collar undone. They talked about various things, and over the second glass of tea, when half was still left, Popov pushed his glass aside, fell silent and said:

"Nikolka, my Zina left me with the child on my hands. She's gone off with some engineer she had an affair with in the past. I haven't any desire to judge her, or to get involved in bad language, but still, it has to be said, she ran off like a bitch, without a word, keeping it dark! I feel ashamed! I picked up a human being from the bottom of the pile at the front. I was concerned for her, loved her and kept her warm, like a fool; I misjudged a woman who lived with me for five years."

And Popov told him all the petty details of their estrangement, which is always so tormenting just because of its pettiness, the details which prevent one from seeing the wood for the trees. Then they began to talk about their children and Gavrilov described his own family life, his three sons and his wife, who was getting on in years but remained the only one for him.

As he left, the commander said:

"Give me something to read, something straightforward, about good people, love—something like *Childhood and Youth*."

Popov had mountains of books heaped up in every corner, but a simple book about ordinary human love, ordinary relationships, life, sunlight, simple human happiness—a book like this was not to be found in his library.

"And that's the literature of the revolution for you,"

Gavrilov said jokingly. "Well, never mind, I'll read Tolstoy
again. The bit about the old gloves at the ball is very good."
Then his face darkened, he was silent and finally said
quietly:

"I didn't tell you, Aleshka, not to waste time in empty
talk. I saw the Chief today, and the specialists at the hospital.
The professors engaged in their professorial wisdom. I don't
want to be cut open. My whole nature rebels. Tomorrow I'm
to go under the knife. Then you come to the hospital and
don't forget the old days. Don't write anything to my wife and
children about it. Good-bye!" and Gavrilov left the room
without shaking hands.

A car stood by the hotel entrance. Gavrilov got in and said:
"Home, to the train," and the car moved off along the
streets. The moon slithered over the rails in the sidings. A dog
ran across, barked and was hidden in the black railroad
silence. A guard stood by the steps of the compartment and remained motionless when the commander entered. An orderly
appeared in the corridor, an attendant put his head out, the
electric light went on and a silent, blue, provincial quiet
descended on the compartment. The commander went through
to his bedroom compartment, took off his boots, put on some
slippers, unbuttoned the collar of his shirt and rang for some
tea. He went into the salon and sat by the table lamp. The
attendant brought some tea, but he left it untouched. The
commander sat over *Childhood and Youth* for a long time,
reading, thinking about the book. Then he went back to
the bedroom, got a writing pad, rang for some ink and began
to write slowly, pondering each phrase. He wrote one letter,
read it through, thought about it and sealed the envelope,
and then he wrote a second, and after a little thought sealed
that one too. And then he hurriedly wrote a third letter, a
short one, and this he sealed without rereading it. A deep
silence reigned in the compartment. The guard by the steps
was motionless. The orderly and the attendant in the corridor made no sound. Time seemed to stand still. The letters
lay in front of the commander for a long while in white
envelopes with the addresses written on them. Then he took
a large envelope, put all the three letters inside, sealed it and

wrote on this envelope: "To be opened in the event of my death."

III

On the day of Gavrilov's death the first snow fell. The city was muffled in icy silence, all white and quiet. Beyond the windows the blue tits, which had flown into town with the snow, scattered it from the branches of trees.

Professor Pavel Ivanovich Kokosov always woke at seven o'clock and this was the time he woke on the day of the operation.

The professor poked his head up out of the blankets, cleared his throat, stretched out a hairy arm and searched blindly on the bedside table for his spectacles, which he then planted on his nose, pushing the prongs into his hair. On a birch tree outside the window a blue tit was quarreling with the snow. The professor put on his dressing gown, pushed his feet into his house shoes and went into the bathroom.

It was quiet in the house when the professor got up but when, grunting a little, he left the bathroom and went to the dining room, his wife, Katerina Pavlovna, was already tinkling a spoon against his glass of tea as she served him with sugar, and the samovar was hissing. The professor came in to drink his tea in his dressing gown and slippers.

"Good morning, Pavel Ivanovich," said his wife.

"Good morning, Katerina Pavlovna," said her husband.

The professor kissed his wife's hand and sat down opposite her, fixing the prongs of his spectacles more comfortably in his hair. Silently he took a gulp of tea and was about to say something again. But the telephone interrupted their usual morning tea drinking. The telephone call was unusual. The professor glanced sternly at his study door where the telephone was ringing, looked suspiciously at his wife, an elderly, plump woman in a Japanese kimono, got up and walked over to the telephone with the air of a man who suspected trouble. He spoke into the telephone in a particularly grumpy, old man's voice:

"Yes, yes, I can hear you. Who is it? What do you want?"

They were ringing from Staff Headquarters and knew the operation was scheduled for half past eight. They wondered if they could be of any assistance and if the professor would like a car to be sent to fetch him. The professor suddenly lost his temper, breathed hard into the receiver and growled:

"I am a public servant, you know. I take no private patients. Let me tell you, sir, that I go to the clinic by streetcar sir. I shall do my duty according to my lights. I see no reason why I should not travel by streetcar today."

He replaced the receiver noisily, sniffed and snuffled and returned to the dining room to the tea and his wife. He sniffed a little longer, bit his mustache and very soon calmed down again. His eyes gazed from behind his glasses with an air of concentration and wisdom. He said quietly:

"When a peasant, Ivan, falls ill in his country village, he lies on the stove for about three weeks, then he says his prayers, coughs and moans, asks all his relatives for advice and finally sets off for the local hospital to see Dr. Pyetr Ivanovich. The doctor has known Ivan for fifteen years and Ivan has taken him a dozen and a half chickens during this time. He has got to know all the doctor's children and has even given one boy a box on the ears. Ivan will come in to see the doctor, and greet him with a chicken. The doctor will examine him, listen to him and if it is necessary he will perform an operation quietly and sensibly and do it no worse than I would. If the operation is not a success and Ivan dies, they will put up a cross to him and that's that. And even if some local inhabitant, say, Anatoly Yurivich Svintsitsky, comes to me and tells me the whole story down to the last detail, I too will examine him, maybe seven times over, get the full picture and say, "Well, my dear sir, go along and live with your ulcer. Take good care and you should live fifty years and if you die, well, that's God's will!" If he tells me to operate, I operate, but if he doesn't want an operation I would never force the issue."

The professor fell silent.

"Today I'm to assist in my own hospital at the operation of a Bolshevik, the Commander Gavrilov."

"That's the one," said Katerina Pavlovna, "the one who

is always in the Bolshevik papers—a terrifying name! Why aren't you operating yourself?"

"Of course, there isn't anything particularly terrifying about it, and as for Lozovsky operating, that's a sign of the times: the young are in fashion and have to make a name for themselves. But it's a fact that no one really knows this patient, even though all our experts examined him, shone lights at him, purged him and looked him over and over in all these consultations. No one knows the man himself—the most important thing of all. They are not dealing with a human being but with a cipher—General Such-and-such, about whom the papers write every day to strike terror into the hearts of the people. And just try slipping up, during this operation—they'll drag your name in the mud through all Europe."

Professor Anatoly Kosmich Lozovsky's room did not look at all like Kokosov's flat. If Kokosov's flat preserved something of the nineties and of the nineteenth century in Russia, Lozovsky's had originated in 1907 and conserved the years between then and 1916. There were heavy curtains, a wide divan, naked bronze women for the candlesticks on the oak desk, walls covered in carpets and on the carpets second-rate pictures from the "World of Art" exhibitions.

Lozovsky was asleep on the divan and not alone, but with a beautiful young woman. His starched collar was lying in a corner on the carpet. Lozovsky woke up, quietly kissed the woman's shoulder and got up energetically to pull the curtain cord. The heavy fabric shifted to one side and a snow-filled day entered the room. Lozovsky looked out at the street, the snow and the sky, cheerfully, as people do when they love the life in their own bodies.

The telephone rang. The professor's telephone hung above the divan behind the wall carpet. He picked up the receiver. "Yes, yes." It was a call from Staff Headquarters asking whether he would like a car to be sent for him.

"Yes, yes, please. You need not worry about the operation, I'm sure it will go splendidly. About the car, that would be fine, especially as I have some business to attend to before the operation. Yes, please, at eight o'clock."

Popov called to see Gavrilov on the morning of the operation. It was still before daybreak and the lamps were on, but
they had no chance to talk because the nurse took Gavrilov
off to the bathroom for an enema. As he went, Gavrilov said:

"Aleshka, you should read Tolstoy's *Youth* on *comme il
faut* and not *comme il faut*.* The old man had the right
feeling for blood!" and these were the last words Popov
heard from the lips of Gavrilov before his death.

Before the operation, the corridor from the operating
theater to Gavrilov's ward was full of hurrying people who
talked in whispers and bustled about without making any
noise. On the evening before, they had stuck a rubber tube
into his esophagus to siphon off the gastric juices and wash
out the stomach—a rubber instrument which produces nausea
and psychic depression, as if it had been invented for lowering a man's self-esteem. Then in the morning he had the
final enema. Gavrilov entered the theater in a hospital robe,
in hospital trousers and blouse made of coarse linen (instead
of buttons the top had tapes), with hospital shoes over his
bare feet (they had changed his linen that morning for the
last time and given him sterilized things to wear). He was
pale, he had lost weight and he was tired when he came in.
In the anteroom people in white robes stood silent, while
spirit lamps hissed and long nickel-plated boxes gleamed. The
theater was very large and painted throughout, walls, ceiling,
floor, in white oil paint. There was an unusual amount of
light in the theater since one wall was made entirely of
window glass and looked out toward the other side of the
river. In the center of the room stood a long white operating
table. Here Kokosov and Lozovsky met Gavrilov. They both
wore white gowns, white caps on their heads which made them
look like chefs, and Kokosov also had a bib around his beard
which left only his eyes free. About ten people in white
gowns stood along the wall.

Gavrilov entered the room calmly with a nurse, silently
bowed to the professors, walked over to the table, looked

* Tolstoy's *Childhood and Youth*, Chapter 31, is entitled "Comme
il Faut."—TRANS.

through the window across the river and clasped his hands behind his back. Another nurse brought in a long nickel-plated box, the sterilizer with the instruments.

Lozovsky asked Kokosov in a whisper:

"Shall we begin, Pavel Ivanovich?"

"Yes, yes, you know . . ." answered Kokosov.

And the professors went to scrub up, to wash their hands thoroughly, using germicide and iodine. The anesthetist examined the mask and touched the bottle he was holding.

"Comrade Gavrilov, let's begin," said Lozovsky. "Please would you mind lying down on the table, and take your shoes off."

Gavrilov looked at the sister and pulled at his blouse with a little embarrassment. She looked at Gavrilov as if he were an object and smiled at him as one smiles at a child. Gavrilov sat on the table, kicked off one shoe and then the other, quickly lay down on the operating table, shifted the bolster and shut his eyes. Then the nurse closed the straps across his legs in a deft and practiced way, attaching the man to the table. The anesthetist put a towel over the eyes, wiped the nose and mouth with Vaseline, fixed the mask over the face, took the patient's hand so that he could feel the pulse, and poured chloroform over the mask. The sweet astringent smell of chloroform began to pervade the room.

The anesthetist noted the time at which the operation was beginning. The professors walked over to the window in silence. The sister began to take out with forceps and arrange on a piece of sterile gauze scalpels, sterile napkins, Pean's forceps, pincers, needles, silk. The anesthetist added some more chloroform. Silence reigned. Then the patient moved his head restlessly and groaned.

"I can't breathe, take it off," said Gavrilov and ground his teeth.

"Please wait awhile," answered the anesthetist.

A few minutes later, the patient began to sing and to talk.

"The ice has gone, free flows the Volga, my golden one, my own," sang the commander and then whispered, "And you, sleep, sleep, sleep." After a pause, he said firmly, "Don't ever give me any cranberry jelly again, I've had enough of it, it's not *comme il faut*." Then suddenly he shouted sternly as he must have shouted in the field, "No turning back! Not a step! I shall shoot! . . . Aleshka, brother, it's full speed ahead, you can't see the ground any more! I remember everything. Then I know what the revolution is and feel its power. And I don't fear death." And again he began to sing: "A carpenter lives over the Urals, over the hills, my golden one, my own . . ."

"How do you feel? You don't feel sleepy?" the anesthetist asked Gavrilov softly.

And Gavrilov answered in an ordinary tone of voice, also softly and conversationally:

"Nothing much, but I can't breathe."

"Wait a little longer," said the anesthetist and added some more chloroform.

Kokosov looked at the clock in a preoccupied way and bent his head over the list of recent deaths in the hospital, reading it through.

Certain organisms react in an idiosyncratic way to certain narcotics. They had already been trying to put Gavrilov to sleep for twenty-seven minutes.

Kokosov called a junior assistant and pushed his face forward to have the spectacles adjusted. The anesthetist whispered to Lozovsky:

"Should we stop the chloroform and try ether?"

Lozovsky replied:

"Let's try the chloroform a little longer. If things go wrong, the operation will have to be postponed. It would be awkward."

Kokosov looked around sternly and then dropped his eyes. The anesthetist added some more chloroform. The professors stood silent.

Gavrilov finally fell asleep in forty-eight minutes. Then the professors dipped their hands in the surgical spirit for the last time. The nurse bared Gavrilov's abdomen and his thin ribs and taut stomach shone in the light.

Professor Kokosov treated the upper abdomen—the operational site—with spirit, petroleum jelly and iodine. The sister gave him sheets to cover Gavrilov's head and legs. She poured half a tin of iodine over Lozovsky's hands.

Lozovsky took a scalpel and passed it over the skin. Blood

spurted out and the skin opened up. Fat escaped from under the skin, yellow fat like mutton fat, lying in layers with strands of blood vessels. Lozovsky cut the human flesh once more, cut the fascia, showing white, layered with purplish muscle. Kokosov closed the blood vessels with forceps, exhibiting an unexpected deftness in spite of his bearlike appearance.

With another knife Lozovsky cut through the peritoneum, put the knife aside and wiped the blood with sterile gauze. Inside the incision the intestine could be seen and the milky-blue sac of the stomach. Lozovsky put his hand into the entrails, turned the stomach and compressed it.

On the shining flesh of the stomach, in the place where the ulcer should have been, there was a scar—white, as if made of wax, rather like the larva of a dung beetle—which showed that the ulcer had already healed and that the operation was pointless.

But in this moment, in the moment when Gavrilov's stomach was in Lozovsky's hand, the anesthetist cried:

"The pulse, the pulse!"

"Respiration!" Kokosov seemed to echo mechanically.

Then one could see how Kokosov's eyes, between his hair, through his spectacles, became very angry and Lozovsky's eyes, at the corners of his glasses with the firm nose piece, narrowed, grew deeper, concentrated, became one extraordinarily sharp eye.

The patient had no pulse, his heart was not beating, there was no respiration and his legs began to grow cold.

This was the result of shock. The organism which had rejected chloroform had been poisoned by the chloroform. The signs showed categorically that this man would never stand up again, that he must die, but that by artificial means, by using oxygen, camphor, saline solution, his final death might be postponed by an hour, by ten or thirty hours, not longer, and that he would never recover consciousness—that he was essentially already dead.

It was clear that Gavrilov must die on the operating table, under the knife.

Professor Kokosov turned his face so that the nurse might adjust his spectacles, and shouted:

"Open the window! Camphor! Saline!"

The silent group of assistants became even more silent. As if nothing had happened, Kokosov bent over the instruments on the table in silence and Lozovsky bent his head beside him.

"Pavel Ivanovich," Lozovsky whispered angrily.

"Well?" Kokosov answered out loud.

"Pavel Ivanovich," Lozovsky said even more softly and without a trace of anger.

"Well?" Kokosov answered and said, "Carry on with the operation!"

The two professors both straightened up and glanced at one another. Lozovsky's eyes had merged into one eye and the other's had slipped from behind the glasses. For a moment, Lozovsky drew away from Kokosov as if he had been struck or as if he wanted to get things into perspective. His eye seemed to double, to wander and then return to itself, and was even sharper and clearer. He whispered:

"Pavel Ivanovich . . ."

And his hands approached the wound. He did not stitch but just tacked the inner cavity, then pulled the skin together and began to stitch the upper integument alone. He gave an order:

"Free his hands. Artificial respiration!"

The enormous window had been opened and the frost of the first snow entered the room. The man had already had a camphor injection. Kokosov and the anesthetist bent Gavrilov's arms back and raised them in the air, forcing the man to breathe artificially. Lozovsky went on stitching the wound. Then he called:

"Saline!"

The sister stuck two thick needles almost the size of cigarettes into the chest, so that a weak saline solution could be introduced into the man's bloodstream to keep up the blood pressure. The man's face was blue and lifeless and his lips purple.

Then they untied Gavrilov from the table, put him on a little wheeled stretcher and returned him to his room. His heart was beating and he was breathing, but he did not regain consciousness, unless perhaps at the last moment, when the heart that had been treated with camphor and salt ceased to beat—after thirty-seven hours—and the doctors abandoned the use of camphor and let him die. It is possible, because although no one was allowed near him until the last moment except the two professors and the nurses, yet an hour before the commander's death was officially announced a neighboring patient accidentally overheard strange sounds coming from his room: a man seemed to be tapping, as men in prison cells tap to one another. Over there lay a living dead man, full of camphor, because in medicine it is against professional ethics to allow a patient to die under the surgeon's knife.

The operation began at 8:39 and Gavrilov was wheeled out at 11:11. Then the porter out in the corridor said that Professor Lozovsky had received two telephone calls from House No. 1. The professor went over to the office where the telephone was and stood for a moment by the window, looking at the first fall of snow. He bit his nails and then went over to the instrument and was connected to that system which has some thirty or forty lines, bowed to the receiver, and said that the operation had been successful, but that the patient was very weak and that the medical officers considered his condition to be critical. He asked to be excused as he could not come at that moment.

Gavrilov died—that is, Professor Lozovsky left the room with a sheet of white paper and, bowing his head, announced in a sad and solemn voice that the sick commander in chief, Citizen Nikolay Ivanovich Gavrilov, had died at 1:17 A.M., to everyone's great sorrow.

Three-quarters of an hour later, when it was nearly two o'clock in the morning, groups of Red Army men entered the hospital yard and stood on guard at all the exits, entrances and stairways. Clouds were creeping over the sky and a full moon hurried after them, weary of hurrying. Professor Lozovsky was going in a special limousine to House No. 1. The Rolls-Royce entered the griffined gateway noiselessly and passed the guards who opened the door when the car stopped. Lozovsky went into the study where three telephones stood on the red-topped desk and behind it on the wall were the serried ranks of bells.

The subject of conversation which took place in this study

is not known, but it lasted for three minutes only. Lozovsky left the study, the porch, the yard very hurriedly with his coat and hat in his hands, and he looked rather like a Hoffmann hero. There was no car now and Lozovsky walked along, staggering a little, as if he were drunk. The streets reeled under the moon in the motionless desert of the night, along with Lozovsky.

Professor Lozovsky left the study in House No. 1. The man who never stoops remained in the study. He stood over the table, leaned on the table, propped himself up on his fists. His head was lowered. He stood still for a long time. He had been torn away from his papers and his formulas. Then he moved. His movements were rectangular and formal, like the clear statements he dictated each evening to his secretary. He began to move very fast. He rang a bell and picked up the telephone. He said to the man on duty, "An open sports car!" And into the telephone he said to someone who must have been asleep, to one of the triumvirate, in a faint voice, "Andrey! My dear chap, a man has died. Kolya Gavrilov has died. We have lost our warrior brother. Call Potapov, would you?"

To the chauffeur, the man who never stoops said, "The hospital!"

Guards stood in the dark gates. The house was mute as houses must be in the presence of death.

The man who never stoops walked along the dark corridors to Commander Gavrilov's room. He went in and the commander's corpse lay on the bed in a stifling odor of camphor.

Everyone left and only the man and Gavrilov's body remained in the room. The man sat on the bed at the feet of the corpse. Gavrilov's arms lay under the blanket at his sides. The man sat bowed beside the body for a long time, without stirring. There was silence in the room. Then the man took Gavrilov's hand, held it and said:

"Farewell, comrade! Farewell, brother!" and he left the room with head bowed and said, without looking at anyone, "Open the ventilator. You can't breathe in there," as he left again by way of the dark corridors.

I V

On the evening after Commander Gavrilov's funeral, when the military brass bands had thundered by and the flags had been lowered in mourning, thousands of people had walked in the procession and the man's corpse had been left to grow cold in the earth together with the earth, Popov fell asleep in his room and woke up at the table without knowing what time it was. It was dark in the room and Natasha was crying softly. Popov bent over his daughter, picked her up in his arms and began to walk up and down the room with her.

A white moon, weary of hurrying, pushed its light in through the window. Natasha clambered out of his arms and stood on the windowsill.

In Popov's pocket lay the letter Gavrilov had written on the night before the operation. It read:

"Aleshka, brother, after all I knew I would die. Forgive me, but you're no longer so very young. When I was rocking your little girl I began to think. My wife is getting on too, and you've known her twenty years. I've written to her. You write to her as well. Start living together, get married. Bring the children up. Forgive me, Aleshka."

Natasha was standing on the windowsill and Popov could see that her lips were folded in a little pipe, her cheeks inflated; she was looking at the moon, aiming at it and blowing at it.

"What are you doing, Natasha?" her father asked her.

"I want to put out the light of the moon," Natasha answered.

The full moon, like a merchant's wife, was sailing beyond the clouds, weary with hurrying.

It was the hour at which the metropolitan machinery comes to life and the factory sirens begin to hoot. The sirens hooted for a long time, slowly, first one then another, and a third, many of them, merging in a gray wail above the town. Clearly this was the wail of the soul of the town, frozen by the moon.

1927

Above
the Ravine

The ravine was deep and overgrown. Its slopes of yellow clay, covered with reddish pines, descended precipitously and a stream flowed at the very bottom. Above, a pine forest stretched to the left and to the right, a dense and ancient forest, full of lichen and alder thickets.

It was rare for a man to pass this way.

Trees were uprooted by storms, floods, by the passing of time, and they lay where they had fallen, cluttering the ground and rotting so that they gave off a pungent sweetish smell of rotting pinewood. There was a bear's lair at the bottom of the ravine and there were many wolves in the forest.

A pine had fallen and remained for many years with its roots in the air, balancing on the side of a sheer, dirty yellow slope. Its roots looked like a petrified octopus and were overgrown with lichen and juniper.

Two large gray birds, a male and a female, built themselves a nest in these roots.

These birds were large and heavy and their feathers were thick, grayish-yellow and brown. Their wings were short, wide and powerful, and their great claws were covered with black down. Their large, square heads were set on short, thick necks, their predatory beaks were hooked and yellow, and their eyes were round, stern and ominous.

The female was smaller than the male. Her legs seemed more slender and beautiful and there was a certain grace in the curves of her neck. The male was forbidding, angular. One of his wings, the left one, did not fold correctly. It had been like that from the time when he had fought the other males for the female bird.

The nest was arranged among the roots. There was a sheer drop beneath it on three sides. The sky lay outspread above it and a few broken roots. All around and down below lay bones washed by the rain and bleached by the sun. The nest itself was laid with pebbles and clay and lined with down.

The female always sat in the nest.

The male bird moved about on a root above the ravine in his lonely way, and he could see far into the distance and down below, or else he sat with head drawn in and wings hanging heavily.

II

These two great birds first met in this same place, not far from the ravine.

The spring was already in the air. Snow was melting down the slopes, and in the forest and the glades it had become gray-looking and mellow. The smell of the pines was strong and the stream had come to life at the bottom of the ravine. In the daytime the sun was quite warm. Twilight was long, green-hued and full of watchful sound. Wolves hunted in packs and males fought for females.

They met in a forest clearing at twilight.

The spring, the sun, the gentle breeze filled the body of the male with an unknown longing. Before this he had flown or sat still, cried out or remained silent, flown fast or slow because there were reasons for these actions either in his environment or within himself. When he felt the pangs of hunger he flew off in search of a hare, to kill it and devour it; when the sun was blinding or the wind was strong he took shelter, and when he caught sight of a stealthy wolf he flew away quickly.

Now it was different.

It was no longer hunger or self-preservation that drove him to fly, to sit, to call out or to be silent. He was under the sway of something beyond himself and his awareness.

When twilight came he rose from his place and seemed to fly off in a mist without being aware of the reason. He flew from clearing to clearing, moving his great wings noiselessly and gazing keenly into the green obscurity which kept him on his guard.

And when one evening he saw birds of his own kind with a female among them, he flung himself down into the clearing without knowing why he had to do so, and he experienced a sensation of great strength and a great hatred for the other males.

He walked beside the female slowly, stamping, his wings spread wide, his head tilted in the air, and he watched the males, slant-eyed. One of them, the one who had been victorious before, made efforts to impede him and then fell upon him, beak ready for attack. They became involved in a long, silent and cruel combat. They flew upon one another, fought with their wings, their breasts, their claws, giving out resounding cries and tearing at one another.

His enemy proved the weaker and moved away, and again he rushed toward the female and walked around her, limping slightly and dragging his bloody left wing along the ground.

Pines surrounded the clearing, the ground was strewn with needles and the evening sky turned a deep blue.

The female was indifferent toward him and all the others. She walked calmly about the clearing, scratched the earth, caught a mouse and ate it quietly. She seemed to pay no attention to the males.

It was like this all night.

But when the night began to pale and the lilac-green streaks of dawn appeared in the east, she walked up to him, the one who had subdued all the others, and she leaned against his breast, touched his wounded wing gently with her beak, as if sniffing it and healing it, and then slowly rose above the ground and flew off toward the ravine.

And he flew after her, moving his wounded wing clumsily but unaware of it, and calling drunkenly.

She flew down by the roots of the pine just where afterward they built their nest. The male settled beside her. He seemed undecided and even confused.

The female walked around him several times and sniffed at him again. Then she pressed her breast to the ground, spread out her legs, raised her tail, narrowed her eyes and froze in this position. The male flung himself upon her, snatching at her plumes with his beak, beating his heavy wings on the ground. His veins were filled with such a splendid torment, such a strong joy, that he was blinded and felt nothing but this sweet torment, calling out on a deep note and rousing an echo in the ravine which disturbed the hour before the dawn.

The female remained submissive.

The red ribbon of the dawn lay along the east and the snow in the forest clearings became lilac-colored.

III

In winter the pine trees stood motionless and their trunks turned brown. The snow lay deep, blown toward the sides of the ravine in great heaps; the sky was gray, the days short and never quite clear of twilight. At night tree trunks creaked and boughs snapped in the frost. In the stillness a pale moon shone down and it seemed to make the frost grow colder.

The nights were tormenting because of the frost and the phosphorescent light of the moon. The birds sat wedged in their nest, pressing close to one another to get warm, but still the frost penetrated their wings and reached their bodies, chilling their legs, their backs and the part by their beaks. The wandering moonlight disquieted them as if reminding them that the whole world consists of one huge wolf's eye and therefore shines so fearfully.

The birds did not sleep.

They moved clumsily in the nest, changing places, and their own wide-open eyes shone green. If they had known how to think they would probably have longed for morning.

About an hour before dawn, when the moon disappeared and light began to show slightly, the birds began to feel hungry. They experienced an unpleasant, bitter taste in their mouths and from time to time their crops constricted painfully.

When the morning finally turned gray, the male flew off in search of prey, flying slowly with his wings spread wide and beating them infrequently. He gazed sharply at the ground. Usually he hunted hares. Sometimes he found nothing for a long while above the ravine and he would fly far away from the nest, as far as five miles, until he found himself over the wide white expanse of what was in summer the Kama River. When there were no hares, he attacked young foxes and magpies, although their flesh was unpalatable. The foxes defended themselves stubbornly, biting fiercely, and had to be attacked carefully and cunningly. He had to strike at their necks straightaway with his beak, near the head, and, catching their backs with his claws, rise in the air; in the air the fox no longer struggles.

The male flew back to his nest with his prey and together they devoured the whole animal at once. They ate only once a day and took their fill until it was difficult to move and their crops hung downward. They even ate blood-stained snow. The bones the female cast down below them.

The male settled on one of the roots, shrinking into himself or bristling up to get more comfortable, and felt how warmly his blood was circulating after the meal, enjoying the sensation of juices flowing in his gut.

The female sat in the nest.

Toward evening, the male gave his cry for some unknown reason.

"Oo-hoo!" he cried in a guttural voice as if the sound in his throat were passing through water.

Sometimes wolves would spy him sitting there alone and some hungry wolf would begin clambering up the precipitous slope.

The female grew anxious and called out in fear, but the male gazed downward calmly with his wide heavy eyes, watching the wolf as it climbed up slowly, fell and flew downward, sweeping off lumps of snow, turning somersaults and shrilling in pain.

And twilight slowly crept on.

IV

As the days grew longer in March, the sun felt warm again, the snow became discolored and melted, the green twilight lingered a long time, wolves hunted in packs and there was more prey because all the inhabitants of the forest began to experience an unrest before the spring, which tormented and bewitched them, so that they wandered through the clearings, along the slopes and in the woodlands, without being able to stop themselves or to resist the unrest of early spring. And they were easily caught.

The male bird brought all his prey to the female and ate very little himself, only the parts she left for him. Usually these were the entrails, the meat around the breast muscles, the skin and heads, although the female always ate the eyes because they were the tastiest morsel.

In the daytime the male sat on the roots of the tree.

The sun shone. The breeze was soft and gentle. And now the black, swift stream thundered at the bottom of the ravine, its banks sharply defined against the snow.

He felt hungry. He sat with his eyes closed, his head drawn into his neck. His external appearance revealed a submissiveness, a weary expectation and a comical guilt which ill assorted with his stern expression.

Toward evening he became more animated and experienced a deep unrest. He raised himself on his legs, stretched his neck, opened his round eyes wide, stretched his wings and then folded them again, beating the air. Then he huddled up, drew in his head, screwed up his eyes and gave his call:

"Oo-hoo-hoo!" he cried out in a sinister way, frightening the other creatures in the woods.

And an echo in the ravine replied:

"Oo-oo . . ."

In the greenish-blue twilight the sky became studded with large, new-looking stars.

The oily smell of pinewood rose in the air. The stream grew quiet in the night frost. Far-off birds called in their mating place. Yet a watchful silence seemed to reign.

When it became quite dark and the night was a dark

blue, the male bird carefully spread out his large legs, unused to walking on the ground, and went stealthily and apologetically into the nest to the female. A splendid and powerful lust drew him toward her.

He sat down beside her and stroked her plumes with his beak. And as before he had a comical apologetic air.

The female bird responded trustingly to his caresses and seemed weak and gentle. Yet her great power over him could be discerned behind her gentleness.

In the language of the instincts the female said to the male:

"Yes. Now."

And he fell upon her, faint with passion. And she yielded herself to him.

V

So it was for a week or a week and a half.

Then when the male came to her at night, she said:

"No. Enough now."

Her instinct told her that it was enough and that now a new period was beginning—the birth of the young.

And the male, as if guilty at not having foreseen the female's command, the command of the instinct within her, left her, to return at the end of the year.

VI

From spring until September, all through the summer, the male and female were absorbed in the splendid and essential business of birth—until September, when the birds flew away.

The spring and summer unfolded with myriad flowers that burned with a hot flame. The pines smelled oily and were decked out with cones. There was an odor of wormwood. Everything bloomed and ripened: reeds, chicory, harebells, buttercups, mountain ash, pansies, prickly thistles.

In May the nights were blue.

In June they were greenish-white.

The dawns and the sunsets flamed in red conflagrations

and at night layers of silver-white mist passed over the depths of the ravine, rubbing out the contours of the pines.

At first the nest contained five gray eggs with green speckles. Then the fledglings appeared. They had large heads and disproportionately large yellow mouths, and were covered in gray down. They squeaked pitifully, stretching their long necks out of the nest, and they ate a great deal.

By June they could already fly about, although they moved their wings inexpertly and clumsily and still had large heads and squeaked.

The hen bird was always at their side, preoccupied, ruffled and cantankerous.

The male could not think, yet felt obscurely a pride in fulfilling the climax of his life work with great happiness. His whole life was instinctive and his will and sensation centered on the fledglings.

He took risks in his hunt for prey.

He had to provide a great deal, since both the young birds and the hen were voracious. He was forced to fly far afield, sometimes as far as the Kama, to catch seagulls there, which always bustled around great white strange beasts with many eyes that went on the water, making a peculiar noise and smelling like forest fires—the steamers.

He fed the fledglings himself. He tore pieces of meat apart and gave it to them. Then he watched attentively with his round eyes as the fledglings snatched the pieces, opening their beaks wide, choking, swaying with the strain and swallowing the meat whole.

Sometimes one of the young birds would fall out of the nest and down the slope. Then the male would quickly and solicitously fly after the young bird, calling and grumbling. He would pick it up carefully in his claws and return it, frightened and bewildered to the nest. Then he would stroke its feathers for a long time in the nest, lifting his own legs high and carefully and never ceasing to call out in solicitude.

They did not sleep at night.

He sat on one of the roots of the tree, gazed sharply into the gloom and guarded his fledglings and the mother bird from harm.

The stars shone overhead.

And sometimes, as if experiencing the fullness and beauty of life, he called sternly and menacingly, stirring the echoes. "Oo-hoo-hoo-hoo!" he cried, frightening the night.

VII

During the winter he lived in order to survive and in spring and summer in order to reproduce himself. He did not know how to think. He did as he did because this was the will of God, of the instinct which held sway over him.

He lived through the winter in order to eat and not to die. The winters were cold and terrifying.

In the spring he reproduced his own kind.

Then the hot blood coursed through his veins, it was quiet, the sun shone and the stars, and he kept wanting to stretch himself, close his eyes, beat the air with his wings and call out joyfully for no reason.

VIII

In autumn the birds flew away. The old birds took leave of their young for good and with complete indifference.

It rained in the autumn, mists formed and the sky was low overhead. The nights were wearisome, damp and dark. The two old birds sat together in their damp nest, finding it hard to sleep, feeling the cold and moving clumsily. Their eyes shone like little yellow-green lights.

The male did not give his call any longer.

IX

So passed thirteen years of their lives.

X

Then the male bird died.

In his youth he had damaged his wing when he fought to get the female. As the years passed, it became more and more difficult for him to hunt and he had to fly farther and farther afield, while at night he could not fall asleep, feeling a sharp and painful ache in his wing which was frightening because in the early days he had not been aware of his wing and now it had become strangely important and tormenting.

He did not sleep at night, and his wing hung down, as if he were rejecting it. And in the morning, hardly able to wield it, he set off in search of prey.

The female bird left him.

Just before spring one twilight evening she flew away from the nest.

The male spent all night searching for her and only managed to find her at dawn. She was with a young strong male who was gently calling beside her. Then the old bird felt that everything he had had in his life was over. He rushed to attack the young male but fought without conviction, feebly. The other fell upon him powerfully and lustily, tearing at his flesh and threatening him. The hen bird watched the combat with indifference, exactly as she had watched another combat many years ago.

The old bird was vanquished.

He flew away to his nest and settled quietly on the root of the tree, torn, bloody, with a blinded eye. He felt he had settled his account with life. He had lived in order to eat and to reproduce himself. Now nothing was left but to die. His instinct probably informed him of this, since he sat for two whole days, his head drawn into his body, silent and motionless above the precipitous slope.

Then he died peacefully and unawares. He fell down below and lay there with his twisted legs in the air.

This was at night. The stars were new and birds called in the forest at their mating places.

A brown owl called.

The male lay at the bottom of the ravine for five days. He began to decompose and gave off a foul bitter odor.

A wolf found him and devoured him.

1915

The
Bielkonsky
Estate

I

For a long time the sun shone through the drawing-room windows across the bare, autumnal park. Jackdaws were calling over the steppe in the empty autumn silence. He had spent his whole life in this house and now he was to leave it forever. The president of the council, Ivan Koloturov, had brought the last order himself and the others, strangers, were already installed in the kitchen.

He got up in the early-morning light. Day set in, golden and clear, with a fathomless blue firmness in the sky; long ago, his forefathers had gone hunting with their borzois on such days. The fields were naked now, dead arrows of rye sticking out here and there, and the wolves were probably on the prowl again. Only yesterday evening they nailed up a plaque on the front door: BIELKONSKY COMMITTEE FOR POOR RELIEF. And they made a noise in the salon all night arranging things. The drawing room was exactly the same and in the study the gilt spines of the books still gleamed behind glass. Was it possible that the poison of books, their sweetness, would be lost?

Count Prozorovsky got up in the blue morning light and went out into the open fields, where he wandered all day, drank the wine of autumn to the lees and listened to the jackdaws' chorus. When he was a child and had listened to the

39

autumnal carnival of the birds, he had clapped his hands and shouted out a nursery rhyme about weddings at the top of his voice. There never had been any wedding and now his days were numbered. He had lived for love; there had been a great deal of it. There had been pain and now there was grief. There was the poison of Moscow, of books and of women, and the melancholy of the Bielkonsky estate, for he had always spent his autumns here. He wandered through the open pathless fields. The aspens were burning in brownish-purple tints down in the valleys and at his back stood the white house on rising ground among the lilac thickets of the park. He was growing bald at the temples and his hair was turning gray. Time does not stand still and the past never returns.

He met a peasant in the fields, a primordial, everlasting peasant with a cartload of sacks, wearing a sheepskin jacket. The peasant doffed his cap and stopped the old nag while the squire passed.

"Good day, your excellency," he said, smacking his lips, pulling at the reins, starting off and then again pausing and calling out:

"Sir, here a moment, I want a word with you."

He turned back. The old peasant's face was overgrown with hair and he was wrinkled.

"What are you going to do now, sir?"

"It's hard to say."

"When are you leaving? They're taking our bread away, these committees for poor relief. We've got no matches, no factory goods—I'm using sticks. The order is not to sell bread—I take it to the station secretly. It all started in Moscow. Eh? Thirty-five, thirty-five, and what can you buy with that! Still, it's all good fun. Have a smoke, sir."

He did not smoke, but he rolled some shag. The steppe lay all around and no one saw or heard how the peasant was sorry for him. He shook his hand in farewell, turned abruptly and went home. The water in the pond was like a blue mirror —the water there was always cold and transparent as glass. It had still to freeze over finally for the winter. The sun was settling into the west.

He went into his study and, sitting down at his desk,

pulled out a drawer full of letters: you could not take a whole lifetime away with you. He shook the contents out onto the table and went over to the fireplace in the drawing room. There was a mug of milk and some bread on one of the occasional tables. He lit the fire, burned his papers, standing beside the flame, eating his bread and drinking the milk, for he was now hungry. Blue evening shadows had entered the room and beyond the windows rose the lilac smoke. The fire burned yellow. The milk was a little sour and the bread stale.

There was the sound of boots in the corridor and Ivan Koloturov, the president, came in wearing a topcoat, with a revolver in his belt. Ivan Koloturov . . . They had played together as boys, and then he had become a thoughtful, hard-working, businesslike peasant. He handed over a paper silently and stood there in the middle of the room.

The message was typed on a Remington: "To the land-owner Prozorovsky. The Bielkonsky Committee for Poor Relief demand your immediate departure from the Soviet Bielkonsky Estate and its environs. President: I. Koloturov."

"I shall leave this evening."

"There will be no horse."

"Then I'll go on foot."

"As you please. Don't take anything." Koloturov turned his back, paused for a moment and then left the room.

At just that moment the clock chimed the three-quarters, the clock made by a famous master craftsman in the seventeenth century, which had first stood in the Kremlin Palace in Moscow and then accompanied the counts of Vadkovsky on their travels in the Caucasus. How many times had the clock ticked in order to bear two whole centuries away? He sat down by the window, leaning on the marble sill, gazing for an hour or more motionless across the bare park, musing and recalling the past. He was interrupted by Koloturov, who came in with two others. They went into the study and silently began to try to lift the desk, and then something cracked.

Count Prozorovsky got up and began to hurry. He put on his wide gray overcoat, his felt hat, and left by way of the terrace. He walked over the rustling leaves, past the stables, down into the gully and up the other side. Then he felt tired and decided he must go more slowly, since he still had ten miles to go and he had never before had to walk. Everything was really very simple and it was only terrifying because of its simplicity.

The sun had set and the western sky was ablaze. The last flock of jackdaws flew by and the autumnal silence of the steppe came down. He walked with a firm and even gait along the cart track. He had never felt so free, walking unencumbered, not knowing where or why. Somewhere very far off in the steppe some dogs were barking. The night grew dark, autumnal, silent, and there was a sharp frost.

He walked about four miles without knowing it and then paused a moment to tie his bootlace. Then suddenly he felt an enormous weariness and an aching in his legs, for he must have walked some twenty miles that day. A hamlet lay ahead. In his student days he had ridden to visit a young soldier's wife here in secret and spent the night with her, but now nothing would make him turn to her. The hamlet seemed to lie close to the ground, littered with great haystacks and smelling of bread and dung. He was greeted by the barking of dogs on the outskirts of the village, a whole pack rolling out at his feet like dark shadows.

He walked up to the first window where a night light was burning, knocked and after some time someone answered:

"Who's there?"

"Give me a night's lodging, kind people."

"Who is it?"

"A passerby."

"All right, in a moment."

A barefoot peasant, in long pink underwear, came out with a light in his hand and had a look at him.

"Count? Your Excellency. Come on in!"

They laid a whole heap of straw on the floor. A cricket chirruped. There was a smell of smoke and dung.

"Lie down, Count. Sleep away. God bless you."

The peasant climbed up onto the stove, sighed, whispered something to his wife, grunted discontentedly and then called out:

"Sleep away, Count, but in the morning you must leave before daylight so that no one will see you. You know yourself times are hard. After all, you're still the squire. We have to put an end to all that. My wife will wake you. . . . Now, you go to sleep."

The cricket chirruped and some piglets grunted in the corner. He lay down without undressing, using his hat for a pillow, and at once a cockroach was crawling on his neck. Far off in the steppe, with its corn, its haystacks and shocks of straw, its thatched hovels infested with lice, fleas, cockroaches, reeking with smoke, where people lived with their calves and pigs, the count lay on his straw bed restlessly because of the fleas, and thought how in a few centuries people would write about the contemporary scene with affection, nostalgia and melancholy as a manifestation of all that is most beautiful and lofty in the human spirit. A piglet approached him, sniffed and disappeared. A bright star low in the sky gazed in through the window out of an infinite universe. The village cocks began to crow.

He did not notice how he fell asleep. At daybreak the woman woke him and led him out the back way. The light was blue and cold and the grass was frosty. He walked off quickly, waving his stick, with the collar of his coat turned up. The vault of the sky was surprisingly blue and deep. At the station he squeezed his way into a heated wagon along with the black marketeers and the sacks of flour. In this way he set out, huddled against the wall and covered with white flour, for Moscow.

I I

Ivan Koloturov, the president, was a man who had spent some twenty years getting up before daybreak and doing manual work. He spent the time digging, harrowing, hammering, mending, planing with his two great, horny, unyielding hands. On getting up he primed himself with bread and potato and left the cottage to start doing something with wood or stones, with metal or earth or with the animals. He was a hard worker and an honest and sensible man. As far back as 1905 (coming from the station he gave a lift on the back of his horse to a man in a master craftsman's jacket) he had been told that we are all equal before God, that the land belonged to the peasants and had been stolen by the land-

owners and that the time would come when it would be
necessary to take matters in hand. Ivan Koloturov did not
grasp very clearly what would have to be done, but when
the revolution reached the steppe he was one of the first to
stand up and do something about it. He felt some depression.
He wanted everything to be done honestly, and he only
knew how to do things with his hands. He was chosen to sit
on the rural district council. He was used to getting up early
and getting to work at once, but now he had nothing to do
until ten, when he went to the committee office and signed
papers with the greatest difficulty. Even this was not work, for
the papers came and went without his orders and he did not
understand them but only signed them. He wanted action. In
the spring he returned home to get the plowing done. In the
autumn he was elected president of the Committee for Poor
Relief and lodged in the count's house. He took to wearing a
soldier's overcoat and stuck a revolver in his belt.

He would call at his cottage in the evening and his wife
would wave her elbows and greet him gloomily as she stood
over her cooking. The children sat on the stove and the
piglets grunted in the corner. The night light smoked.

"So you don't even eat with us after the grub you get over
there? Turning into a lord now?"

He kept quiet and sat on the bench under the icons.

"Just look at the people you're mixed up with. All our
worst enemies have got together."

"Shut up, you fool! You don't understand anything, so
keep quiet!"

"You're ashamed of me and keep away."

"Come and live with me."

"That I won't."

"Fool."

"You've learned to bark, all right. Take some stew then.
Or aren't you used to it after the pork over there?"

It was true that he had eaten his fill and she had hit the
mark when she guessed it was pork. He breathed hard.

"You're an utter fool."

He had come to talk about their smallholding and to discuss things, but left with nothing settled. The woman had
caught him on the raw, since peasants with a good name stood

aloof and only those with nothing to lose had joined the committee. He crossed the village and the park and saw a light in the stables. He went to have a look around and found some men playing cards and smoking. He watched for a while, and said:

"That's not such a good idea. You'll set the place on fire."

"I like that. Why should you protect someone else's property!"

"It's not someone else's—it's ours."

He turned and left and they shouted after him:

"Have you got the key to the wine cellar? There's alcohol down there. If you don't give it to us, we'll break the door down!"

It was dark and silent in the house and the count was still living in the drawing room. The large rooms were strange and eerie to the president. He went into the office, which used to be the dining room, and lit a lamp. He was constantly preoccupied with cleanliness. There were some lumps of earth from his boots on the floor and he could not understand why the shoes of the gentry left no trace. He got down on his knees, picked up the lumps, flung them out the window, fetched a brush and swept the floor. Then he went to the kitchen, lay down on a bench without undressing and could not get off to sleep for a long time.

He got up early, before anyone else, and wandered around the estate. The men were still playing cards.

"Aren't you asleep?"

"I've had my fill."

He woke the herdsman. He came out and stood there swearing because he had been wakened.

"Mind your own business. I know when to get up!"

The morning was clear, blue and frosty. The light went on in the drawing room. He saw the count coming out on the terrace and making for the steppe.

At ten he sat down in the office and started on the useless and laborious task of listing how much wheat and rye each peasant possessed—useless, because he already knew exactly how much each man in the village had and they knew that he knew, and it was laborious because there was so much writing to do. There was a telephone call from town with an order to give the count notice to leave immediately. He spent a whole hour typing the order out.

The count left in the evening. They started moving the furniture around and tore off a bit of plywood at the back of the desk. They wanted to move the clock into the office, but someone noticed that it had only one hand. No one knew that such an antique clock should only have one hand, which indicated the passage of every five minutes. In the old days perhaps minutes were not so valuable. Finally they realized the clock could be taken out of its case, and Ivan Koloturov said, "Take the clock out of the case. Tell the carpenter to fix shelves in it. It will do as a cupboard for the office. And mind your feet!"

His wife came running in during the evening. There had been an incident. A girl had been raped the night before either by their own people or by some man from Moscow who was trying to steal flour. She put the blame on the committee and stood by the window, shouting abuse at the top of her voice. Ivan Koloturov drove her away with a clout over her ear, and she walked off howling.

It was quite dark and silent in the house. Outside, the dairymaids sang loudly. He went into the study, tried out the softness of the divan, noticed an electric torch and played with it, lighting up the walls. Then he caught sight of the clock in the drawing room and wondered how to get rid of it. He took it away and threw it into the water closet. A crowd of men gathered in the other half of the house and someone began to strum on the piano. Ivan Koloturov would have liked to drive them out and avoid any rowdiness, but he did not dare. Suddenly he felt very sorry for himself and for his wife and wanted to be home on the stove.

They rang the bell for supper. He crept stealthily to the wine cellar, filled up a large mug and drank it down. He managed to lock the door again, but not to reach his home. In the park he fell on the ground and lay there a long time, trying to get up, trying to tell someone about something, to explain something, but he fell asleep. A dark and coldhearted autumnal night moved over the cold, wild and empty steppe.

1918

Death Beckons

I

The hay in June gives off a smell really rather like cheap scent and yet there is no sweeter smell and at night, in June, the silver birches add a bitter odor and the daybreak, in June, is crystal clear.

Alena was born in a house in the woods where she knew the sky, pine trees, sand and a river, and received all that the earth grants to a human being to keep forever. There were meadows on both sides of the river and Alena knew, because her mother told her, that yellow St.-John's-wort, which flowers in June, with the little warts on its stems and leaves, makes an infusion which is good for the chest, and yellow nipplewort is a remedy for headaches and colds, and pink-and-white cinquefoil is good for cuts, and the century plant is also good for cuts, and spicy sage is good for toothache and sore throats, and as for camomile, it cures toothache and with it you can abort an infant from the womb, and she knew that sweet mint is good for sore throats and chest complaints, and the orange-colored juice from the roots of the greater celandine is good for warts, that the only plant good for snake bite is star grass with its humble blue flower and the purple thorny thistle which grows on the slopes can drive devils out of cottages. Alena and her mother gathered these plants before the hay was cut in June—they all flowered in June, except the thorny

47

purple thistle, an August bloom. She and her mother distilled the plants for the winter.

Alena was born in June and she retained the memory of the sweet-smelling June hay and the labor of the June harvest all her life.

When she was still a little girl, she learned that death beckons.

Near the house in the woods there was an embankment, and an iron bridge spanned the river. Trains ran over the bridge, rattling. In the spring, at high tide, people got to the other side of the river by walking over this bridge. Before Easter, when spring was in tumult, when the snows were melting and sunlight dazzled, the forest hummed with the mating calls of birds, and on one such dazzling day, a student from the other side of the river was walking along the embankment. He was young and healthy, with a cap over his curly fair hair; he wore polished boots and he came up to the window laughing, and asked for a drink.

"What a wonderful day! What wonderful air! Is it all right to go over the bridge?"

He laughed aloud in a carefree way; he was handsome, young and strong, with the collar of his dark-blue shirt undone and a drop of sweat on his white neck.

"Oh, what bliss it is today, Aunt Arina!"

He glanced at Alena, smiled and said:

"Is this your daughter? What a beauty she is going to be!"

Mother addressed this student by his name and patronymic and told him not to look down as he crossed the bridge because in spring the water flows fast and you can get giddy. The student doffed his cap, shook his curls and went off. He got as far as the middle of the bridge and flung himself into the water. It was a miracle he was saved: the water pushed him against a pier left from the old bridge.

And in the evening the mother told her daughter that death attracts us like a magnet, flood waters beckon, earth beckons from a height, from the church bell tower, we are drawn under the train and out of the train. When she was a little girl, Alena could not understand this—not that evening when the flood water roared outside and the smell of fresh earth blew in through the open window. But she understood it later when she was a young woman. Some springs later she was standing on the bridge herself when she felt the strong attraction of the water, of what was unknown and deathly, and then she became wiser and more profound and understood that death beckons everywhere and that life consists in this— blood, earth, God beckoning us.

The girl went beyond the river to the village at festival times; she sang songs and danced in chorus with the other girls and met a boy and fell in love and there would have been a wedding, only her mother suddenly became obstinate and then confessed to her daughter:

"Alena, my dear, your sweetheart is your own brother. I sinned. It happened a long time ago, I was young, it was at the hay making. I sinned with his father. Your father had been called up. I sinned." She spoke softly and wiped the corners of her once beautiful lips with the edge of her kerchief.

The mother made her confession and Alena stopped going out on the hillside and spent her evenings near the house. At night, she listened intently for the sound of the quail, watched the river mist, and once more experienced the feeling that death beckons, sin beckons; the sinful attracts us as much as the blessed and death is the end of everything.

So her youth passed in a thatched cottage, where, under the sky, there were pine trees, sand, the river with its meadows, its flowers and grasses.

I I

Then there was her life.

All of us love once and love is always unhappy, since it cannot but be so and must be so, because after having loved, a person becomes a complete human being, cleansed by suffering. The beauty and joy of love consist in its mystery. And no one knew how Alena grieved at night, young and solitary, with her young body—alone in June during those nights of the hay making. That was why she stayed unmarried until after the appointed period of twenty years, when girls are seldom taken to wife any more, and that was why she never showed anyone her church remembrance book, where, on the

first page, was the name Alexey, servant of God, her first sweetheart and her blood brother. She helped her mother to
gather grasses and followed behind her father along the
railway track with a lamp and a green flag, and sat spinning
endlessly in the winter evenings. So time passed until her
twenty-fourth year. She began to experience God sharply and
the mysteries of death, went to church and prayed from dawn
to dusk—the religious is after all always concerned with the
physical and carnal. From that April when her mother told
her about how death beckons, fifteen years elapsed. And
Alena, the little girl, became a beautiful, strong, suntanned,
broad young woman, with black eyes that looked modestly
downward.

The same young student who had once laughed at the
window with his collar undone, happy and confident, had
already had time to change his life radically, as many Russian
gentlefolk did. He made an unhappy marriage and went from
place to place all over Russia and abroad, homesick the while
for his country estate and a quiet, sensible life. He separated
from his wife after no short time and with difficulty, and
spent on this all the money he had been left to make a life
for himself. Finally, he returned to his estate in Marin Brod
and settled down alone in the old house, burying himself in
books. He was now a mature man with a thick beard, eyes
that already looked tired and a sad smile.

And Alena went to live with him. The moral code of our
people is strict and simple: everyone must get married in the
spring of his life, give birth and then die. All who deviate
from this way must arrange their lives as best they can: it is
no sin for an unmarried girl to go and work for a widower,
nor for postmen from the station to visit a widow, and no
one will criticize them. After all, the corn grows and the
ears of corn ripen; after all, in spring horses neigh in the
fields, birds mate by their nesting places; and maidens sing on
the hillside.

Alena went to Mass, cried a little quietly at home, and
then she took her trunk on her shoulder and went on foot
over the river to the Marin Brod estate; as she left, she paused
on the threshold, glanced around the cottage and said quietly:

"Well, good-bye. I'm going now." And so she left and no one passed judgment on her or felt she sinned.

It was June once more. Quails called in the rye fields, the sky was green, the sun set in the west and a crystal sickle rose in the east. She walked slowly and, picking ears of corn, sucked the bittersweet juice from the unripe grains.

III

She lived on Polunin's estate with him for five years.

She arrived in the evening, put her trunk down on a bench in the kitchen and went to his study. Polunin was sitting at the table. She said:

"Here I am, sir. I've arrived," and, like her mother, she wiped the corner of her lips which were still very beautiful, with her kerchief.

Polunin was of those Russian gentlefolk who seek for truth and for God and he had asked Alena to come, both because he had grown to love her, and also because he thought to find what was honest and genuine in her, to rest himself with her and to build an orderly and steadfast life with her. They live together on the estate and looked after it alone. Polunin taught Alena to read and write and he read *The Lives of the Saints* with her, becoming absorbed himself in his search for something genuinely Russian.

Six months later, their daughter, Natalya, was born and Alena gave herself up to the child, experiencing life through her and in her. Her life was simple and serious, as was Polunin's: she got up at dawn, said her prayers, went to milk the cows, prepared their dinner, milked the cows again in the afternoon, took care of the child, fed it, swaddled it and washed it. No one came to see her and she went nowhere except to church. In the winter they became snowbound after the blizzard; in the spring the river reached their doors; in the autumn it rained and the days became empty, clear and cold. Polunin sat at his books, chopped wood, spoke about truth and probably did not notice that sometimes his words about goodness became hard and malicious: people grow old.

Year succeeded year. Springtime plays a great part in the lives of men. Alena had one more June smelling of different grasses, with bitter birch dawns and a crystal sickle above the horizon. The little girl, Natalya, died.

Death beckons. Natalya died in April and Alena's life became empty. Yet God remained with her in her heart. She and Polunin went to bury her over the bridge—the river was in flood. They walked back in silence, side by side, and paused for a moment on the bridge—perhaps each one recalled his youth—and walked slowly on. At home it was deserted, damp and dark.

When June came around, Alena decided to go. Death beckons, beckons one to jump into the flood water, beckons in the distance, with finality, to make one walk, walk, walk—and there are people who go.

Her life lay behind and there she left June with its grasses, her sweetheart, Alexey, her daughter, Natalya, Polunin perhaps, her mother's secret; ahead lay death, God and the open road.

She said to Polunin in the morning:

"I'm going tomorrow. Good-bye."

"Where are you going?"

"Oh . . . to the monasteries . . . it doesn't matter where . . . to the holy places." And she went. She took her trunk back to her mother's cottage and at dawn set off through the fields, through the sea of corn, tasted the bittersweet grains of rye, gazed into the sky, went from one bell tower to the next, experienced to the full the smell of June and thought, as she looked at the road, that plantain is for cuts and herpes, and the dark-blue stars for snakebite.

In the monasteries, she said her prayers and took holy bread in remembrance of the dead.

She only sinned once, in a monastery guesthouse, in a dark corridor; sin is sweet in the presence of God and death beckons.

1918

A
Thousand
Years

"Let the dead bury their dead"

His brother, Constantine, arrived toward evening and talked that night with Vilyashev. He walked in, tall, thin, muffled in an overcoat, with his kepi in his hand. They did not light the candles. They talked for only a short while and Constantine went away almost immediately.

"She died quietly and peacefully. She believed in God. It's impossible to break away from what has been. One is surrounded by hunger, scurvy, typhus. People are like beasts. Utter depression reigns. As you see, I'm living in a hut. The house has been taken over—it's a stranger's now. We are strangers and they are strangers."

Constantine said shortly and quietly, "There were the three of us in the world: I, you and Natalya. *Finita*. I walked from the station and traveled in the pig wagon. I couldn't get here in time for the funeral."

"We buried her yesterday. She knew she was going to die. She didn't want to go anywhere or leave this place."

"She was an old maid. Her whole life was centered on this place."

Constantine went out without a word of farewell. The next time the younger Vilyashev saw his brother was again in the evening; they had both spent the whole day wandering in the dry valleys. There was nothing for them to talk about.

The sunrise was yellow and dull. Vilyashev noticed a golden eagle at sunrise on the mound. The eagle was perched on the flat summit of the mound, and it was tearing at a dove. Catching sight of Vilyashev, it flew off into the waste of sky toward the east, sending a lonely, guttural cry over the spring fields. This lonely, sorrowful cry remained in his memory for a long time.

From a hillock by the mound there was a view for about ten miles around—meadows, young woods, villages and white belfries. A red sun appeared over the meadowlands and pink mists came crawling in. A morning frost crisp with icicles hung about the hedges. It was spring, the sky hung in a deep-blue cupola over the earth, kindly winds blew, exciting as half-dreams. The earth was swollen and breathed like a satyr. Migrating birds flew by night; at dawn the cranes called by the barrow and then their voices sounded glassy, transparent and mournful. The tumultuous abundance of spring was on its way—the unchanging and preeminent.

Bells tolled above the spring earth. Typhus, hunger and death walked the villages and huts. The blind huts stood as before, their rotten thatch waving in the wind as it had waved five hundred years ago when it was removed each spring and carried deeper into the forest, toward the east. There was death in each hut. In all of them someone in high fever under the icons was yielding up his soul to God in the same way that he had lived—quietly, cruelly. There was hunger in each hut. Each hut was lighted with torches in the evenings, and they made fire by striking flints, as had been done five hundred years before. The living carried the dead to church, and the spring bells tolled. The living in their confusion walked the fields in procession behind the Cross, and they went around the villages, sprinkling them with holy water and blessing the hedgerows; they prayed for the corn, and that they might be spared from death, and the noise of the bells broke on the spring air. At twilight the songs of the young women still rang out: at this hour they came to the mound in their bright homespun garments and sang old songs, since spring was coming and the time was ripe for childbirth. The young men had left for the cruel war; now they were stationed near Uralsk, near Ufa, near Archangel. This spring the old men would come out to plow the earth.

Vilyashev—Prince Vilyashev, his ancient title descended from Monomakh*—stood downcast on the hill and gazed into the distance. He was a warrior. He had no thoughts. He felt pain because he knew that everything was ended. Five hundred years ago perhaps, his ancestor stood as he did now, but with a sword, in a coat of mail, leaning on his spear; even his mustache was probably like Constantine's. His whole life was spread out before him. Natalya died from famine-typhus; she recognized her death and welcomed it. Neither Constantine, the eldest, nor he, nor Natalya, the youngest, were needed. The nest lay ruined—the nest of the birds of prey. They had been a plundering people. The Vilyashevs had been strong; now their strength was powerless.

Leaving the mound, Vilyashev set out for the river Oka, over ten miles away. He wandered about the whole day, walking over the fields and through the valleys. He was heavily built, broad across the shoulders, with a beard down to his waist—a warrior. The snow still lay in the gullies and streams ran noisily in their rocky beds. The swollen earth stuck to his boots, and the sky was warm and huge, as it is in spring. The Oka poured itself out in a wide expanse. A wind passed over the river and there was a kind of dreaminess in the wind, as in the young Russian girl who has not yet experienced passion. One wanted to stretch and relax one's muscles; Vilyashev felt grief and a stirring half-sleep, an anxiety. A Russian feels nostalgia for distances; rivers beckon like wide roads to new places: the old blood was still alive. Vilyashev lay prone on the ground with his head on his hands, motionless. The hill above the Oka was bald and the wind caressed Vilyashev gently. Larks shrilled overhead. From the right, from the left, from behind, came the noise of birds, for the spring air carried all sounds clearly, but from the river came a severe silence, and it was only at dusk that the echo of bells from over the water moaned above it and was carried for many miles along the river. Vilyashev lay a long time, down-

* Prince of Pereyaslavl and Lord of Rostov, Vladimir Monomakh drove Khan Ofrak beyond the Iron Gates to the Caucasus.

cast, motionless—a warrior plunged in gloom—then he got
up swiftly and swiftly walked back. The wind caressed his
beard.

He met his brother by the mound. The sky was overspread
with a leaden evening tinge; the young birches and firs below
the mound became ghostly and somber. For a few minutes the
whole world waxed yellow like a marsh plant, then it turned
green and began to go blue quickly, like indigo. A purple
line gleamed in the west, mist crawled over the valley, geese
cried as they flew past, a bittern moaned, and the silence of
a spring night fell, that silence which does not lose a single
sound but merges them into the expectant drone of spring—
expectant as spring itself. His brother, Prince Constantine,
was making straight for the mound, a walking stick in his
hand. He was wearing his cap and his English overcoat with
the collar turned up. He reached it and began to smoke; the
little light illuminated his eagle nose and bony forehead, and
his gray eyes, shining cold and calm like November.

"In spring, during the migrations, something draws a
man away like a bird. How did Natalya die?"

"She died at daybreak, fully conscious; she lived uncon-
scious, hating and despising."

"Look about you." Constantine was silent a moment. "I
was thinking, tomorrow is the Annunciation! Look."

The barrow was a dark stain, last year's grass barely
rustled, air bubbled out of the earth, an earthen gas of some
sort. A smell of rot rose up. The sky beyond the mound was
lowering, and the valley stretched out, deserted and boundless.
The air grew damper and colder. In the old days there had
been a pathway through the valley.

"Can you hear it?"

"What?"

"The earth is groaning."

"Yes, it's waking. Spring. Earth's joy."

"No. I don't mean that . . . but mourning. It smells of
rot. Tomorrow is the Annunciation, a great holiday. I was
thinking, look about you. People have become crazed, savages; death, hunger, barbarism prevail. People have become
crazed from horror and bloodshed. People still believe in
God and carry the dead forth when they should be burned—

and idolatry still exists. They still believe in satyrs, witches, in the devil and in God. People seek to rid themselves of spotted typhus with processions of the Cross. I stood the whole way in the train to avoid infection. People think of nothing but bread. On the way I wanted to sleep but a lady in a little hat kept swimming before my eyes and she repeated rapturously that she was going to her sister's to drink a little milk. I felt nauseated; she didn't say 'bread,' 'meat,' 'milk,' but used all the diminutives. 'My darling butterkins, I shall eat you up!' Savagery, the people are becoming savage, the whole world is atavistic. Remind yourself of the history of all times and all peoples: sectarianism, chicanery, stupidity, superstition, cannibalism. Not so long ago, in the Thirty Years' War, there was cannibalism in Europe; they boiled and ate human flesh. . . . Brotherhood, equality, freedom. . . . If brotherhood must be brought in by force . . . then . . . better . . . do without. . . . I'm lonely, brother. I feel grieved and lonely. How does man differ from the beasts?"

Constantine took off his kepi. His bony forehead was pale, greenish in the evening gloom, his eyes were sunken. For a moment the face resembled a skull, but the prince moved his head, glanced westward, and his nose became a predatory beak: something birdlike, predatory, cruel passed across his face. Constantine took a piece of bread from his coat pocket and passed it to his brother.

"Eat it. You're hungry."

A bell could be heard tolling in the valley, and the dogs were barking beside the huts. The wind passed with a wide wing.

"Listen. I was thinking of the Annunciation. . . . I pictured to myself how . . . slowly the red dawn broke in the east. Dreaming forests stood around, marshes and swamps. In the valleys and woods, wolves howled. Wagons squeaked, horses neighed, people shouted. The wild Russian tribe had gone to collect tribute and was now returning by the valley path from Oka to Desna and Sozh. Slowly the red evening sky began to glow. The prince made his camp on the hill; the young prince, his son, was dying in the slow evening sunset. They prayed to the gods, burned maidens and youths on the fire, threw people into the water to the water spirit,

called on Jesus, on Perun, the Thunder God, and the Blessed
Virgin, to save the young prince. The young prince was dying;
he died in the terrible spring sunset. Then they killed his
horse and his wives, and made the mound. Now, in the
prince's camp there was an Arab, the learned Arab Ibn
Sadiph. He wore a white turban, was lean as an arrow,
supple as an arrow, dusky as resin, with the eyes and nose of
an eagle. Ibn Sadiph had mounted to Kama along the Volga
to the Bulgars, and was now making his way from Russia
through Kiev and Tsargrad. Ibn Sadiph was wandering over
the world, since he had seen everything except countries and
people. . . . Ibn Sadiph climbed the hill. They were burning
a pyre on the hill; on a log lay a naked girl with a gash in
her left breast. The fire licked her feet; frowning bearded
people with swords in their hands stood around; the ancient
shaman priest circled in front of the fire and shouted
frenziedly. Ibn Sadiph turned and left the pyre, and walked
down the valley road to the river. The sunset was growing
dim. Legible stars were in the sky and legible stars were
reflected in the water. The Arab glanced at the stars in the
sky and at the stars in the water, always equally precious and
phantomlike, and said, 'Woe, Woe.' Wolves howled over the
river. That night the Arab went to the prince. The prince was
supervising the feast for the dead. The Arab raised his arms
to heaven, his white robes rose like wings, and he said in a
voice like an eagle's cry: 'This is the night when exactly one
thousand years ago in Nazareth the Archangel told the Blessed
Virgin of the advent of your God, Jesus. Woe. One thousand
years!' So said Ibn Sadiph. No one in the camp had heard of
the Annunciation, of that bright day when a bird will not
weave its nest. . . . Do you hear, brother? Bells are ringing.
Can you hear how the dogs bark? . . . And over the earth as
before come hunger, death, barbarism, cannibalism. I feel
full of dread."

Dogs barked at the bottom of the hill beside the huts. The
night grew more blue and colder. Prince Constantine sat back
on his heels, leaning on his stick, but got up almost at once.

"It's late and cold now. Let's go. It's very uncanny. I
don't believe in anything. Savagery. What are we? What are
our sensations when savages surround us? It's lonely. I'm

lonely, brother. No one needs us. Not so long ago our ancestors whipped peasants in the stables, took girls to bed on their wedding nights. I curse them too. Beasts . . . Ibn Sadiph!" the prince shouted hollowly, bitterly, wildly. "A thousand years. I shall probably go from here to Moscow on foot."

"I have the strength of a warrior, Constantine," Vilyashev said softly. "I want to break, to uproot, and they have dealt with me as with a child."

The mound was left behind. They walked along the hill. The abundant swollen earth clung to their shoes and hampered their movements. Geese called in the gloom, astride the night. A mist hung blue over the valley. They entered the village. It was silent. A dog barked behind the wall. They walked noiselessly.

"There's typhus and barbarism in each hut," said Constantine, straining for sounds.

Beyond the huts on the road out of the village young women were singing the church troparion for the Annunciation. In the expectant spring evening the melody sounded solemnly simple and wise. And probably they felt that this troparion was unchanging as the spring was unchanging, with its law of birth. They stood a long while, taking the weight off one soaked foot after the other. Both probably felt that in spite of everything, a clear blood flows in man's veins.

"Good. Mournful. This will not die," said Vilyashev. "It has come down to us through the ages."

"Wonderfully good. Strangely good. Fearfully good!" answered Prince Constantine.

The girls turned the corner in their bright skirts and passed by in orderly pairs, singing:

> *Virgin Mother of God, rejoice! . . .*
> *Blessed Mary, the Lord be with Thee. . . .*
> *Blessed art Thou among women. . . .*

It smelled of the damp, abundant, swollen earth. The girls walked slowly. The brothers stood there a long while and went off quietly. The midnight cocks were crowing. Over the hill rose the last crescent moon before Easter, throwing deep shadows.

It was dark, damp and cold in the hut as it had been on the day of Natalya's death, when doors had banged unceasingly. The brothers went to their different rooms quickly, without talking or lighting the candles, and Constantine lay down on Natalya's bed.

At daybreak Constantine roused Vilyashev.

"I'm going. Good-bye. *Finita*. I will leave Russia and Europe. They called our fathers birds of prey here: with their borzoi dogs they hunted wolves, people, hares. Woe. Ibn Sadiph."

Constantine lighted the candle on the table and walked up and down the room. Vilyashev was amazed: across the whitewashed wall, distorted by the blue light of dawn, fell his brother's blue shadow, incredibly blue, as if laundry bluing had been spilled on the wall, and his brother, Prince Constantine, looked like a dead man.

1919

Wormwood

On their way back they climbed the bare height toward the excavations. A bitter scent of wormwood reached them. The wormwood had overgrown the hilltop in a dusty silver net and smelled bitter and dry. From that desolate height there was a view for forty miles all around; the Volga flowed just beyond the hills and farther off in the distance lay a fading town with a few lights and a fading stockade of chimneys. Dryness came on the wind from the steppe.

They stopped to take leave of one another and suddenly they saw naked women running from the valley in the direction of the excavations. They were running in a single line at a steady unhurried pace, their hair unplaited, black shadows on the pubic bone, feather-grass brooms in their hands. Silently the women ran up to the excavations, circled the ancient ruins and turned back to the ravine, the valley and the village beyond, raising the wormwood dust.

Baudek said:

"Fifteen miles away you have the big river port, but here people have beliefs which go back a thousand years. Young girls run around the boundary of their fields, exorcizing spirits with their chaste bodies. This is the week of Peter of Midsummer. Who would conceive of it—Peter of Midsummer!

That's better than the excavations. It's midnight now. Perhaps they are bewitching us. It's their secret."

Again dryness came on the wind from the steppe. In the unbounded sky a star fell; it was July, and the season of shooting stars was at hand. Crickets chirped with their dry, sudden music. The bitter scent of wormwood was very strong.

They took leave of one another. Saying good-bye, Baudek retained her hand a moment and said dully:

"Natalya, extraordinary one, when will you be mine?"

Presently Natalya answered quietly:

"Don't, Flor."

Baudek set off for the tents. Natalya went back to the ravine and walked down the narrow path, overgrown with snowball trees and maples, down to the farmstead and the agricultural commune. Night could not assuage the thirst of the day's ashes. The night too was full of thirst and sultry heat; the grass, the valleys, the Volga and the air all shone dry like tarnished silver. Dry dust rose from the pebbly path.

Svirid lay by the stables. He gazed into the sky, humming:

> *Volga, Volga, mother riv-ver!*
> *Smash the Kalchik with your fist!*
> *Volga, Volga, mighty riv-ver!*
> *Smash the communist with your fist!* . . .

Noticing Natalya, he said:

"It's night, Comrade Natalya, and still impossible to sleep. I feel like a game of cards. All the communists are out in the fields. You've been out to the excavations? They say they're excavating a town. We're living in such times now, there's nothing they can't dig up. Yes . . ."

And he began again:

> *Volga, Volga, mother riv-ver.* . . .

"The newspapers have come from town. What a smell of wormwood there is. This is the country of wormwood."

Natalya entered the small square reading room (the old landowners had used it as a sitting room) and lighted a candle. The dull oily light was reflected on the yellowing wooden pillars. The little cupboards with their fancy cloths and the revolving whatnots still stood about as before, and the windows were hung with homemade lace curtains. The low furniture was arranged with a careful and naïve orderliness.

She bent her head, and her heavy plaits fell forward, as she read the newspapers. The newspapers from the town were printed on brown paper and the others, from Moscow, were printed on dark-blue paper made from shavings, and they were all full of sedition and bitterness. No metal. Shortages. Only hunger, death, lies, terror and horror.

Semyon Ivanovich, an old revolutionary, with a beard like Marx's, came in, dropped into an armchair and lighted a cigarette nervously.

"Natalya?"

"Yes."

"I've been to town. You can't imagine what it's like. There's nothing to be had! When winter comes they'll all die of starvation and cold. It seems that in Russia there's no acid of any kind, and without acid you can't smelt steel, and without steel you can't make files, and so there is nothing to sharpen saws with, and you can't saw wood—all on account of this acid! It's dreadful. Can you feel the fear in the air, the dreadful, hollow silence? Look about you; death is more natural than life or birth. Death is everywhere—hunger, scurvy, typhus, smallpox, cholera. . . . The forest and ravines are teeming with cutthroats. Can you hear the deadly silence? Death. There are villages in the steppe where the people are all dead and rotting, with no one to bury the corpses, and at night deserters and dogs grovel in the stench. . . . The Russian people! . . ."

In Natalya's room on the top floor there stood a crucifix in the corner with tufts of grass decorating it. The mirror, on the fat redwood dressing table with all its old useless odds and ends, was cracked and blurred. The open drawer in the dressing table smelled of wax and contained a few fragments of bright silk material—it used to be a young girl's room in the old days, belonging to the daughter of the landowner. There were rugs and mats on the floor. Outside the window lay the wide stretch of the Volga, and beyond the river and the meadows, the steppe, the Medinsky forest, the Volga district, and one could imagine how in winter all this empty expanse would be under snow. Natalya stood a long while at the window plaiting her hair over again, and then she threw off her sarafan,* so that she was in her white shift. She thought about the archaeologist, Baudek, about Semyon Ivanovich, about herself, about the revolution and its bitterness, and about her own bitterness.

The martins announced the dawn, flying and singing in the yellowish, dry gloom. The last bat flew away. At dawn the scent of wormwood grew very strong and Natalya understood: It is not only July that smells of the bitter, fairy-tale scene of the wormwood on the steppe, but all our days. The bitterness of wormwood is the bitterness of every day. But it is with wormwood that country women drive devils and unclean spirits from their huts. The Russian people . . . she remembered them. In April on a small station on the steppe where there was only sky, steppe, five poplars, the railroad and a station shed, she had noticed three people, two peasants and a child. They all wore bast shoes, the old man had a short fur coat, the child was half-naked. Their noses seemed to suggest that both Chuvash and Tartar blood flowed in their veins. All three had thin, haggard faces. The broad yellow sunset glimmered. The old man's face resembled a hut, his hair falling on both sides like a thatched roof, his half-blind eyes (the dull windows) stared motionless into the west, as though he were a thousand years old. And these eyes held a boundless indifference, or perhaps the unfathomable wisdom af ages. Seeing them, Natalya thought: these are the authentic Russian people, these thin, gray people saturated with dirt and sweat, with faces as stark as huts, with hair like thatch. The old man stared into the west, the other sat motionless, his head on his bent knee. The little girl slept, tossing about on the asphalt, spattered with spittle and the husks of sunflower seeds. They were silent. It filled one with dread and weariness only to look at them, those people by whom and in whose name the revolution was being made. . . . A people without history—what else is the history of the Russian people?—a people who have composed folk tales, songs and choruses. . . .

* The sarafan was the national costume of Russian women, worn with an embroidered headdress.—TRANS.

Later on these peasants wandered by chance into the agricultural commune; they sang like pilgrims, bowed, begged
alms, told their story. They were from Vladimirsk, hunger
had driven them, they were on the steppe for the first time
and were now wandering about the steppe in the name of
Christ. At home they had left their huts boarded up, and had
eaten everything, even the horses. Natalya had seen lice
dropping from them.

In the yard the women went out to milk and the milk pails
clattered. The horses were driven in from their night quarters.
Semyon Ivanovich, who had not slept all night, was oiling a
cart with Svirid and was getting ready to fetch the hay from
the water meadows. The chickens, now growing up, were
bustling about. Day had come, turning the earth to ash with
its heat. It was time to drink the heat to the dregs, so that in
the evening she could go in search of that other wormwood,
Baudek's wormwood, the bitterness and the joy—for Natalya
had never yet experienced the joy of this wormwood, brought
to her by the days when one must live, now or never.

II

The Volga curved sharply and a desolate hill jutted over
the river, quite bare except for the white hazels crowded at
its base. It stood high above the Volga, a lonely landmark for
forty miles around. The ages preserved their name in it, for it
was called Uvek.*

On the summit of Uvek, people had noticed ruins and
barrows, and the archaeologist Baudek had come to excavate
them, taking charge of a workmen's association of peasants
from Tver, men who formerly got a living from the Volga
boats. The excavations had been going on for three weeks,
and the centuries were being unearthed. They found the
remains of an ancient town on Uvek, stone remains of a
system for raising water, foundations of buildings, canals. All
this had been preserved under limestone and black earth, left
by neither Scythians nor Bulgars, but by some unknown
people who came here from the Asiatic steppes to found
a town and vanish out of history forever. And after these

* In Russian the word for "age" is *vek*.—Trans.

unknown men, the Scythians had been here and they left their barrows. In the barrows, in stone sepulchers, in stone tombs, lay human skeletons, in clothing which disintegrated at the touch like ash, and there would be a scepter, a silver vase containing Arab coins, with pitchers and plates decorated with riders and hunters, which had once held food and drink. The bones of a horse lay at the feet of a dead man, and there was a saddle worked in gold, ivory and precious stones, and the leather had become mummified. Everything was dead in the stone sepulchers; they smelled of nothing and every time they were entered your thoughts became clear and calm and sorrow entered your heart. The summit of Uvek grew bare in the ash-dry heat of day, wormwood began to grow in a dusty silver net and it gave off a scent of bitterness. Ages passed.

Ages teach their lessons like the stars and Baudek knew the joy of bitterness. The archaeologist's values had become confused through his involvement with the past. A thing always tells less about life than about art, and the art of living is itself art. Baudek regarded life as an art, like all artists.

The men digging on Uvek woke at dawn and boiled water in a pot. They excavated. At midday dinner was brought from the commune. They rested. They dug again till the evening light faded. Then they made a campfire and sat around it, talking and singing songs. . . . Across the ravine, in the village, men plowed, mowed, ate, drank and slept in order to live—just as at the foot of the ravine in the commune they also worked, ate and slept. And in addition they all wished to taste tranquillity and happiness, and they did. A burning July was in progress, turning the days to ash, and as always the days were too translucent and wearying, while the nights brought peace and the unrest that belongs to night alone.

One group dug up the earth, a dry mixture of sand and clay, mixed with flints and belemnite; another carried it away in wheelbarrows and sieved it. They dug down to the stone entrance. Baudek and his assistants carefully sorted the stones. The sepulcher was dark. It smelled of nothing. The tomb stood on raised ground. They lighted torches. They made sketches. They lighted magnesium flares and took photographs. It was all very still and quiet. They lifted the 350-pound lid covered with verdigris.

"This man has probably lain here for two thousand years —twenty centuries."

Others on the edge of the ravine were excavating the remains of some sort of circular edifice, the stones still uncovered by time and lying exposed above ground. Around this ruin the girls had been running during the night.

Uvek dropped sheer. At its foot flowed the Volga in a wide, desolate expanse, a free river, and beyond the water meadows, the crest of Medin bristled, and the Medinsky forest. . . . No one on Uvek except the peasants from the village knew that deserters had reached Medin. They were a brigand army of peasants, they had thrown up mud huts, raised their tents, sent lookouts into the thickets. They formed an army with machine guns and rifles, and they were ready, if pressed, to descend on the steppes, raise a rebellion and march on the towns.

III

The sun revolved along its fiery pathway. The day wearied with the heat and the quivering silence; the horizon trembled in minute shivers, like liquid glass. At midday, during the rest hour, Natalya went up to the scene of the excavations and sat with Baudek in the sun on an upturned wheelbarrow amid the heaps of earth. The sun burned, and on the wheelbarrows, the black earth, the stones, the tents and the grass there was a haze like bright shreds of silk.

Natalya talked about the heat, about the revolution, about the days they lived in. She had felt and accepted the revolution with her whole heart and wanted to work for it—and the present days had brought wormwood, and smelled of wormwood. She talked like Semyon Ivanovich. And because Baudek put his head on her knees and the collar of his embroidered shirt lay open, baring his neck, and because of the heat, she experienced another kind of wormwood of which she said nothing. Again she began to talk like Semyon Ivanovich.

Baudek lay on his back, his gray eyes half closed. He held Natalya's hand and when she stopped speaking in the languorous heat, he said:

"Russia. The revolution. Yes. It smells of wormwood, of

the waters of life and death. Yes. Everything is in ruins. There
are no roads leading out. Yes . . . Think of the Russian fairy
tale about the waters of life and death. The foolish lad Ivan
was quite ruined, he had nothing left, he could not even die.
Yet Ivan prevailed, because truth was on his side and truth
battles against falsehood. Every kind of falsehood will be
conquered. All fairy tales grow out of sorrow, fear and falsehood, and the denouement is always reached through truth.
Look about you: Russia is now the scene of a fairy tale. The
people create tales, the people create revolutions, and the
revolution has begun like a fairy tale. Famine and death are
fabulous, surely? Are not the deaths of towns fabulous, or
their retreat into the seventeenth century? Look about you:
we are living through a fairy tale. There is a scent of wormwood, because it is all a fairy tale. And we too have our fairy
tale—your hands smell of wormwood."

Baudek put Natalya's hand to his eyes and gently kissed
her palm. Natalya sat bowed, her plaits hanging forward, and
again she had a strong sensation that for her the revolution
was bound up with joy, a turbulent joy, one that goes together
with grief, the bitterness of wormwood. A fairy tale. All were
figures in a fairy tale: Uvek, Medin, Semyon Ivanovich with
his beard like Marx—Marx, the Old Man of the Sea, evil as a
wizard.

Wheelbarrows, tents, earth, Uvek, Volga, the far distance.
All gleamed, burned and shone with patches of haze. It was
fiery, desolate and silent all around. The sun was approaching
three o'clock and gradually the diggers emerged from the
shade of the wheelbarrows and out of the pits, dressed in whatever chance offered—pink shorts, trousers of sacking, old mats
over their backs. They yawned, screwed up their faces, drank
water from pails, rolled themselves something to smoke.

One sat down opposite Baudek, began to smoke, and
scratching his bare hairy chest, said slowly:

"About time to start, Florich. . . . The horse has got to be
harnessed. We must lay Mikhail down somewhere. He's broken
out in a rash. Let's hope it won't be the end of him."

Toward evening the crickets began to sing. Natalya was in
the kitchen garden, carrying pails, watering the vegetables.
The sweat stood out in drops on her brow and her body,

tense under the weight of the pail, ached sweetly with un-
expended strength. Drops of water splashed on her bare feet
and the coolness brought rest. Toward evening in the cherry
orchard the hedge sparrow began to sing and then it stopped,
for it had remembered July. The last bees flew lazily in the
golden air on their way to the hive. She went to the orchard
and ate the black juicy cherries: the juice was like blood. In
among the bushes grew blue bellflowers and honeyflowers.
She plucked them from habit and made a wreath. Upstairs in
her young girl's room, she sorted the bits of silken stuff in the
dressing-table drawer and breathed in the smell of wax and
the old stale scent. She saw her room with new eyes: it was
full of a greenish twilight. Faint, quivering shadows stole over
the floor and the dark-blue walls with their ingenious old-
fashioned patterns absorbed you into their ancient tranquillity, simply and easily. She stood over the basin, splashing
in the cold water.

She heard the footsteps of Semyon Ivanovich, going in the
other direction, walked down to the foot of the ravine and lay
in the grass with her eyes closed.

The sun went down in a wide yellow sky.

IV

Late at night Baudek and Natalya came to the scene of
the excavations. There was a campfire near the tents, and they
were heating water. The fire burned brightly, crackling and
sending off sparks, and if anything, it seemed to make the
night more close, black and distinct. Far away on the steppe,
heat lightning gleamed. They were warming the pot on the
fire; some of them were sitting, others lying down.

"The dew is honeydew on that night and full of virtue,
and the grass has a special healing power. The ferns flower on
that night, brothers. And you must look where you're going
in the forest, because the trees walk from one place to
another. . . . Yes . . ."

They were silent.

Someone got up to look at the pot and a contorted
shadow crawled over the hill to fall down the ravine. Another
took a cinder and, throwing it from one hand to the other,

lighted a cigarette. It was very quiet for a moment and the crickets could be heard clearly. Behind the fire, a flash of lightning flamed up on the steppe and its dead light rose and faded clearly. The breeze blew restfully and without heat; it was obvious a thunderstorm was coming from the steppe.

Natalya and Baudek did not approach the fire but sat on the wheelbarrows.

"I was telling you, brothers, it was a bad idea to dig up these places. Because this place on Uvek is mysterious and always smells of wormwood. In the time of Stepan Timofeyevich,* a tower used to stand here on the very summit, and a Persian princess was imprisoned there, and this Persian princess, whose beauty no words can express, used to turn herself into a magpie. She flew over the steppe, troubling the people, savage as a wolf, bringing darkness in her wake. It all happened long ago. . . . Stepan Timofeyevich heard of this; he went to the tower and looked in at the window—the princess lay fast asleep—and he never realized that this was only her body lying there without the soul. The soul was flying over the earth in the shape of a magpie. Stepan Timofeyevich fetched a priest and sprinkled the windows with holy water. . . . Well, from that time the restless soul flies over Uvek, weeping, for it can't be united with her body, and beats against the stones. The tower has collapsed. Stepan Timofeyevich is nailed to a mountain in the Caucasus and she still sorrows, weeping. . . . This is a desolate, mysterious place. Sometimes girls seek the beauty of the Persian woman, naked, at night in Midsummer, though they have no knowledge of the secret. . . . And the wormwood grows here and should be left to grow."

Someone answered:

"Still, now Stepan Timofeyevich, the Ataman Razin, has come down from the mountain, and so we can dig. It's the revel-ution now, the people's rising."

"He's come down, come down, all right, my son," said the first, "but he hasn't reached these parts yet. All in good time, all in good time . . . About the revel-ution, you say right, it's

* Stenka Razin, a Robin Hood-like character, celebrated in song and story.

our revel-ution, a rebellion, the time has come. . . . Everything in its place . . ."

"Yes . . ."

One of the diggers got up and made for the tent. He noticed Baudek and said dryly:

"You were listening too, Florich. There's no call for you to listen to our peasant talk. . . . We say all manner of things."

They were quiet again. Some took up different positions casually and began to smoke.

"The times are good. . . . So long, friends. Don't get me wrong. Good-bye, sir."

And the old man with his white beard and white trousers, barefoot, got up and walked with unhurried steps down the valley toward the village, vanishing in the gloom.

The lightning gleamed nearer, more often and more distinctly, the night grew steadily blacker and deeper. The stars grew dim. The wind turned the leaves and blew cool. The first thunderclap sounded from the boundless distance.

Natalya sat perched on an upturned wheelbarrow, leaning with her hands on the bottom, her head bent down, the glow of the fire dimly lighting up her figure. She felt with every corner of her body an enormous joy, a joyful torment, sweet pain, and she understood the bitter grief of wormwood—a wonderful sweetness, a measureless and extraordinary joy. Each time Baudek happened to brush against her, she was scorched with wormwood and the magic water of life.

It was impossible to sleep that night.

The storm broke with a downpour of rain, with thunder and lightning. It caught Baudek and Natalya by the ruins of the Persian princess' tower. Natalya drank the wormwood, the witch's grief which the Persian princess had left on Uvek.

V

The dawn broke purple and red. At break of day soldiers arrived from the town and mounted machine guns on Uvek.

1920

At the Gates

Some years ago Olga Nikolayevna Zhmukhin, a merchant's wife, had a water tower built at the foot of the Sibrin Hill. This water tower is called Olga Nikolayevna for short. Olga Nikolayevna no longer produces any water, but still hoots at eight, two and four o'clock, hoots near the Sibrin Hill. On the other side of the town, Ivan Petrovich Bekesh, the clerk, wakes up in the mornings to the sound of the hooting, and while half awake he experiences a marvelous sorrow touched with pain, which burns like life itself and the springtime of our days. Ivan Petrovich once spent a couple of days on the Volga and it seems to him that Olga Nikolayevna hoots just like *Caucasus and Mercury*. Everyone knows how the Volga aches in spring with the sweetest sorrow and how the impulse comes to embrace the whole world in the rose-cold spring dawn. Ivan Petrovich drinks his carrot tea and goes off to work in the finance department. His life is poor.

Olga Nikolayevna was built at the foot of the Sibrin Hill. On this hill, beyond the rampart, near the Kremlin Gates, there was a club, once a social club and now a communist club. When Olga Nikolayevna hooted at two o'clock, Dr. Andrey Andreyevich Viralsky would arrive for luncheon. In the old days, just before he arrived, the waiter at the buffet would tell the boy to "freshen them up," and then the boy would lick the

sandwiches to freshen them up before giving them to the
doctor along with a carafe of vodka. But now they gave the
doctor an empty carafe and he filled it himself from a flask
in his waistcoat pocket. As always, after luncheon the doctor
would call through the ventilator across the street into his
own backyard:

"Ilya, the horses!" and then he would go off to see his
patients while propping up his paunch on his walking stick.

It was Christmas.

Someone came along, a certain snob, and gave instructions
that everyone should feel the occasion, hide their poverty, give
up their petty preoccupations and thoughts for a week, so
that they might feel all the more acutely—in their darned and
patched-up state—their poverty, their squalor, their bored
depression and their habital condition. However, human
happiness is always happiness and is always blessed. It was
Christmas.

Olga Nikolayevna did not hoot at four because it was
Christmas. The real Olga Nikolayevna had died two Christ-
mases ago from fright when her smoked geese and some
of her furs were requisitioned. Handwritten notices were hanging on the walls of the club. The waiter knew that on Christmas Eve the cavalry orchestra would be playing at the military commissar's house in honor of his wife's birthday, and
on the first and fourth days of the holiday at the club, and on
New Year's Eve, the men of the battalion were arranging a
trip out of town. On Christmas Eve everyone went to St.
John's Church to see the new churchwarden—the divisional
commander, Comrade Tanatar, a handsome Kabardian, with
a leather jacket and spurs on his boots. He sold the candles
and took the plate around. People killed chickens, bartered
shirts for butter and baked sweet pies with white beet instead
of sugar—the chemist shops had been empty since a week
before the holiday.

And it was freezing and there was a blizzard. In Viralsky's
stone house, silent as a coffer on the Sibrin Hill, it was only
possible to live in two rooms, as the rest were filled with frost
and rime. And on the first day, on the first night of Christmas,
Olga heard the coming of the frost. The frost really came
cracking with a sound of frozen diamonds, the night was blue

and biting like glass, and the moon seemed to have been tossed in by accident. Olga wore her fur coat as usual. She stood by the hinged ventilator and listened. The frost was coming, crunching away here and there in the empty drawing room, and the steps of passersby squeaked in many tracks in the street. Then the waxlike morning came—the air in the frost-bound sun was yellow like wax, like the face of a corpse. The barometer fell to thirty-two; Ilya said the birds were falling from the air. And in the morning, Comrade Tanatar sped past, his greatcoat flung over his shoulders. In the evening, someone telephoned and said a snowstorm was coming from the Urals, and the blizzard came that night. For a few moments, Olga felt extraordinarily well—as one does in a snowstorm when everything circles around, whistles and sings. But all the same, witchcraft really must exist, since the flying hair of the snowstorm looked just like the hair of a witch. The blizzard rushed headlong, danced, howled, groaned and shouted over the fields, the hills, over the Sibrin Hill and in the empty drawing room. Everything was white and white and white. The hair of the storm stood on end and within it houses, alleys, trees descended and ascended and swayed. Everything sang, groaned, shouted, above the house and in the house, and in the house it was only possible to stay in one corner by the stove. Olga thought the revolution was like the blizzard and the people in it were like snowflakes. Olga thought she had died in the blizzard. Olga wore her fur coat and boots, and she huddled against the stove as she had done for many days now, tired of thinking and tired of reading.

Olga was reading Ivan Petrovich Bekesh's diary in the snowstorm.

Five icon lamps hung before Olga. The divan was hollowed out by all this sitting by the stove and it was heaped with fur coats. The tiles gleamed dimly from time to time. Behind the wall in the empty rooms the blizzard howled.

July 11th, 1913
    . . . a ball . . . given by Olga Nikolayevna Zhmukhin.
    We dressed up and set off with the Volinsky girl. The party was in full swing. The elderly people were in two small rooms and our crowd was quite separate, isolated

from prying eyes. Samuel Tanatar settled me down next
to him and the Volinsky girl was opposite. I had only
just sat down and taken a glass when she began begging
that "we shouldn't drink too much. . . ." She promised
to spend the evening with me and let me see her home
on condition I didn't get drunk. In less than half an
hour, they began to fool about and shout "bring the
wine." There was singing, shouting and breaking of
crockery. . . . One's organism began to demand that one
should drink a little less. . . . I began to get a little
tipsy myself. In order not to get drunk, I went up to the
Volinsky girl. "Well, am I to see you home, or Tanatar?" She had been sitting beside him and was talking
about being escorted back. "I don't know," she said and
added, "Vanya, after all, you're drunk." I answered, "All
right," and went into the other room, where Dr. Viralsky,
the father of my dearest Olga, was sitting. He saw me
and sat me down beside him and silently offered me
something in a glass. To spite the Volinsky girl I drank
it and became drunk there and then. My friends took
me into the garden, gave me some seltzer water and
went away. I sat on a bench and cried for a long time,
wondering why on earth I had got so drunk, and thinking about Olga Viralsky, whom alone I loved. . . .
Why had I got so drunk? I had ruined the whole evening, ruined everything. I was not alone for long. The
Volinsky girl arrived, sat down next to me and began
to lecture me: "You shouldn't drink so much wine." I
had not lost my powers of reasoning and said, "It wasn't
my fault. It was Samuel's fault—I heard you arrange
to walk home with him. And so having heard everything
and made my point, I'm sitting here blind drunk. The
things we wanted to do are impossible now because I'm
drunk." She leaned close to me and put her arms around
me. I kissed her hands. "Forgive me, forgive me!" and
implored her not to leave me, adding, "I know we are
seeing each other for the last time." And then I tore
myself away from her and from Tanatar (who had been
with us all the time). . . . She didn't want to let me go,
but I tore myself away. Tanatar caught me and sat me
down beside her again. She embraced me and said,
"Vanya, if you love me, you won't commit suicide," and

holding me more wildly and tightly, she kissed me on
the mouth . . . and grew still. . . . There was so much
sympathy, despair, frenzy, passion and such supreme
love in this kiss . . . minute after minute passed and each
was an eternity, and each was full of memories (memories of Olga Viralsky). . . . Yes! In this kiss she gave me
a fantastic illusion of happiness, only an illusion—but
still happiness! When she left me (to dance), I caught
sight of Tanatar and drove him away, shouting, "You
absolute swine! You've wrecked my happiness!" At this
point I even burst into tears. "I don't want to know
you any more. . . ." Tanatar bathed my head and gave
me another seltzer water, which made me sick. They
decided unanimously to put me to bed. But no, devil
take it, I wouldn't go with anyone except the Volinsky
girl. . . . She helped me (I couldn't manage it alone) to
get to bed and then tried to leave, but that was not what
I wanted. I held on to her and sang:

"Don't leave me, stay with me, I feel so happy and
so gay."

She stood there in front of me. I saw her beautiful
attractive figure and saw her thick gold gleaming hair
(a chignon), teeth as white as snow behind the bright
sensitive lips . . . and an electric current passed through
me. . . . Yes, happiness was so near, so near (Tanatar had
it). . . . Oh, happiness!

July 12th, 1913

I woke up about one the next day and immediately
caught sight of Vasya Fedorov. He was sleeping in an
interesting way—his head on the pillow and the rest
of him on the dirty floor. I glanced in the mirror and—
heavens!—jumped away again. My suit was crumpled
and stained with sickness and I was covered in fluff from
the eiderdown. We tidied up and went out into the
garden. There we met Tanatar; he passed us in silence,
coming from far down the garden, where he had probably slept. He looked awful. The front of his suit was
stained with sickness, and the back was covered with
earth as if someone had been dragging him around by
his feet. Then we met the girls, who were coming out of
the summerhouse, where they had been sleeping. Grad-

ually we all met again. And how we laughed! First the
lunatic Fedorov described how last night, when he could
hardly stand, he had made his way somehow to the
summerhouse, where the girls had just settled down, and
wished them good night, taking the first dress he could
lay hands on, along with a jacket and hat, dressing up
and dancing. One young man we knew less well spent
all the supper interval and half the dance sitting with
the hostess, Olga. Nikolayevna, in the phaeton out in
the yard, where the servants brought them supper and
wine, all this to the accompaniment of kisses and *très
piquante* conversation. The girls told how they had not
yet all got undressed when Tanatar broke in, drunk as
a coot, and announced he had come to sleep with them.
Of course, the girls got scared and hid under the
blankets. He remained cold and ugly to all their requests
and commands that he should free the summerhouse of
his presence. Then the girls, ignoring the conventions,
jumped out of bed, seized him and pushed him out . . .
Immediately after Tanatar, the lunatic Fedorov had
arrived and there was a lot of laughter, because he was
charming and not ugly like Tanatar.

Happiness! Happiness and laughter! Somewhere a story the
nurse used to tell her in childhood was lost—the snowstorm's
hair, the snowy crest must be shorn with a sharp knife and then
her granddaughter, the snow maiden, would be killed. A drop
of cold white snow maiden's blood would fall and this blood
brought happiness—happiness. . . . Believe me, if you go out
into the snowstorm and lie in wait for the storm's granddaughter, who circles endlessly in a white chorus, then there
will be happiness.

Well, and if you don't believe in anything?

Happiness! Happiness!

Olga knew she was this snow maiden. They had killed her.
The blizzard sped along; they spoke of it last night on the
telephone. The furs were lying on the divan. Five icon lamps
were burning and the tiles gleamed from time to time. Dr.
Viralsky was snoring. The diary fell to her knees and her tears
fell. About him. Her head dropped into her hands.

Well, and if you don't believe in anything? If they have

killed you, like the snow maiden? If you don't bake pies with
beet instead of sugar, as the doctor says, even if that would
please your father. No, they hadn't killed her, but he had.
Fairy tales are mindless and there is no venom in them. Olga
Viralsky's life was very simple: high school, lessons, Red
Front . . . Don't judge what you can't understand . . . and
he, that one . . . A dark Army stable, the odor of horses, a
dim lamp on the wall, the head of a horse and his own head,
dark as pitch, a black beard, black brows, black eyes, red lips
—pain, pain, horror and ugliness. That was all.

The diary fell on her knees and her tears fell. The icon
lamps burned; her eyes were like lamps in autumn rain. Her
head dropped into her hands. Heaviness, pain.

The telephone rang.

"Yes?"

"Dr. Fedorov."

"Well, and if you don't believe in anything? No, it's impossible to go on living. There's nothing but philistinism.
There are no fairy tales, none."

Christmas. . . .

Pies. Mutton pies made with mutton fat. Sweets made of
vegetable marrow. And dumplings. . . . A ball. A masked ball
on the fourth day of Christmas.

"Olga, Olga Andreyevna. This hurts me very much, I love
you very much. . . . You mustn't grieve . . . Olenka . . . What
does it matter, we keep alive on various carbohydrates. No,
I don't mean that. Olenka, Olenka, you must pluck up courage. It's very empty. . . ."

Tanatar? Don't, don't, don't!

"No, Vasya. It's nothing. I've only got what they call
neurasthenia, I expect. And it's depressing in a worn-out dress
with down-at-the-heels boots, depressing to feel ashamed of
them and to be happy about a pound of mutton. There isn't
anything."

Olga bent her head. Her comb was sewn up very neatly
with a thread, so it didn't show at all and looked as pretty as
before.

Dr. Viralsky came out of his room in his fur coat and boots
and went over to the stove.

"I've brought a little mutton, Olenka. Shall we fry it and spoil ourselves a bit or use it for soup? Tell Ilya."

"Papa, what did Olga Nikolayevna Zhmukhin die of?"

"From a heart attack. She took fright when they searched the house. They found her dead under the bed. . . . Why?"

"What sort of a person was she?"

"What sort of a person? . . . A loose woman . . . but generous. . . . Tell him to fry it."

The doctor yawned sweetly.

11

Toward Christmas Eve a man was sent around to distribute the following advertisement:

If you wish to obtain the following goods, namely:

Sugar (lump)	1000 r. per lb.		
Sugar (granulated)	800	" "	"
Mutton	450	" "	"
Pork	700	" "	"
Meat (Circassian)	250	" "	"
Meat (Russian)	225	" "	"
Meat (horse)	100	" "	"

Tell our messenger what you want and in what quantity at 6 o'clock and all the items listed will be delivered immediately. There is no deposit, we rely on your honesty.

Well wishers.

We request that this not be taken as a joke.

Christmas Eve . . .

A large, clear star should arise on Christmas Eve and weld everything together, but no such star arises.

Dr. Fedorov's mother was baking pies, and she was happy because in the evening there would be a star and there would be dumplings, because there would be no potatoes, and most important of all, because of Vasya, her one and only son and her all. There would be napkins and a cloth and kerosene and a sweet and dumplings such as existed nowhere else in the whole town.

Next to happiness lies the greatest sorrow: so it was for the mother. Next to sorrow lies the greatest happiness: so it was for Dr. Fedorov. The doctor chopped wood and kept the stove going for his mother and his heart contracted with tenderness and love for his mother. Mama, Mama in an apron, an old lady, anxious, happy and unhappy—about the dumplings, the sweet pie and the pie made with mutton fat.

There was a ball at the military commissar's on Christmas Eve, an orchestra, waiters, geese, pork, hot punch, biscuits, pies, sweets, a magic lantern, forfeits, charades, postman's knock and speeches—a gathering of the third estate, namely, of the intelligentsia and members of the Communist Party.

Ivan Petrovich Bekesh had nothing extra on Christmas Eve, because if there were people who knew how to get something edible in the hungry town, Ivan Petrovich did not, and he had to eat the potatoes they had rationed out so they would not die until about spring, along with his mother, his godmother and his wife and child, rotten potatoes measured out to last until about July 15th inclusive.

On Christmas Eve, Dr. Fedorov and the writer Jacob Kaminin made their way toward Bekesh's house across the small side streets which were thickly fenced, along squeaky snow in the dark-blue twilight and in a red patch of sunset, along the outskirts of the town where the houses were buried roof and all and where the empty fields lay. On this Christmas Eve Bekesh was playing *vingt-et-un* with his wife, his mother and his godmother and he asked his guests into his study, where there was a double bed, a Japanese fan and a table with postcards on it arranged neatly and symmetrically. Kaminin nearly reached the ceiling and he sat down to the table with his hat on. Ivan Petrovich knew why the doctor and the writer had called on him, but he asked:

"What brings you here? It's been a long time!"

"We came on foot," answered Kaminin.

"Yes . . ."

"Ha ha! Of course!"

"Do light up. The shag is fresh."

"How are you?"

"Hm . . . What we do is of no great concern. We live, munch bread . . . as a matter of fact there isn't much bread. . . . No, well, we live as we can."

They were silent awhile. They lighted up and inhaled.

"We have come about the diaries."

"Ah, about the diaries. Yes. I don't go back on my word . . . only . . ."

"Then you will sell."

"I won't go back on my word, but what use are they to you? Just trifles."

"I need them," said Kaminin and inhaled.

(For Olga, dear Olga Viralsky, Fedorov thought painfully and sharply.)

"Of course, as material, for a writer . . ."

"Yes, as material."

"But may I ask what interests you about them, Jacob Sergeyevich?"

"Well, a great deal, you know, yes. . . ."

"Are you going to write a novel?"

"Well, I don't know about that. Perhaps."

They fell silent again.

"Well . . ."

"Oh, but you know, I can't for that price."

"What price?"

"The one we settled for. I'm only selling them to you because you are a writer. I would never sell them to anyone else at any price."

"No one else would buy them. Not even for wrapping paper."

"That's true! That's absolutely true! But don't forget it's my whole soul. My whole life is there. . . ."

"Yes."

"You want to pay one thousand rubles?"

"You named the price yourself."

"No, I made a mistake. I can't do it for a thousand."

Dr. Fedorov noticed that Bekesh had begun to tremble and there was sweat on his brow. He sat unnaturally and made jerky movements as if he were on hinges. In this jerking and the drop of sweat on his brow there was something cringing, something calculated, groveling. Jacob Kaminin, who had written fifteen books, looked rather like Don Quixote, sitting there with his hat on, with bony legs, smoking in a bored way, and speaking in an unhurried and bored way too.

(Olenka, Olenka, dear one, my precious, and Fedorov's heart contracted with love and pain.)

"Well, you show me the diaries."

Ivan Petrovich made a jerky movement as if to get up but remained seated.

"Honestly, I don't know where they are. . . . I think they're in the trunk and then you have some of them. Let's leave it. Let's talk of something else."

"No, let's get it over with. . . ."

"Well, all right, I'll have a look in a minute." Ivan Petrovich crawled under the table and produced a bundle of notebooks.

(Oh, but there is something very vile about this. Very vile. And if one doesn't believe in anything?)

Dr. Fedorov lowered his eyes painfully. Kaminin rolled another cigar and began to untie the bundle.

"Do smoke. This shag is strong. How much then?"

"My poems are there too. . . ."

"Yes. How much, then?"

"The price? Honestly, I'm not selling. . . . I don't know how much. . . ."

(Painful. Painful. Human poverty. And if one doesn't believe in anything? . . . Olga doesn't believe in anything—and her comb is sewn neatly so that no one would notice. And at home there is Mother. She is making dumplings, an old lady in an old apron and her pince-nez are stuck together with sealing wax. . . . Dumplings like none other in the whole town —for him, for Dr. Fedorov. The diary is for Olga Viralsky.)

"Listen, it's late, and I've got a headache. Hurry up and get it over with." This from the doctor.

Ivan Petrovich was watching Kaminin leaf through the books and suddenly his face became tender, attractive and clear.

"All right! I'll give in, Jacob Sergeyevich! Only leave me this one small notebook. Here I described my love for Olga Viralsky and it was her words—a precious memory. My first love . . . What do you want it for? Most important to me are her words. She wrote them in in pencil. Leave this."

"Well, all right, I'll leave it," Kaminin said.

"No, this one too!" said the doctor painfully.

"Leave it, Doctor, no matter," said Kaminin.

"Vasya, after all, you're a childhood friend. Leave it," said Bekesh.

"Either . . . Oh, all right. It doesn't matter. All this is very painful."

"My very soul. And so cheap," said Bekesh.

They started to walk back again in silence along solitary lanes, between fences, through the snow in the blue twilight. Only the icon screen of the west gradually became tarnished and the twilight hammered into the hard sky the heads of the nails of the Christmas stars. They met a woman in a shawl, a beautiful woman, carrying an ornamented yoke and buckets. Jacob Sergeyevich followed her with his eyes for a long time and then stopped, his long legs wide apart, looking simultaneously like Don Quixote and a large pair of scissors, and he said:

"Do smoke. . . . There is beauty in everything painful. What a beautiful woman, yes. . . . You know, I've managed to lay my hands on a hundred pounds of cod liver oil and potatoes and so I can survive another couple of years for the sake of beauty. I must write another book. I've written fifteen books and I wrote each book with a new woman. I think my wife and Tanatar are having an affair. . . . And now Olga Andreyevna Viralsky has made her appearance. She is very beautiful. . . . What a beautiful woman that was with the yoke."

"That's Bekesh's wife," said Fedorov.

"Really? But Bekesh is already selling his diaries while I still have some cod liver oil."

"Jacob Sergeyevich! Aren't you afraid of what you are doing?"

"What's that? After all, I have to write a book."

The writer Kaminin did not disclose that besides the oil and potatoes he also had some denatured alcohol. His wife was not at home. Without undressing and still wearing his hat,

Kaminin peeled some potatoes with a damaged antique saber and boiled them. Drawing his lips to one side in a convulsive gesture, he drank some alcohol, drank some cod liver oil, lay down on the divan and fell asleep with a clear and calm expression on his face, but with his lips twisted wryly as before.

At Dr. Fedorov's there were dumplings. They had a pie, napkins, a large lamp, and his mother said in her excited and preoccupied way: "Do have some, Vasya, my dear, take a little more, my dear boy."

Dr. Fedorov ate the good things, but there were not enough dumplings to satisfy him and Mama had not had time to comb her hair and take off her apron for the holiday. . . .

The festive season was in full swing, the season in which the she-devil dances out her final witchcraft—before the coming of spring, of the sun of happiness. . . .

They brought Dr. Fedorov a letter in this odd style:

SOVIET———

DEPT. OF LAB.

POPOVKY VILLAGE

Certification Card

Given to the citizen refugee of Popovky village Anton Joseph Panaschuky, because he wishes to be vaccinated to avoid catching cholera on his way, and also to his mother, Anna Pavlovna Panaschuky, who is in town, which the village Soviet endorsed.

CHAIRMAN,–I. PTITSYN

(Stamped)

Here is an extract from the writer's notebook:

Late at night, in the blizzard, depressed, a mother goes into her child's room; the boy is asleep, she roots about in the pockets of his shorts and sorts out the endless bits of string, screws, nails, cotton reels—and begins to cry.

A superficially smart lady from Astrakhan impulsively gives her lover a ring, and then, coming to her senses and afraid of a row with her husband, goes to the lost-property office about it.

A thanksgiving service for the good health of the horse Bucephalus.

III

How does the story continue?

On the first day of Christmas people get dressed up and pay calls. And on the first, the second, the third and the fourth days of Christmas one must go to bed at four, be happy, have a good time, arrange soirees, five-o'clock teas and dances, pay court to the ladies, become transformed—and remain as one always is, suffer as one always does—and not suffer as usual. On the first day everyone went to the Communist Club. Tanatar spent the day giving young ladies troika rides all over the town. Tanatar, the handsome Kabardian, spent the night of Christmas Eve lying beside the icons in the empty family house, and he looked like a large, tired black cat. The icon lamps were burning and the silver gleamed. Comrade Tanatar lay curled up as if about to leap to his feet. His eyes, black under their brows in a dry, dark face, reflected in their despair and suffering the yellow anguish of the icon lamps. His wife appeared in the doorway—pale, white—and said softly, "Get up, Samuel!" and Tanatar contracted still more, drawing close to the floor, in distress, frantic and suffering.

Once at the front, in the Volga district, in the limestone, Tanatar had accidentally squashed a black lizard under his boot—its entrails and its eyes had popped out—and, if his wife had seen that lizard she would have noticed that Samuel's eyes that Christmas night looked like the eyes of the lizard on that other day in the steppe. "Get up, Samuel!" His wife wandered about that night, pale, white, around the dark rooms, from the room with the icons to the kitchen, where the orderlies were laughing and playing cards.

In the corridor the night light was smoking. The corridor was littered with saddles, sabers, overcoats, horse blankets, and there was the acrid smell of horse sweat.

"Get up, Samuel!"

The blizzard still raged. The same blizzard which had revealed to Olga the secret of the snowstorm's snowy granddaughter: witchcraft must after all exist. It was difficult to wander about that night. The wind tore itself off the roofs and turned somersaults, circling in frenzy, rushing over the waste ground and the fences. The snow swayed like the waves of the sea and it was not possible to walk but only to crawl in that mist of snow, that whirlwind of snow, in its cries, moans and howls, in a white obscurity, in white funeral dirges. Three people were wandering about that night on the Sibrin Hill near the house of Andrey Andreyevich Viralsky. Tanatar left his house and it must have seemed to him that the white witch—the snowstorm—seized him by the throat with icy hands. He hunched his shoulders and his birdlike face with its crooked nose advanced, so that again it looked as if the man were ready to leap forward like an animal. He explored the little crossing and mews waist-deep in snow and then took up a position by the invisible Viralsky house—you could only see a step or two ahead. The blizzard came from the foot of the hill, from the fields, and sought to break into the houses and streets with a great shout. Out of the blizzard a man walked right into Tanatar.

In the howling of the blizzard their voices were drowned.

"Who's that?"

"Commander of the cavalry division. Dr. Fedorov." The words were drowned. Tanatar contracted still further into himself and Fedorov could not make out whether Tanatar shouted out loud, whether it was the noise of the storm or whether his own inflamed thoughts put the words together:

"Are you spying on Olga? I'll not give Olga up! Olga is mine! Don't you know me—Tanatar? Tanatar will kill you!"

They parted, but, frightened, met up once again, and having met, they encountered one another a third time by the fence. In the blizzard, huddled against the fence, stood a white woman. And when they had passed her, Tanatar whispered in Fedorov's ear, clearly and softly, wafting warmth against his ear, "That's my wife. My wife. A pale invalid. She watches everything, knows everything and keeps silent. Anemia. Dr. Fedorov, Vasya, how depressing it all is! Vasya, there's nothing to live for. I'm like a beast, without culture, knowing nothing. . . . And my wife—she keeps silent and knows everything. . . .

She says that we must love our fellow men, we must love
each last Ivan Bekesh . . . they have forgotten man!"

They passed two little streets and met Bekesh. Ivan Petrovich was standing by a curbstone, resting a sack against it, and
when he recognized his friends, he called out gaily:

"Oh, you gave me a fright! I've bought some bread for the
holiday. I'm carrying it home in the dark, so it doesn't get
stolen."

And the blizzard raged on. . . . During the blizzard they
all went to Jacob Kaminin's, drank tea from soup plates,
peeled potatoes with the antique saber, sent out for home-
brewed brandy, and in the storm, to the accompaniment of
raucous cries and laughter, played *chemin de fer*. That whole
night and all next day the writer Jacob Kaminin and the
military expert Samuel Tanatar stood at the antique round
table, since they could not play sitting down. Oil lamps were
burning and then a gray mist showed itself, the oil lamps went
out and the day began. The table was littered with cards,
thousand-ruble-notes, glasses, plates, potatoes and tobacco. Tanatar had already sent a messenger home twice to his pale, white
wife for thousand-ruble-notes from Army funds. Other people
would leave the table and take a nap on the divan, getting
up an hour later to play again. Just before daybreak, in the
first light, the women vanished and returned again at noon.
The room was like the heads of the players: the room had
grown old with insomnia, as in their heads the smoke of cigars
circled around, the smell of spirits produced exhaustion. In
weary concentration, the round table, the divan with its rug
and dusty smell, the oil lamps, were imprinted on the brain—
there must be hope. It was as gray in the head of the writer
Jacob Kaminin as in the smoke-filled room, and in Tanatar's
dark head it was even darker, far darker. Dr. Fedorov had
long ago fallen asleep on the divan. Jacob Kaminin must have
been right when he said to all the newcomers:

"Do smoke. You know, cards are unique, a miracle on
earth. It must be so. That's why we can go without sleep for
them at night. A miracle. Which of us does not dream of a
miracle? The queen of spades, the king of clubs and the nine.
Unique. A miracle. And beautiful. The other miracle is
woman."

As he played, Kaminin crossed things out in his pocket diary.

"And the calendar is a miracle too."

After they had had their sleep, toward noon, the women returned and boiled potatoes for the players. Irina, Kaminin's wife, did not peel potatoes for her husband but for Tanatar. Kaminin peeled his own with the antique saber, hardly able to stand any longer on his thin legs, in riding breeches, with eyes as clear as a saint's. And Irina came and bent her head, not on her husband's shoulder but on Tanatar's.

"Did you lose?" she asked quietly.

"Lost everything." Tanatar smiled naïvely. "Army cash."

"A lot?"

"Two."

"Thousand?"

"Yes."

"Who won?"

"I don't remember. Jacob, I think. But it's probably all gone on drink by now."

"Come to my room. I'll settle you down."

"All right, if you like." Tanatar smiled faintly. "Is the storm still blowing?"

"No, it's quietened down." Irina . . . No one had seen an ancient Assyrian but everyone imagined they must have been like Irina—breasts like goblets, eyes like almonds and hair like that of a stone Ahriman, like a horse's mane, plaits across her breast, her face and her body almost square, almost of stone and light as a circus rider's. Irina had been a circus rider somewhere in Odessa.

The men drank up what was left and poked about in odd corners like flies in autumn, in their overcoats and furs, trying to find somewhere to sleep. The women were getting their clothes ready for a fancy-dress ball in the evening. The cards went to the kitchen where the orderlies were sitting. Kaminin went on writing in his pocket diary, at the table where they had been playing, and he sipped the leavings in the glasses. Prince Trubetzkoy, an adjutant, sat with him and they talked lazily. Until 1917, the prince had owned several streets in Moscow and others in the Tambov, Voronezh and Poltava districts, while Kaminin had owned by the laws of Polish inheritance a whole town in the western region and could hardly recall in what districts he owned forests, sawmills, smelting works, mines and factories.

"Send for another bottle of cognac, Prince."

"We ought to take a bath now and eat strawberries with white wine," Trubetzkoy answered lazily.

"Fresh strawberries? Yes. When you're playing and drinking vintage champagne, at first there's nothing so refreshing as fruit and berries, but afterward, you know, sour cabbage and ham are better."

Kaminin was copying out dates and said again:

"Let's send out for another bottle of cognac, Prince."

"Really, this cognac is just home brew."

"Let's send for home brew, then."

"With red pepper and a steak. Have you any bread?"

"There's no bread, but that doesn't matter. We can have the meat raw, Prince."

Kaminin wrote in a final date, gazed at his diary for a long time and then got up, set his thin legs wide apart and put his hands not on his waist but in his armpits.

Tanatar lay in Irina's room among the cushions on the divan, covered with a rug and with his head on Irina's knees. He was pale, with half-closed, ashen eyes. Kaminin and Fedorov walked into the room along with the twilight. Everything was in the balance. Kaminin held the balance for a long while and finally he said:

"Do smoke, Tanatar. Irina, I've got to write a new book. The coppice is still green, the birch coppice, but I can take it to make paper. Everything for the book, for beauty. Beauty. Irina, you are with Tanatar now and I need a new wife—for my book. Let's discuss it. Good, evil, truth, falsehood—all nonsense. Beauty. Everything must be settled very simply. . . . I want to invite—I propose to ask Olga Andreyevna Viralsky to be my wife."

Twilight came down. The windowpanes and the air behind them grew dark-blue in the frost. The church bells were ringing. No one moved and no one said anything.

"Olga Andreyevna Viralsky. It must be put very simply. Beauty. For the sake of the book. Everything is very simple."

Twilight—twilight, gray and dark blue. Shadows searched the corners of the room. Irina's face was the face of an Assyrian.

"Irina! After all, we've got some cod liver oil. And we won't die, the three of us, Irina. . . ."

"Tell us about yourself, Jacob."

"What's there to tell? There's no life, only beauty. Something wonderful does exist. One must walk away from life."

"Call Olga, Jacob. Sometimes we can all three drink together. Two drunken women!"

Twilight. Gray. Tanatar bounced up like a spring, like a ball.

"A troika! Vodka! We'll go find Olga Andreyevna."

The orderlies sped up in the divisional troika and sledge. Tanatar rushed about the room and got dressed up like a coachman. He carried Irina in his arms and yelled without rhyme or reason, "Anarataira!"

Tanatar stood up like a coachman and Fedorov and Kaminin sat in the sledge.

"Let's go!"

The horses crumpled a silver dust, the sledge squeaked, the houses slanted and the house on the Sibrin Hill appeared, dark and morose as always. Fedorov stayed with the horses. Kaminin and Tanatar went in. Tanatar remained in the cold drawing room. Kaminin went into Olga's room.

When Kaminin left Olga's room, he tripped in the dark drawing room and fell. As he got up he made out Tanatar; Tanatar lay crouched as if to spring, like a black cat, on the floor. Did he hear Tanatar's whisper?

"After all, miracles do exist. We shouldn't treat mysteries like that. Olga, Olga. We shouldn't."

That evening Comrade Tanatar raced about the town in the troika for a long time, giving everyone rides—Irina, the girls, the drunken Kaminin, the drunken Trubetzkoy, the men.

The masked ball was held in the Communist Club.

Olga Andreyevna Viralsky's comb was neatly stitched so that it did not show, but Olga Andreyevna was not at the ball; some little girl was there whose comb was also stitched. The military band thundered out Viennese waltzes and mazurkas. The lamps were bright but smoked a little. The men, especially those of the cavalry regiment, stamped about with their spurs and sabers, and were the life and soul of the party. The women came as Night, Spring (with paper flowers), Birch Trees, Ukrainians (with glass beads from the Christmas trees), Tyroleans, and there was a Cucumber and a Domino. And because the public baths in the town were not heated and the black marketeer had long ago transported all the perfume to the villages, it smelled mostly of powder and sweat, a specifically feminine smell, since the men mostly reeked of shag. They thundered with their spurs and danced away, twisting their heads from side to side and going to the buffet for tea in the intervals. The ladies did not go to the buffet and the men told stories there.

"Maria Ivanovna said yesterday that she was going as Night and her sister was going as a Cucumber. I went up to Maria Ivanovna and there was a Cupid next to her. I thought it was Claudia and said, 'Why aren't you a Cucumber?' The Cupid spat out, 'You're an insolent wretch! Ha ha!' "

"That's nothing. But one of the fairies has a ribbon . . ."

The orchestra broke into a gavotte.

There was a little girl at the ball. She was there with her sister. The sister wore a cheap new dress and was eagerly waiting for her partner, anxiously, and for some reason, angrily. The little girl was in her way. She was small, thin and had red hands, a pale face and a poor dress, her stockings were mended and she had unusual eyes, clear and bright. The little girl looked openly and gently at the people around her, laughed sweetly and asked her sister something. Her sister answered unwillingly and briefly and looked at her crossly. The little girl laughed in an unusual way, sweetly, openly and gaily. The little girl laughed and was happy. But a post-office clerk came up to her sister and they started to join in the gavotte. Dr. Fedorov watched the little girl closely.

She was left alone. For a moment her face showed fright and misery and then she began to wander quietly around the rooms, looking and watching. Misery showed in her eyes; she no longer smiled and her eyes gazed around slowly and quietly. Dr. Fedorov probably did not notice that he was talking out loud:

"There's time for that yet. It will come. Later. Don't you worry, don't worry."

Dr. Fedorov came up to the little girl, his arms outstretched.

"Don't be miserable. Let's go and dance. Let's go and have some tea. Come along!"

The little girl ran away from the strange doctor, through the dancing couples, through the gavotte, and suddenly burst into loud and bitter tears. And Dr. Fedorov began to cry as well, falling with his chest across a table where they were selling tickets and homemade sweets, and hiding his wet face in his hands, in the books of tickets.

Dr. Fedorov was given some water. People surrounded him. The gavotte stopped. The most concerned and gentle was Tanatar. When Tanatar was settling Dr. Fedorov in his sledge, the little girl with her sister and the clerk came out of the entrance. And lifting up the little girl, the sister was saying angrily:

"Stupid. Crybaby."

She saw Dr. Fedorov and whispered angrily to the clerk: "And he's a . . ."

IV

A very long time ago, a long time ago, I last took up my pen to note in my diary anything that stimulated me. I say "a long time ago," although only a fortnight has gone by since then—but what a great deal has been lived through, what a great deal. . . .

First, there was my getting to know Olga Nikolayevna Zhmukhin more intimately. It all happened quite incredibly as things do in fairy tales. To have had the opportunity and let it slip would have seemed preposterous. Well, I took the opportunity. Up to then we had played cards with her several times. Seeing that she said nothing, I was in a nightmare of trepidation and debated with myself how to approach her. . . . A chance came my way . . . I went to see her secretly . . . it was embarrassing. She did not welcome me with open arms but rather coldly and shyly. She even said, "Vanya, why have you come to see me? After all, it's embarrassing." After this I flung myself on her like a bloodthirsty beast, but then she said:

"Why should we get our hands dirty? Let's go on the bed. . . ." I nearly let out a cry of joy. . . . All right, but I would take what was mine in the next few days. . . . After that day about three more dragged by in the same mood. On the last two days I was at her place with Fedorov and Samuel Tanatar. I don't say much about that nasty business. . . . I've hesitated for a long time whether to write it down but not because I was afraid my godmother might happen to see it, not at all, but because this step was the first in my life. . . . My first visit, when I was alone, was comparatively better than when I was with my friends. As always on such occasions, it all started with begging and imploring (very persistent we were) and finally turned into a wild bacchanalia. We turned up drunk. Olga Nikolayevna and I laughed a lot; Fedorov kept crying and Tanatar kept praying. . . . It turned out that they were virgins and Fedorov couldn't manage and stayed that way. . . . It couldn't have been better. We played the Gramophone, drank tea and then embraced a bit and sipped a little wine. . . . "Live and enjoy yourself," as some learned man has said. . . .

Again the diary fell into her lap and it was painful. Oh, God, give us something clean. Oh, God, take away pain, lies, dirt. . . .

In the daylight the frosty air was as yellow as wax—yellow like the waxen sun. The frost fans and mares' tails on the windowpanes grew yellow in the sunlight. A lusty cold, a silence, emptiness, waxen rays settling on the stone floor indoors. The barometer stood at thirty-two—out there beyond the frozen window. Ilya had told them that morning that there were frozen gulls lying in the yard.

The diary fell into her lap and her tears fell. An empty day.

Again the telephone rang. . . .

It was New Year's Eve. The military were arranging a party in the Kaminin country house, now a Soviet estate. For several days they had been heating the colonnaded house, which was a century old, but it was still damp and cold. Since the house had been plundered, they could not find any electric lamps and had to light it with oil lamps. The orchestra played unmusically in the gloom, making mistakes, but still it did play up in the gallery, in the white ballroom. Some had gone off in the morning to take sledge rides and walks in the country and others arrived at suppertime. Every town has the type of young girl whose only aim is to have a good time, and there were many like this at the party. In the evening in the woods, a group of skiers lighted two candles on a gay Christmas tree in a clearing. Then they danced around it and set fire to the tree. Night came, deep and silent, with hoarfrost and myriad stars. They served supper in the bedraggled drawing room and the oil lamps were lighted. People in coats, furs, hats, sang songs, ate and drank. The orchestra played very loudly but no one danced. After supper they had more to drink. There was an incident. Kaminin, the former owner of the house, opened a secret cupboard full of drinks. Some of the wine had gone sour, some of the cognac and vodka had evaporated, but it was all drunk to shouts of "Hurrah," "When you die, they'll bury you" and "Gaudeamus." There proved to be more wine, cognac and vodka (never mind the evaporation) in the cupboard than would be needed before a cavalry attack. It was terribly gay and some of the girls got up on the mantelpiece and so onto the back of the military, who pretended to be fiery steeds: this was called a cavalry attack. The attack proceeded with squeals through the dark rooms. Some played *chemin de fer* at the round table in the drawing room. Whispers and squeals could be heard in all the dark rooms. The orchestra blared away in the distance, but in the drawing room tobacco smoke rose in the air. There was a fireplace there too and new cavalry pairs set off while the oil lamps smoked. Kaminin was thumbing through a book by the window in the drawing room. The book was the New Testament and, setting his feet wide apart, Kaminin stood by the oil lamp and read aloud at a venture:

" 'He who is a hireling and not a shepherd, whose own

the sheep are not, sees the wolf coming and leaves the sheep and flees; and the wolf snatches them and scatters them. He flees because he is a hireling and cares nothing for the sheep.' "

A girl jumped off the mantelpiece and screamed.

Someone said:

"*B-Banque!*"

Tanatar came up to Kaminin and said quietly:

"Go on reading, for me."

The telephone rang. The ringing sounded in Olga's desert-like room (in the yellow desert) abruptly and strangely, and Samuel's voice came over the receiver:

"Olga. Forgive me. I feel very hurt and very depressed. Olga . . . forgive me—for everything. I shall pay for my sins. You know that there is no life left for us, we are dying, we must die. Forgive me. Perhaps my filth is some dream of paradise. I speak with my heart's blood."

And Olga answered softly:

"Yes, I forgive you. Yes, yes, I forgive you. I forgive you for everything now and have forgiven you. There's nothing left. . . ."

When Tanatar rang Olga, Olga Nikolayevna hooted near the hill and Andrey Andreyevich was probably shouting through the ventilator at the club:

"Ilya! The horses!"

The girl leaped from the mantelpiece and screamed. Someone said:

"*B-Banque!*"

Tanatar came up to Kaminin and said quietly:

"Go on reading, for me."

"For you? All right. This is from Matthew:

" 'From the fig tree learn its lesson: as soon as its branch becomes tender and puts forth leaves, you know that summer is near. So also, when you see all these things, you know that He is near, at the very gates.' "

Kaminin came to an end and rocked drunkenly. Tanatar gazed at him intently.

"Would you like me to read you some more?"

"Here you are. Go ahead."

"I don't need the book. I can remember it without. It's

from Matthew too: " 'Let the dead bury their dead.' It's in Chapter 8. 'Let the dead—' ' "

Tanatar turned sharply and left the room. The lavatory in the house was out of order and the men went out through the back door. Tanatar went out there. The moon was rising over the earth and the village dogs were barking. Trubetzkoy was poking his head in the snow and sticking two fingers down his gullet. Another man was lying in the snow to cool off. The two of them began to smoke.

Tanatar walked down the veranda steps and strolled a little way along the path.

"What a filthy mess they've made of it all. . . ."

The revolver jumped in his hand very quickly and the sound was loud, although Tanatar himself probably did not hear it. . . .

Only one woman followed Comrade Tanatar's red mahogany coffin, to the sound of the "Internationale" and funeral marches. She was mournful, thin—white and pale. His wife, who knew everything.

Night. Blue murk. Snow. Stars. Silence.

Near the clearing in the woods little disheveled Christmas trees wrapped in snow pressed close to the earth beside the stern pines. One Christmas tree was scorched and gave off an acrid smell. Silence. Stillness. The stars were bright and there were myriad stars. A star fell. Silence. Hours passed. Blue murk. Then something stirred in the field by the dry gullies and one faint gust and then another and another from the blizzard ran between the disheveled Christmas trees, circled about and disappeared. Someone began to draw a dark dull sleeve across the stars from the north. Then the snow maidens began to run forward again—one, two, five. Two met, their trains entwined, melted into one another and died away. The forest answered them: a cry rose up in the forest, the pines moved in a strict minuet, last year's boughs crackled and fell. And silence again. Then the snow maidens began to run afresh, to circle about—one, two, a hundred—arising and dying away. The pines bowed their heads in a new minuet. There was shouting, whistling, howling. The dull sleeve dropped grains from heaven. The snow maidens became con-fused, there was not enough room, they ran into the field—myriads of them.

And the blizzard came. The dead maidens, born of the storm, rushed on for thousands of miles over the fields, over the forests and rivers, over the towns, dying, dying in groans, in laughter, in yells and in sobs.

This blizzard was not announced over the telephone. It came from the Volga district and passed over Elets, Kursk, Suma and Poltava.

It was white, white, white.

Dr. Andrey Viralsky did not visit his patients during a blizzard and he sat reading Mayne Reid all day. The doctor wore his fur coat, his hat and his boots, and at three he came out of his room for dinner. He had cabbage stew with mutton. He looked at Olga in silence, frowning, and said:

"These are difficult times, Olga. You have had a rest. You should get yourself a job—as a teacher, perhaps. The holidays are over! We must work, and anyway, work makes it less de-pressing and boring. . . . Have a little more mutton. . . ."

As for Ivan Petrovich Bekesh. He went to Kaminin about his diaries and ended by saying he had given them away for very little and could he have some more money. Kaminin replied that he had not bought the diaries for himself but for Olga Andreyevna Viralsky.

Olga met Kaminin at the Ministry of Labor in the morn-ing. A girl with black eyes like a sheep's and ribs like the sides of a sledge was registering just in front of them.

"What is your profession?" the woman clerk asked the girl.

"I'm a political émigrée," the girl answered. "Until 1917 I was living beyond the pale. Sophia Pindrink."

"Ah . . . ha!"

Kaminin registered next.

"What is your profession?"

"I'm a writer."

And the clerk made a note in the corresponding column: "Copy writer."

1920

The
Tale of
St. Petersburg
or the Holy Rock

CHAPTER ONE

The centuries are stacked in sober layers like packs of cards. The packs of the centuries are encrusted with years, and the years are shuffled into ages—in Chinese cards. "No seller of idols bows down to the gods, for he knows what they are made of." How, then, should the centuries bow down? Should they bow to the centuries? They know what has gone into their making: no wonder the fashions of years can be sorted out like suits of cards. "Yung Lo, the third emperor of the Ta Ming dynasty, passed here on his way to make war against the Mongolians, supporters of the Yuan dynasty and exiled from China by his father, Hung Wu": this is engraved upon blocks of white marble. Yung Lo—did he justify his life with this inscription, since nothing more is left of him? And the Emperor K'ang-hsi passed there likewise on the thirteenth day of the second moon, in sixteen hundred and ninety-six, according to European chronology, to destroy men and horses by famine in Shamo. Shamo means the same as Gobi. Shamo is Gobi, a desert. And since there is an inscription on a white marble plaque, the name of the village is preserved for history—Sudetoi. In Sudetoi his mother was born, and her feet were not bound tight when she was eight years old, as was the custom with the aristocracy, because she was of the people.

The centuries are stacked in sober layers like packs of cards. What fortuneteller from Kolomna in St. Petersburg can throw down the cards so that history will repeat itself, so that the years will repeat the cards of the centuries and come up exactly the same a second time? Two thousand years ago, two centuries before the European era, the Emperor Shih Huang Ti, of the Ch'in dynasty, cut off the Middle Kingdom from the world by means of the Great Wall of China, which extends for a thousand *li*—Shih Huang Ti, who abolished all ranks and insignia, all noblemen, thus dealing "a death blow to feudalism"; on becoming the Great Khan he "opened a window," like Peter the Great of the Romanov dynasty, who remained an emperor but did not live long enough to become a Great Khan.

The first Peter of the Romanov dynasty and the first Tsar of the Russian Plain, Peter Alexeyevich Romanov, in his paradise at St. Petersburg, once spent the whole day drinking at Senator Shafirov's, in his "palace" on the Kaivusari-Fomin island, and went sailing in a skiff along the river Neva to the inn called Austeria on Perusin island to drink out the night there. By this time the ice on Lake Ladoga had melted, navigation had been reopened and the emperor perceived an irregularity: despite the quiet expanse of the river, the dim white night and the dim white stars in the sky, the buoys on the river Neva were not lit up and the lighthouse was not lit up on Vasilyevsky island. Peter sat in the stern, drunk and silent. Puffed up with vindictiveness and debauchery, he shouted drunkenly:

"What are the circumstances? . . . What are the circumstances, eh? . . . What are the circum-cum-stances! . . ."

It was very quiet and deserted on the river Neva, and before looking into the womanish eyes of the Tsar, Senator Shafirov gazed around him in a mouselike way. A belch rose from the drunken bag of his body.

"Your majesty, I am at your service. . . ."

"Wha-at are the circumstances! . . . Again and again regulations are made for the establishment of communications, and again and again I behold no lights on the buoys or in the lighthouse, in defiance of the order in which it is decreed that there should be red lights on the right and green on the left, to mark the waterway!"

Shafirov said:

"Your majesty, in view of the fact that the nights are light and there are stars in the sky—"

The Tsar said:

"Your Excellency. In view of the fact that the heavenly lamps are lighted by the Lord God, they serve God, and therefore are not responsible to man. And *sondern,* since lamps in the lighthouse are lighted by mortal men, they serve man! What are the circumstances?"

This first emperor, Peter Alexeyevich, and the drunken Shafirov huddled like a sack in the boat, did not succeed in reaching the Austeria that night even though they "ste-arred" (as seamen say) by the buoy lights (for he thrashed out those green and red lights on the backs of the men responsible and at the same time thrashed out bravado in himself when he gazed on the lights). And Tsar Peter was right, since lamps kindled by men's hands have a human meaning when they lead the way. Although at dawn a cold fog crawled over St. Petersburg and both the stars and the lights were hidden in it, yet it is possible that only the clouds would have come and the rain drizzled. Then the stars would have vanished altogether and only the lights kindled by men's hands would have remained.

Confucius said:

"No seller of idols bows down to the gods, for he knows what they are made of."

The stone wall runs over the hillsides, and vanishes from sight to the left and to the right. Time has already ruined the stone wall, Shih Huang Ti and Yung Lo and Tamerlane and many others passed here, and under the wall where the lizards were always gleaming, white nettles grow. Stones, sky, desert, to the west—China, to the east—Mongolia, the land of the Tamerlanes. He did not know then (how could he?) that over there, beyond Gobi, beyond Altai, beyond Turkestan, lay a second Middle Kingdom. . . . By the little stream Sai-hi he was born and lived in the limestone which had been tunneled out by men as though by swallows and which stank of human dirt and human sweat. Overhead, in the limestone, his fathers sowed *goakin* and *sargo,* labored like ants in the fields, every one of which could be covered with a straw mat. He was a boy with a womanish walk, and would leave the darkness of the limestone dwellings and run to the wall with a basket, to the Great Gates, where caravans passed along the Argali-Kiang to Urga, and there he collected camel, horse and human dung, so that he could take it to his fathers in the field for manuring the earth under the kaoliang. From there, from these gates in the wall, already in ruins, the town of Dushekoi could be seen with its stone towers, also in ruins, and whenever he stopped to rest, the boy would be stung by nettles, living his secret life, and he would catch lizards, which were sacred creatures, and he would squeeze their silver bellies to watch their entrails crawl out at their mouths. The fathers came in from the fields toward nightfall, when it was as dark as in the limestone. By that time the child had learned how to eat with chopsticks instead of with his fingers, and he no longer went about stark naked, but he was still afraid of the cave, the one over there, "to the west in the limestone," where his father would go to ponder in the presence of his ancestors, about toil, about the best death, about the crops, where an old woman kept house and where the idols stood. It was night, and the boy slept on a straw mat covered by a sour-smelling cotton-wool quilt. In all his childhood . . . the boy . . . had not seen . . . a single tree, as he lived beyond the wall, where Mongolia became the land of the Tamerlanes. The boy did not know what idols are made of.

Later the boy discovered why it was forbidden to squeeze lizards' bellies. The boy discovered the meaning of his father's toil, he understood what it meant to plow a field by hand, to bring manure from Argali-Kiang by hand, to strip each clump of maize and kaoliang by hand, so as not to starve and to live in the limestone, and he learned to work. He discovered about yang and yin, about the Two Powers. He came to realize that both the world and his kin lay within the will of Lao-tzu, and for him it was that once the Great Wall was built, since Lao-tzu spoke about Tao, the Great Way. The womanish walk remained with him for the rest of his life, but his eyes grew dim and began to resemble a worn Chinese coin. Although he had learned that "the world is not the real world," he still knew how to sow grain, which tires the body, and he conquered "the Four Shu and the Five Tsan," which tires the mind. He learned "the fountain of knowledge and the river flowing thence." He pondered the Eight Hua, symbolized by the four straight long ones and the eight short, where the true meaning of the passive yin is revealed, that "man is a product of Nature and therefore should not violate her laws," and, like everyone, he finished the *Shih-ching,* the Book of Odes. And still Dushekoi gazes into Mongolia, as Mongolia, smiling at Gobi, stares into Dushekoi.

Who knows what might have been?

The centuries are stacked in sober layers like packs of cards: in the packs of the centuries the years come exactly the same a second time, since history repeats itself. The Great Wall of China stood for two thousand years. Who knows every path followed by every man, and who knows why fate has ordained that such a man should live his life now, at the present time? This is in the limestone village. Men came to the limestone village from Yun-Chzhoi, from Tsupun, even from Peking, the beggar-rich people, who have no possessions only that they may possess all, to speak of I-he-da-tsuan, of Hun-Den-Chzhao, of Sha-Gu, of "the Truth and Harmony of the Great Fist," of the "Red Lantern," of the extermination of devils, of their delight that grain already cost so and so much and labor remained cheap, of the news that there were foreign devils in Peking (Yang-kuei-tze), as at home, and how the empress (ts! tss! . . . shsh! . . .), the empress Tsu-Hsi was betrayed—poor wife—the empress. They lighted red lanterns in the caves and his father omitted to visit his ancestors. They would sit by the lantern, and it looked as though their teeth were bigger than they should be, as though they hung suspended in their mouths. They went away singing songs and each time his father took him by the hand and impressed upon him: "No one knows about this!" But the war song of the departing men rang out in the night:

> *Tien-da-tien-men-kai!*
> *Di-da-di-men-kai!*

Who knew the names in the limestone village? The name of Dr. Sun Yat-sen or of General Yuan Shih-kai? The day came when everyone learned that the empress Tsu-Hsi was no more in the Middle Kingdom, and that the three-year-old Pu-Yi must soon abdicate. On that day no one went into the fields, on that day the caravans stopped at the Argali-Kiang, and everything seemed new like a festival, and only the wall and the lizards were the same. Afterward, all day and all night, people with red lanterns and with faces like posters, carrying rifles, swords, even bows, came in crowds, singly and in battle array, walking over the stone wall through the gates toward Peking. His father went with them, taking the sword of his ancestors, with dragons on its hilt, which had always hung in the idol temple. Then, it is true, grain became dear, there was not enough tea to go around, shut away in the south, and one night someone trampled down their family field. And at that time his father returned to his ancestors; they carried his head on a stake, and his body was pierced with a pike from the place where the head had been and through the rectum. Two men bore the ends of the pike on their shoulders, and then it looked as though his father were crawling through the air, as he had crawled when stripping the clumps of kaolin, and they carried him for a long time along the Argali river and in the sour-smelling streets of Dushekoi. Many were honored with such a death in those days, and then all his relations had to run where best they could, sheltered by those who only yesterday had helped to carry his father's body. The people with faces like posters and their pigtails cut off passed on and on through the gates. Someone sat two guns on the wall and fired all day into Dushekoi and into the limestone. A random shot hit the mound on the stream Sai-hi and the toil of many years perished in an hour, and then the people on foot threw themselves on the guns, and pillars were set up where the gaping mouths of decapitated heads hung for a long time in the moist half-light of the gates. And then the great night of Blood and Death began—the nineteenth night of the sixth moon—and the latest news came in: the three-year-old Huang-Chzhin, the most yellow monarch Pu-Yi, had abdicated. Then people went out of the gates.

His name was Li Yan, and he was in Dushekoi and in Peking. He witnessed everything but did not understand anything, although an eyewitness. And then he ran for thousands of li, through Timur Mongolia, across Urga and Kyakhta, and in his memory Vladivostok, Port Said and the oceans grew confused. He passed the white marble plaque where is 'written how "Yung Lo, the third emperor of the Ta Ming dynasty, passed here on his way to make war against the Mongolians, supporters of the Yuan dynasty," how here the soldiers and the horses of the Emperor K'ang-hsi perished. But he did not know this; his only thought was that his mother came from here, from the village of Sudetoi; here his mother had caught lizards when she was little, his mother, whom he, like all the others, had abandoned as a woman. And with him went tens upon tens of others, men who had lost all, abandoned all—fathers, mothers, sons and native lands.

"No seller of idols bows down to the gods, for he knows what they are made of."

CHAPTER TWO

"Thou art Peter, and upon this rock shall I build my church." Peter is the rock and the provincial city of St. Petersburg is the Holy Rock City. But a definition should be given in one word only. St. Peter's Burg is defined in three words: Holy Rock City. There is no single defining word, and therefore St. Petersburg is a fiction. But on the river Neva, as desolate as the Irtysh, there stood a city, truly a city of granite. A stone city and a provincial city, and because it was stone and provincial it was obviously un-Russian, since all Russian provincial towns were mellow like peasant women, and were littered with sunflower-seed husks, smelled of herring tails, and there were benches where the bright petticoats of women rested, women mellow as the provincial citizens, who were dying an excremental death. The perspectives of the St. Petersburg streets were so constructed that when they came to an end they leaped beyond the streets into metaphysics. And that day, which was an ordinary Finland day on the river Neva, as desolate as the Irtysh and as a day in Finland, a solitary barge hooted for a long time, throwing back many echoes, as always happens in the lake district—echoes from the palaces, from the Stock Exchange and from the Peter and Paul Fortress—and then a car passed over Trinity Bridge into the perspectives of the streets, to cut the lines of the perspectives, to begin man's working day, and to leap from the ends, from the very ends of the streets—into metaphysics. There is a poetry of stone and silence. Such Finland days clothe the granite with moss. Green grass broke through the granite, and on the Nevsky Prospect green grass broke through the flagstones. Then palaces became moribund museums, and is not a monument (like that of Peter at the Admiralty) the monument of the provincials—that house which stands decrepit in Goncharnaya Street. There is indeed a beauty dying, and the granite town was beautiful, beautiful in its desolate granite, its bridges, its perspectives, its ruins, in the stir of its provincials, in its emptiness, in the mute echoes of its desolation, its lakeside river, the ordinary un-Russian Finland days. And out there, where the roads from the little towns in the Moscow district crowded together, on the Russian, the Moscow side, in an alley, at a little crossroad, in a two-story house with all its windows broken, in a deserted and abandoned house, there was a shop on the ground floor, and through the window an open inner door could be seen looking onto the yard behind the house. In the shop spiders' webs were hanging, and there was a litter of bricks and broken glass. . . .

"Thou art Peter, and upon this rock shall I build my church."

Along the Russo-European plain a glorious revolution came, and the winds of this fierce blizzard stripped the husk from all dead things—death to the half-alive. The predictions of the Russian sectarians came to pass. The first emperor of the Russian plain originated a paradise for his delectation on the rotting marsh—St. Petersburg. The last emperor surrendered the imperial St. Petersburg of the rotting marsh to the peasants' Moscow (the word Moscow means "Dark Waters," and dark waters are always stormy). It is left for St. Petersburg to leap from the *rectilinear* street into the mists of metaphysics, the fumes rising from the marsh. That same Finland day promised to remain till night and with a misty night to destroy the straight lines of the street, to cloud with mist. And that day the car must cut along the streets, to conclude man's working day—the St. Petersburger's day— Ivan Ivanovich Ivanov's, like many others in Russia. Ivan Ivanovich was a brother. Ivan Ivanovich was an intellectual. He was a pro-fess-or. The car distracted Ivan Ivanovich's thoughts—by the Smolny, along the Nevsky Prospect, on Gorokhovaya Street—the car, where Ivan Ivanovich sat in a corner, surrounded by mirrors, on cushions, with his briefcase. The car set off once more into the desolate washes of the Neva, as desolate as the Irtysh, across the expanse of Trinity Bridge, to turn into the approach bridge of the Peter and Paul Fortress and so into the Fortress, to fade there beside the cathedral, beside the headquarters. On the cathedral a monk hovered close to the steeple. Then on the Fortress the gun was fired to indicate the hour, and the palaces threw back the echo against the Fortress. Ivan Ivanovich sat in his office in the outer courtyard for a long time, there in the office with wooden chairs and a table covered with oilcloth, and men from the bastions and prisons were brought before him, in the name of their consciences: for two people to stand facing one another with two truths, so that one man and one truth should return to prison. A Chinese Red Army man was brought by another Chinese Red Army man from head- quarters, and this Chinese Red Army man waited his turn a long time because there was no interpreter, and nothing of much importance was noted in his papers, only that English gold coins were found in the possession of a Red Army man of such and such a light-infantry battalion—while other men kept passing him on their way to the table, to talk or to stand silent at the table. . . . In the engineer's house, in his study, a bed stood behind a screen, and some time ago a bed had stood in the same position in the same engineer's room in London. There had been an underground meeting of revo- lutionaries in London then. And just as on that occasion in London, on meeting here in St. Petersburg once a year as usual, on shaking hands, Ivan Ivanovich had gone up to bed quietly and begun feeling the sheets.

"What is it?" the engineer asked.

"I am looking to see if perhaps the sheets are damp. Don't catch cold."

The engineer and Ivan Ivanovich had known each other as children, from the days when they played bone marbles in an authentically provincial little town. Masks of Chinese devils grimaced in the engineer's study—bone, bronze and porcelain—grimaced with a cold solidity: and there was a chilly Venetian window in the study, looking out on the white nights with the cool white study walls. The engineer . . . was forbidden to sit with round shoulders. On that white night the engineer had music—he invited musicians and guests. Ivan Ivanovich did not join the company, he shunned crowds, he disliked people, he sat in the study, alone in the darkness. And the engineer realized that the music had dumbfounded Ivan Ivanovich—that he was dumbfounded as only a chosen few who understand, can be dumbfounded; in the cool study where the devil masks grimaced coldly, real—human—warmth descended on an armchair and radiated there. Then the engineer who sat by the window hunched his shoulders in the white night, and Ivan Ivanovich came up and stood behind him, leaning against his shoulder.

"I feel I am the master of the earth," the engineer said. "And you? Still the same? A guest?"

"Yes. Yes, a guest!"

"Petersburg—a new architectural problem, a roofless town, with skating rinks on the top floors . . . silence, deathliness. . . . A guest?" The engineer gazed into the white night and into the streets. "Yesterday I ate some bread made from moss. A guest? Metaphysics?"

"Yes, a guest. Do you remember how we walked along the country roads in Bruges? We discussed the world, then. I did not go to Moscow: blood, factory smoke, the workers' hands. I look centuries ahead! And I remain a guest! . . ." Ivan Ivanovich pressed the engineer's shoulder hard; the engineer felt the warmth of his body through his jacket. "How big you are, Andrey . . . there's the same silence in Bruges . . . what music!"

"Where?"

"Over there, in the sitting room, the piano, I don't see realities."

That night . . . over there, in the misty ends of the street, the car leaped from the ends of the streets, from the reality of the streets . . . into mistiness, into mist, because . . . St. Petersburg . . . is mysteriously definable, that is, a fiction, that is, a mist, and yet remains stone. The engineer went out to his guests and said:

"Do you know who was with me in the study just now, who was my guest?" and fell silent. "Ivanov—Ivan [Ivanovich]" and was silent, waiting for the name to lash across the room.

"He was listening to the music, he knows music well, he is a guest on earth."

A woman went up to the engineer, they leaned toward each other in the embrasure of the window (down below there, the car leaped off the end), the woman's shoulder touched the engineer's softly, such an age-old, such a beautiful peerless wine is woman. The Chinese devils—bone, bronze and porcelain—grimaced.

In a house . . . at home . . . Ivan Ivanovich Ivanov . . . lived like a black beetle in a crevice. He feared open spaces. He liked books, he read lying down. He had no mistress, he did not wipe away the cobwebs. In the little room there were books, and the screen by the bed was made of books, and the sheets on the bed were aired. The car pushed its way into the mist. The doors were locked and barricaded with shelves of books. Ivan Ivanovich . . . lay . . . in a corner on the bed . . . and he *saw* an enormous chessboard: this board did not exist in reality. The world, the smoke of the factories, the hands of the workers, blood, millions of men, red flame of Russia, Europe—standing like an iceberg on its side in the Atlantic, the Stone Guest, clambering . . . thunderously . . . with his horse . . . onto the board. The sheets were aired, dimness in the room, and here in the dry sheets, among the pillows, the thought: I!—aaa-I! *The Stone Guest:*—with vodka: "Your excellency. Again and again Russia is dragged to Golgotha. What are the circumstances?" *The Guest:* "There is no Russia, sire, no St. Petersburg, only . . . the world." *The Stone Guest:* "Let us drink to art, your excellency. Won't you drink?" "No." "And for the prisoners in the Alexis Ravelin in the Peter and Paul Fortress, no, once again?" "No." "Because you are already drunk, perhaps?" "You are pleased to joke, sire; the prisoner in the Alexis Ravelin . . . is I—I!" In the dry sheets, the hot pillows, in a corner . . . comes the thought: aaa-I!—I . . . am the world!

"Thou art . . . Peter."

The Chinaman stood to one side, the Chinaman's face was like the face of the Chinese devil in the engineer's study; in the office there were wooden chairs and a table covered with oilcloth. The Chinaman walked to one side, in a womanish walk, he wore a Russian soldier's tunic without a belt. The car stood behind the window grating. The Chinaman's face was . . . all teeth, strange teeth, the jaw of a horse; with these he grinned: who will understand? In the office there were cobwebs on the windows, which means there were flies. People walked up to the table. The engineer came up: the engineer must not sit with round shoulders.

"I assert that a deeply national well-being, a vital movement from the depths exists in Russia, and that this has nothing whatever in common with European syndicalism. In Russia an anarchistic revolt exists in the name of no-government, against every kind of government. I assert that Russia must experience and is experiencing a fever of *Peterism,* of Petersburgism, a fever of ideas, theories, mathematical catholicism. I assert Bolshevism and Stenka Razinism, and renounce communism. I assert that the Russian will conquer in Russia —throwing off the fever of Peterism. The Alexis Ravelin. Engineer Andrey Ludogovsky." Such was the writing in the protocol.

Ivan Ivanovich said in English: "Remember, Andrey? We played bone marbles. But my own brother, I . . ."

And then on the Chinaman's face—all teeth—prominent teeth, the whole face a question, the blinkers fell from his eyes, so that the eyes could speak. The general order became confused. The Chinaman was swaying from right to left by the table and saying in English everything he knew all at once, and it was a great deal: "I want my native land. Nin kei Yuan Shih-kai, president! I want my country! I fought in the south. I want my country!" An insubordinate chunk . . . of hot . . . humanity . . . exploded within the office.

To the chessboard with the Chinaman! On the quays, grass has sprung up through the stones, the Finland days dress the granite with moss: the palaces have become moribund museums. Peter I went from the Admiralty to Goncharnaya Street, where a house collapsed: the house had crushed people then. The car—over bridges, quays (the bridge at the Peter and Paul Fortress was up)—the car, over the expanse of the Neva, which was like the Irtysh, and through the region of lakes and open skies. In a house . . . at home . . . in the window . . . through the window . . . over the roofs . . . over the Neva . . . by the seashore . . . in the room . . . the red wound of sunset. The red wound of sunset yellowed the color of pomegranate skins, to *yellow jaundice*. There will be mists tonight. Yellow jaundice? Onto the chessboard with the Chinaman! The sunset . . . *was dying!* . . . Somewhere far off a solitary barge hooted. Books, books, books . . . the sunset lay in pomegranate skins on the shelves, and the laundress had not blued the pillowcases. There will be mist tonight. Ivan Ivanovich did not have a woman—a fever again. "Quinine is yellow, I think, yellow—quinine skin?" Bells.

"Please bring some black coffee, strong"—to the maid. She was a maid—a woman: "You must come tonight. . . ."

"Remember, Andrey? We played bone marbles. But my own brother, I sent my own brother to be shot, dear Andrey!" "Peter's fever, St. Petersburgism? The Bolshevik will bite one's head right off. So what? There is no Bolshevik, there is no Russia. Savages! There is only . . . the world!" *The Stone Guest:* "We must drink to art, your excellency. Will you drink coffee?" "Yes, coffee." "Because you are drunk as it is, perhaps?" "I assert that there is no communism in Russia, in Russia you have . . . Bolsheviks. The Alexis Ravelin. Engineer Andrey Ludogovsky." *The Stone Guest:* "Stop it, your excellency. Let's drink to art! To hell with it! While strength and will remain to us." *The Guest:* "Wait a moment, excellency! Everything is . . . I! Do you hear, Andrey, everything is: aaa-I! . . . dear Andrey!"

"Stay, Lisa, for a minute."

"I've aired the sheets, sir."

"I'm feverish, Lisa. I'm lonely here. Do sit down."

"But, sir . . ."

"Sit down, Lisa, we'll talk."

"But, sir! . . . I'd better come later."

"Sit down, Lisa!"

"Remember, Andrey? We played bone marbles. . . . I've two brothers. One has been shot, and the other . . ." The Chinaman crawled on all fours over the map of Europe, the Red Army man Liyanov (why has the Chinaman no pigtail?). The sheets are dry, on the chessboard—the world, the hands of the workers, factory smoke, Europe—an iceberg on its side in the Atlantic. There is no St. Petersburg (the Chinaman is on all fours on the iceberg). And there is no chessboard—Lisa's hair has hidden the chessboard, and Lisa's lips are . . . drawn tight in disdain. "Again and again we shall be dragged to Golgotha! . . ."

"Thou art Peter and upon this rock shall I build my church:—I—aaa-I."

"Oh, sir, quickly, please."

A bluish-green mist rose above the Neva and wreathed the Fortress. And below it, below the mist . . . gleamed the sunset, the color of orange peel, and in the midst, in the yellow sunset, a devil-angel-monk, like a terrible black bird, floated on the spire above the Fortress. The Fortress swam away in the mist.

In a communal cell . . . some were lying down with newspapers, others played chess with bread pellets. The Chinaman with the womanish walk and large nostrils above a horse-like jaw, a prostitute's jaw, a deathly smile on his face, approached everyone in turn, was silent for long stretches, smiling, and then said, half questioning, half asserting: "Depressing. . . ." Everyone understood that this meant . . . depressing. . . . Another Chinaman, the guard, stood by the Judas hole, and from time to time he whispered into the Judas hole:

"*Ni yo zhi tsui?*" How old are you?

"*Wo erh dze wu.*" Twenty-five, the Chinaman would answer from the cell.

And then the guard would say in Russian:

"Go-o! Must not talk-ing!" Only to whisper again in five minutes:

"*Ni hao?*" Are you well? . . .

The engineer Ludogovsky—the engineer must not stoop—played chess all evening at the table among the crockery, teapots and tin mugs. The chessmen were shaped from bread pellets. It was of no account to the Chinaman where he sat; he liked to sit on the floor in the corner, and to sing something there, something very disquieting, something monotonous, like the baying of a dog at the moon. An hour after the roll call they always came to call men out.

During this hour the men always talked and no one went to sleep, although they all lay on their bedboards, as if bedboards and sleep together gave them . . . a chance not to be called out that night.

Engineer Ludogovsky was telling them:

"After death life does not die away immediately in the body. Everyone knows that the hair and nails of dead men continue to grow for several months. One of the last things to die away is the activity of the brain. Four weeks after death, the dead man still sees and hears and perhaps can feel the taste of rot in his mouth. . . . He can't move, he can't tell you what is happening. Gradually the nerves of the arms and legs fail—and then the legs and arms are lost to consciousness and perception. The brain begins to decay last, and then the eardrum takes in the last sound, for the last time the outer cortex of the brain associates thoughts of death, of love, of eternity, of God (for it's impossible to think of anything else then, when you're faced with eternity; there are no human relationships then), and the thought fades—as long ago the eyes faded, grew glassy, became fish's eyes—the thought fades, disintegrates, as the brain disintegrated and rotted away. The worm crawls through the sockets of the eyes—then the eyes have vanished forever. After death a new and terrible life sets in. To some this is . . . ghastly, but to me. . . . A curious thought, St. Petersburg. . . ."

But the engineer did not finish, he turned to the wall, lifted his coat collar, would not answer: the engineer must not grimace. No one spoke. Then in the corner the Chinaman started counting fragments of glass, began wailing like a dog at the moon, sang a war song:

Tien-da-tien-men-kai!
Di-da-di-men-kai!
Zho-sue-tien shen' kui!
Wo tsin shi-fu lai!

The Chinese guard whispered through the Judas hole:
"*Nin kuei hsing?*" Your honorable name?

The chessmen shaped from bread pellets were left on a table in the cell for the night. That night the Chinaman ate the chessmen made from bread pellets.

And that night by the palaces on the Winter Canal, in the mist shrouding the perspectives of the streets, out of the green water, there swam forth the twelve plump sisters of fever, the Catherines, Annes, Elizabeths, Alexandras, Marys—empresses —to swim on the river Neva, which was like the Irtysh, to the Peter and Paul Fortress, to pluck grass from the granite, scatter scurvy, hear the old debate of Alexis and Peter, the groan of the poet Rileyev, the military marches of Nikolay Palkin, to investigate the tales of the lakes, to watch how on the river Neva red communication lights burn on the right, and on the left, white, and to see there in the mist . . . through the mist . . . rising from the mist the Great Wall of China, built by the Emperor Shih Huang Ti two centuries before the European era.

"*Nin kuei hsing?*" Your honorable name? the Judas hole whispered.

"*Wo hsing Li Yan.*"

It was the hour at which they came to call men out. The Chinaman went up to Ludogovsky, settled down on all fours by the bedboard, the horse's jaw looming in the half-light, grinning, grimacing:

"De-plessing?"

The twelve sisters of fever swam along the Neva, the fog crawled in at windows. Then the lock thundered, making the men press close against the bedboards, draw close in despair: "But don't you see, I'm lying down, lying on the bedboard, I'm asleep, not I, not aaa-I—not me!"

The Red Army man went out. The lock thundered, lowering the vaults, narrowing the cell. One could smoke and so avoid stifling. Quinine, quinine, mist, fever. Impossible to see . . . the Neva's bottom is deep where the twelve sisters lie. Red Army man Liyanov . . . "de-plessing!" "The centuries lie down gravely in packs of cards. The packs of the centuries repeat the years once and twice, to shuffle the years for the ages—in Chinese cards. No seller of idols bows down to the gods, for he knows what they are made of. How should the years bow down? Should they bow down to the years? They know what has gone to their making: no wonder the fashions of years can be sorted in suits." "Peter is the rock, and the provincial city of St. Petersburg is Holy Rock City. But St. Petersburg is three, and therefore it is fiction: the perspectives of St. Petersburg streets were so constructed that at their ends they leaped beyond the streets—into metaphysics."

"(No) (thou) (seller) (art) (of idols) (Peter). . . ."

"Some quinine, some quinine! . . . De-plessing! . . ."

Then the lock thundered, making the men press close against the bedboards, draw close to one another in despair: "But don't you see I'm lying down, lying on the bedboard, I'm asleep, what for? I'm asleep, aaa-I! . . . What for?"

Engineer Ludogovsky, Smirnov, Petrov . . .

". . . But I'm lying down, on the bedboard, I'm asleep, not I, not aaa-I—not me-e! . . ."

Corridors, stairs, a step. Darkness. An electric lamp. Darkness. An electric lamp. The splash of water, stairs, a step. Light, a cellar . . . and: two Chinamen—oh, what slanting eyes! And who touched the face, pressing it in, smashing the bridge of the nose, a face, like a poster, with inset teeth? (And the walk of the Chinaman . . . was womanish. . . .) The engineer must not grimace. . . .

Ugh-ha! . . .

This was all. The last thought . . . the last function of the cortex of the brain . . . in a few weeks . . . became . . .
                    a dehumanized thought . . .
                                        as phosphorus cleansed the cortex of the brain, in murky water . . . in green water . . . in running water. Fog, some quinine, some quinine!

CHAPTER THREE, THE LAST . . .
AS ST. PETERSBURG . . . IS . . . THREE

The boy . . . in all his childhood . . . did not see . . . a
single tree, for he lived beyond the Great Wall, already in
Mongolia, the land of the Tamerlanes. In St. Petersburg, out
there, where the roads from the little towns in the Moscow
district crowded together, the Russian road, the Moscow road,
the Serpukhovsky road, on the Russian, the Moscow side, in an
alley, at a little crossroad, in a two-story house with all its
windows broken, in a deserted and abandoned house, there
was a shop on the ground floor, and through the window an
open inner door could be seen looking onto the yard behind
the house . . . there the slender poplars were chopped down.
The Chinaman—with his own hands—sawed up the slender
poplars and stripped the bark. The Chinaman—with his own
hands—picked up all the stones and pebbles. The Russians
had abandoned the house, having made it filthy in a typical
Russian way: the Chinaman—with his own hands—picked up
all the human excrement from off the floors, the window
ledges, the fireplaces, the drains, the corridors, to manure the
earth. Around the yard were brick party walls, and elder grew
against one of these. The Chinaman piled all the stones, tins,
bits of iron and of glass in neat piles by the wall. The Chinaman dug beds and sowed the beds with maize, millet and
potato. It was a gray Finland day in the lake country. The
Chinaman rose with the yellow dawn . . . and the whole live-
long day . . . he raked and stripped every little clod, every
grass blade, with his own hands. And the whole day the
Chinaman sang the rebellious war song of China, which
sounds so unbelievably mournful in Russian ears:

> *Tien-da-tien-men-kai!*
> *Di-da-di-men-kai!*
> *Zho-sue-tien shen' kui!*
> *Wo tsin shi-fu lai!*

a song which told how "the sky should open the heavenly
portals, to surprise the sleep of the heavenly spirits, as the Fist
of Truth and Harmony and the Light of the Red Lantern

would sweep all before them with a single broom. And the star Chzhi-Yui, uniting with the star Nu-Si, would aid them, would save and protect them from the foreign cannon." It was a gray day. Urchins from the neighboring houses whom the Chinaman had driven out of the yard, where they played at being Yudenich and played cards, climbed the wall, and hung there like swallows in a row, shouting:

"Hey, get on, cross-eyed devil! Who cut your pigtail off?"

"Just wait, we'll steal your potatoes!"

But the Chinaman did not hear them, and on the whole the urchins were interested most in the sight of this man with a womanish walk, laboring like an ant in his little square backyard—alone, alien to everyone, slant-eyed.

It was a gray day in the lake country in Finland. It came in with a dawn yellow as the bark of quinine and went away like translucent vetch pods. In the evening the Chinaman lay alone on the stove of one small room which had escaped damage, lay covered with a sour-smelling blanket—his cell smelled as once it had smelled in the limestone cave. The Chinaman lay open-eyed with a glassy stare, writhing as he masturbated. Who knows what the Chinaman was thinking? And in the hushed white night, somewhere in a nearby Mozhaisk alley, a mouth organ screeched and screeched, and a woman's voice sang:

> *If hills of gold were mine*
> *And rivers full of wine . . .*
> *For a glance of love I'd give them . . .*

And if that evening, with compasses great enough for a third of the globe, if one were to stride with these huge compasses to the east, across Turkestan, Altai, Gobi—then, there, in China, in Peking (Ivan Ivanovich Ivanov was a brother!)—in Peking, in China . . .

A White Guardsman, an officer of the Imperial Army and a gentleman, the émigré Peter Ivanovich Ivanov was passing through the Hatamen gate. In the earthy passage of the gates through which the people passed it was dark and damp. Peter Ivanovich turned to the left. Walking along the wide square flagstones, under the high walls of the medieval fortifications by the moat filled with green water, and then across the stone bridge over the canal, he came to the western gate Tang-p'en-men, and there along the steep slope of a grassy path he mounted the wall onto the battlements, silent and deserted above the town. What a strange scene for the eyes of a European! The European is accustomed to the square immensities of gray buildings, welded together by the squares of the streets. The rays of the sun shone from a deep-blue sky, reflected bold purple shadows from the moats, the battlements, the banana trees, gleamed brightly in the laquered tiles of the roofs and rippled in the golden-yellow, bright-blue, red miraculous fire of pagodas, temples, kiosks, towers, spiraled porticoes, cut off far in the distance by the dark, piercing line of the walls and the green dimness of the canal: down there, a busy throng . . . people . . . a Chinese town . . . of merchants, vendors, poor people and beggars . . . the shuffle of the crowd, the cries of mules and asses. Here on the wall above the town . . . silent, deserted. The émigré, an officer and a gentleman, in an officer's coat with gold buttons (this was all his baggage) sat down by a granite stone. This gray officer's coat with gold buttons . . . was the officer's whole baggage. He had no boots. And it was summer. How many miles or Chinese li he had walked! The officer leaned against the granite stone and pulled his cap with its white cockade further over his face, so that his eyes would not be dazzled. Here in this deserted spot, in the sun and by daylight, the officer, Peter Ivanovich, slept.

In the later afternoon, toward evening, the officer walked in the crowd between the gates Kuang-dzu and Sha-Ku. Peasants with mules and asses were selling meat, game, onions, sargo, and both the men and women smoked frail pipes of tobacco until a customer arrived. Disdainfully, unhurriedly, the gentlemen walked by with their fans. The drone and shuffle of the crowd floated . . . to the mauve sky. At the pavilion where a guard stood, posts with crossbars were dug into the ground: on these posts in bamboo cages—a head in each cage—lay the heads of dead men. The officer stopped to see what remained of these people: their mouths were ugly in a gay grimace, all alike, their teeth . . . clenched . . . convulsively, with blood which was still fresh dripping from the cages, and the officer felt nauseated with the smell of fresh flesh. This was the place for the execution of political offenders. And over there at the gates, by the wall under the chestnuts—some sitting, some standing, some lying down—were beggars, lepers, jugglers, hypnotists, old men. And lords and ladies came walking or riding past them, riding on horses or carried in chairs by men. The officer went and stood by the beggars and, half-stretching out his right hand, sang out in Russian:

"A-alms, for the sa-ake of Christ! . . ."

A White Army man, an officer of the Russian Army and a gentleman, an émigré, a brother, Peter Ivanovich Ivanov.

1922

The
Cheshire Cheese

MY FRIEND,

Your letter from England took exactly a year to get
here and goodness only knows how it reached me in the
end. I wonder where you are now. You tell me how London,
as always, gathers up all its endings and beginnings—those of
its streets, subways, music halls, pubs, nights in the docks and
Hyde Park, the City, Piccadilly, Pall Mall—and leads them
back into the stone centuries of Westminster Abbey, and the
grandfather chair by the fireplace with whiskey and soda in
the misty evenings. No wonder their Parliament has been
sitting for about eight centuries in a monastery! I well remember my amazement at civilization when—it was just a
trifling thing—I found it impossible to cross the road between
Tottenham Court Road and Oxford Street because it was so
full of taxis, buses and cars, and then I noticed the crates
being lifted by cranes over the rooftops, and I was told to
cross the street by the underground subway for pedestrians.
I remember, too, that feeling of pride and gratitude to
humanity for its human and spiritual culture which I twice
experienced in London. Once it happened by the columns
of the British Museum, when I left the silence of its halls
after my communion with the whole history of mankind

toward the age of what is best in humanity, and in the gloom below I saw all the books that had ever been published in the world. Another time in Westminster Abbey, near Newton's tomb—there in the twilight of centuries on the stone of the walls and under the stone of the floor—even Newton is only a tiny link in the grandiose scheme called humanity and created by man, and the flagstone set in the floor over Newton's remains and bearing his name has already been half erased by the feet of the people walking over him. I remember that after Westminster Abbey, we went to The Cheshire Cheese, a favorite tavern of Dickens. A parrot squawked in a cage, we were given some of the pie Dickens had once enjoyed, and finished our luncheon with the cheese from which the tavern derives its name. When we were leaving, the landlord saw we were foreigners and made us a present of a book of three hundred pages, which told the history of the tavern from 1647. It described who had frequented the place—poets, artists, Dukes of York, killing time on days of London fog—and related how a gentleman had kissed a beautiful lady on the staircase and with what result, and also gave in detail the place and hour when Dickens sat there and the page in *A Tale of Two Cities* where he describes the tavern. The landlord of the tavern was proud to tell us, with a bow, that he too worked for culture. . . .

Well . . . and how am I living now?

The steppe surrounds us in all directions. The sun rises on the steppe and sets on the steppe. The railroad is about sixty miles away and the nearest village about ten. In spring the steppe is a riot of tulips and waist-deep grasses, and then it becomes scorched and there is only dry earth with an occasional patch of feather grass or wormwood. In winter we are snowbound, the Pole Star shines overhead and the scoop of the Great Bear cannot exhaust all the melancholy we experience on the steppe. There is a ravine in the steppe which cannot be seen from a mile to the left or the right, and our farmstead stands in this ravine. We don't plow, but we have a huge garden around the slopes of the ravine, about thirty acres. We have made a stream which runs above the ravine into a pond and two camels keep walking around and around to pump up water for watering the garden; we have six cows, two camels and a horse. In spring the garden is in bloom and then one's head aches with the song of nightingales and the smell of apple blossom. In autumn everything smells of apples, and mountains of apples are piled up everywhere, on the tables, the windowsills, the floor, in outhouses and attics. . . . Our house stands near the pond among poplars, a low house with a wooden roof, whitewashed outside like cottages in the Ukraine, and the little terrace overhangs the precipice and the garden, overlooking a thicket of trees, and in spring there comes a commotion of nightingales. The rooms are low in the house, the seats by the stoves are big, the doors squeak and I imagine the house will now keep the smell of the steppe forever, and wormwood and summer heat. There is a revolution in Russia, all the roads have been deserted, only very rarely does a Kirghiz horseman appear for a moment on the horizon, and then he vanishes beyond the ravines. No one comes here and we go nowhere. We have no bread and make bread with apples and milk. We go on living as before, the five of us. There is my husband's mother, who is a member of the Geographical Association, an entomologist—she does research work and she still writes—my husband, I, my husband's brother, Nicholas, an artist, and his wife, Olga. We live a friendly, cheerful life. My husband spends his days on the slope of the ravine where the sun rises and he has an apiary there and he keeps some writing paper in a hut. Sometimes he fires a shot from his rifle during the day and that's our signal —I go to join him and we sunbathe, or I hear the hard, bony steps of his pointer on the terrace and the pointer has a piece of paper in his mouth with one word on it: "Come." After sunset, in the evening we sit in silence on the terrace, my husband on the steps leading down to the ravine, and I feel the dew settling on my dress. . . . I wake with the sun and always find Mother in her room, with a magnifying glass screwed to her eye and a pen in her hand, bent over her butterflies and beetles—if you could hear what extraordinary things she tells us about butterflies. . . . Our days are full of work. In the morning, Olga and I milk the cows and one of us drives them into the field, the men bring the water, we prepare the morning meal, then we have to go and work in the garden. In spring we dug trenches all around the apple trees, then waged a war on worms and now it's time to gather the apples. . . . Soon the winter will come, we shan't go anywhere, we shall all get together in our little house, the blizzards will blow and it will be very good. We don't know what is going on in the world, we live without money, on the first rung of the cultural ladder, and I don't know how and when I shall be able to send off this letter. . . . Now it's autumn and by the European calendar, September, the days are wonderfully fine, the garden has grown yellow, the steppe opened out even farther, the days are like silent deserts, the sun is blinding, but a little chill is creeping in, there is frost at night and the enormous sky is covered with stars. In the evening the four of us go walking for several miles on the steppe. The men take their rifles with them because the birds are migrating and there's a chance of hitting a bustard, and also because of the wolves, which have begun to raid the farmstead. When we get back, my husband and I go to sleep by the apiary near the apple trees and the honey, and Olga and Nicholas go to the hayloft among the dry spring grasses. . . .

FROM THE DIARY OF OLGA, THE WIFE OF THE PAINTER NICHOLAS. *September 5th, 1918*

Yesterday Mother told us about her scientific expedition to Mongolia, and Maria remembered her days in England. Later we took a walk on the steppe and heard the wolves howling. I had bad dreams at night. I dreamed of London streets, of Trafalgar Square, but they seemed to be in a Mongolian desert, dead and overlaid with sand. The fountain by Nelson's column had dried up and the granite was cracked. Mongols rode on horseback along the streets and then an Englishman in a bowler hat with an umbrella passed by. Now I feel this dream is very like reality. How frightening the steppe and the wilderness all around! When the Kirghiz ride up and stop for a rest, they take raw rotting meat from under their saddles and devour it with their teeth. When we make preparations to visit a human habitation—this year we have only done it twice—it's far more complicated than making the journey from our nearest station to Petersburg, which is over a thousand miles away. . . . The day was sunny, empty, clear and dead, there was a frost, we slept after burrowing deep in the hay and then at night on the hill above, the wolves were howling. . . . At day-break, making an awkward movement, again I felt the child move in me, my wonderful, unknown child. . . . Then the day passed as usual in work and various problems. I like our days because we are friendly and cheerful. At one o'clock we all meet for dinner and always joke, we women play patience and the brothers play a game of chess. I suppose the dream is not really like our life. In the dream, Mongolia had devoured London, but we are like the builders of colonies, bringing culture into the lands of the savages.

September 7th

I was picking the last apples—Antonovka apples—in the garden today and as I reached up to the topmost branches I slipped a little and again I felt the child turn inside me. How happy that makes me! I left the garden and went to find my husband, who was with the camels, and leaned against him. We sat on the wheel which the camels move around and I know we experienced joy. Then, like naughty children, we hurried to mend the wheel, mended it, went back into the garden to pick apples and did not go to dinner until late. And after dinner we didn't linger in the house but went back into the garden. Maria noticed something and wagged her finger at me and I stuck out my tongue. By evening we had brought in a whole mountain of apples. In the evening, Andrey, who is an eccentric inventor, gave Maria and me a bottle of home-made perfume, very good too, smelling of apple blossom and wormwood, like our whole life; he wrote on the jar, "Per-fume—Our Life." We sat indoors; I was sewing for the future child, Mama played patience, the men made wax candles for the winter and we all made jokes. At night we saw far off on the steppe the glow of a fire. What did it mean? The men became worried and began to talk about the revolution and peasant uprisings—we all welcome the revolution as it will wake up this feudal Russia. . . .

September 8th

This morning our unpeopled existence was disrupted. At dawn five Kirghiz horsemen arrived with English military rifles. Always in the past it was a long time before they could be persuaded to ride into the yard and enter the house. This time, they left their horses in the middle of the yard, flung them some hay from the barn, entered the house and sat down in our dining room like Europeans, not on the floor but on the chairs, and they were very ceremonious and silent. Mama brought them some dried apples, but they refused to eat. Andrey offered them some honey and cider but they refused again, even the cider, although it was explained to them that this was alcohol. They all sat as one, their crooked legs thrust out and their arms resting on them, as if they were thinking some great thoughts. They were all alike, with narrow, slanting, little eyes, with conical fur hats, louse-ridden. Soon the whole room became impregnated with the decaying smell of the unwashed, of sweat and sour milk. They did not stay long. They rose as silently, went out to their horses, bound some of our hay to their saddles and sped off into the steppe. Andrey and Nicholas did not like their visit but Mama thinks there is no point in expecting decency from savages, and the fact that they had cast off their usual mask of cowardice and abasement and showed themselves, however awkwardly, to be citizens, was a good sign. . . .

Today was a transparent, empty autumn day and in the morning I saw the cranes move in an arrow toward the south; they always make one feel melancholy, stir up one's soul with a yearning to join them. The leaves are beginning to fall in the garden, it's becoming bare, space is opening out much more than usual, and one can hear forgotten apples falling. Toward evening it began to rain and the sky clouded over. A damp wind has begun to blow, encircling and penetrating everything. The night is black as black and it's impossible to see anything. And now the steppe is frightening, wet, dark and empty. The garden is rustling in an evil, sinister way. We are all in the dining room, each with his own task, and I'm sitting in the corner, writing. On evenings like this one should be particularly friendly. I shall finish writing this and sew for the child, and tonight we won't be sleeping in the hayloft but will settle down in the house as we do in the winter. . . . How unpleasantly the dogs are barking, there must be wolves again. . . . A shot! Andrey has gone to see what is the matter. . . .

II

In executive committees, in extraordinary commissions, in Army headquarters, in squares, on country roads, along the railroad, in stations, in villages, farms, fields, steppes, ravines, rivers, by night, in fog, in rain, in autumn, with a thousand voices, people went from place to place, crawled, dragged guns, carts, cattle, shouted, sang songs, prayed, wept, swore, slept on the roadways, in the ravines, on the steppe, blazing campfires, villages, fields, towns, died with a cup in their hands, sleepy, cheerful, sick, were killed by typhus, guns, famine—from the Urals and the steppe marched pale-blue men in English overcoats with Old Believers' crosses and with beards. From Moscow and Petersburg, from towns and machines the Reds marched in workmen's jackets, with stars, but without prayers. The guns were set on hills and let off along the expanse of rivers, through fog, into the towns. Obstinate villages blazed with tongues of flame. People buried themselves along with bread in the fields, by canals, ravines and rivers. People went without sleep for weeks and fell asleep forever through insomnia and others slept for weeks. In the fields, under the autumn sun and stars, wild horses wandered and wolves, people, fear, chaos. . . .

In executive committees, in extraordinary commissions, in the security service, in Army headquarters, telephones roared, couriers crowded round, shag rose in clouds, orders were written, news was received, treachery discovered, heroism and stupidity passed as trifles; they slept on tables, ate and worked in one and the same place, shot men in the yard, hung posters on the front door, and people who were hoarse yelled from the front doors, from columns, yelled, yelled at those who were going, going, going past. . . .

In executive committees, in extraordinary commissions, in Army headquarters, papers piled up for history, papers about a bridge blown up somewhere and a hundred sailors heroically going to their death, about a detachment going to their death, about a piece of land lost here, gained there, about a dirty night somewhere, about the Pale Blue Coats hanging a commissar, about a new Red Army of a thousand men going to their deaths for the sake of a glorious future, shaven men in workmen's jackets, about a Kirghiz gang marauding, plundering, raping, murdering and setting fire.

First came the brave sunny days of an Indian summer, when the sun rose over a dark-blue heavenly crust, gossamer flew over the fields and the earth grew still in the hard blue air—that was by day, and by night the stars shone, filled with fresh life after the summer, and a crescent moon shone, reborn after June. Then came the rains; the world and the steppe grew gray and moist. Then the frosts clamped on the damp grayness of the steppe and the snow fell, only to creep along the gullies, turning to mud. The snow began to fall at night, as usual, but at dawn it would thaw, and for a moment our hearts would be touched with courage. Red Army men marched along the streets mixing snow and mud together, and the campfires on the square had not yet burned out after their night's rest, the smoke hanging over the ground; the air was dark blue as on all winter mornings. Secretary of the executive committee, wearing felt boots for the winter, put some wood on the stove before settling down to his business. Among thousands of documents there was one in which the chairman of a rural district council made a report on his district:

I must also report that a hundred armed Kirghiz passed about a fortnight ago across the wasteland; they plundered the peasant farms and took prisoners, whom they murdered afterward on the steppe. They must have raped all the women; as for cattle, they did not steal it so much as drive it away, and they have done goodness only knows what. They have attacked sixteen farms and three villages. We have set the peasants to catch the cattle on the steppe. What is to be done?

Outside the window the snow was melting and the soldiers began to sing a song about how the maidens labored. The snow thawed, a puddle appeared on the square, the earth grew gray like the face of an old woman in tears. The small stove in the room began to warm up. The boldness which always strikes people on the first day of winter passed with the thawing snow into the humdrum working day, and the soldiers' song died away at the bend in the road to the steppe. The executive committee already knew about the Kirghiz— one dull dawn on a hillock on the wet steppe a machine gun had blown them to pieces together with their horses, giving them to the wolves—and the secretary pushed the paper from the rural council under the baize cloth. . . . The telephone rang in the chairman's study and a telegram came from head-quarters about an order for supplies. . . .

Somewhere on the steppe in these terrible days, the sun, as it set among the rustling feather grass beyond the ravines in a terrible red glow, lit up a hillock, and on the hillock there was a camp of nomad Asiatics, wild and savage. A campfire was burning on the hill, and the savages sat around the fire in furs, wearing conical hats, and they had dull, dead faces like the steppe and all the wormwood civilization of the steppe. These people were as silent as the steppe. Only the horses, wandering in the ravine, sometimes let out a neigh and sud-denly galloped into the steppe, beating up the dust and the silence. During the day's halt, these people had littered the ground by the fire with human rubbish; horse dung lay around, saddles, rifles, camping utensils. The fire smelled of dung since that is what was burning there. For a long time they cooked the carcass of a horse and then they ate it, holding the meat in their hands. So the sun passed in a red wound toward the future sky studded with stars, with ice, for the fire to smolder for a long time and melt, ominously red, on the steppe. . . . The next dawn caught the Kirghiz many miles away from the campfire and it was an empty, transparent, boundless autumn day, in silence, a scrunching like glass, with the cranes calling, with the melancholy of the cranes. And this day too ended in rain, damp, grayness. The Kirghiz sat as silently as before by their campfire in the steppe, their legs under them, in conical hats, the fire smoldered with dung and smoke as before and the horses wandered about in the murk. The night came in black gloom, with frost and an orphan wind. The wolves began to howl early and the horses ap-proached the fire, standing in a circle, their backs to the steppe, their heads toward the people, watchful and afraid. Again they set off at night. By this halt there was a haystack—

the kind into which Russians hurled Kirghiz horse thieves and set fire to them—and someone riding off flung a brand in the haystack and it flared up, a landmark for another night. . . .

On the hill above the ravine it was quiet and peaceful down among the trees. A light shone through the windows, strange and alien to the Kirghiz. The dogs began to bark. The horsemen stood motionless, the horses dropped their heads, the wind rustled in the trees below with an orphaned sound. The horsemen approached nearer and began to dismount. One of them, who sat like all Kirghiz, crouching over his horse, a long-maned squat little creature, held the rifle away from himself and, frowning, shot into the sky. Then, one by one, noiselessly, the Kirghiz began to creep downhill with their knives and rifles through the bushes. The one who had fired the shot remained behind with the horses, which stood in a circle, their backs to the steppe, their heads bent, with the broad mares in the center.

Someone shouted calmly from below:

"Hey! Who's firing up there?"

There was silence for a long time and then suddenly in a great burst of flame the hayloft caught fire and the roof crackled with flames. Then a woman gave a wild piercing scream, an imploring scream.

"Let me go, let me go! I'm pregnant, let me go, I'm preg—"

The Kirghiz on guard saw three men dragging a woman along the ground, seize her by her arms and her legs and pull her down from the porch. The Kirghiz changed his grip on the reins and made a sound with his lips. The screams quietened down. People were silently running to and fro in the light of the flames. Then the woman screamed again. Four men rolled a cask uphill, and without waiting for the others, they began to drink up there, holding their hats under the tap and gulping from their hats. The blaze grew more powerful in the black murk, and jackdaws flew on the wind and rain, and a live raven, awakened by the fire, croaked above the dark steppe.

Again a woman yelled:

"Help, let me go, I'll die! . . ."

The woman rushed out of the darkness into the firelight and began to run. About ten men chased her and brought her down by the bonfire. Then someone who was disfigured and bleeding, a man unnoticed up to this moment, dragged himself along by the arms from the porch, and stretched out his hand and fired into the group of Kirghiz—and then the guard, scarcely taking aim, fired, and saw the bullet smash the man's head.

It rained all night and the new dawn came with gray damp mist, wind. . . . The new dawn discovered the Kirghiz in a new halting place. The campfire reeked as before, the people sat as silently as before, their legs drawn up under them; the horses wandered about, eating the withered grass. . . . Several more dawns passed, and then on one cheerless dawn gunfire burst out from two sides of the encampment, to leave a hash of human bones to the vultures and the wolves. At the farm a few days later, three women and two Red Army soldiers buried two men. Two men and one prematurely born dead infant. After the burial the commissar wrote, shaking his head dubiously:

"They killed two men"—after pondering, he changed this to three—"raped two young women and an old woman; ate a mare, burned a shed. . . ."

Snow fell over the steppe again, and again it thawed, and the snow turned to mud; it spread over the black earth and the soldiers' feet sank ankle deep. At night the soldiers blended into a whole, the light of the campfire, the snow, the dirt and their own bodies. At dawn the soldiers advanced into the gloom the steppe and the snow. . . . At headquarters, in executive-committee offices, the telephone rang unceasingly.

III

It was March in London and already there had been fog for a week. There were days when buses, streetcars, taxis, cars were forced to come to a halt because of the fog; the city grew quiet and people walked about the streets in the yellow mist, feeling their way along the walls of houses. The city grew quiet. People sat at home by the fireplace with blankets over their shoulders and in woolen underwear. Men and women drank whiskey and soda to warm themselves and to kill time. The city waited for the wind to blow from the sea. The street lamps burned all day but were useless in the fog. Newspapers increased their circulation.

A solitary man, a Russian, who, however, had come to resemble an Englishman, was accustomed to waken to the screeching of metal, to the metallic din of machinery, to the hissing of cars outside, but now, during these days of fog, he woke in a yellow morning and, still half asleep, heard a distant bell chiming, as in Russia: once he had cursed Russia for this chiming of bells instead of the screeching of machinery. A bell rang out in the yellow fog in the muffled city, and what new spirit was it that crept out of this sound and this fog? Like all Englishmen, he ate porridge and bacon at breakfast and drank coffee with toast and marmalade. But unlike all Englishmen, he was not connected with the city—this was a characteristic which remained from his Russian days—and, in a black coat, feeling his way along the walls, from corner to corner, he made his way to the British Museum, and in these twilight halls left the present for the furthest recesses of the catacombs of human history; and like all Russians he measured the history of mankind by Russia, although she was somewhere there, abandoned and unknown like China, and even though the man had forgotten how to talk Russian, the English language having torn his native tongue out by the roots. Books spoke truly enough of the terrible senility of the human race. And so the lunch hour came round, as he sat with his books, and then he went out again into the fog, walked to Kingsway, toward the churches in the Strand and then to Fleet Street—the street of world newspapers and of Dickens. By decree of "the old world" and on account of English conservatism, this street looked as it had four hundred years ago, and the man entered The Cheshire Cheese through an archway in a mews. The fire was burning, the room was empty and the parrot shouted something. With their side whiskers, the waiters were as important as ministers. At the bar along the corridor, an Irishman had already had a good many drinks, as the fog induces depression, and now he was whistling "It's a long way to Tipperary" and only drinking whiskey. He was standing there propped up against the bar, his legs wide apart in their bold checked gray trousers, and he interrupted his whistling to say:

"Fog, fog! Take a look at this photo of my daughter and this is her sweetheart, a clerk in the city—that's important!"

The man from Russia was no longer young. English fogs, business, streets in which all the houses are alike, were sharply reflected in his close-shaven face with its grayish tan, neither a very healthy nor a very sickly face, but one in which will power showed in each vein, and only his eyes retained the Russian melancholy of fields and Russian senility. Another Russian, just like himself, was going to meet him in the tavern. They entered together. They took off their black overcoats simultaneously and hung them up side by side on hooks where Dickens too had hung his coat. They sat opposite one another at a table with a white cloth, on benches with high backs. Their gray heads facing one another in the setting of the benches were like the old English portraits of benevolent drunkards in the National Gallery, and the backs of these benches, yellowed with age, eaten with woodworm, were carved with gay words, initials, dates, which preserved the memory of whole centuries, and indeed there came from these benches encrusted with centuries a smell of old cheese, a smell just faintly reminiscent of sweat. The attendant waiter silently set two pints of beer before them and walked away to fetch two plates of pigeon pie to accompany two more pints, and then he was to give them still two more pints after the cheese.

And because it was foggy outside and the city was quiet, because they were old men who were Russian and lonely, and because the waiter had just decided to serve their third order of beer, they had a long Russian conversation, and because they were Russians their talk was about Russia. Their pipe tobacco, like all English tobacco, smelled exotically of countries beyond the seas and of navigation—it's not for nothing that Englishmen are sailors and their tobacco is called "a whiff of the sea." The labor of Englishmen is not drenched in the smell of cheese, but of tobacco. The Russians ate their cheese slowly and spent a long time talking. . . .

"I'll tell you a story. It took place more than four years ago in 1918, in Russia, in the Volga district, in the southeast, when the steppe was in revolt and the Czechoslovaks were on the march. A family, friends of mine, lived there on a farm and they were lively healthy people. The old man, a mining engineer, died, and his wife became the head of the family. She had two sons, who were married to beautiful Russian women, and one of them, Olga, was expecting a baby. The five of them lived on the steppe, engaged in cultural pursuits and worked hard. The Kirghiz plundered their farm, killed the sons, raped the mother and both the daughters-in-law, right there before the very eyes of the dying husbands. Olga miscarried on the day after this happened, and the other, Maria, became pregnant soon after that night. . . . And just imagine this Russian woman, who loved her husband, whose husband was killed by the men who raped her, and who did not know right up to the birth of the child who the father was—the husband who would never return and this son his one memory, or her violators, who had sullied her body and her soul. She gave birth to a little, slant-eyed Kirghiz, red, like all newborn babies, and when they slapped his bottom he gulped and let out a cry like all newborn babies. . . . How did the mother accept this child? She lay in the pangs of labor and when it was over she asked for the baby. They were afraid to show it to her; they gave her the baby and she clasped it to her breast and was as radiant as all mothers who first take their baby in their arms, in that joyful moment of existence when still unaccustomed to the mystery of birth. . . . That's life. Olga's unborn child was killed and, you know, she used to come quietly, secretly to Maria to caress and fondle her baby. That's life, life—a terrible tragedy! . . . I wandered around London with Maria when she was a young girl and we came here—it was here she talked about the grandeur of human culture. This tavern amazed her; half-joking, half-serious, she was ready to kiss this wall and the stones of the Houses of Parliament, as a temple of culture. . . . How far more ancient, more meaningful and more terrifying is man's life. . . ."

The parrot gave a gay laugh over in his cage. And the Irishman who had mentioned his daughter changed his seat to chat with the parrot. The waiter placed a box of cigars and the bill before the two Russians. A family of American tourists came in. The Russians got up, took their coats, bowed and went out into the fog. On the corner they took leave of one another and the fog swallowed them up after a couple of steps. The town was silent.

In his flat at home, the old man changed into his dressing gown, lighted the fire, settled himself in a low armchair by the fire, lighted a pipe and sat there like that for a long time, tired, decrepit, as old men in Russia always do in a Russian way. Then he fetched a siphon of soda and a bottle of whiskey, put them on the arm of the chair and again sat down, with a writing pad, and began to write on his knees. The fire began to go out—it was burning as feebly as the decrepit old man. . . . Toward seven the old man began to change into a dinner jacket and again set off into the fog, now in a black coat and top hat. At Russell Square—the students' place—the elevator carried him ten flights down underground. He took the tube to Piccadilly Circus and made his way to Pall Mall. Night had settled over the town. The street lamps burned steadily and made the fog turn brown. For a moment a cascade of lights on placards and advertisements burst through the fog, but still nothing could be seen except a few passersby walking a couple of steps ahead or just behind, making a shuffling sound in the street.

The old man was home again by eleven and got into his pajamas for bed, as all English people do. He did not put on the electric light and there was only a glow from the fire in the grate. And once again in the unusual silence which now replaced the screeching of iron and steel, a church bell sounded and reminded him of Russia. Lying there in his bed in flannel sheets and woolen pajamas in the English way, the old man thought about Russia, about his native land, in the way of old people when old age has to justify everything and an entire past life, and the old man realized that nothing would be justified if he did not carry his bones to his own earth.

The fog hung over the town. The town and everyone in it was waiting for a wind to blow from the sea and drive the fog away from London. If you were to gaze down on London from Parliament Hill, from the hill where once the rebels watched for the Houses of Parliament to burst into flames, then the mists over London lighted up from within by millions of electric lamps, London under the fog, might seem to be a city living on the ocean bed, a phantasmagoric, a Russian city, a Kitezh, a drowned city. . . .

The birds were stirring all night on the steppe, for they had stopped to rest in their flight to the north. The night was dark, but already it was as warm as in spring. The snow thawed fast, in a few days, and now the streams were noisy, the grass was quickening, the birds began to fly off—the spring had come in rapidly and they had to hurry. In the evening there was a shower of rain, soon over, and by midnight it was quite clear again. The crescent moon rose, the stars took their places in a new design, in readiness for June, when they would be renewed. A row of geese honked on the hill by the stream; farther away a watching crane screamed, and the birds muttered to one another as they fell asleep. The stream descended in a waterfall. It was necessary to be quick. Three women worked all night on the dam, cheerfully and boldly. They were making haste to mend the dam so that the water would not burst it. They chopped wood with an ax, carted earth, stamped down the piles. Just before dawn, as always, it became even darker for a few minutes and soon the east was streaked with lilac. The sound of birds beating their wings was heard, as they rose from the earth to fly north toward their nests.

1923

The
Old House

I

On the terrace of this house there was a doorpost with a great
many pencil marks, each initialed and bearing a date. Whenever the house was redecorated (in the old days, before it was
pulled down), instructions were always given that these dates
should not be painted over, and they are preserved to this day:
K. M. APRIL 1861, K. M. APRIL 29, '62—each of the two letters
representing a name and each year mounting higher. Then
after twenty-five years had elapsed, the years stopped and
reappeared again low down on the door. The initials K. M.
stood for Katiusha Malinin, who was their grandmother, and
they were written high up because in her youth Katerina
Ivanovna who was the head of the house, had been tall and
well-proportioned. And it happened that the eldest girl in
each generation, whose initials appeared after each quarter
of a century at the bottom of the door, would reach as high as
Katerina Ivanovna. And the last person—N. K. APRIL 11, 1924
—was first marked near the floor on May 7 (the lilac must
already have been in bloom on the terrace) in the year 1908.
N. K.—Nonna Kalitinin—the last of the family; the dates of
her notches appeared in the years 1914, 1917, 1919, 1920, 1924.

Katerina Ivanovna, née Malinìn, who married a Kor-
shunov (and she was nicknamed "the Old Kite" until she

died) died on October 25, 1917, by the old calendar. The family was then carried on by the Kalitinins.

This house, as the person whose dates appeared first in 1917 and 1919 remembered only vaguely, was part of Katerina Ivanovna's dowry. They lived then in the Great Moscow Road (now Lenin Street), where they owned a business, and they only came to the house to spend the summer holidays on the banks of the Volga. They moved here altogether when they lost their money and then Katerina Ivanovna's husband died. The marks on the door were made in the spring, when they first used the terrace after the winter months.

This terrace stood on posts which were about fourteen feet high. Below the terrace grew poplars, white acacia and lilacs, and for some seventy feet beyond that, as far as the embankment and the Volga, there were timber warehouses, logs bound in eights, in twelves, battens, firewood—this was the Korshunov-Kalitinin livelihood—and beyond the embankment wall flowed the Volga, wide and free each spring, sandy and chalky each autumn. It was possible to throw a pebble from the terrace into the Volga and cast out care. Stone storehouses separated the terrace from the road and in the old days they held enough stocks of salt for the whole town, and then, later, when kerosene appeared, they were full of kerosene, which was first called photogen, then photonaphthalene and only finally, kerosene. After they lost their money, before 1914, the storehouses were full of sacking and coal, an adjunct to the timber landing stage, where they traded logs in lots of five. If one glanced at the house from the sloping drive leading to the street—because houses are built along the waterway—it looked as if the house were askew. On the left, the ground came up to the windows, while on the right, under a row of windows, there was a whole floor for storage and quarters for the watchmen, and the storehouses themselves were three stories high. By 1923 the storehouse had collapsed. It looked as if the ocher-colored house had made a desperate effort to jump into the Volga and, failing, remained there, the blood-red bricks of the façade disfiguring it, while half the building crouched close to the earth, frozen in its forward leap. The house was built of stone. It was cumbersome, echoing . . . Katerina Ivanovna's dowry.

The first memory of this house related to the time when Katerina Ivanovna's husband, their grandfather, lay dying. This took place in the years when the signs of this generation had only recently appeared on the door, and they remembered that their grandfather died slowly of a painful illness. In his gloomy study (the windows were always curtained) there was a stifling smell from the mahogany commode, which looked like his throne. Grandfather could not walk. He lay there, supported on high pillows, with sweets hidden under them. The memory of their sweetness in the stifling smell of the mahogany always remained and if one of them were to come across this mahogany commode throne among the rubbish of some market place even twenty years later, it would be impossible not to recognize it. But below the terrace on the little promenade, white acacia and white lilac bloomed riotously each spring, and below the terrace, below the embankment wall, the Volga—the mother of all Russian rivers—spread itself tumultuously, carrying the open spaces, the barges and steamers, their hoots, and storms and songs—the Volga boat song—and people and bargemen. The old man lay dying in the spring, and in the spring it was impossible not to absorb the violence and freedom of the earth, this earth hurrying intoxicated with bird cherry, lilacs, acacia, songs, troops of bargemen, hooting. Katerina Ivanovna walked about the house, weeping loudly for her husband in front of everyone, and she went to town with an umbrella and a bonnet, taking a pair of shaft horses, and she did the accounts, listed the securities, counted the bills of exchange, went to the landing stage with a walking stick, to see the bailiff, Mikhail Arsenteyevich.

Either the fact was remembered, or a legend grew up, that Pugachev was once in this house and that the cellars under the house (they were large and blocked up) used to shelter brigands and money forgers and had underground passages. And the boys did not care that grandmother would have to go to the bank and the law courts; for the boys, the ones whose dates began to appear in the nineties, it was essential to dig down into these cellars, to poke around them for so long that finally they themselves had to be dug out, standing on guard with kitchen knives at night (until they fell asleep

at their posts), on the watch for money forgers at the door of
the storehouse, wondering how to bring Pugachev to life again
and each of them hoping to become a Khlopysha (Pugachev's
memory was vividly alive along the Volga in those days and
the boys learned about him from the bargemen). Katerina
Ivanovna would come back from the bank and begin to cry
on the terrace for her dead husband and because he had left
all their affairs on her shoulders and she would punish the
boys with her umbrella or by shutting them up in the storehouse. It was dark and damp in the storehouse, the windows
were covered with wire netting, and the storehouse had two
floors. There were trunks with goods in the storehouse, there
were jars of jam and dried provisions, scales hung there on
which you could swing, there was kvass in a barrel—swinging
on the scales, the boys were not miserable in the storehouse.
They ate jam and drank kvass. Once (after Easter) there were
some open bottles of wine closed with glass stoppers; they
drank wine and nibbled candied fruit. When girls got locked
in with the boys, it was bad, because the girls took their
punishment seriously, cried, and would not allow feasting and
celebrating (on pain of telling tales). There were a great many
girls and boys because Katerina Ivanovna had eleven children,
of whom seven lived to grow up—and the boys kept aloof
from the girls. Katerina Ivanovna's sons and daughters in
those years were scattered all over Russia (and even abroad),
and they only descended on her in the spring to leave their
children with her for the summer. And sometimes when the
gang of children disappeared, then those left in the house no
longer discriminated between the sexes, and the story was
handed down of how Boris and Nadya poisoned Andreyevna,
the cook (more of Nadya later, because this was Boris' first
love).

It was spring again, when houses were being redecorated
all along the streets, when asphalt was smoking at the crossroads and lilac rioted beside the fences—and Boris and
Nadezhda decided to be house-painters and to paint some walls
with laundry bluing. Boris was in shorts with slits at the sides
and no pockets and he went to get some bluing from the
kitchen, which was Andreyevna's domain. He took it down
from the shelf, but she came into the kitchen at just that

moment. He hid the bluing bag in the slit in his shorts but Andreyevna demanded, as Granny did, "Show me your hands!" And the bluing bag fell out through the leg of his shorts. Andreyevna was not friends with Boris and said she would tell Granny. Boris returned in disgrace to Nadya, who was waiting for him with a bowl of water, in which the paint was to be mixed. Boris said, "Andreyevna's a fool. She told me to go away." Granny was not at home and it was terrible when a plan could not be carried out, so Boris said quickly:

"We'll poison Andreyevna. She'll be a martyr and go to paradise—it won't matter to her and it will be convenient for us because then she won't tell tales to Granny and we can get the bluing."

And because Granny had gone off to the courts with her companion, Darya Ermilovna, and because they really meant business, Boris soon succeeded in proving that the best thing to do was to poison Andreyevna, and in convincing Nadezhda that this would be the most convenient for all concerned. Granny had a dark, severe-looking bedroom with a whole collection of wonderful things in it and she had a little shelf there with medicines and poisons, for stomach upsets, colds, toothache, hangovers, migraine and nerves (although Katerina Ivanovna did not accept "nerves" any more than she would admit that the world was round and she herself "like a louse perched on its head"). Boris made his way to this cupboard and the plan was to tip some sort of capsule with some mysterious drops in it over the sugar which stood in the canister on the kitchen shelf. Andreyevna was not there that minute. Boris climbed onto the stove, where Ivanich the coachman was sleeping (what wonderful stories Ivanich could tell about horses and about Pugachev, and his favorite expression was: "Don't touch, child!"). Boris even enticed Nadya up there, so that they could watch Andreyevna take the poison and die. Andreyevna's fate was predestined by the stove and the stove responded to her with a flame which spread over her ugly face, already almost blue with lupus. She came into the kitchen and the children knew she drank a hundred cups of tea a day. She took down the sugar, opened the box, and the children sat quiet as mice on the stove. Andreyevna called out angrily:

"Nyushka, you wretch, what have you been splashing into the sugar?"

Nyushka, the maid, answered from the corridor:

"I haven't been near your sugar."

Then Andreyevna muttered something, poured some boiling water from the kettle into a mug and sat down at the table, still muttering. She took out a huge piece of sugar, just the one which had been moistened worse than the rest. Boris was silent; Nadya's eyes were double their usual size from tears. Andreyevna began to bring the sugar to her mouth. And then Nadya began to cry and squeaked out:

"Andreyevna dear, don't eat it, you'll die. Don't go to paradise, live with us!"

With her lupus-scarred face, Andreyevna cried furiously:

"Wh—a—at?"

"We took some poison from Granny's shelf. Don't eat it, you'll die! You wouldn't let us have the bluing bag."

Nadya was crying. Boris took the disclosure oddly: he fell on his back, kicked his legs in the air and squealed blissfully. It so happened that Katerina Ivanovna returned at this moment and Nadya and Boris, having run the gauntlet of Granny's umbrella, spent a long time in the storehouse. Boris put away the jam with gusto and Nadya endured the punishment, cried and said she was sorry. . . .

Over in the house in the silence of the large rooms, the bustle of the day quietened down, candles burned under bell glasses on the terrace, moths circled them, and Granny sat alone at the samovar—Katerina Ivanovna—and in the doorway, just by the dates marking their height, stood Ivanich, the watchman, or the cook, Andreyevna. Those whose names appeared immediately below K.M., the parents, were scattered all over Russia—an engineer; a manufacturer; a city lawyer; a revolutionary and a woman revolutionary; an actress; two sons had gone over the embankment wall to rags and tatters; embittered alcoholics. . . .

Boris, whose dates rose along with those of the third generation, remembered this house only bit by bit—his grandfather's death, springtime, the storehouse, the money forgers. He exchanged his shorts for the long gray flannels of the highschool boy in town, hundreds of miles off, where his father

whiled away his days, a halfhearted revolutionary, always forgetting, and when he remembered, sternly judging that house
on the Volga. And he arrived there once again in long trousers
and a jacket, in another spring when the lilac was rioting once
more, caldrons of asphalt were warming and the Volga hooted
with open spaces and bargemen. And from some other town
in another part of Russia there arrived, as well, not a little
girl with two plaits, an eternal enemy to sessions in the storehouse, but an adolescent with long plaits in a brown dress
and a much higher mark on the doorpost—Nadya, a high-
school girl. Boris told her he was a Social Democrat and she
said she was a Socialist Revolutionary, and Boris made her a
present of some poetry in a book with gold stamping and then
they buried themselves in Turgenev's *Rudin* and Boris grieved
for Rudin and Nadya for Natasha. They played croquet and
sometimes, when they had to be on opposite sides, perhaps it
was not by chance that Boris' mallet slipped and his op-
ponent's ball, Nadya's ball, rolled into position. They played
"opinions" and again perhaps only by accident, Boris always
guessed whom Nadya had chosen. The grownups often went
out of town by boat to the Green Island, where they drank
milk, bought sterlets from the fishermen, made fish soup over
a campfire, sang songs and argued (the year '05 passed over the
house, over their grandmother, Katerina Ivanovna, and over
this first childish love). Nadya and Boris were sitting in a boat
and talking (afterward they could not remember what they
were talking about), dragging their feet in the water—everyone had taken off their shoes to walk on the sand, even the
grownups—and the boat heeled over. Nadya staggered and
stumbled into the water. It was not deep, only knee-deep, but
without thinking, Boris jumped into the water, stood in it up
to his waist, picked Nadya up and carried her onto the sand.
Nadya's eyes were surprised and frightened and gazed up into
the sky—and Boris did not notice how his lips moved close to
Nadya's cheek and how he kissed her. He realized it only when
he was lost forever, with no turning back, burning with shame,
bitterness and remorse.

Below the house, where the storehouses were and the
cellars, half underground, there were also some prison-like,
netted-off—what could one call them?—quarters, chambers

that were flooded in winter, and in one of these vaulted cellars
lived the carpenter, Pankrat Ivanich with his family, a man
who went on strike, and then had to go hungry. Boris had a
ruble, a silver one, which Granny had given him along with
a purse so that he should learn how to save, and Boris ordered
a little wooden bookshelf for a ruble. . . . Boris and Nadya sat
in the drawing room, holding hands, and Granny Katerina
Ivanovna passed by. Boris went with Nadya in the evening
to gaze at the moon, the Volga and the silence. They sat down
on a log and Boris took Nadya's hand and then Katerina
Ivanovna's threatening figure appeared over the wall. And
next morning, Nadya had to leave and go back to her parents
and was not even allowed to say good-bye to Boris. In the
drawing room, under the family portraits, striking the floor
with her stick, Granny spoke to Boris and said something
loathsome he could not understand about incest, and that they
were not children and that she and her husband, his grandfather (the one about whom he remembered the taste of sweets
in the stifling atmosphere of his dying), had lived their life
together as no one had and yet had only met twice before the
wedding. . . .

Then Boris saw Nadya ten years later, when they were both
already called by their patronymics, in Moscow, in Nikolayev-
sky station, where crowds of people were passing, luggage was
lying about and trains kept coming and going. Nadya had a
child in her arms and she was traveling to see her husband,
an officer, in a far-off town where he was lying wounded at the
hospital. Boris recognized her from a long way off and saw
how tall, beautiful and well-built she was. She was wearing a
black hat with a veil. She raised her veil to kiss her relative
and began to talk about trifling things, about a porter, her
trunk in the luggage van, and Boris could hear that her voice
was like their Granny's had once been. They took a cab and
drove past the Red Gates to the Nizhigorodsky station. . . .
Over there on the Volga, each spring the Volga was in a
tumult of waters and lilac. The house stood over the landing
stage and below the embankment wall a human crowd surged
violently, along with the tons, the things, the bales, whistles,
along with the burning sky, glazed like the polished whistles.

Two of Katerina Ivanovna's sons had rolled down the jetty, beyond the embankment wall, into tatters, drunkenness, vodka, which could be got there by oxlike toil, expended on lugging great two-hundredweight sacks full of salt and oxhide, by that hard labor which, besides sweat, vodka and a bitter life, also gives one Caspian roach. One of them died without a trace. About the other, the police sent word after a search that it was not certain whether he was dead or not, but if not, then he must be in hiding in the south, since he had been caught with a gang of thieves and robbers that had resisted capture, leaving three unidentified corpses behind—and Katerina Ivanovna did not know whether to put his name on the side of the dead or the living in her thick Church remembrance book, bound in leather and bearing a cross. Her other children went up in the world, as things were understood in those days. One built bridges, and was a railway engineer. By the age of twenty-seven he had grown a fat stomach and his thin wife wrote that he was unfaithful to her with cabaret singers but she received her monthly housekeeping money regularly. Another went abroad to study German philosophy, returned with a patent and opened a chemical-paint factory near Petersburg. He was Katerina Ivanovna's favorite and she secretly sent him some thousands of rubles to "get started." She did not write to his wife except to send her greetings and thanks at Christmas and Easter. A third became a lawyer in Moscow, went abroad in spring, was kind and jovial—Nadya was his daughter—and his wife wrote to her mother-in-law that it was uncivilized to live as she did, to eat such rich food, that it was essential for the organism to have plenty of protein, the capitalist way of life was coming to an end, and it was dishonest to live off capital and that this year they were going to Karlsbad. One of Katerina Ivanovna's daughters remained with her for good. She left only after she got married for two years and then returned, her wings clipped, with a child in her arms, her daughter, Nonna. Katerina Ivanovna died on October 25, 1917. The last marks on the doorpost on the terrace were N. K.—Nonna Kalitinin—starting low down on May 7 (when the lilac must have been in bloom) and growing higher year by year, 1914, 1917, 1919, 1920—1924. . . .

II

Nineteen fourteen and 1915 passed like a curtain before the action of 1918. In 1917 all the beliefs, the folkways, the nations of Russia were conquered. A terrible ice-encrusted thunder swept over Russia and swept everything away, even those who lived in the old house, scattered everything, froze and heated everything in heat waves and ice. Katerina Ivanovna died on October 25, 1917. Those who grew up in the generation after her were scattered over the whole world and not only over Russia. Some recalled the old house somewhere in Algiers, one spoke of it in the town of St. Petersburg in America, Nadezhda remembered it in Blagoveschensk in eastern Siberia, where she was driven along with her husband and the remnants of Kolchak's army. Nineteen twenty-one, when cannibalism reigned in the old town, was a crossroad for these people. As streams pour from huge melting glaciers and carry with them everything that was frozen there, sometimes so that this frozen thing, preserved in the cold, flows along just as it was before—so out of the ice age of 1917 there flowed 1921. The third generation after Katerina Ivarovna, apart from Nadezhda, who remained in Russia, did not think of the old house in the old town. For this generation, the revolution was not glacial, but instead it leaped forward across Russia in action and construction, in projects and their fulfillment. And yet the glacial years must have frozen them in such a way that afterward, in the streams, something of the remembrance of life before the ice age quickened. Nineteen twenty-two and 1924 brought great misery to these people. During these years, people searched for one another and letters arrived as from the grave, letters from Algiers, from the American town of St. Petersburg, written simultaneously in another language and in Russian. And at home, it was necessary to go over and over everything that had been lived through and experienced during these glacial years, in order to build, if not afresh (since in man's life what is new comes only once), but at least for the better.

It was April, 1924, when the twilight is greenish and when the twilight takes away one's peace of mind.

It was April in a village near Moscow and it was twilight. A man whose dates appeared on the doorpost in the third generation was writing in this twilight:

In three-quarters of an hour I shall set out for the station. I arrived in the evening and saw Katya from the street. Some boys ranged themselves in a row as I was at the outskirts of the village, let me pass their ranks and yelled something only they could understand. I felt very bitter, since in these urchin stares I recognized my estrangement from the house where all these uneasy years were lived that held more than sorrow. One loves one's children as one loves the soil and it was bitterly painful to press them to my breast. My wife told me how Anatoly had asked her to write me a letter. He woke up one morning and asked where was Daddy and then he wanted, he insisted that Daddy must come home and asked her to write a letter at once, dictated it himself:

"Write, 'Come quickly, Daddy dear!' " My wife began to cry as she told me about this. Anatoly sat in his high chair. He had annexed *The Hunchbacked Horse* and Katya had *Tom Sawyer*. Anatoly looked at the pictures in the book, Katerina went off to bed, I sat beside her bed and she told me all about how on May 1 they would go for a ride in a car. Anatoly did not want to leave me, but his mother said, "That's enough now, or Daddy will go away again," and he cried, but went off obediently, ". . . only don't go away." And in the morning, in a nightshirt, his tummy bare, Anatoly lay down beside me, put an unlighted cigarette in his mouth and had a smoke. I went to the village and bought them some sweets; the children met me in the street. Anatoly took a sweet and went off with it to have a nap. . . .

Children are frightening. You love them as the soil, as yourself, as life itself. And it's a bitter love. Now, while I'm getting ready to leave, I feel as a man must feel who has cancer and can calculate, pencil in hand, how many weeks, hours, days he has before he dies. I walk about the house, talk, do things and eat. It's not right, I'm a stranger here.

Then this man walked through the fields and woods, the wind ruffled him, mist and darkness enveloped him . . . and in the mist and obscurity there was a smell of bird cherry and nightingales sang. A train crawled out of the mist and up to the stop. Then thoughts came about falsehood and truth, about how a man can never tell everything, understand and explain it to himself, so that he could be certain this was the truth. In these unhappy days of parting with his wife, neither she nor he knew how to speak the truth to one another, a truth which might dissipate their sadness, as if it really belonged to someone else, and might bring them peace of mind and some justification. The train went off in the mist and it was a good thing they did not put on the light in the carriage.

At the end of April, there was already a strong suggestion of the stifling heat of summer in Moscow, which greeted him with its lights and noisy pavements, with bursts of laughter at the crossroads. A streetcar which had also revived after the ice age went by, creaking slowly. He unlocked the door of the house with a latchkey: the room smelled unlived in, the books were covered with dust, some bread on the windowsill was stale. The porter came and brought a batch of letters and among these there was one about money from the old town which he had quite forgotten—he had an invitation to give a lecture there. His childhood came back to him and he began to think how in all these years he had not once remembered that town and that house and how he did not know who was living there or whether any of his relatives were still there or whether the house itself had survived. He sent off a telegram that same evening agreeing to come and in two days' time the train bore him toward the steppe, the Volga and the old house.

He was in an international carriage on the train, which went along the broken sleepers and the iced-over stations, a stranger. It was spacious, unhurried and solitary and in this solitude came thoughts about the frailty of life, its transitory nature, about children like the earth. His own childhood came back to him, the landing stage on the Volga beyond the embankment wall, where you overheard the stories told about Pugachev, which the days of the year 1917 had brought back to life. And then again he thought about the soil, children, years passing and the dust of summer days. Every few miles the view from the window became more steppelike and open; the train went to the places where cannibalism had been rife. When it reached the old town, urchins at the station were selling lilies of the valley, white acacia and lilac, as they had done in his youth.

The man, whose dates were either preserved or not on the doorpost of the old house in this town, did not go to this house that evening, but to the hotel, where he took a room, both because it was a long way to the old house and because he did not know who was living there. He took a walk on the little promenade and gazed out at the Volga and at the distant stretches of the Volga below the hill.

In the morning he walked over to the old house. He went by side streets where he had once run around as a boy and where the thunderous dray horses from the quay had ridden by. Now it was empty in these places, the grass grew between the stones, and behind the fences, beyond the half-ruined gates and railings, lilac and white acacia grew riotously. There were no people about, stone storehouses and granaries stood doorless, gaping and empty, covered with last year's white weed and wormwood. The Volga opened out in a wide expanse, free and tumultuous as every spring, just beyond the old cathedral (the one where, in the porch, one of Pugachev's guns was still lying). And the Volga, like the lanes by the old cathedral, was deserted and silent. Where the barges once stood and crowds had thronged together, there was nothing now, and the embankment had been washed away by the water. As the man began to walk down the drive, he heard the Volga echo with the croaking of frogs, which had never been heard just there before, and somewhere nearby, oblivious of the daytime and crazed with night, a nightingale sang. The driveway was broken and torn by the wind.

But the house seemed to stand as before, except that the side where the storehouses used to be had collapsed and spilled over into the Volga. And then it became clear that the ashes of the passing years had scattered over the house as well. There was not a single fence around; the yard that had once held great loads of timber, descending in steps to the Volga, now lay like a lichen-covered dog, gray, overlaid with weed and wormwood. The roof over the terrace had been ripped off, but calm was wafted from the terrace, the lilac and acacia underneath had become overgrown, had penetrated into the yard, filled the empty spaces, riotously and gaily as always in spring. The steps at the main door were broken and the front door itself hung in the air—the man entered by the back way.

There on the stairs, in the chill, he met an old man, a cobbler by trade with a boot in his hand.

"Who lives here?" he asked. But before the old man could reply, a tall and strong young girl with a pail in her hand came toward them and she at once brought to mind both the old portrait of Katerina Ivanovna and Nadya as well—the Nadya of those days of their youth. The newcomer felt his heart beating fast; he remembered Nadya and his childhood and could not understand who it was standing there.

"Hullo, we've been waiting a long time for you already," she said, and her voice was Nadya's voice and Grandmother's. "Where are your things? Give them to me, I'll take them."

"Nonna, has he come?" someone called from above.

There was no roof over the terrace any longer, the lilac grew riotously down below and the Volga flowed even more widely. In the principal rooms of the house lived the carpenter, Pankrat Ivanich, who had moved up from the basement, the cobbler, a girl telephonist, two stevedores and two women students. And in the far-off rooms, where no one used to live before or only Katerina Ivanovna's hangers-on, lived her daughter, the one who had left home for just two years to have her wings clipped through love, and with her lived her daughter, Nonna. When the spring came, Nonna moved out of these rooms and made herself a dwelling on the staircase under the terrace, where only the Volga was visible from the window, and a girl friend of hers lived with her after leaving her parents' home. Nonna had her work there and it looked oddly like a scene from the contemporary theater. A bed was fixed at the bend of the staircase like a bird's nest, the rest of the floor descended in the wide steps of the stairs like an amphitheater and so there was no need for chairs. On the walls, Nonna had hung old family portraits—Katerina Ivanovna in her youth looked as Nonna did in the third generation. Nonna's toilet table hung over the drop of the stairs. A volume of Plekhanov lay open beside a saucepan filled with millet porridge.

On the terrace door where they had marked their height, the marks were still preserved. This man of the third generation found his last mark, stood beneath it and experienced a painful sensation—he had grown shorter by nearly three inches. Nonna went off with the bucket, suddenly burst merrily into a factory song, quickly returnd and put the bucket down again.

"Are you measuring yourself?" she asked. "I do it every year as well." She stood by the door, straightened her back and it was clear she had grown over an inch again and so surpassed by three inches Katerina Ivanovna's last mark in 1862. She said:

"I'm the tallest in the family!"

Nonna's mother, Olga, came in and Nonna went off with the pail, singing her unfamiliar song. Olga sat at the terrace balustrade and he stood facing the Volga.

"Nonna sings well," he said.

"Yes, not bad; she studies at the conservatory and also at the VUS*—what outlandish words they use nowadays," Olga said in a dull voice.

"How did you live?"

"Oh, well, we had our share of cannibalism. What can one say about how we lived? . . . Nonna doesn't lose heart, she sings and studies, she's obstinate, takes after her Granny. But I can't understand it. Either it's youth, or the times, but she's a sort of communist, everything new attracts her, she keeps going to meetings, that's how she came to buy a ticket to hear your lecture. How did we live? It's better to forget. I keep quarreling with Nonna."

"Is there nothing of Granny's left?"

"Nothing—just junk."

"There were antiques, bead embroideries, china, utensils, books—is there nothing left?"

"Nothing—everything was swept away. Nonna collects things, ask her. I must complain to you about her: she doesn't treat me well, takes no notice of me; it's a good thing Mother

* VUS, Russian initials for Higher Educational Institution.—Trans.

died or she would have cursed her. She's a member of the Komsomol—what a word!"

Nonna came in with a samovar and said:

"I measured myself, but I didn't make a notch. I must mark the place."

He got up and began to wander around the rooms, where everything looked different and the same. The cobbler now lived in Katerina Ivanovna's room, where the shelf with the poisons had been. He went back to the terrace. Olga was asking Nonna:

"Have you been with that Pankrat again?"

Nonna said:

"You know Pankrat Ivanich lives with us now and Mother keeps going on at me because I see him and she can't forget that he used to live in our basement."

It began to feel depressing and dull, his own thoughts returned, he fell silent and began to drink his tea.

In the evening, Nonna came in the boat to fetch him and took him to the islands. They talked about trifling things; she told him about her work and her friends, about exams and student meetings. The Volga was wide and benevolent— Nonna did the rowing.

"Well, how do the students take things and what do they think? What songs do they sing?"

"They still sing the old songs about the beautiful things in life. The students are all right and we've all got to build everything up afresh, everything has broken down. I try to spend all my time at the University. At home everything is dead and dreary, wrecked, everything belongs to the past and they go on hissing away. I only go to see Pankrat Ivanich; the things he dreamed of all his life are coming about. But I shall go a different way. Do you know how we lived? The jobs I had to take? I had to buy and sell things, go up the Volga for flour, mutton, kerosene. I went on the steamers and worked in the communal association on boats. I worked on the tow-path, and chopped wood; for a month each year I lived in the forest and cut down wood for the winter. I worked as a stevedore unloading barges and wagons. I went to fetch contraband flour from beyond the Volga from the Germans —I went over there a girl and came back pregnant. I've dug trenches. Life was a stubborn struggle. This life taught me how to understand life. I'll manage to survive anywhere now! Here I am learning singing and studying law when I could command a ship! Mother is falling to pieces like the old house while I can swim three miles across the Volga. . . ."

"Yes, the house has fallen to pieces."

"Do you know what I nearly did? I wanted to rent the house last spring—I've got friends—and to redecorate it through the communal association, with our own hands, of course, to fling out all the riffraff of years like summer snow, so that the house would not collapse. . . . I'll take it over yet. I feel a strange tie between me and the house. I keep collecting everything that's left, old rags, useless books, oddments. I found a pair of pincers about a hundred years old for straightening out tallow candles and I treasure them, the remnants of a culture I haven't got any more. I shall take the house in hand, only there'll be no more trading on the wharf. I shall plant green trees and bushes in all the yards, so there won't be the smallest path left and no one can see what's what!"

Nonna scooped up some water in her hand and drank it.

"Why are you drinking river water?"

"It doesn't matter—one does sometimes," and she began to sing an unfamiliar song.

"What are you singing?"

"It's a robber song, supposed to have been composed in the time of Pugachev. I wrote an essay on Pugachev once, he was a good man, I like people like that. . . ."

"You look very much like your grandmother, only times have changed and she used to get quite annoyed about Pugachev."

They got back late. Nonna tied up the boat, they came around the wall, she straightened up, cleared her throat and suddenly it was again quite clear that this was Nadya, a long time ago, in this same place, when the day after Granny started talking about incest. . . . Nonna went on ahead out of habit, her step was firm, she was beautiful and strong. They did not go into the house but went to the hotel to fetch his things. Nonna would not hear of getting a porter and carried the case on her shoulder. Someone was lying snoring near the house. Nonna put the case down, went over and Granny's voice could be heard:

"Hey, you rascal! Drunk as a coot again. Up you get!"

Someone stirred in the gloom and Nonna reappeared, not alone but supporting the cobbler by his collar, the one who lived in her grandmother's bedroom. She picked the case up with her other hand and went on ahead again. The night was dark. Beyond the terrace, the Volga lay spread out in the gloom, silent, with just a faint splashing of water by the broken embankment wall.

And memories came back. . . .

Each spring when there was a reunion in Granny's house, the marks on the door grew higher, and below the terrace the lilac grew and the Volga was in tumult beyond the wall. Beyond the wall, on the open water, stood hundreds of barges, fishing boats, steamers and every kind of craft. Under the Clock Tower Wharf there was a market on the barges, and Katerina Ivanovna herself took her grandchildren there into all the wonder of wooden painted dolls, whistles, spoons, mugs, little horses ("a horse to decorate the roof is a silent sign that we have far to go"—Kluev).

The anchor chains were like fishy whiskers going from the barges, gangways stretched across the embankment—good for swings—and hundreds of people, bargemen, tramps, women, hauled bales of flour, onions, hemp on their backs—in the powerful smell of Caspian roach, Volga water and fresh air.

Under Granny's embankment stood willow barges full of timber and firewood. Bargemen and women porters moved these loads in barrows and pushed them in wheelbarrows, one after the other, in a line, taking the wood ashore and making batches of five, whole fantastic dominoes, where they used to hide in games of hide and seek at the risk of being covered over with wood. Under the embankment, the frogs croaked all together and men and women squealed, bathing in the dull water and then drying off after their dip, eating roach, giving it a knock first on a post or a stone. In the bars and little kiosks they sold ring-shaped rolls and, since beer is bitter, sour cabbage soup. Under the terrace, on the embankment there was a riot of lilac. And over this shining water, over the stones of the jetties, over the houses and huts, over the thousandfold crowd of this semi-Asiatic town—each morning there rose a burning golden sun which decked the heavens with the same glaze that covered the clay-and-willow cockerel whistles. Along with the sun below the embankment, a human roar arose, loaders shouted and porters and hawkers shouted louder still:

Mead, co-o-old mead!
Onions, onions, green onions!

Steamers hooted and heartrending, incomprehensible yells came over the megaphones from the barges. And at night, when the water grew quiet and the sky was first painted with a slow red sunset and later when it was decked in stars, on the other side of the wall among the timber on the ground, people rested and talked, talked about the robbery that had brought a heap of money to cheer Rykavishnikov and Bugrov, told stories, talked about Emelian Ivanich Pugachev (Pugachev's gun was still lying nearby up on the hill by the old cathedral), and sometimes it seemed that Pugachev had been around just recently, say last year, and had made himself known over there on Sokolov Hill, had called the keeper of the wharf:

"Do you recognize me, Ivan Sidorov, or not?"

"I have never had the opportunity of seeing you before. I didn't recognize you," said Ivan Sidorov.

Then Emelian Pugachev took a paper from his pocket.

"I am the murdered Czar, Peter III, and it is so written in this paper here."

Ivan Sidorov first fell on his knees, then kissed his hand and said:

"I recognize you, sire, it was my foolishness, I'm old and blind."

Emelian Ivanich said:

"Stand up, Ivan Sidorov. It does not become a working man to crouch at anyone's feet," and then:

"Now tell me, who in this place is against the working man?"

"A landowner there is, our lord and master, and he is against the working man. He lives in his house and drinks our blood."

"Bring the lord here," said Emelian Pugachev.

They brought this lord, who wept and had no wish to part with his life—his life was sweet. But Emelian Pugachev said to him:

"I'm loath to hang you, since the life in you is still a human life, but there is no help for it, as you are the landowner here, the lord and master."

Emelian Pugachev frowned, his glance like a falcon's, and shouted:

"Gentlemen, hang this wretch upon the blasted aspen tree!"

Sometimes the new moon rose at night and filled the Volga reaches with mist, chilling the free Volga water. The smell of white acacia crept down the hill, the dew penetrated to one's shoulder blades, and it was rather scaring to mount the cubes of timber, with the day's warmth caught up inside one, because it felt as if Emelian Pugachev would come in a minute, stand there and say—

Nonna came, sat on the balustrade and folded her arms. And then this man whose dates had first appeared on this terrace thirty years ago suddenly realized that the truth which brings relief had come to him. He understood that life is alive with life, with the earth, with the fact that each spring the earth brings forth blossoms, cannot but do so and will do so as long as life endures. He felt the sharp pain of the wish that here on this terrace—on precisely this terrace, in this forgotten town, in this forgotten house which still held ties of family and blood—his daughter, Katya, and his son, Anatoly, should stand by this doorpost to be measured, until they grew up; even if he himself were not there, let a new life go on. And then, for a moment, in this bold and happy renunciation, came pain, because everything passes, everything flows by.

Below the terrace, just as in Grandmother's day, the lilac was in tumult, making one's head ache with its strong scent, and blending with the scent of lilac, just perceptibly, came a smell of decay because they emptied slops and garbage over the terrace balustrade.

1924

The Unborn Story

This was a radio station at Spitsbergen, latitude 78° north, and it was December, night-bound for half a year. Snow lay all around, stones, ice, mountains and night, a night of many weeks, a gray night through which to sleep for weeks. There were three of them at the meteorological station. They had buried a fourth the day before, and eight months ago a fifth, a sixth and a seventh, who had died of scurvy. A boat had last called at this place a year and four months ago and it was this boat which had brought them there. It was only possible to bury someone in the earth when the snow melted in June. The man who had just died was put in a tarpaulin and covered over with ice, so that the dogs could not get at him and devour him. They had planned to remain for a year. In the summer, a boat called to pick them up and they had exchanged messages over the radio, but the boat could not make its way through the ice. Because their comrades had died and because those who remained alive had collected eggs and killed some seals, they did not go hungry. But they had no paper left and the whole point of their expedition, a record of the weather conditions, was disrupted. So that their days should not become completely meaningless, the head of the radio station telegraphed Green Harbor with summaries of the forecasts three times a day. It had been the 24th of December yesterday when they buried their friend—Christmas Eve. The remaining three met in the evening. There was the chief, a workman and a mechanic, and all three were Norwegians from Tromsö. They dressed up and the chief produced punch and whiskey. They were drunk by midnight when they received a greeting from the radio station at Spitsbergen and the chief replied:

"Go to hell!"

They had put their comrade in a mound of ice, they were drunk and they sat silent because everything had already been said. The chief set the radio to pick up Christiania; but all the stations in the world had gone crazy that night and from the places, thousands of miles away, where normally people lived, now nothing was to be heard: they got snatches of concerts, of speeches, of greetings, and in the middle of the Toreador song came a talk on "millions of working American men," until the chief again let the whole world hear his:

"Go to hell!"

On this meteorological station, cut off by ice and mountain for hundreds of miles from the nearest human habitation, they still had some siphons for making soda water and the three men were drinking whiskey and soda. They were drunk. The chief picked up a siphon and started running after the other two and soaking them in soda water, as if he were shooting at them with a gun. All three roared with laughter.

Then they all went to bed. And the chief, who was no longer young, a corpulent, slow-moving man, must have seen many drunken dreams in his sleep. He dreamed they were all back in Tromsö with their families and wives, in a restaurant, and the man who had just died was there with them. It was a tormenting dream and he kept on trying to see that the conversation did not touch on the death of the man who had died. As soon as they began to talk about the man, he would interrupt and change the subject, so as to avoid causing the dead man's wife any pain, and each time he would lean over the man's shoulder and whisper:

"Softly, softly. Your wife doesn't know that you are dead, Victoria doesn't know...."

The electrician (the one who had died last year) said, "Do you remember, Edward, how we went to hunt the bear, before

I died." But the chief interrupted him, splashed soda water, laughed to cover up and said, "Hey, electrician, yes, you died eight months ago but Edward was alive then and he never went hunting bears with corpses." And then he whispered to the dead man, "Softly, softly, Edward, Victoria doesn't know you are dead!" They were drinking Swedish punch in the restaurant in Tromsö.

The chief woke up in a fit of anxiety, drank some water and went over to the window. The window was covered in great thick mares' tails of frost, but you could still see the crescent moon, which shone for weeks on end, and on the other side were the columns of the northern lights. His head had never felt so clear and their whole appalling situation never seemed so clear, nor their courage—three of them dying in the snow. He glanced at himself and at his two comrades with the engineer's mathematical calculating eye which he had always retained since his college days, and he realized that both he and they were no longer quite normal, they were half mad, each had his breaking point, each was too worn out for healthy living and would first of all have to go from Spitsbergen to a psychiatric hospital. He went up to the receiving set and moved the knob over all the wave lengths. All world radios were already preoccupied with daily events and were passing on summaries from different agencies. He looked at his watch. In Europe and Norway it would already be light, in the Mediterranean it was day, morning. It was cold in the little house, below zero. He poured some seal oil into the fireplace, lighted it, and lay down again in his sleeping bag. Before he fell asleep, his thoughts again became confused in a drunken way. It was as if his head was a radio, which was receiving all wave lengths simultaneously. He felt giddy, his thoughts became sticky, melted, crawled about like worms, became muddled, floated into confusion . . . disappeared . . . and he fell asleep.

And in his dream he saw:

. . . a cypress by a stream with steppingstones to make it easy to fetch water. A hill rose up behind and the bare summits of the hills were in a lilac mist, girdled with forest and with the white remains of snow in their hollows. Beneath the hill was the blue sea—blue in the distance and green by the shore among the rocks. A stony path led to the stream, its stones wet with morning dew, and this path went down to the seashore. Beyond the trees—cypresses, flowering Judas trees, chestnuts—there was a mosque, and in this eastern morning hour a muezzin was calling out some incomprehensible words like the cries of a camel on the steppe. The sun, a splendid golden sun was shining over the whole world, the mist rose from the mountain hollows, and a girl came up to the stream with a pitcher on her shoulder to fetch water. And the girl smiled at the sun and at the sea and held the palm of her hand above her eyes to shield her from the sunlight, and her sunburned legs were bare. . . .

In the morning the workman came in, lighted the lamp, kindled the fire, warmed up the coffee. The chief woke up slowly and lay in his sleeping bag for a long time. He asked:

"What's the temperature, the atmospheric pressure, the wind force?"

"Forty-two degrees of frost, the pressure is—"

The mechanic had already set the dynamo. He called through the doorway:

"One fox got caught."

Then the chief began to get dressed quickly, drank some seltzer instead of coffee and went up to the apparatus. Who knows whether in delirium, when thoughts float like ice floes, crack, crawl over one another, the human brain is not a broken receiving set? And perhaps in as little as ten years or so people will not switch on radio sets but brains? The chief switched on the power pack, so that he could shout all the more loudly into space, and he shouted:

"Radio station Spitsbergen, Tromsö, Christiania. Temperature, forty-two degrees of heat, the oranges are in bloom, the almond blossom is over already. We are catching tigers. The sun is shining like hell for forty-eight hours a day. . . ."

Spitsbergen—Green Harbor began to ask:

"Has something terrible happened? Is anyone ill?"

At noon the radio station replied:

"The temperature is lower, thirty-eight degrees of heat. During the last day four men were born and a fifth is expected in the evening. The newborn are buried in the snow."

In the evening a telegraph message came from Green Harbor:

"A doctor is by the set. State the symptoms of the illness, how many of you are alive and well, what medication you have."

The chief replied to this radiotelegram:

"The workers of Russia, Italy, France and America have declared a world strike, everyone is alive and well, another one will be born in a minute, the medication will be left for the dead."

The chief switched off the set, went to his room, undressed, changed his underwear, got dressed in fresh clothes, lay down in his sleeping bag and shot himself.

It is true that the day was sunny in the morning, mists rose from the sea and the hollows in the hills, the mountains disappeared in golden azure, a muezzin gave his call and a girl came up to the stream with a pitcher on her shoulder, filled it with ice-cold water, carried it to a little flat-roofed house dug out of the lilac hillside, near a plane tree. The girl was probably not thinking about anything except that she must hurry with the water and then make some meat pies and take them to her fisherman father down on the shore. She was certainly not thinking about the Arctic or about the mad radio engineer, and it is quite likely that the girl got some bedbug bites in the hay where she slept at night. . . . And I, the author, was taking a cab that night from Dmitrovka to Povarskaya. The cabby was not much good and said nothing, having passed some remarks on the price of oats. To save a bit of mileage he began to crawl up Leontevsky and we crossed Tverskaya. I glanced at the sky, at the stars, and caught sight of the Pole star, which was very bright, although the moon was full, and my thoughts fixed on the Pole star and on the moon. I did not spend much time thinking about the Pole star or about all the events I have described above, but the moon held my attention until we reached Povarskaya. I wanted to search out a word for the moon which no one had used before. Round, green, full—no; dry, frosted, icy—no; indifferent, calm, callous, kind, foolish—no. Wait a moment; it shines on me here in Moscow, and it shines in Madrid, and in Paris, and in Spitsbergen; perhaps some friend of mine is looking at it in

Madrid, and in Paris, and in Spitsbergen; perhaps some friend of mine is looking at it in London and thinking of me. . . . The moon is like a ruble (if the moon is reflected in the sea, one can say "the ruble of the moon has been changed into silver coins by the water"—that's not bad); the moon is like a pot. . . . No, it's impossible to invent anything new, everything has already been said, whatever word you find, someone else has used it already. So I ended up not finding any word for the moon.

1925

The
Human Wind

Ten years of human life—when you look back over a decade it is as if it had all happened yesterday, everything is there down to the last detail, the wrinkles around the eyes, the smell of the room. But every decade a fifth of the human race, millions of people, go into the earth to rot and feed the worms. In this decade millions of people are born, grow, live, travel, reproduce themselves, riot at full tide in spring, multiply in summer, rest in the fine enameled days of Indian summer and are consumed in red winter sunsets. And every period of human life, each land, each town, each house and room has its characteristic smell, and so does each man, each family and race. At times, quite often in fact, decades cross and fuse, yet for each given man it is not the events that take place in towns and countries in any historical epoch, but the wrinkles around the eyes and the smell of a room that are more real and meaningful.

Certain characteristic winds blow over every land.

This man, Ivan Ivanovich Ivanov, remembered life in the shape of a town with wooden sidewalks, wooden fences along the streets, a gate into the yard, an oppressive lived-in smell along the passageway, low-ceilinged rooms overlooking the weeds in the yard. His life knew the breath of the wind which is saturated with human living. A sofa with many hollows stood in his room, and behind it cigarette butts had been collecting for a long, long time. The books on his table changed occasionally, but the tablecloth was never changed. There was a desk, and ash had discolored the green baize, changing it to yellow—it was impossible to blow the ash away. Weeds and nettles, henbane and burdock bloomed in the garden beyond the low window. His life had felt the breath of the wind which is saturated with human living, and this wind became trapped in his room.

In this room there always remained the memory of a foul autumn evening, permeated with the smell of humanity down to the choking in the throat—this was the evening on which he had thrown his wife out. Before this moment, there had been the wild grasses at dawn, the water meadows in spring, and nights when they said, "I love you, I love you, forever!" When daybreak came suddenly in the dawn-lit world there had been the sun, the world and the lake of her eyes in which the sun and the world might drown—she encompassed the world and the sun. They were happy as people are happy when a child was born to them, a new Ivan. In the evening the mother's eyes were beautiful with all the maternal beauty of the world. He went in to her in the evening while the child lay sleeping, the new Ivan, and he would kiss her pale hand. All this had been experienced. Then came that foul evening, an evening when a man feels lonely and terrified on earth because of the stifling oppression of human nature.

It was not evening but midnight. The autumn rain was pouring down outside and you could not see a step ahead. A candle was burning on the desk and dripping onto the baize cloth which was never changed. Her eyes were swollen and there were wrinkles around her eyes. He was standing by the desk and she was standing by the door.

She said:

"Ivan, can't you understand, it's not true, forgive me. It was just an infatuation. After all, we have known real happiness together, and we loved each other."

Ivan Ivanovich bent over the candle and reread, syllable by syllable, the note she had written on a scrap of paper, which he had already gone over dozens and dozens of times: "Nikolay, I know it's just an infatuation but I can't live

without you. My husband will be out today and the gate unlocked. Come about eleven when everyone is asleep. . . ."

Ivan Ivanovich put the hand holding the scrap of paper
into his pocket, turned away from the light and said slowly,
stressing each syllable:

"Forgiveness has nothing to do with it. The word isn't
appropriate. I'm not concerned with infatuations. And it's
not a question of infatuation at all. The plain fact is that you
lay naked in my bed with a naked man. Get out!"

"Ivan! We have a child, a son!"

Ivan Ivanovich was sarcastic:

"I don't have to let you beget bastards. Get out!"

Then the wrinkles around her eyes vanished and there
were only her eyes, full of hatred, scorn and humiliation. She
whispered distinctly and clearly:

"You're beneath contempt! I'm in love, in love, and I love
him and not you!"

Ivan Ivanovich made no reply, and for a moment he was
at a loss. She turned sharply and slammed the door as she
went. He did not follow her. It was quiet outside the room.
He stood there motionless. It was quiet inside the room. About
a quarter of an hour must have passed. Then he rushed to the
door. There was no one there, the child's bed was empty and
a candle was burning on the chair beside the bed. The door
was open. He rushed into the corridor and into its stifling
lived-in smell. The front door was open as well. He rushed
out into the yard and the rain. The gate was open. Then he
shouted helplessly, in a humiliated and pitiful way:

"Alenoushka . . ."

No one answered. The street was swallowed in gloom and
rain.

Then the next morning a peasant woman brought a note
—"Ivan Ivanovich, please would you"—and he was asked to
send just her things and the child's with this woman. He collected all her things, spent all day on the task, and the woman
helped him. Twice she went away to have tea and a meal, but
he never thought of eating and, when the woman left him,
spent the time composing an enormous letter. In the evening,
the woman took the things away in a handcart and tucked the
letter inside her bodice. Ivan Ivanovich helped her get the

cart into the street and told her to be sure not to forget to bring him a reply, as he shook her by the hand. The woman was embarrassed by the handshake and said thoughtfully as she pulled her hand away:

"What's it to me? If I'm told to, I'll bring a letter back. After all, my feet are my own." There was no reply either that day or the next, or the day after. But on that day he heard that she had left town by train, with all her things, presumably forever. And she really did leave forever. Ivan Ivanovich never saw her again. A year later he heard that she was living in Moscow somewhere and three years later he heard that she had given birth to another child, a boy called Nikolay. The boy's surname was his, Ivan Ivanovich Ivanov's—Nikolay Ivanov.

The cigarette ends behind the hollowed leather sofa collected more and more.

II

This woman, the mother of the two boys and Ivan Ivanovich's wife, understood love as do many women who want to follow a man's every step and know each thought he has—in reality preventing a man from living, from thinking and working—because they have lost all that is their own and principally their own self-respect. Such love affairs inevitably collapse because even the slavery of love is still slavery and there is no way to build on such love. There is a symbol for each man's life and each love. In the years after she left her husband, this woman's life was like a very bright-patterned red kerchief or a gypsy's shawl which someone had wound around his hand and then waved in the wind beside suburban houses, candles, empty dawns. This shawl came to smell of various tobaccos and perfumes but the smell of human living was caught up in it from the days of the past. Then this waving shawl fell to the ground in a very dirty Moscow suburb, in a stifling odor of human garbage. Her son Ivan lived in the country with her sister. Nikolay first lived with her and then she put him in an orphanage. Seven years after he was born. Nikolay first experienced the misery of epilepsy in an echoing corridor of the stone asylum. And then the mother realized that this father who had not even given his son a name was no good, since only such men dare to give birth to sick children. In fact, by that time she had long felt that she herself was no good because she too had dared to give birth to this child (the judgment of humanity cannot be and should not be as strict as a man's own sense of guilt). . . .

Then the mother died. She died with dignity because she was able to leave her children with love and respect for her—both Ivan, who lived far away and was well, and Nikolay, who lived nearby behind the asylum wall and suffered from epilepsy. She died of some sort of typhus but the full significance of her death lay in the fact that she had lived through everything she expected life to give her.

The children did not know each other. And it was only after some years that Nikolay received a letter from Ivan in the country. His brother wrote suggesting they might be friends and brothers to one another again. Nikolay wrote back. Ivan wrote about the river which flowed nearby, the hayloft in the yard, his school friends, about birds and the open fields. Nikolay wrote about the corridors, about the industrial school, about his daily life in the dormitory. After a good many letters Nikolay mentioned his illness. They often wrote about their mother and each told the other in minute detail whatever he could remember about her, for she remained a sacred symbol of motherhood for them. When Ivan turned fourteen his aunt told him about his father and Ivan wrote to Nikolay to say that their father was alive. This piece of news had a strange effect on Nikolay (or perhaps it had just the natural effect) and he began to wonder about his father. Nikolay buried his dreams about his father deep in his heart, cherished his memory and a tenderness toward him, for he was well versed in hiding his feelings in the asylum. Ivan wrote to his father and the father replied at great length and with affection. Ivan sent the letter on to Nikolay. Nikolay wrote to Ivan Ivanovich Ivanov and he did not reply. . . .

(Here it must be mentioned in parentheses that these last days of Ivan and Nikolay's life brought them into the midst of the great Russian revolution.)

III

Ten years in a man's life is not so very long, and yet ten years can be an immense length of time. More and more cigarette ends collected behind Ivan Ivanovich Ivanov's sofa with many hollows and, as before, the town with its wooden sidewalks lay out there, with wooden fences along the streets, a gate into the yard, an oppressive lived-in smell along the passage and weeds beyond the windows. What Ivan Ivanovich was or might have been is not important—a grammar-school teacher or a country statistician—for his life felt the breath of the wind which is saturated with human living. And there as the years passed on, in one of the decades, Ivan Ivanovich called his son Ivan's letter to mind. He had received the letter one morning and it began, "My dear Papa, how are you? . . ." Ivan Ivanovich felt ten years younger that day and remembered the sun, the wild grasses at dawn, the shallows in summer, and only recalled very faintly the moment on the terrible night when he walked from one open door to another, to the gate, and shouted into the gloom of the street: Alenoushka! That day he kept wanting to shout again, only loudly, and with a final conviction of forgiveness, and joyfully. Happily he wrote a long reply to his son. Another letter soon came about that time, from Nikolay, and it began in the same way as Ivan's: "My dear Papa, how are you? . . ." And then he wanted to shout again, his blood clamored for it, to shout in hatred, with the full force of that foul night, reeking of human nature: "Get out, get out! I don't want any bastards!"

It was twilight one autumn when the heavy rain makes the smell in the passage even more oppressive (the revolution had already begun) and the candles have to be lighted early. There was a noise at the gate and the sound of a stick tapping up the steps of the porch. The front door opened and someone asked quietly:

"Please, would you be kind enough to tell me if Ivan Ivanovich Ivanov lives here?"

"Yes, I live here," Ivan Ivanovich answered.

A man of medium height entered the room and the stick he carried had a rubber knob such as cripples have. He was round-shouldered. And his face in the half-light, with its fine mustaches like strings, seemed very pale and very tired. This is how Ivan Ivanovich was to remember the man afterward. This man took a step forward and then stopped on the threshold, hesistant and happy. He said:

"Are you Ivan Ivanovich?" Then he began to cry, stretched out his arms, and the stick fell to the floor.

"Papa, it's me, your son Nikolay."

Ivan Ivanovich was standing by the desk (the same one on which the cloth had faded) and he did not offer his hand but turned away from Nikolay. He felt the whole night of twenty years ago entering the room again. He said quietly:

"Sit down. What can I do for you?"

Nikolay made no reply and sat down on a chair by the door hurriedly and submissively.

"What can I do for you?" Ivan Ivanovich said more loudly.

Nikolay did not understand the question and before he could answer, Ivan Ivanovich shouted, screamed at him:

"What can I do for you?"

"I'm so sorry, I don't under—"

Ivan Ivanovich dragged an armchair from the desk and sat down opposite Nikolay, his arms propped against the arms of the chair. Ivan Ivanovich picked up the stick and handed it to Nikolay. Nikolay took it. Ivan Ivanovich looked intently at Nikolay and narrowed his eyes.

"Excuse me, I don't know your patronymic," Ivan Ivanovich whispered, narrowing his eyes still more. "I don't know your patronymic," he said more loudly. "Excuse me, we must have an explanation, to end this misunderstanding. I don't know who your—" Ivan Ivanovich interrupted himself and pulled a packet of cigarettes out of his pocket. "Do you smoke? No; well, forgive me, but I have not the honor of knowing who your father is."

Nikolay got up. Ivan Ivanovich got up too. The stick fell down again. Ivan Ivanovich quickly gave it to Nikolay. Ivan Ivanovich's eyes were screwed up.

"Yes, yes, forgive me. I have not the honor. It's nothing to do with me; I have not the honor of knowing with whom your mother slept to get you!"

Nikolay stopped listening. He walked out of the room. He

went quickly, limping on his right leg, holding the stick in his right hand, and his right shoulder was higher than the other as happens only with very sick people.

"Yes, yes, I have not the honor! I have not the honor!" Ivan Ivanovich shouted after him.

The brothers, Ivan and Nikolay, had arranged to meet in the town where their father lived. Nikolay arrived a few hours before Ivan. Ivan drove to the hotel from the station and was told that his brother was already there. They had never seen each other. A candle was burning in the room when Ivan entered. He was tall, healthy-looking, and he wore a regimental commander's uniform. A candle was burning, but he could not see anyone in the room. He asked the porter, "Where's my brother?" And the porter said that he had not been out. Then Ivan caught sight of a man on the floor behind the table. The man was clinging to the back of a chair. Ivan was encumbered with the straps of his sword and revolver but he was a strong man and lifted his brother up in his arms.

"Nikolay, what is it, my dear fellow," he asked anxiously. "Did you have a fit?"

Nikolay answered calmly:

"No, it's not a fit. I'm all right. I went"—the words came painfully—"I went to see Ivan Ivanovich Ivanov, your father. He told me that our mother was a—that he doesn't know who my father is, or, as he put it, with whom my mother slept to get me."

"What, our mother . . ."

The candle was burning on the table. The strong man put his arm around the weak man's shoulders. Beyond the window the streets were swallowed up in gloom. There were some cigarette ends on the table by the candle. The strong man sat down quickly on the floor beside the weak one. This was the brothers' first meeting. These two men had never seen one another but they knew all about one another from the first days of conscious childhood, and they talked about their mother, whom one of them had known. The man who lived in that town, whom they had come to see, who had had the temerity to attack their mother's memory, they referred to coldly: he was no good.

In country towns the wooden sidewalks serve not only to keep people out of the mud, but also as a grapevine for local news. And this man, Ivan Ivanovich Ivanov, whose life was saturated with the smell of human nature, was to experience yet another night like the one when all the doors were open, a night of infatuation like the infatuation which years ago had taken his wife away from him. The streets were swallowed in gloom, the earth wept with rain and Ivan Ivanovich stood by the gate waiting for his son, Ivan, who was just around the corner in a room at the Moscow Hotel. And the father shouted, "Ivanyshka!" into the darkness. Ivan did not come to see his father. In the morning, Ivan Ivanovich saw his son at the railway station, really for the first and last time. The father stood among a crowd of people. Two people passed: a lame man leaning on a rubber-tipped stick, who was being led by a tall and healthy officer, a fair-haired, suntanned, healthy, calm man, harnessed to the straps of his saber and revolver. The father saw that his eyes were extraordinarily like the eyes of his mother, like the lakes where once he had drowned the whole world and the sun. The train left quickly, with a whistle, a puff of smoke, the sound of the engine. The father went along the wooden sidewalks beside the wooden fences. There was a wind in the streets. A decrepit, gray-haired man walked along the wooden sidewalks, along the streets.

At home in the passage there was a smell of human living.

I V

The judgment of humanity cannot be and should not be as strict as a man's own sense of guilt.

1925

A
Story
Without a Name

Human biology has ordained that it is very difficult to kill a
man but it is even more difficult to undergo the experience
of death.

It was twilight in the aspen thicket and it was raining.
Very fine, gray, damp drops of rain fell down. The aspens had
grown yellow and there was a rustling from the Judas trees as
the damp leaves dropped to the ground. Inside the ravine
there was a broken bridge, moisture, and a road led out of it.
A potato field, half dug up, invaded one side. The road went
by the aspens, the ruts swelling with mud, and entered the
field, and there was a church steeple on the horizon. This
thicket—a triangular corner of Judas tree gallows—adjoined a
real forest. It was twilight, and the small rain fell. The clouds
seemed to brush against the tops of the aspens. It would be
impossible to walk along the bridge, along the road through
the thicket and the potato field, without sinking up to the
knees in mud. Then the twilight was filled with the cuttle-ink
blood of night, with shadows and gloom, and nothing could
be seen any longer. . . .

And after decades had elapsed, after many years with
their various roads of every kind, this thicket in a rainy twilight was always to leave an imprint on the mind, as it fell
into a gloom where nothing could be seen any longer—a state

where nothing could be seen was always to be remembered. In the evenings, after the daylight road and the rivers of the Moscow streets, it was necessary to take the elevator to the third floor of the House of Soviets, the one on the corner of Tverskaya and Mokhovaya. If the electric light was not on, the dark-blue atmosphere of the streets entered the room, and a red banner splashed the blue gloom above the Kremlin and the Central Executive Committee building. The standard itself could not be seen but only this crimson-red color in a black sky. And the thousandfold city bore the fragments of its roaring into the different parts of the House of Soviets.

II

All this happened twenty years ago.

There are three protagonists in this story. He, she and the third man, whom they killed and who stood between them.

The third man was an agent provocateur, who had sent people to the gallows for money, betrayed the revolution and dishonored it and its ideas. He and she volunteered to kill this man for whom there is no name but traitor. This was in the days of the defeat of the revolution in 1905, and the man's sentence had to be extreme. There was no need to preach to the converted, when their comrade sold men to the gallows, sent men to their death in battle and was responsible for years of human torture in prisons and deportation camps—there was nothing to discuss. She had never seen this agent provocateur. She went straight from the underground headquarters in the countryside where her father, who was a deacon, was living. It was June. He—his name was Andrey—arrived to see her; she was his sweetheart. The third man did not know anything about this, as he did not know Andrey's legal name. He was to arrive at a railway stop about three miles from the deacon's village and to contact Andrey in the little wood, first on the right away from the railroad, beyond a small gully.

It was June. How can one find the words to describe a first love? The love which is as white as lily of the valley and as heavy in its springtime as the dark brown of buckwheat, weighty enough to turn the world, a love that knows nothing except the clasp of hands and the eyes of the other, looking forward for all time, a love (both she and he knew this and proved it over twenty years) which is (and remains forever) unique. It was June, with the hay being mown and corn crakes calling in the twilight. Her auburn hair was blown by an auburn breeze and her white dress was lightly touched by the wind and the evening dew. The neckband of his embroidered shirt was wide open, and one could not imagine how his crumpled cap stayed on the back of his head. After the mowing was over for the day, the deacon foolishly lectured them on the benefits of family life, and with naïve slyness he praised his daughter's good qualities like a merchant praising his wares. They played merrily at being lovers in his presence. Then the deacon went to sleep in an outbuilding and they went into the fields. In the presence of the deacon, she had placed her hand gently on his shoulder, but here in the fields they walked at least three inches apart, in a love like March icicles underfoot and with no intimate talk.

They never once spoke of the fact that they had to kill a man. The day came when he told her at twilight that they must go that night. They went to bed when the hens settled down and an hour later met again behind the barns among the pine trees. His cap was on the back of his head as before and she appeared out of the shadows in her white dress shining blue in the darkness and with a white nunlike kerchief. She had a little bundle in her hand.

"What are you taking?"

"I've brought a little bread for the road."

Then he set his cap straight and said nothing. She glanced at him, her face inclining toward him. She straightened, slowly untied the kerchief and flung the bits of bread into the bushes, while he said nothing.

"Let's go," she said.

They walked along a forest path in silence. The honey of June filled the wood, far off an owl called, and the trees stood in a solid wall. They walked side by side. Sometimes he offered her his hand, to help her, and she took his hand trustingly. They had to hurry, because of the train, and they walked quickly. The thought that in an hour he would have to use the revolver in his pocket to kill a man never once entered his mind, because he had to kill a scoundrel who had ceased to be a man for him. He did not know what she was thinking, and never learned. She walked beside him, the only one, his love, and her head in the white kerchief was stubbornly bent low, as when she volunteered to kill the agent provocateur. They left the forest for the fields again. In the distance, they could see the light of the station and then they hurried. He went ahead and she followed him step by step. They reached the aspen thicket. The aspens rustled like Judas trees, the pinewood stood in a black wall beyond, there was a smell of potato flowers from the field, patches of starlight appeared in the ash-colored sky of a Russian June.

They stopped there. She was to remain in the thicket and he had to go on toward the pines. In the distance, they could hear the noise of the train as it left the station. They had about ten minutes to wait. He sat down on the grass beside an aspen. She sat down obediently by his side.

"You were right. It would be nice to have some bread now."

She did not reply.

"Is your revolver ready?" he asked.

In silence she stretched out her hand which held the revolver.

"If I don't succeed in killing him, you have to shoot. If I am seriously wounded, you are to shoot me."

She bowed her head in acquiescence and said nothing. They did not talk any more. He lighted a cigarette, smoked it down to a stub, spat firmly, settled his cap and got up. She got up too.

He gave her his hand. She squeezed it lightly, pulled it toward her and kissed him on the lips with the calm of a maiden, for the first and last time in their lives. He pulled at his cap again, turned sharply and disappeared among the dark aspens. When he had walked a good way, he glanced back. He saw her white dress as she ran down into the ravine, toward the bridge, toward the alder, and she was running with determination.

He walked on farther toward the pine trees. The corn crakes called in the field and the night continued in profound calm.

The third man, in a straw hat and a coat, came from the embankment into the mist of the gully, toward the pines. He approached the pine trees. Andrey met him there.

"It it you, Kondraty?" the man asked Andrey.

"Yes," answered Andrey, "let's go." They set off side by side. It seemed to Andrey that the man always managed to walk a step behind him, and when he put his hands in his pockets, he pressed close to him.

"What's the matter with you, Kondraty?" the third man asked.

Andrey made no reply. He stepped back a pace, snatched the revolver from his pocket and shot the agent provocateur point-blank in the chest. The other smiled and sat down on the ground, helplessly raising his arms. In his right hand he held a Browning. Andrey shot a second time into the smiling face. The man fell back like a sack of flour. Andrey left, walking fast. He walked on like this for about a hundred paces. Then he returned to the corpse, bent over him, touched him with his foot. The unnaturally bent leg straightened out and the dead man's face was smiling. Andrey gave him another push and began to search his pockets very carefully like someone afraid of a contagious disease. At this moment she walked up to the pine trees, looked attentively at the dead man and at Andrey and then went to the edge of the wood and stood with her back to the pines.

Andrey went up to her and she walked ahead in silence. They went on like that, she ahead and he behind. They walked all the miles back without taking a rest. Daybreak appeared over the earth, the east was suffused with a crimson dawn and the crescent moon which had risen toward daybreak shed fresh dew. The solemnity of the silence gave warning of the sunrise. They did not exchange a word the whole way and entered the house noiselessly.

III

They never afterward spoke to one another when they were alone. She woke him the next morning laughing gaily, the deacon went on talking his kindly nonsense over lunch and she was loving in her gestures like a future bride. Then the deacon went away, they were left alone and were silent. So three days passed, the time they had calculated they must wait in order to leave no trace, but in these three days not even a rumor reached their village. On the fourth day, the deacon drove them to the station, kissed them both warmly on the platform, made the sign of the cross, gave them his blessing, and then, in Moscow, they went their different ways still without a word to one another.

The country road, an autumnal thicket, a bridge over a gully, a potato field were imprinted on the mind forever. The aspens had grown yellow and there was a rustling from the Judas trees as the damp leaves dropped to the ground. Everything was swollen with autumn mud and the mud came to one's knees. . . . Then the twilight was filled with the cuttle-ink blood of night and everything was plunged in gloom and nothing could be seen any longer. . . . The memory of this autumnal thicket of aspens and Judas trees was not left from the night when he killed a man, because then it had been a honeyed June of hay-harvesting. The memory was left from a night when (according to the ancient law of nature which drives a murderer to return to the scene of his crime) he came in a dark autumnal half-light to spend a vigil at the place where he had murdered love. . . . An autumnal thicket, twilight, rain and then a gloom in which nothing could be seen. . . . In the evenings, after the daylight road and the rivers of the Moscow streets, it was necessary to take the elevator to the third floor of the House of Soviets. If the electric light was not on, the dark-blue atmosphere of the streets entered the room and a red banner splashed the blue gloom above the Kremlin and the Central Executive Committee building—the standard for whose sake an aspen thicket lay buried in the mind.

1926

A
Story
About How Stories
Come To Be Written

I met the writer Tagaki quite by chance in Tokyo. Someone introduced him to me at a gathering in one of those literary Japanese houses and then we never met again. We exchanged a few words which I have now forgotten. I only remember that he had a Russian wife. He was very smart in the Japanese fashion, with a calculated and studied simplicity. His kimono was absolutely simple and so were his pattens (those little wooden platforms the Japanese wear instead of shoes). He held a straw hat in his hands and his hands were beautiful. He spoke Russian. He was dark, short, slight and handsome, insofar as a Japanese can seem handsome to the European. I was told that he had become famous through a novel in which he described a European woman.

I would have forgotten all about him as one forgets other chance acquaintances, had it not been that . . .

In the archives of the consulate in the Japanese town K., I came across the papers of Sophia Vasilyevna Gnedikh-Tagaki, who was applying for repatriation. My compatriot, Comrade Dzhurba, a secretary at the consulate, took me up into the hills above the town of K., to Maiyu-Sun, where there was a temple of the fox. We drove by car, then took an elevator, and finally had to walk along footpaths and woodland paths and over rocks to the summit of the mountain, through cedar thickets, into the silence, where a Buddhist bell tolled in a melancholy way. The fox is the god of cunning and treachery; if the spirit of the fox enters a man, then that man's race is accursed. A monasterylike temple stood on a little platform, with a sheer drop down the cliff face on three sides, in the shade of cedars, with a sanctuary for the foxes among its altars. It was very quiet there and the widest of horizons opened on a chain of hill crests and the Great Ocean, which disappeared into nothingness in the infinitude of that horizon. Yet not far from the temple, higher still in the hills, we found a small inn, where we could drink cold ale. With some ale, to the sound of the cedars and above the ocean, two compatriots can have a very good talk. And it was there that Comrade Dzhurba told me the story which reminded me of the writer Tagaki, and which is the reason why I am writing this story.

It was on Maiyu-Sun that I began to think about how stories come to be written.

Yes, how do stories come to be written?

That evening I picked out the paper on which Sophia Vasilyevna Gnedikh-Tagaki had written her autobiography from the day she was born, because she had not understood correctly the requirement which demands that those seeking repatriation should give some autobiographical information. The biography of this woman—for me—begins from the moment when the boat docked at Port Tsuruga. It is a short and unusual biography, distinguishing her from thousands of provincial Russian women, whose biographies should be compiled statistically, since they are as identical as two peas: first love, injured innocence, happiness, a husband, a child for posterity and very little else. . . .

II

He and She come into my story. I once stayed in Vladivostok in the last week of August and I shall always remember Vladivostok as a town of golden days, wide-open spaces, with a stiff sea breeze, with a dark-blue ocean and a dark-blue sky and blue distances—and that dry emptiness which reminded me of Norway, since in both these places, the land breaks off into the ocean in bald, ridged stones, isolated, with solitary pines. Really, this is just an introduction, a nature description to fill out the personalities of the main characters. She— Sophia Vasilyevna Gnedikh—was born in Vladivostok and grew up there. I am trying to imagine it. . . .

She finished high school so that she might become a teacher until she could find someone to become engaged to—she was exactly like thousands of other young girls in old Russia. She knew just as much of Pushkin as was necessary for her course at school, and she probably got muddled over the meaning of the words "ethics" and "aesthetics," just as I once did when I was showing off in an essay on Pushkin in the sixth grade. Of course, she never realized that Pushkin begins just where the schoolbooks end, nor did it ever occur to her that people consider their own particular fragment of knowledge to be the standard by which all things are measured, so that anything both above and below seems either a little silly or downright silly, especially if the person in question is a little on the stupid side himself. She read the whole of Chekhov, because his works appeared in the supplements of the journal *Neva,* which her father read, and Chekhov knew that this young girl was, "God forgive us, a little silly." But as Pushkin has come to mind, this girl might have been (and I want her to have been) silly as poetry can be silly, and it is right for an eighteen-year-old to be silly. She had her own opinions on beauty (Japanese kimonos are very beautiful, particularly those which the Japanese never wear and only make for export), on propriety (she stopped greeting the ensign Ivantsov most properly after he had gossiped about their rendezvous), on knowledge (she knew that Pushkin and Chekhov, the great writers, are, first of all, unusual people and, secondly, that they are now as obsolete as mammoths, because nowadays nothing unusual happens, because a man may not be a prophet in his own land, or in his own time). . . . But if, by a literary convention, we fill out our characters with descriptions of nature so that they come alive on the page, then let this girl be a little silly, God forgive us, and in the name of poetry let her be clear and transparent as the sky, the sea and stones of the far eastern Russian coast.

Sophia Vasilyevna managed to write her autobiography in such a way that neither the consul nor I could extract anything extraordinary. The only thing that amazed us, and I was not very amazed, was that the woman should have managed to miss the experiences we had known during those years. As everyone knows, the Imperial Japanese Army was in the Russian Far East in 1920 in order to occupy this region and was driven out by the partisans; there is not a word about this in the biography.

He was a staff officer in the Imperial Japanese Army of occupation. He was lodging in the same house in Vladivostok where she had a room.

Here are some extracts from the autobiography:

> . . . he was always called the "macaco" . . . Everyone was very surprised because he took two baths a day, wore silk underwear and pajamas at night . . . Then people came to respect him . . . In the evenings he always sat at home and read Russian books aloud, poetry and stories by contemporary writers unfamiliar to me—Brusov and Bunin. He spoke Russian well, with only the one flaw—he pronounced an *l* as an *r*. This is what led to our becoming acquainted. I was standing by the door; he was reading poetry and then began to sing softly:
>
> "Night breathed . . ."

I could not restrain myself and burst out laughing. He opened the door before I could walk in and said in his strange accent:

"Excuse me, it is not polite to invite mademoiselle. Will you allow me to visit you?"

I was very embarrassed, did not understand him and with a brief apology entered my own room.

Next day he paid me a visit. He presented me with a very large box of chocolates and said:

"I beg you to allow me the honor of a visit. Please have a chocolate. What do you think of the weather?" still in his odd accent.

The Japanese officer proved to be a man with serious intentions and quite unlike the young ensign, who made ap-

pointments in dark corners and pestered her for kisses. He
invited her to the first row at the theater and afterward did not
entice her into a café. Sophia wrote her mama a letter about
this officer's serious intentions. She described in detail in her
autobiographical account how, one evening, when the officer
had been sitting with her, he suddenly grew quiet, his face
became livid, his eyes bloodshot, and he immediately left the
room. She realized he was overcome with passion and spent
a long time crying into her pillow, feeling how physically terrifying this racially strange Japanese man was for her. "But
later, it was just these outbursts of passion, which he was so
able to control, that began to stimulate my feminine curi-
osity." She fell in love with him. He proposed—in the style
of Turgenev—wearing a dress uniform and white gloves, one
morning in the holidays, in the presence of the owners of the
house. He offered his hand and his heart according to all the
European rules.

He told me that in a week's time he was leaving for
Japan because soon the Red partisans would be arriving
in town, and he asked me to follow him. By the regulations of the Japanese Army, officers were not allowed
to marry aliens and officers on the general staff were not
allowed to marry at all until a certain time. Therefore,
he asked me to keep our engagement a strict secret until
he could obtain his discharge from the Army and live
with his parents in the country in Japan. He left me
1,500 yen and a letter of recommendation so that I
might make the journey to his country. I gave my con-
sent. . . .

The Japanese were hated along the whole far eastern
Russian coast. The Japanese caught Bolsheviks and killed
them. They burned some in the boilers of battle cruisers,
others they shot to death and burned in the morgue, situated
on one of the hilltops. The partisans used all their guile to
annihilate the Japanese: Kolchak and Somenov died, the Reds
from Moscow poured down like mighty lava. Sophia Vasilyevna did not mention a word of all this.

III

And it is just at this point that Sophia's independent biography begins, from the day when she set foot on the Japanese archipelago, a biography confirming the laws of large figures—with statistical exceptions.

I have not been to Tsuruga but I know about the Japanese police. The Japanese themselves call their police dogs. They have a demoralizing effect because they are in a hurry, because they speak Russian quite incredibly, start their inquiries with full details of your maternal grandmother's name, explaining that "the Japanese police wish to know everything" and try pincerlike to extract "the object of your visit." The Japanese police rummage among your belongings according to their special search methods no less drastically than they delve into your heart and soul. Tsuruga is a provincial port without a single European house, only Japanese huts, a port reeking of cuttlefish, which are gutted, pressed (to process them) and dried right there in the harbor itself. Apart from the police, everything became even more confused in this provincial Japan because the gesture which in Vladivostok means "come here," in Tsuruga means "go away," while the faces of the inhabitants are expressionless according to the Japanese convention that one must conceal one's feelings and show nothing even in one's eyes.

Sophia Vasilyevna was apparently asked about "the object of her visit," but was allowed to forget the details of her maternal grandmother's name. She writes briefly about this: "They began to question me about the object of my visit. I was arrested. I spent all day in the police station. They kept asking me about my relations with Tagaki and about why he had given me a recommendation. Then I admitted that I was his bride, because they said that if I did not, they would send me back on the next ship. As soon as I confessed, they left me alone and brought me some rice and two chopsticks, which I did not then know how to manage."

That same evening her bridegroom, Tagaki-San, arrived in Tsuruga. She saw him through the window and he went to speak to the chief of police. He was questioned about the young girl. He took it like a man and admitted she was his bride. They offered him the chance of returning her to Russia. He refused. He was told he would be discharged from the Army and banished; this he already knew. Then both he and she were allowed to go. He kissed her hand in the style of Turgenev and did not reproach her. He settled her in a train, told her that his brother would meet her at Osaka and that he himself was "a little busy" just now. He was hidden by the dusk, and the train left for the dark hills; she was abandoned in the cruelest solitude, which emphasized the more that he, Tagaki, was the only one in the whole world, well-loved, loyal, to whom she was beholden for everything, without understanding anything. It was brightly lighted in the carriage, but everything outside was swallowed in gloom. Everything surrounding her was frightening and incomprehensible, as when the Japanese traveling with her, both the men and the women, began to get undressed before going to sleep, quite unashamed to go naked, or when they started selling hot tea in little bottles and supper in pinewood boxes, with rice, fish, radish, with a paper serviette, a toothpick and two chopsticks. Then the light in the carriage went out and the people fell asleep. She did not sleep all night, feeling lonely, bewildered and scared. She could not understand anything. At Osaka, she left the carriage last and immediately there was a man standing in front of her in a spotted brown kimono and wooden pattens; he offended her because he hissed something and after bowing, hands on knees, gave her a visiting card and did not shake hands. She did not know that this was the usual Japanese greeting. She had been ready to rush into her relative's arms, and he did not even shake hands. She stood there blushing at the insult. He did not speak a word of Russian. He touched her shoulder and pointed to the exit. They went off. They got into a car. The town deafened and blinded her, an enormous town beside which Vladivostok was like a village. Then went to a restaurant where they were given an English breakfast; she could not understand why she had to eat fruit before ham and eggs. Barely touching her shoulder, he showed her what she must do, saying not a word and rarely smiling. After breakfast, he took her to the toilet and did not leave her—she had no idea that in Japan toilets are the same for men and women. In embarrassment she made a gesture that he should leave—he did not understand and began to urinate.

They then got into another train and he bought her a *bento,* a lunchbox, coffee, and he pushed two chopsticks into her hands, and she used them for the first time in her life.

At twilight they left the train. Outside the station he sat her in a ricksha and her cheeks flushed from the intolerable sensation a European experiences when he rides on a ricksha for the first time—but she no longer had any will of her own. First by way of the crowded town, then along paths and cedar alleys, past little houses concealed by flowers and greenery, the ricksha carried them uphill, toward the sea that lay below great cliffs. Beneath a sheer drop, on a little platform overlooking the sea, near the harbor, amid green trees, there stood a small house, where they stopped. An old man and an old woman came out of this house and some children and a young woman, all in kimonos, and they all bowed from the waist and did not offer their hands. At first she was not allowed into the house. Her bridegroom's brother pointed to her shoes; she did not understand—and so he sat her down on a step, almost by force, and untied her shoes. On the threshold the women fell on their knees before her and requested her to enter. The whole house seemed like a toy. In the farthest room a wall was drawn back and a wide view opened out over the sea, the sky, the cliffs leaping toward the sea. On this side the house was close to a ravine. There were a great many little bowls on trays on the floor and a cushion lay before each tray. They all sat down on these cushions to have their supper.

In a day's time, Tagaki-San arrived. He entered the house in a kimono and she hardly recognized this man, who first bowed to his father and brother, then to his mother and only last of all to her. She was ready to run to him and embrace him. He held his hand back a moment thoughtfully, then gave it and kissed hers. He arrived in the morning. He announced that he had been in Tokyo, that he had been discharged from the Army and as a punishment, banished for two years to the country, but that he had been given permission to spend this time in his father's house; they would not be able to leave this house on the cliff for two years. She was happy. He brought her a great many kimonos from Tokyo. The same day they went to the police station to register the marriage. She went in a blue kimono with a Japanese hair-style and the obi, the sash, got in the way of her breathing and hurt her breast, while her sandal rubbed a blister between the toes on her foot. She became Tagaki-Okusun instead of Sophia Gnedikh. And the only way in which she could repay the husband she loved was not with gratitude but with real passion, at night, on the floor, in their night kimonos, when she gave herself to him and in the pauses between tenderness, pain and passion. The sea roared at high tide down below.

I V

In the autumn, everyone went away and left the newly wed couple together. He was sent crates of English, Russian and Japanese books from Tokyo. In her confession she said hardly anything about how she spent her time. One can imagine that in autumn the winds blew from the sea, the cliffs echoed and it was cold and lonely for the two of them as they sat by the fireside for whole hours, days and weeks. She had already learned the greeting *O-yasumi-nasai,* to say good-bye with *sayonara,* to reply to thanks with *go-itasima-site* and to ask people to wait while she fetched her husband: *Choto-mato-kudasai.* In her spare time she learned that rice, like bread, can be prepared in many different ways and that just as Europeans know little about cooking rice, so the Japanese know little about baking bread. From the books sent to her husband, she discovered that Pushkin begins just where the schoolbooks end and that Pushkin did not die like a mammoth, but is alive and will remain alive. And she discovered from the books and from her husband that the greatest thought and literature in the world is Russian. Their time passed in a strict rural discipline—a somewhat cold discipline. In the morning, her husband sat down on the floor beside the stove with his books, she boiled rice and made pasties, they drank tea, ate salted plums and rice without salt. Her husband had few needs and would have been content with rice alone for months on end, but she cooked a Russian dinner. In the morning, she went to town shopping and was very surprised that in Japan they do not sell whole chickens, but separate wings, legs, breasts and skin. At twilight, they would go out walking, either by the sea or into the hills to a little shrine there. She was already used to walking in wooden sandals and to bowing to the neighbors from the waist, hands on knees, in the Japanese fashion. In the evenings, they sat over their books. Many nights passed in passionate lovemaking. Her husband was a passionate man and excelled in lovemaking according to the culture of his ancestors, a culture alien to a European, as when on their first married day, his mother, without a word, made her a present of erotic pictures painted on silk, comprehensively representing sexual love. She loved, respected and feared her husband, respected him because he was omnipotent, courteous, taciturn and knew everything, loved and feared him for his passion, which burned her out, subdued her utterly, left her powerless, but not him. In the daytime, her husband was rather silent, preoccupied, and just a little strict in his courtesy. She really knew very little about him and nothing at all about his family—somewhere his father owned a silk-manufacturing factory.

Sometimes he had friends to visit him from Tokyo or Kyoto and then he would ask her to dress and receive the guests in the European fashion. They drank saki, the Japanese vodka, with their guests. Their eyes grew bloodshot with the second glass, they talked endlessly and then got tipsy, sang songs and left for town before daybreak.

They lived a very solitary life, the snowless winter gave way to the heat of summer, the sea tumbled below at high tide and in stormy weather, and then grew blue and quiet at low tide. One might say her days resembled a rosary made of jasper beads, but it was not really so. It is possible to count these beads, fingering them on the thread as European and Buddhist monks do, but she could not count her days, even if they were days of jasper.

This is how one could end the story of how stories come to be written.

A year went by and another year and another. His term of banishment came to an end, but they lived by the sea for another year. Then suddenly a great many people began to invade their quiet life. These people bowed profoundly before her and her husband; they photographed him with his books and with her beside him and asked her for her impressions of Japan. It felt to her as if all these people were descending on them like dried peas from a sack. She discovered that her husband had written a famous novel. People kept showing her magazines with photographs of herself and of him, taken in their house, near the house, on the walk to the little shrine, on the walk to the sea—she in a Japanese kimono or in European dress.

She could speak a little Japanese now. She played her part as the wife of a famous writer and did not notice an insidious change in herself as gradually she stopped being nervous of the alien people around her and learned that these people were ready to serve her and to treat her with respect. But she did not know her husband's famous novel or what it was about. She did ask her husband; he in his polite taciturn way offered her no reply. It was not very essential for her to know about the novel and she forgot to insist. Their jasperlike days vanished. A boy now boiled the rice and waited on them, and she drove to town by car, giving the chauffeur orders in Japanese. When the father came to visit them, he bowed to his son's wife with even greater respect than she offered him. Sophia Vasilyevna would have made a very good wife for the writer Tagaki. Heinrich Heine's wife once asked one of his friends: "They say Henri has written something new?"

But Sophia discovered the subject matter of her husband's novel. They were visited by the correspondent of a city newspaper who could speak Russian. He arrived when her husband was away. They went for a walk by the sea. And there by the sea in the course of trivial conversation, she asked him to what he attributed the success of her husband's novel and what he considered its most essential element.

V

And that is all. I bought a copy of her husband's book in the town of K. the day after I had found Sophia Vasilyevna Gnedikh-Tagaki's autobiography. My friend Takahasi gave me its theme in translation. I have the book with me now in

Moscow. I did not invent the fourth part of this story but simply reproduced what my friend Takahasi-San told me. The writer Tagaki made a note each day of his observations on his wife all through his years of banishment, observations on this Russian girl who did not know that the greatness of Russia begins when the high-school syllabus is over and that the greatness of Russian culture—of a subject that is caviare to the general—consists in the ability to reason things out. Japanese morality is not embarrassed by the naked body, or by natural, human bodily functions, or by the sexual act. Tagaki-San's novel was written with a clinical wealth of detail: he contemplated in the Russian manner, on the nature of his wife's thoughts, her body, the way she spent her time. That day on the seashore the newspaper correspondent, in his conversation with Tagaki-Okusun, the wife of the writer, set up for her not a mirror but the philosophy of mirrors and she saw herself coming to life on paper. It was not important that the novel described in clinical detail how she shuddered in passion and how there was a disturbance of her belly—the frightening part—the part that frightened her began after this. She came to realize that her whole life and every single detail in it was material for observation and that her husband was spying on her at every moment of her life; this is the point at which her fear began and became the cruel accompaniment of everything she did and experienced. And she made a request through the consulate to return home to Vladivostok. I have read and reread her autobiography with great care. It was written by one person, all at one time, spontaneously. Those parts of this rather silly woman's autobiography where, for no reason at all, she describes her childhood, her schooldays in Vladivostok and even the Japanese days, are naïvely written, like letters from one sixth-grade girl to another, in the style of a light novelette or set composition. But the last part, the part describing her life with her husband, for this the woman found authentic words of simplicity and clarity, just as she found the means to act simply and clearly. She gave up the rank of a famous writer's wife, love and the touching jasper days, and she returned to Vladivostok to live the humdrum life of a primary-school teacher.

And that is all.

She . . . lived out her autobiography and I wrote her biography.

He . . . wrote a splendid novel.

It is not for me to judge people, but to reflect about everything and, among other things, about how stories come to be written.

The fox is the god of cunning and treachery. If the spirit of the fox enters a man, then that man's race is accursed. The fox is the writer's god.

1926

The
Big Heart

CHAPTER ONE

To Europeans all Chinese have the same face. In their government concessions, Europeans check their lists with a dash when one Chinaman has earned about a hundred *dayans* and goes off home to Chefv after selling his job to his brother or a friend for two *dayans,* along with his passport. And so non-European eyes and non-European ears would be needed to catch this brief exchange by the factory fence:

"Are you a Mongol?"

"No, I'm Chinese. I want to be with Russia. How about you? Are you a Mongol?"

"Yes, I am. A Mongol *boy* from Shin-Barga is going on your train. We both come from Shin-Barga, from Kwot-ulang. Let me take your place."

". . . *Shang ho.*"

There was a Chinese town on this side of the fence, an anthill of a Chinese town. The street was thronged with people, rickshas, lanterns, pagodas, posters bearing sentences in ideograms written in bold, lacquered colors—red, blue, yellow, black. In the little shops along the street they were making parasols, gluing fans together and frying fish and onion in soybean oil. The men walked along in skirtlike black gowns with ideograms on the back, and the women in dark-blue quilted trousers with their little feet disfigured by pattens of beauty. In the temple, when they prayed, they tossed a coin into the box beside the god who looked like a devil, and beat a gong so that the devil-god might hear their prayers. The din of gongs, calls, whistles, squeals, howls and ricksha bells hung over the anthill street. The resinous smell from the temples intermingled with the smell of soybean oil. Wafted from the factory and along the street there came the creeping scent of consecrated incense, the odor of excrement of people and of pigs, the smell of garlic, ginger, sweetmeats. The lanterns and the red-painted shop signs near the brothel flew on the dusty wind. There was no sky over the street. The sky was covered with dragon banners, the signs and ideograms hanging across the street from house to house.

If to an Englishman the Chinese all have one face, a thousand Chinese eyes find the faces of Englishmen very distinctive, down to the last detail, to the pin in the tie and the filling in the tooth. The Englishmen sat in the rickshas, with traveling rugs over their legs. The faces of the Englishmen were even more impassive than the faces of Chinese Buddhas. The ricksha boys were stripped to the waist and ran at a rapid gallop. The crowd made way for the Englishmen's rickshas. The Englishmen were set down at the factory gates.

"There are thirty-two oil-pressing plants in this town," one Englishman said to the other. "It's seventeen kilometers to the main line from here. We'll make a branch line here. And we'll increase the general rate by one two-hundredth of a *dayan* on every thirty-six pounds. Add it up, Smith. How much will that bring the company?"

Mr. Smith answered from his ricksha.

"All right, Mr. Grey. I know that hundredths of a *dayan* can be converted into hundreds of *dayans* and it's always easy to turn *dayans* into pounds sterling."

On the other side of the fence there was the plant for pressing oil from soybeans and processing them. On the factory gates, beside a Chinese poster, there was a small English notice, blue on white enamel:—Ltd., etc. The factory yard was piled high with mountains of soybeans covered with matting. The Chinese were working naked in the wooden barracks in the main part of the factory, in a temperature of 40° above zero Reaumur (122° Fahrenheit, 50° Centigrade). The beans were steaming in vats. The Chinese lugged them in barrows on their backs, not on wheels. The steaming beans sent up a cloud of white steam. And the temperature of the steam according to Reaumur must have been higher than 40°. From the steam there came the stifling, overwhelming smell of beans. Naked men dragged the steamed beans along the ground in baskets made of rice straw. Two naked men poured the beans into the presses, the sinews of their naked bodies turning livid, exhausted human haunches quivering under the weight of the heavy baskets. When the man emptied the basket, he returned to fetch another and then the man who had taken the basket leaped into the press and danced on the beans—a wild and rapid dance—scalding his feet in the steam of the beans. One round cake of beans was piled on another, on and on, as high as the ceiling, as far as the crack in the ceiling that let in the light. And then the Chinese squeezed these round cakes in a screw press—like dray horses they pressed forward with their chests against the shafts in the capstan. They squeezed out the beans to produce oil, which ran down in greenish rivulets. The men toiled at the capstan, chests against the shafts, turning them—and their skins were marked with crawling purple sinews, while sweat poured off them, a greenish color in the tumultuous steam.

One of the Englishmen held his nose and stepped out of the pressing factory.

Old women or young girls, naked save for loin cloths, stood inside the drums in the milling department, where the beans were crushed into grits. They revolved along with the drums inside them sweeping up the waste and sorting the beans. The women who do this work, old women and young girls alike, change every three months, since people die after three months of such labor. The women are bought for this work from their fathers or their sons, on condition that wages are paid in advance to their fathers or their sons.

CHAPTER TWO

There was no snow, and the ground was stony. The sun carved warmth and color out of the sky, and it was difficult to know whether it was being done with an ax or a chisel. In the sun it was twenty degrees and in the shade there was twenty degrees of frost. The shadows were lilac as if the frost were lilac, and where the sun was driving down, its rays were not golden but blue and withered. It is beyond understanding how such a sun can warm, and one could invent theories to account for the peculiarity of color and line in Oriental art in terms of this blue sun and blue light. The air was so transparent that perspectives became confused. There was no snow and the ground was stony, yellow and withered. And the sky above was yellow and withered too. The mounds in the distance, on the left and on the right of the railway track—as if someone had spilled out hills of sand with great accuracy from slits in the sky—these mounds were yellow, tarnished, useless the dwellings of the *Hunhuzi*.

Ahead lay the blue summits of the great Hingan—China on this side and Mongolia over there. Farther on were the Urals and Russia, an enormous land of many peoples who have traveled on into justice. Farther still, there was Europe and England.

A very short train was standing at the platform—made up of three sleepers, a dining car, a flat car for automobiles—and its engine was headed for Mongolia. The blinds were down in the observation car and there was a red-carpeted gangway from the step to the platform. Observation cars exist so that people can sit there and admire the scenery as it falls away behind the train. An observation car is the last carriage in a train and at the back there is a sort of terrace where one can sit and watch everything flowing past. This observation car was covered in shiny blue paint and if you examined it attentively you would see that the paint concealed steel plates —the car was armored up to the windows so that if the *Hunhuzi* attacked, the people inside could take shelter on the floor. A detachment of Chinese soldiers in fur hats and quilted trousers was standing on the platform in front of the observation car.

It was noon. The sun was hacking at the earth. The night before, an incredible, cruel, red moon was ascendant, a moon, which the Chinese people's philosophy of life leads one to expect, and so also something mysterious that prevents one from understanding the passivity of the Republic of the Blue Sun—but now it was noon.

The Englishmen entered the observation car by way of the red carpet—tall, pale-faced men in beaver-lined coats and fur hats. The one in front, who was the tallest, said to the stationmaster, "The train will leave at exactly a quarter to one."

The stationmaster answered:

"As you wish, Mr. Grey."

A boy in white gloves and jacket bowed low to the Englishmen in the corridor—Englishmen are not able to distinguish the faces of people of the yellow race. The boy helped them off with their coats. The air was blue and reddish-brown in the salon of the observation car, which was decorated in blue plush and reddish-brown leather. The Englishmen sat down in armchairs. The boy poured out whiskey and sodas before luncheon.

"All right!" said Mr. Grey gaily. "We'll bring a branch line out here. The Japanese are building a line parallel to ours but in a more southerly direction. We shall carry out a minor project, Mr. Smith, and we will lay out branch lines to the north and south of our main line. We will double the rates on the northern branches, and as for the southern ones, well, we'll carry freight at less than cost price to please the Japanese, so that they need not go to the trouble of building railways!"

At precisely a quarter to one, the Chinese soldiers placed their rifles at the ready, a horn gave out a mournful orphaned call, and the train started off. Mr. Grey went out into the little terrace of the observation car and waved to the saluting soldiers. He surveyed the terrain with an indifferent glance— the soybeans in sacks of matting near the station warehouse, the station shanty, the ox yoked to a two-wheeler cart near the crossing, the Chinese standing beside the ox, the mounds in the distance, *fanzas* scattered over the plain and surrounded by earthen ramparts against the marauding *Hunhuzi*.

After that the order of the day proceeded for Mr. Grey as ordained by Englishmen since the creation of the British Empire. Luncheon was served as usual by boys who waited in white gloves and white dinner jackets. After that the day passed in the observation car.

It is not, in fact, true that all Englishmen's trousers are creased in rectilinear lines like the parting of their hair nor that the heels of their shoes are as hard as their cheekbones. One of the Englishmen, Mr. Smith, wore his hair brushed back like a Russian student and it was the same color as the student's hair, for it was tow-colored. He was wearing puttees and a gray traveling suit, both very crumpled. Mr. Grey sat facing the window, watching the sleepers run by. His gray suit, once brilliantly cut, still preserved the marks of a good tailor despite the creases, and it encased Mr. Grey's hardy frame, an excellent example of masculine physique, voluntarily acquired and just a little too nervous. There was also a small man in khaki, bespectacled, leaning back in his armchair, legs crossed, reading the newspaper with the air of a philosopher. Mr. Grey could only sit with a straight back, but this man found it hard not to lean against the back of his chair. He was a philosopher and a bookworm.

Mr. Smith stood behind Mr. Grey.

This was an armored train, and an armored train always creaks heavily over the rails, swaying slowly on its solid-steel casing. It was also an express train and rushed forward with all its might. The train was, in fact, traversing a desert or, at any rate, a colony. The founders of colonies were sitting in the observation car and it is quite unnecessary for such people to wear helmets and sport Mausers in their belts. These men traveled in Russian beaver-lined coats among the mounds in the frosty landscape.

The view from the windows of the observation car was poverty-stricken—desert, mounds like the breasts of Chinese women, nipples pointing at the sky. And there was the strangeness of the sun's heat and the frosted shade, so that it was necessary to open the carriage door from time to time and cool the air, which had been heated by the sun. The little fortresses of the *fanzas* showed up more and more rarely in the valleys.

The train was heading for the passes of the great Hingan. Beyond these lay Mongolia, the land of Timur, a land totally unknown to Englishmen, a land of khans, *hoshuns*, Huns, Beilés, Bargouts, Daurs, Haratsins, of frightful steppes and deserts. This was a land unknown to any man, a land of ancient riches and of ancient civilization, of the greatest conquerors and lawgivers—now a land of sand, scorched by the sun, with an unknown, undecipherable history.

"You are fond of philosophizing, Mr. Smith," said Mr. Grey. "My own philosophy is a simple one. I can only reflect on things that have been created by human hands. The bridge we have just crossed seems far more poetic to me than all the Chinese lanterns or the views of Hingan that you have set your heart on photographing."

Smith answered loudly, "But all the lanterns were made by human hands as well!"

"And all for nothing, believe me," answered Mr. Grey. "I keep feeling the inconvenience of all these natives talking in a damn-fool language, which no one can understand, and having their own set of customs. What I mean is that poetry is what is made by European hands, a bridge like the one we have just crossed. It's quite true that the simple philosophy of our philosopher"—Mr. Grey waved a hand in the direction of the man in khaki, reading his newspaper—"is very much to the point in its simplicity. We shall arrive at the Mongolian khan's—I believe that's what they call their princes—and he has his own army of three hundred horsemen, his own lamasery and his own little bank, where he prints money on a press stolen from Russia during the revolution. We'll arrive, dine with the khan in his palace, I'll make him a present of a watch, a cigar box and an English race horse. . . . His title is He Who Sits upon a Tiger Skin. I'll give him a couple of Bengal tiger skins. . . . In return I'll invite him to dinner here in the dining car and we shall never set eyes on one another again. I'll have no further use for him. But our philosopher will visit him once more and again partake of horse meat with his fingers. Then he will calmly propose to him and his courtiers that he should just generally organize their little bank and we may even become shareholders in it, perhaps. And that's all. The khan and his armies will have no place of retreat. We shall have a base, garrisoned by the horsemen of the khan, a descendant of Tamerlane and the Russian Tartars, and then the Russian communists can yell blue murder from Urga and Moscow to their heart's content. That's our philosopher's philosophy, since he understands straightforward bookkeeping and—what is it you call it in Parliament?—the theory of finance capital. I shall have the khan and his horsemen in my pocket."

The third man, the philosopher in khaki, rose clumsily from his easy chair, pushing his glasses onto his forehead, and it was plain how painstakingly this khaki had been crumpled during its span of existence by sitting around in every kind of chair. The philosopher just stood there awhile, hands in pockets, saying nothing, and then went off to the lavatory.

Mr. Smith flung away a match with an expansive gesture and blew smoke out of his pipe.

"Well," said Mr. Smith, "you have a point there, Mr. Grey. What we have here is the poetry of conflict, of cunning and organization. If you have decided to build a railway into Mongolia, you must lay the right foundation. But wouldn't you yourself become intoxicated with a storm at sea, or love for your wife, or even for some little Japanese girl? You'll take possession of this khan's—this feudal baron's—steppes and that will be that. But I want to see for myself how the centuries-old sands of Mongolia, how the Mongolian droves of horses run from the train in fear, I want to learn to eat as the Mongols do without feeling a spasm of nausea contract my throat. And I want to understand the music of Chinese drums. . . . When we thunder across the Hingan today, I shall have the train stopped at the very summit and go to look at the view, because it will be me, Richard Smith, an ordinary Englishman, standing there at the top of the Hingan Pass. . . . You were saying that a tunnel will have to be made for the new line. I shall come here then so that I can see for myself how human labor penetrates into the bowels of the earth. Tomorrow, or whenever it is we reach the steppe, I shall visit the Mongolian monasteries to have a look at the lamas, and tomorrow I shall also visit our anthracite mines to watch the Chinese at work."

Mr. Grey gave a sarcastic smile.

"If I'm not mistaken, I saw you hold your nose this morning in our oil-pressing factory?"

The philosopher in khaki came back from his visit to the lavatory.

"Don't you think, gentlemen, that you're talking just for

the sake of talking, when we have more practical work on hand? For example, it's time for a drink, and after a whiskey we've got to tackle the thoroughly boring task of calculating the freight rates for the northern and southern branch lines, and also to consider what sums we have to sacrifice on the presents for the khan and his nobles. My philosophizing only amounts to this—when it is a question of money, accounts must be kept, that's all. . . . Did either of you see about getting an interpreter? We'll need one when the time comes to talk with the Mongolians."

Mr. Grey got up and straightened his square-shaped feet. Englishmen have flat feet and his tan, thick-soled boots were turned up at the toes.

A strange sun shone out there beyond the windows, a sun unlikely to be bighearted or kindhearted. A really beggarly earth lay out there beyond the windows, wretchedly barren, without a single bush, strewn with sand, covered with de-hydrated dunes. The great Hingan alone rose ahead, a chain of blue mountains dividing desert from desert. There were people living among the dunes on both sides of the Hingan, scattered and separated from one another by ten kilometers, living in the wilderness, in penury, in the harshest labor. The sun was traveling across the yellow sky in the same direction as the train, racing the train. It was depressing because it looked as if the same landscape was running beside the steely scream of the armored train. Mr. Grey and the bookkeeper were sitting at the table going over the accounts, the figures, with enormous red Parker fountain pens in their hands. Charts and maps were spread out. Mr. Smith, in a melancholy mood, took out a miniature music box from his waistcoat pocket—the kind that can play only one tune, in this case, "It's a Long Way to Tipperary." Mr. Smith wound it up, held it to his ear, listened, taking a melancholy delight in the music. When the spring ran down, he wound it up again. The sun passed the train on its eternal journey and vanished beyond the Hingan.

That was how the day passed in the observation car.

The dining car separated the observation car from the other three carriages. In those carriages, apart from the people, there had also settled down a stern sense of authority, circumspection, a serious air, and briefcases, adding machines, rugs, maps, blueprints. This was the office in transit of the directors of communication and transport. The train was traveling along with a committee for a revision of the route and messengers, looking like withered bamboo leaves, and wearing the shortest of little white jackets, stood at the doors, awaiting instructions. On hard chairs, at tables covered with green felt, sat these directors in all their authority, surrounded by pencils, adding machines and blue cigar smoke. It was here that reports were prepared and problems worked out, and the most complicated bookkeeping and mathematics went on about tariffs and freight miles. These people, responsible for the plans, the air of reliability and the cigar smoke, absorbed in their plans, their reliability and their cigar smoke, were all dressed very respectably in formal blue suits. The order had already been given—each head of a department was to go to see the chiefs in the observation car after five-o'clock tea. What really mattered was how to adjust one's jacket and make some apt remark when with the chiefs. For these three carriages, the penetrating sun, the beggarly mounds and the Chinese were neither here nor there. They had few needs, but one of the most important was to transfer their air of security to the observation car. The reliable speed of the fast-moving train was due to them, to the reliability of their bookkeeping and their calculations of freight-mile hours.

The dining car was situated between these carriages and the observation car. The sun had raced the train and was dipping toward Hingan. Soon it would vanish behind Hingan and leave the landscape to the incredible cruelty of the moon, the moon which determines the nocturnal philosophy of the Chinese people, according to European conceptions. Dinner would be served at seven and then everyone from both the observation car and the other three carriages would meet in the dining car. Meanwhile this car was in semidarkness. In this half-light the boys were arranging plates, spoons, forks, wineglasses and goblets, and the napkins, made up to resemble rosettes, loomed over the plates. The stove was red-hot in the kitchen. Beef, turkey, fish was set out on the zinc-topped table. It was very hot in the kitchen. A Chinese chef in a white cap was burning to a crisp by the stove, with a helper working beside him. There was no philosophy there and no air of solidity. People were chopping up meat so that it could be particularly well cooked for some other people who were to assemble with all the confidence of those who know how to wield a knife and a fork. Beyond the window the moon rose. The senior chef gazed out into the darkness, holding a hand covered with fragments of meat above his eyes, and he said:

"We're just passing Hu-Kei-Shan. I spent my boyhood here. I know every hillock, every burrow of this tarabagan—" But he could not finish what he was saying because he was interrupted by the sizzling oil and it was his job to supervise the oil, the meat, the sauces.

"Ada-Bekir," the senior chef said quietly, inaudibly into the sizzling oil, "if the Mongolians snatch Shin-Barga and Hichun-Barga from the Chinese, if you take Ha-Ha-Golen, Han-Chandamaniulang, Tsun-Utsushima-Chin, the lands of Hu-Kei-Shan will follow you. . . ."

The junior chef was pounding the meat with the butt of a knife to make it more tender, and he was silent, head bent. The senior chef knew how to distinguish the faces of the East and he knew why the lips of his helper were so tightly drawn and his eyes so narrowed: to him and the other Chinese, the Mongol Ada-Bekir was a hero, while to the Englishmen he was just another boy. Both the chefs were decked out in white caps. The junior chef gazed slowly out of the window and perhaps in answer to his own thoughts, he said:

"You Chinese have a parable about how a man began to build himself a *fanza*. He had a great many friends who all gave him their advice about how to build his house and he paid heed to all and did as they suggested, but he never finished building his house. That's what happens even when a man takes only the advice of friends."

Then a boy, a waiter in the observation car, came in and he said:

"Ada-Bekir, I have news for you."

"What is it?" asked Ada-Bekir.

"The eldest Englishman, Grey, told me that I am to be their interpreter when they go for their talks with our khan.

You'll see that I shall have to remain behind in the steppe after that, or the Englishmen will destroy me."

"That's all right, then. You can conduct the Englishmen to the khan and then disappear. Are the Englishmen still sitting over their charts and maps?" asked Ada-Bekir. "The train is to stop at the pass because the Englishmen want to take a walk up there. They are waiting for me there. I shall leave the train and take our secret paths to the steppe. By night I can cover a good fifty miles on horseback across the steppe and I shall be able to reach Daura before the Englishmen get there to see the khan. We shall not give the Barga away to the Englishmen. You will leave the train and remain in Daura."

For the Englishmen the order of the evening proceeded as ordained by Englishmen since the creation of the British Empire. No open spaces could be seen through the window. They could not see that the train had begun to crawl by way of valleys, precipices, bridges up to the passes, to the eternal snow, the cold, deserts of cold, frozen over by the moon.

However, at the open summit of the pass, the train stopped as the Englishmen had ordered. It was really time for the Englishmen to go to bed but all the same they left their carriages to walk in the snow. To the left and to the right of the track, in the blue snow under the moon, the wooded summits of the hills vanished into obscurity. But behind them and ahead China and Mongolia loomed in their immense expanses. The moon cast its light in forty degrees of frost and the snow formed a hard crust, hard as stone underfoot. Mr. Smith walked on ahead across the snow and said aloud:

"The savage is still in me, the ancient Saxon that once burned, pillaged, raped, fought and conquered with his fist. Before us lies a land of the cruelest warriors and the cruelest blood. We are going out to conquer this land. I know nothing about this land—but why today do such countries no longer exist anywhere, countries where one could force men to go on all fours with a club, force women to submit to love with a club, force them to strip with a club! I know I should be the last ever to let this happen and yet sometimes this stirs the blood. What open spaces, what a moon, what far horizons! Why, we are standing on the summit of such ancient mountains that men once crawled here when Britannia was not yet

in her mother's womb. And now I, an Englishman, am standing here and I feel a yearning to become a savage!"

Mr. Smith's words were very convincing but the silent bite
of the frost was more convincing still. The Englishmen shrank
into themselves in the frost and their heels crunched over the
snow. Very soon they abandoned the grandeurs of nature and
went back into their compartment. The conductor ran from
carriage to carriage, waving his lamp, and the train began to
move slowly, to gain momentum. The rails were abandoned
to the silence of the night and the moon shone on the snow.
Then a man rose up from the snow close to the sleepers. He
looked about him and then gave a piercing whistle through
two fingers, as they do in the steppe. From the left, out of the
dark ruffled pines, came an answering, reassuring whistle.
Horsemen rode out from the shelter of the dark pines. They
led spare horses by the halter. On one of these saddles a man's
clothing was piled. The man who had left the train put on
fleece-lined trousers, high felt boots, a goatskin robe, a conical
hat and became a Mongol, indistinguishable from the men
who had ridden up to meet him. The thick-maned, squat
horses were cold and tossed their manes restlessly from time
to time. These men sped along the edges of the precipices,
taking mountain paths known to them alone.

CHAPTER THREE

A horseman was standing by the railroad crossing. His
horse was shaggy, squat, and had a large head; the horse gazed
terrified at the train standing in the station. A Mongol sat
on this horse, in the way of all Mongols, hunched over, legs
drawn up high, not beautifully, yet at the same time looking
absolutely one with the horse. The Mongol gazed at the train
with indifference and could remain gazing in this way for
hours, motionless, unblinking. Some people left the train and
made for the automobile standing in front of the station;
the Mongol blinked rapidly. These people seated themselves
in the car and then the Mongol's horse, flinging its legs higher
than its lowered head, raced impetuously through the tiny
Chinese hamlet in front of the station and through the
Mongol hamlet and out into the steppe.

On the train, the Englishmen in the observation car had examined their Brownings carefully and then put them in the pockets of their fur coats. They were already in their fur coats and hats. The third man's fur coat was wide open, the khaki protruding; his spectacles looked angry and he was talking to the fourth man. This fourth man stood at the door, hat in hand, dressed in a railway clerk's uniform, and he had a Russian face. This Russian's face was flushed and worried.

"Hell and damnation!" the bookkeeper-philosopher exclaimed. "You're an engineer and we entrusted you with the district, and it calls for the utmost responsibility. And here you are telling me that your agent has run off and that you have no good trustworthy interpreter of your own. We have no idea how well our boy can speak Mongolian."

The engineer answered in a low voice:

"It's almost impossible to work here. The Mongols wreck all our work. I've been preparing this agent for several months and he was absolutely loyal. I was talking to him only yesterday evening. At night he disappeared. I've no idea where he's got to and no one has seen him."

He was interrupted by the bookkeeper-philosopher:

"But how did the Mongols find out we were coming? Were there any telegrams? Did this fellow know about our coming?"

"I've already shown you the telegrams. As I reported, one was for Ada-Bekir, a young Mongol who is suspected of harboring revolutionary ideas and who has been to Urga and Russia—but we can't make anything of that telegram."

"All right, go and see about the cars. We're leaving in two minutes."

When this railway chief had left the observation car, the bookkeeper-philosopher said thoughtfully:

"Some sort of nonsense. It's impossible to make head or tail of it. Gentlemen, apparently last night a young chef who is suspected of being a Mongol escaped from the train. But we're going just the same! Boy!" the bookkeeper-philosopher shouted. "See that you are warmly dressed; you're to come with us and interpret for us with the khan."

The sun hacked at the earth. It was hot in the sun and frosty in the shade, and the shadows were lilac, as if the frost were lilac too. Beyond the railroad crossing lay the boundless steppe, shadowless, scorched by sun and frost. The Englishmen, the railway chief and the interpreter took the first car. The Chinese guards had the second. The cars gave a roar, turned and, propelled by a force incomprehensible to the Mongol, approached the crossing where the horseman had been waiting. In both the Chinese and the Mongol hamlets, dogs and little children scattered wildly, screaming and shouting. In the Mongol hamlet the horses climbed the walls, sheep and oxen ran in front of the cars and could not turn aside at their hooting. And only a caravan of camels, beyond the walls enclosing the village, remained unperturbed by the cars, continuing their slow walk into the long trail across the desert, the bells about their serpentine necks tinkling slowly. The cars traced their course over the earth with authoritative impetuosity.

There were narrow lanes in both the hamlets. In the Chinese hamlet, bright lacquer, bright colors, the sound of gongs and voices, a crowd of people, and in the Mongolian, the invariable color of the desert, burned out by the silent sun. All was dusty and impregnated with the smell of an Asiatic town—sour and rotten. Beyond the encompassing wall the steppe at once spread out—there lay the boundless expanse of the steppe, desert wastes that appeared to be untrodden by man's foot, untouched, primeval, the great plateau of the steppe, undulating slightly with its hillocks, creased by a few ravines, the plateau of the steppe burned to ashes by the sun and like the faces of the Mongol people—wide and boundless as far as the eye could reach.

"If the English gentlemen would like, we could go by way of a Mongolian monastery, where the English gentlemen could see some Mongolian lamas," the boy-interpreter told them.

The Englishmen decided to call there on the return journey.

Mr. Smith was holding forth:

"You know, the Mongols dedicate every firstborn son to be a lama. The lamas loaf about in their monasteries, doing nothing and subsisting on charity. The lamas are believed to be half-sacred and according to the Mongolian code of morals, all their women are sent to the lamas for sacred copulation.

It wouldn't be so bad at all to spend two or three months as a lama."

In the distance they could see on a hillock a red-painted block of wood surrounded by a pack of dogs.

"What's that?" asked Mr. Smith.

The interpreter answered unwillingly and said it was a Mongolian cemetery.

"Oh, I've read about that!" cried Mr. Smith. "The Mongolians throw their corpses out into the steppe and the dogs eat them up. These dogs are sacred. Let's go and have a look."

The cars made for the wooden blocks and the dogs made way unwillingly. Nearby, there lay a human corpse, for some reason without its head, unclothed, torn by the dogs. Mr. Smith asked Mr. Grey to immortalize him beside this corpse in a photograph.

And again with resolute impetuosity the cars raced across the steppe. It was cold, the cars were bound for Daura, for Kwot-ulang, the capital of the *hoshun* of Shin-Barga. The sun was hacking at the earth, flinging the horizons wide, but it was cold in the car, since to the Englishman the Mongolian sun has a small and cruel heart. They had to huddle down into their furs and be silent awhile; they were able to contemplate in silence the thousands of kilometers that stretched in all directions and the thousands of years that these deserts had been traversed by Mongols, Adjiks, Tartars, Huns, in golden and bloody epochs, enticing even Alexander of Macedon into these wastes, once the most powerful on earth and now annihilated by the cruel desert sun. At one point they caught a glimpse far off in the steppe of a horseman on high ground, who at once vanished into a ravine where a column of gray smoke rose in the air. And then far ahead, hardly discernible, another column of smoke rose up. And who knows, maybe in this steppe without telegraph poles, these columns of smoke might have been the telegrams of centuries?

After some hours the cars reached the dead silence of a *hoshun*'s domain in the steppe. They entered as the plague might enter, because life seemed dead in this place with its crowded clay lanes, gray as the steppe, without a man, a horse, a sound, and only silent unseeing merchants, their legs tucked under them, sitting motionless at the doors of their shops. The earth of the streets, beaten down by the innumerable hoofs of horse and oxen, and by innumerable feet, forged iron-hard by frost, echoed beneath the passing cars, but neither the streets nor the clay houses saw the cars or wished to see them.

The cars drove toward the fortress where the Hun lived. A rampart of heavy gray stone surrounded the fortress. Moats in which the water was frozen entrenched the fortress. The cars approached a drawbridge which was down at the gates over the moat. The Englishmen's Chinese guards held their rifles at the ready. The iron-girt gates were silent and tight shut. The interpreter and the railway chief got out first and went up to the gates with half a dozen visiting cards. The Englishmen dismounted.

And the Englishmen saw, on a post, to the right of the fortress drawbridge, a stake, and a head impaled on this stake. The head must have been chopped off only that day or the night before, for the blood had not darkened yet, nor coagulated. The face was terrible, with a gaping mouth—the face of a man tortured to death.

The fortress gates were now open. The Englishmen looked distraught and Mr. Smith forgot about his photographic apparatus.

"Mr. Grey, Mr. Grey," the railway chief began to whisper distractedly, "there's something I must tell you—"

"Let us go in, gentlemen," said Mr. Grey with excessive calm, "and you can make your report to me later!"

The third Englishman, the philosopher-bookkeeper, went on ahead of Mr. Grey. The Englishmen crossed the bridge and went through the gates, through the first inner court and through the second.

"Mr. Grey," the railway chief whispered again.

"You will make your report to me later, sir," Mr. Grey shouted in a whisper.

They went through the second court and a third gateway. It was difficult for the Englishmen to see what was going on around them. Mechanically, and not by chance, their hands were in their pockets where their revolvers lay. In that moment, and not by chance, their faces resembled the masks once worn in miracle plays, fixed and muzzled through English self-control. They proceeded on their way, surrounded by a

crowd of Mongols, and the national odor of the Mongols, a
sour odor, had already enveloped them. The Englishmen
proceeded in their masks. The Hun's private mansion stood
beyond the third gateway. The leopard skins on which he
sat were spread out inside. The Englishmen, having seen the
eyes of the impaled head, could see nothing else. They could
not see that the mansion where the Hun held his court was
like many a Russian house such as might have been owned by
a fairly well-to-do merchant. It had an iron roof, a small
raised porch and a little balcony with panes of colored glass
in the windows. They could not see that the tiny yard was
swept clean and sprinkled with sand, nor that the house had
a sun-trap on raised ground like peasant cottages. The steps
of the porch were carpeted. The Hun stood on a carpet embroidered with gold thread, he wore a mandarin's cap, his
mustaches drooped in fine long gray strings, and he was
dressed in a skirtlike gown of celestial blue. He was surrounded by a crowd of courtiers, military commanders, coun-
selors, ministers, barons, counts, *beilehs* and *beises*. Mr. Grey
wanted to observe the Hun's face: it was dry and burned out
like the stones of the desert and as expressionless. The Hun,
without any change of expression, without looking at his
guests, on account of either his great age or his rank, bowed
with his sand-colored eyes alone, which looked down and
then closed. The Englishmen bowed to the Hun from the
waist. The crowd of courtiers returned this bow from the
waist. The Hun held out his hand to Mr. Grey (how did
the Hun know that Mr. Grey was the senior among the
Englishmen?), held out his hand so that Mr. Grey might shake
it reverently; the hand had no strength in it. It was difficult for
the Englishmen to see clearly and they did not see that the
man who had been their cook's assistant the day before was
now standing beside the Hun among his retinue. He was
dressed in a lilac-colored caftan and a curved saber was thrust
through his belt. He stepped forward, bowed and spoke to the
Englishmen's interpreter, who had up to now been their
waiter:

"Tell the English dogs," said this sweet-voiced Mongol as
he bent double, bowing low, "tell them that the lord of Shin-

Barga, who sits upon a leopard skin, invites them to his private chambers to the ceremony of the samovar."

The Englishmen did not understand what their dragoman was saying. The railway chief looked at Mr. Grey imploringly and then followed him with the crowd into the house, where the leopard skins were spread out. . . .

It might have been possible to walk around the fortress and take a look at the frozen past. The Englishmen could not look—the eyes of the impaled head stood in the way. It is possible to muse over these vestiges or rudiments of government, of feudalism, which reflect in epitome each and every aspect of each and every government. The Englishmen passed the first gates and noticed there only the impaled human head which had been chopped off and hung there through the judgment and decree of the Hun. The Hun lived behind the walls of his fortress and it was of no account that the walls would collapse under the first shot of a field cannon; he lived guarded by his army, his race horses in the paddock; he had kennels and kept falcons, with which he loved to ride to the hunt. In the inner yard there were subterranean dungeons where men were tortured by the judgment and decree of the Hun, and, as it happened, there too was the printing press which had been stolen from Russia during the revolution, the press on which the moneys and decrees of the Hun were printed. In the third court were the Hun's private chambers, his harem, his wives, his children, while in the first and in the second court, and within the fortress walls, were the living quarters of his horsemen. Inside the first gates in the first courtyard, with the barracks on the left, there was a clay-daubed building which looked like a worker's hostel and there the Hun's government offices were installed, his judicial, tax and financial institutions. Bulky folios were stored there, written in the Chinese fashion with a brush, folios containing the history of Shin-Barga and the Hun, traditions, documents of war and treaties of peace with the neighboring tribes, lists of tributaries, charters of lineages and the nobility, records of what was due to the Hun and from whom and from what *ulang,* for his judgments, his troops, his administration, what was due to him in money, in horses, oxen and forced labor—

one could see any government reflected there in epitome.
But it was not possible for the Englishmen, wearing muzzles
of nerves, to think. . . .

In the Hun's reception room, with its many leopard skins,
a Dutch stove was burning, which had become very Russian-
ized during the years of its wanderings from Holland to
Russia and Mongolia: it was friendly and comfortable with
its cracked tiles, painted with figures of green sheep and
shepherds and bearing German proverbs. In the alcove by
the stove the walls were covered with a dozen or more clocks,
some of which were silent, while others ticked away in every
tone down to bass. The main walls were hung with the
aphorisms of the great men of Mongolia and China. The Hun
was enthroned on a leopard skin. The Englishmen stood
before him among the throng of courtiers. The servants
brought in chairs and a round table, dark with age.

Mr. Grey, through the interpreter, delivered a long speech
which he had prepared beforehand. He spoke quietly. This
was the beginning of his speech:

"Great Hun, Great One who sits upon a leopard skin as on
a throne! We, the directors of the new railroad, have come to
bow before you and your grandees, have come to bring you
gifts and to arrive at an amicable agreement with you, that
we may in future live in amity and peace under your guidance
and in accordance with your counsels. The whole point is that
our road abuts on your domain, passes through your land,
and we . . ."

The Hun's face was like a stone burned by the sun. He
sat with his eyes cast down; his eyes were covered by their
yellow lids and could not be seen. The Hun was immobile and
impenetrable.

The servants set out on the round table small, round
Chinese bowls and cups with chopsticks beside them, but in
the Englishmen's places they put forks which had never been
washed or cleaned. When the interpreter had finished trans-
lating Mr. Grey's speech, the Hun rose from his leopard skin,
walked up to the ideograms of an aphorism on one of the
walls, contemplated the saying for a long time with his unseeing eyes and said:

"This manuscript was presented to me by the Chinese Emperor Pu Yi, who is now living without a throne, having renounced his throne when he was three. The Emperor Pu Yi wrote to me and said, 'I have heard the birds sing and the voices of birds are everywhere the same; why then do men speak with different voices and with different words?' "

The Hun then went to take his place at the round table. There was one solitary bottle of cognac on the table, which was not genuine but made at Fudidyan. The Hun and his guests sat around the table in the European way on chairs and taborets. And an endless array of Chinese food was brought to the table—trepang, rotten eggs, so rotten they were green and transparent, the abortions of pigs in soybean oil and dozens of similar dishes, uneatable to Europeans. The Englishman told the Hun, through the interpreter, that in addition to some leopard skins, he was making him a present of an all-white English race horse. To show that he heard, the Hun slowly blinked his eyes. His hands were slow, dry, narrow, and the fingers were beautifully and unusually long, which is considered aristocratic among Europeans.

But these Chinese dishes were only the beginning of the dinner. The Englishmen were lost in the maze of little cups and bowls standing before them. The eyes of the impaled head stared at them from each bowl of trepang or frogs or soybean oil. Then the servants brought in a samovar, the progenitor of the Russian samovar, made of copper, covered in verdigris, hissing and boiling, and they put embers in its flue with a scoop. On wooden trenchers, the servants brought wafer-thin slices of horseflesh, pork, goosemeat, chicken, bustards, wild boar and wild goat. And the Hun with his own hands placed the meat in the boiling water of the samovar. The Hun sprinkled in some salt. The Hun put in pepper, ginger, onion, garlic. The Hun poured soybean oil into the mixture. All this boiled in the samovar. And then the Hun took the meat out of the samovar with his own hands and placed some before each guest, so that his guests should eat it, in the Mongolian way now, with their hands. The Hun's eyes were unblinking. The clocks on the walls sounded in different ways—in deep tones, like a cuckoo, high-pitched or hoarse. The Hun said through the interpreter that he was making Mr. Grey a present of his best white race horse. Mr. Grey invited the Hun to dinner next day on the train. The Hun blinked slowly to show that he heard. Mr. Grey, within his muzzle, from afar, through the interpreter, expressed his interest in the Hun's bank and its currency and suggested that he might become a shareholder. The Hun was unblinking and showed he did not hear.

Then Mr. Grey received a note under the table from the railway chief, written in pencil: "Mr. Grey, your excellency, I consider it absolutely necessary to disturb you. That head impaled on the stake is the head of my agent who vanished last night." Mr. Grey glanced around at his companions. They were pale and choking on the horseflesh. His first impulse was to get up and run, but he continued to sit there. He could not see anything any longer. He picked the horsemeat up in his fingers submissively. Then he drank Mongolian tea made with salt, wheat and mutton fat. And, submissively, he inspected the Hun's ancient arsenal, the swords, spears, bows, and examined the bow and arrows that, according to tradition, once belonged to Timur, one of whose descendants the Hun claimed to be. The Hun sat motionless and his unblinking eyes were desert-like. The Hun ate nothing, but his courtiers deftly snatched the hot meat with their bare hands and neatly filled their mouths with it, bending over the table, belching a little and licking their fingers. The Englishmen ate quickly without looking at what they were eating. They no longer said anything. The Hun wound up a Gramophone which played Chinese records—the very degeneracy of music to the European ear. The clocks gave their cuckoo calls and chimed low.

Then the servants brought in the visiting cards of the Hun and his courtiers on copper salvers and these were four times larger than usual since they were written in ideograms. The dinner ceremony came to an end and the Englishmen were free to leave.

The Englishmen made their way to the exit hurriedly, in a stampede, heads bowed, with hurried farewells. The Hun and his suite escorted them to the gates. The Englishmen did not see their Chinese guard lifting their rifles to attention. They got into the cars. When the empty street of the hamlet had been left behind, and the steppe opened out its white landscape, Mr. Grey stopped the car and got out. He shoved two fingers into his mouth, vomited, and then drank some castor oil diluted with coffee from a Thermos. Mr. Grey's face was pale, his eyes brimming with tears, his face had aged by thirty years or so and revealed that he was far from young. Then the others got out and made themselves sick as well. The boy-interpreter stood by the mudguard of a car and said calmly:

"The English gentlemen wanted to call at a Mongolian monastery on the way back, to see the lamas. Should I turn in there?"

Mr. Grey waved his hand feebly and said:

"No, no, that will do. I've seen it already. I want to get back to the train. As quickly as possible, please."

And the car tore up the distance with impetuous speed but without dependability. The frost just before sunset was being hacked out by hard cold and not by the sun. The Englishmen sat huddled down, their noses hidden behind their coat collars, their hands thrust deeper into their pockets. . . .

Out in the naked steppe, behind low moats, stood the temples of a Mongolian monastery. A hunchback lama, eaten up with smallpox and syphilis, was growing cold beside the gates. To the left and the right of the altar, in the first temple, were a pair of gods, terrifying and inhuman, yet anthropomorphic, hewn out of wood and twice the height of a man. Their tongues and tusks were sticking out, their eyes were rolling out of the sockets in rage, bloodstained, their eyebrows were horrible, they had horns on their foreheads, they held enormous swords and clubs in their hands, while under their feet, contorted in torment, were two little human figurines. These devil-like gods were guarding the altar from evil spirits and evil men, driving them off, frightening them away in terror of their own terrible visages. The hunchback lama grew cold beside the gates. Then he entered the temple and beat a gong so that the gods might hear his prayer and know he was zealously on guard. . . .

The Englishmen's cars raced on toward the train. . . .

In the evening, the Englishmen were tired out and sat
about the observation car in their pajamas after a bath. The
car had been well heated so that they could warm up after
the frosts of the day. A reinforced detachment of Chinese
guards surrounded the car. The Englishmen were silent.

"Well, and how about your plans now?" Mr. Grey said
wearily to the philosopher-bookkeeper. "Our boy-interpreter
has run off too, hasn't he? Do you think they'll impale him as
well? Or is he just a Mongol agent? The railway chief said
the interpreters kept calling us dogs of Englishmen and,
unfortunately, he knows a few words of Mongolian! What
about the plans now?"

The philosopher-bookkeeper was angry. His face no longer
looked at all sleepy, there was no drooping there now and no
resemblance to the color of his khaki. His spectacles sat firmly
on his nose.

"After all," he said, "we have other means which will be
more effective in the case of savages. Let's see what results we
get from the dinner here tomorrow. I intend to have a heart-
to-heart talk with the Mongol here and no jokes about
chopped-off heads. As for our being dogs—"

"All the same," Mr. Grey interrupted, "the dogs in the
steppe have devoured an agent of ours whom we paid well, by
all accounts."

"As for our being dogs," the philosopher-bookkeeper continued, "we can't hope to make anything of their morals, so
let's leave that alone. The population here is such and such—
take a look at the figures in my memorandum—the cattle
such and such, the area of the ground such and such. The
reckoning is obvious. If we chuck on a thousand pounds
sterling—"

But at this point something incomprehensible occurred,
which the Englishmen only understood when the train had
begun to race beyond Hingan, regardless of signals and arrows,
with an unnecessary and hysterical precipitation. . . .

There was the noise of a crowd behind the observation
car. The official on duty came in and announced that the
Mongols had brought the horse presented to Mr. Grey by the
Hun and wanted to make the presentation to him personally.
Mr. Grey went out onto the little platform of the car and then

stepped down onto the station platform. There was a throng of horsemen out there and the horses, in gold- and silver-embroidered shabracks, were snorting at the train. An old man, a grandee of the Hun's, sat his horse as if they had been born together. His face was like the face of the Hun, like the burned-out stones of the desert. And his wild steed was something to be admired, probably one of the best horses in the whole world. The old man dismounted and a groom led the horse over to Mr. Grey, handed him the reins and bowed to Mr. Grey. Mr. Grey began to say in English that he was most grateful to the Hun, but did not finish what he was saying, because a shot rang out alongside. The bullet must have gone straight into the brain of the horse whose halter Mr. Grey was holding, since the horse did not even have time to rear back on its hind legs but fell to the ground instantly, surrounded by horsemen who rose in the air as their mounts reared.

There were no more shots. In a moment the platform was deserted—no Mongols, no Chinese guards—and only the splendid white horse lay there. Mr. Grey weakly gave orders for the train to leave. The horse lay on the platform. There was not a soul on the platform. And then from behind the station hut a man came running with unnatural speed. He began to run for the observation car, stumbled over the white horse, jumped up and leaped into the car. This was the railway chief. The railway chief, the engineer, looked at the Englishmen with eyes that were starting out of his head and whispered, "Hurry, hurry—I escaped from the Mongols, leaped through the window—I've left my wife and children there—quick, quick, let's go, help me!" At this moment the train began to move, the armored steel grinding. A solitary bullet shot through the window of the observation car, breaking the glass and humming. The Englishmen fell to the ground, hugging the carpet. The philosopher-bookkeeper shouted in a high-pitched voice:

"Full speed, full speed ahead! Get going, give her a full head of steam. Hey there! Hurry!"

The railway chief stood over the Englishmen, his face the face of a Yakut, and whispered:

"Quick, quick! I've left my wife and children there! Come on!"

"Full speed ahead!" the philosopher-bookkeeper screamed with a ferocious rage born of cowardice, and then he fell silent, hugging the carpet, hiding his head.

THE LAST CHAPTER

It was night in the steppe, in the black and boundless steppe, its moon like a corpse high overhead, the moon, which to a European seems to predetermine the Asiatic philosophy of existence. To the European the steppe is a desert, but to the Mongol the steppe is his native land. When the Mongol, Ada-Bekir, left the train that night on the Hingan, he galloped all through the night.

Beyond the mountains lay the steppe of impetuous races, the wide expanse of the steppe disappearing into obscurity, the ice-splinter of the moon in the skies, the directing stars, and the snort of the horse, the smell of its sweat, the rushing wind, the reins in the hand, the lowered head of the horse, its ears pressed back, its mane flying in the wind—and the man on the horse embraced an enormous heart and the wind. Through the obscurity of the night and the thousands of kilometers traversed, both heart and mind saw again the days of Tamerlane, the days of Mongolia's freedom and power, the days of a boundless future, days of blood, of sorrow and of joy, saw the steppe aflame with the bonfires of rebellion, heard the gallop of horsemen in the dark, the creaking of oxcarts, sensed the blood of brotherhood and death for brotherhood, for loyalty, duty, freedom, experienced the joy and torment of brotherhood, the bonds of blood and freedom.

The horses sped on until they had no breath left. Then the horsemen changed horses and raced onward, true to their will power and their enormous hearts, re-experiencing the groans, moans, cries and shouts, the shouts of joy and victory, the noise of creaking oxcarts, of galloping horses, of the riotous crowds. At the moment when the sky over the steppe was just beginning to lighten and when it seemed darker than ever in the steppe, as always before dawn, the horsemen reached a halting place. In a ravine, there were a few clay huts inhabited by non-nomadic Mongols, and around these were pitched the sheepskin tents of other nomads from the steppe. No one was asleep there that night, but no light showed. The dogs betrayed the presence of the place by their howling before any sounds from the encampment itself could be heard. The horsemen were met by others, who had ridden far out into the steppe to meet them. The galloping of the horses muffled all thought and feeling except for the real sounds of rebellion, the real noise of insurgents. The men met in one of the clay huts. There was very little room; men sat on *kanas,* stood about inside or outside the door. It was very silent and quiet in the hut, as happens where there is really not very much to discuss.

Discussions were short.

"Now, or never."

"Let every man mount his horse immediately and ride out into the steppe, to every *ulang, hoshun,* hamlet, village. Let the whole steppe take to its horses."

Inside the clay hut no one said very much. They were quiet and taciturn.

The sun had not yet risen over the steppe and the lilac-colored night still lingered. The Hun's fortress was silent. The sentries slept at the gates. Then the horsemen galloped up to the fortress gates. There was a murmur at the gates. "You a Mongol and a traitor?" and a human head went up on a stake. "To the dogs with the corpse. Out on the road which the Englishmen will take. Let them see it." More horsemen rode up. By now the fortress gates had been opened. The horsemen rode in. The Hun was expecting them in his private chambers where the leopard skins were spread. The Hun did not at all resemble a stone burned out by the sun in the desert. He stood upright and gazed like an eagle at those who entered and had risen in rebellion.

"Sit down," the Hun said, and sat down himself, not on a leopard skin but simply on the earthen floor, tucking his legs beneath him. The men sat down around him, also on the ground, also with their legs tucked under them and their arms hanging loose.

"Let us smoke," said the Hun, and slowly he began to light a long, thin pipe, an old pipe, inlaid with silver. The men lighted their pipes. A servant brought in a clay tub of burning embers and set it within the circle formed by the men.

"How about the Englishmen?" the Hun asked.

"You are old, wise and cunning. There was a time when you and the Chinese governed and suppressed us. You know the head of a traitor is already impaled on the stake by your fortress—this is what we tell you."

"Well and good," said the Hun. "But the Englishmen have cannon."

"Yes," they replied, "but we have a just cause and the steppe. We have the sacred custom of hospitality. You will meet the Englishmen and receive them. And they will grasp the significance of the head on the stake. We haven't much choice. You have mentioned the Englishmen in China."

"Very well," said the Hun. "You, Ada-Bekir, was it you who raised the revolt? You came here with the Englishmen and you shall be the one to receive them and guide them. But now I wish to sleep. And you too, lie down and sleep."

The horse under the rider gasped for breath. It was night. The dawn was approaching. The rider and the horse had grown together into one. In the night, in the dark and in the steppe, the rider felt the sounds of revolt, the creaking of oxcarts, the shouts, the galloping of riders. The boundary fires were burning, the horizon smoking, above the steppe in the immense distances, and there came the sound of dogs barking and the mute silence. The horse under the rider gasped for breath.

An enormous sun rose above the steppe. The rider's limbs had grown numb with uninterrupted galloping and the horse gasped for breath. The sun rose up, red, round, enormous, and the rider knew that for him, for a Mongol, this sun had a big and a kind heart.

At that hour, in the Chinese town with the soybean factory, the overseers were waking the Chinese with bamboo sticks, rousing them for work, as they slept on the soybeans in their sacks of matting. . . . In the temple, the faithful dropped a coin into the box for the devil-god and beat the gong, so that the god might hear their prayers. The noises of the day had not yet risen above the anthill streets and from the alley came streaming the stifling smell of opium.

1926

The
Boy from Tralles

For P. A. Pavlenko

Sun and wind.

There is a museum of antiquities in Istanbul behind the Janissary square, between the church of St. Irene and the sultan's Palace of the Old Seraglio. In the quiet of the Greek gallery there is a statue of a shepherd boy from Tralles, which was carved by Myron, a sculptor of antiquity. A curly-headed boy carries his head proudly on a thin neck, he wears a sheepskin cloak over his shoulders and is barefoot. I was shown a photograph; the idea was to surprise me. The curator of the museum took the photograph near Tralles in 1918, and it showed a shepherd boy just like the one Myron had carved two and a half thousand years ago, with the same gesture of the head, the same curls, the same brow, nose, neck and shoulders, the same sheepskin cloak. If this shepherd boy had not been holding a branched staff, one would have thought that it was a photograph of Myron's statue. In the ruins of the desert of Asia Minor, a Greek type was perfectly preserved—Greek life and culture was preserved. And so we are going to Tralles.

Sun and wind.

It was November and so it was cool, rather as it is in Russia toward the second apple harvest. The Keysteyn Dag mountains rose on the horizon. The sky was dark blue. This was our second day's journey on horseback and all around were yellow mounds, stones, the dust of the highway and the uninhabited silence of the desert. Pools of water and camel dung lay beside the ancient wells. The road, which went back to either the time of the Greeks, or perhaps the Roman legions, was empty. The ancient Greek cities abandoned a thousand years ago were in ruins and the Turks had settled alongside the ruins. Dusty poplars rose above these hamlets, inhabited by Turks and Christian Turks. From time to time an eagle flew across the sky. Occasionally broken statues and marble slabs covered in writing appeared instead of boundary stones. The fields had already been harvested. Cartloads of hay were rarer than caravans of camels. These carts and the Turks in them were like the heroes in the stories of the Turkish writer, Reyfik Khalid.

When we camped last night near a well, the donkey was startled by my shot at a jackal and broke the old stirrup on my saddle, as it crashed into our goods and chattels. I had to ride along miserably, because I cannot stand in the stirrups with both feet. And we inquired at each hayloft about where I could get hold of another stirrup. The Turks made no reply. And we grew silent too in the sun and wind.

Then we spent another night beside a well, covering ourselves with sheepskin cloaks. The jackals did not trouble us that time, since there were no people there and the jackals had also left the place.

In the morning, there was sun and wind again. We turned off the highway into a desert of sun-scorched stone, a flat rocky expanse with mounds and before us the mountainous crest of Keysteyn Dag on the horizon. In a hollow under the mountain ahead of us lay the desert of Tralles.

We reached the place toward noon. Where was Tralles? The hollow between the rocks lay silent with its stones, scattered about the hillocks, remnants of human dwellings. We rode into an absolutely empty street. November noons do not carry sounds. I went into a house, as the door was unlocked. There was a basket with coal by the threshold. A fly buzzed as it came to meet me, and grew quiet. There was goat dung

on the clay floor, the threshold step was covered with in-
scriptions: all the human beings, down to the last man, had
abandoned these places in 1921, when the Turks drove the
Greeks from Anatolia. . . .

Could Greece have been like this two thousand years ago
and a thousand five hundred years ago? We preferred to
spend two days in the saddle rather than travel on the
German train to Adana. No rumors of mankind reached this
place. We were in Asia Minor, an Anatolia devoured by goats.
Had lively Greek colonies existed here, and had the epoch of
the flowering of Greek civilization passed through here? They
had been here and they were gone, separated from us by a
great span of time. Once Ephesus was the chief city of bank-
ing; it stood at the beginning of all the banks in the world.
Pergamon, then, was a town of learning with a great library.
Magnesia has gone down in history as a town of actors, drama-
tists and philosophers. Tralles was once a town full of noise,
of poets, artists, musicians, theatrical productions and
Dionysian priestesses. To this day, on the ruined walls of a
town, the poems of Anacreon can be deciphered, carved there,
so it is believed, by the poet himself. Tralles, a town of great
theatrical productions, has had many names—Anthea, Evanthea, Larissa, Antioch. The Seljuks called Tralles Guzel
Hisarom, which means "Beautiful Palace."

Surely Greece was not these ruins, indeed not. History, that
great theatrical producer, has disguised the face of Evanthea
with its sands. It is no joke to say that the goats have devoured
Asia Minor. This flowering land of merchants, poets, philosophers and Dionysian morality did not perish through wars
and the invasions of Assyrians, Persians, Romans, Turks, but
through the invasion of goats, which for centuries devoured
the shoots of trees and finally annihilated woods and groves,
dried up the valleys and rivers and transformed a green
Anatolia into parched sands and stones. Tralles and the surrounding district had remained preserved up to our time, and
historians have said that Hellas still lived on there. But the
theatrical producer has his work to do, and Tralles was
abandoned by the Greeks, forever, in 1921, in the days of the
Greco-Turkish war, when the Turks, with the aid of Russian
heavy artillery, above Smyrna, cast the Greeks into the

Mediterranean Sea, forcing them to flee and to abandon their homes. . . .

This was Evanthea, the joyful land of poets and musicians. I found a crust of dried-up bread on the table in the empty house, and in another house the oil had not yet evaporated in the lamp. This was Anthea, a land of famous plays, a dead Hellas, dead, because nothing new had entered the lives of the Greeks who lived here for the past thousand five hundred years, and the Turks had not plundered since they came in 1921.

A man came riding on a mule toward us down the hill and he was waving. We rode to meet him along a clay road. A broken statue of Aphrodite stood at the crossroads, covered in buffalo hair, for these beasts scratched themselves against the statue. The person who approached us on the mule was an old man in a white cloak and sandals. His mule had no saddle.

I asked him whether it was possible to get a stirrup anywhere thereabouts.

"A stirrup?" asked the old man and thought a moment. "Yes, it's possible. Up on the hill there, there's a street, and in the third house on the right there's a stirrup lying under the bench. Take it."

I galloped off to fetch the stirrup. The house was unlocked and empty. A spindle was stuck into the lintel over the door.

An old copper stirrup lay in the dust under the bench. I picked it up and examined it. It was a stirrup that might have been left there from the days of Alexander the Great.

And I was to see the authentic Hellas. My fellow traveler asked the old man:

"Where is Tralles?"

"Tralles is here," he answered.

The old man led us to a house as empty as the rest. He poured some red wine from a fur-covered bottle into a clay vessel and offered it to us with some goat cheese. The old man was taciturn and dignified. He played the host, he was the patriarch of these parts although he bowed to us with servility. I thought the old man was not altogether normal, as many Russian peasants are not normal in old age. We were resting before going to see the ruins. The old man asked us to wait until the boy came from the hills. I watched the old man. He was extraordinarily handsome, a real grandson of Dionysius in his old cloak, with his gray curls and proud eyes. We asked him what he was doing there and how he, a Greek, had managed to survive, but his reply was vague.

We gave up waiting for the boy from the hills and began to wander around the dead ruins. The old man accompanied us in the guise of a custodian and as a personage in his own right. The old man talked of bygone ages, he knew everything better than our guidebooks, and wandered from century to century in history, but he also talked about each separate house, about who had lived there and what was left there, just as he talked of past centuries. My interpreter told me that the old man talked entirely in the present tense, setting historical time aside. In one house, he took down the lamp and made me a present of it—it was made of black clay and was centuries old.

He pointed at the dust rising in the hills and said it was the boy driving the herd down. He spoke solemnly about the boy.

And a boy approached us, his head set proudly on his thin neck, the same boy whom I had seen in the museum of antiquities at Istanbul. At his feet were goats and watchdogs. He wore across his shoulders a rust-colored sheepskin cloak. He carried a branched staff.

I knew that in the sun and wind I was looking at a real Greek, at the real Hellas, even though the goats have devoured Asia Minor. The theatrical producer had not forgotten that Evanthea had been a city of great plays.

The old man began to speak in a ceremonial voice as he pointed at the boy.

"We are together here. I am alone. I guard these places. The boy from Tralles is still alive. Greece lives on!"

The old man gestured at the mountains like an actor of genius and gazed over my head. He was majestic. And he repeated quietly to himself:

"The boy from Tralles is still alive!"

Sun and wind. It was November and so it was cool, rather as in Russia toward the second apple harvest, when the sun and wind are firm and fragrant like Antonovka apples.

1927

A

Story About

Crystallization

Spring came suddenly in a few nights. For some days there was no sun and it drizzled. The snow disappeared faster at night than during the day. The river broke through the ice and overflowed at night, and sounds changed, so that the voices of people calling from the farther shore could be heard as clearly as those forty paces away. Then from dawn to dusk the sun appeared, and though a light-brown snow still lay in the valleys, the hilltops were dry by afternoon and they were already covered with the first blue crocuses. The day was spacious, full of light, wind and sky. In the gloom of the evening, which was sticky, moist and tender like spring mud, the cranes called to one another just beyond the gardens in the common pastureland, in exactly the same place now as a thousand years ago.

That evening they decided to begin plowing. Dawn was the hour appointed for making a beginning. No one slept that night. From midnight the cocks began to crow, close by, beyond the river, five miles away, as if they wanted to crow over the whole world. In summer the river only comes up to the knees, but now the team of workers had crossed over on a raft, and they had been sitting since evening in the porch, smoking, or lolling on the hay in the stable yard, also smoking. Papa Klementev, nicknamed "Public Enemy No. 1," crossed the river with his daughters. Time hung heavy on his hands; he went from the porch to the stables, back to the porch and out to the tractor drivers, then to the office, where he gazed in some disapproval at the new, bald-headed president—and everywhere, on the porch, with the tractor drivers, in the stables, he said the same thing over and over again:

"They've let things slide since autumn, the fools, so that now we've got to make up for lost time during the frost," and he blinked and screwed up his eyes, grimacing, his nose sticking out from a face overgrown with beard. "They forgot the old proverb, the fools: 'Never put off till tomorrow what you can do today!' They've let things slide, the fools!"

In the office they were checking over and alloting work to the men in the work brigade. At the stables they gave the horses an extra meal, but this only tended to disturb their rest. The cries of birds rose from the fields, where they came in flocks to spend the night. The tractor drivers rode out to work before dawn. All the tractors began to roar simultaneously, and they crawled out of the shed in a row by the light of acetylene flares, like impossible bats.

For Lavrenty this was not just plowing, but a test of everything he had learned during the winter. He had gone over the tractor again and again since about seven in the evening and then had fallen asleep until midnight on the straw beside the tractor, with his sheepskin coat flung over him. Aganka, who was "Public Enemy No. 1's" daughter, woke him.

"Time to get up! I'm going to be your mate!" she said, laughing, as she shook him carefully and lovingly by the shoulder. "Get up, I've got leave to come and help you, with the plow or whatever there is. . . . Come on! It's me, Agasha. . . ."

They rode off into the night. Agasha settled down by his left arm and they breathed close to each other. In the light of the acetylene flares everything seemed strange—the bridge on its high piles, the stream below full of icy mounds of unmelted snow. "Public Enemy No. 1" was standing on the bridge with a staff in his hand. He said nothing, but screwed up his eyes in the glare and looked serious. The field they had to plow lay immediately beyond the pastureland. They drove up quickly, stopped and switched off the ignition. Immediately the night with all its events and sounds became accentuated. They put out the lights and the night grew less dark. Right over their heads the startled wild geese flew away and Agasha repeated the age-old saying: "The geese are on the wing, now it will get light."

Agasha's shoulders trembled. In the village the cocks began to crow and a dog began to bark.

Then it really did begin to grow lighter in the east. Lavrenty and Agasha paced the field, marking the route for the tractor. The hillside had already dried after the snow, but in places the earth still clung to their feet, making their movements clumsy and delightful. Lavrenty's black shoulders seemed still blacker and larger in the darkness, while Agasha's white kerchief was wispy and shone bright. On the other side of the field they stood shoulder to shoulder once more and once more Agasha trembled.

By the time they had returned to the tractor the east was not only mauve but greenish already and over the hill, over all the hills in a cold wide expanse the dawn broke. Lavrenty started up the engine, sat down at the wheel, moved the tractor to the boundary of the field, took his position, dropped the plowshare, moved on again, plowed a couple of meters and stopped. Agasha sat next to him. Lavrenty bent over the newly turned earth, picked up a handful of clods and examined them attentively and carefully as if he were seeing earth for the first time.

"Soil . . ." he said. "The structure of the soil, both physically and chemically, depends among other things on the conditions under which the plowing is done. The soil can become alkalized and incrusted with salts. The alkaline solutions and the crystallization of the salts. . . ."

Lavrenty was really seeing the earth anew, not because it had just emerged from under the snow, but because his new knowledge of the earth as it was after the icy covering of winter came from the pages of books which he had been studying all winter. He fingered the earth dubiously.

There followed a long hard day's work. Lavrenty plowed the earth through sun and wind, paying deep attention to was he was doing. Once or twice the tractor gave trouble, and then Lavrenty climbed into its "heart," armed with keys

and concentration. Agasha bent over the "heart" with him
and then their shoulders would touch and remain motionless
for a moment. Agasha supervised the plowshare. At midday,
she went to fetch their dinner and they ate it sitting on the
tractor—up there they seemed high above the ground, in the
wind and wide expanse of sky. At sunset they ate bread and
salt standing opposite one another.

"Are you tired?" he asked. "We still can't sit on the
ground. You've been on your feet all day. Now have a rest on
the tractor."

The last rays of the sun shone in Agasha's eyes; she was
chewing and smiled playfully and boldly—sit down!—and she
perched on the tractor and ate another "doorstep," a great
thick slice of bread rimed with salt. They drank the icy water
from a bucket. Then they went on working till suddenly they
discovered that the night was black as pitch and the ground
frosty. On the way back Agasha again placed herself next to
Lavrenty, put her hand on his shoulder, dozed and nodded
as they bumped along the furrows. At the bridge they lighted
the acetylene lamp. Agasha settled herself more comfortably
and Lavrenty steered with one hand. Agasha said sleepily:

"Tomorrow the ground will be a bit dryer. . . . We'll get
really going and plow all night . . . only we must get used
to it. . . . Lavrusha, do you really love me?" and without waiting for a reply she dozed off again.

The windows in the office were blazing with light and the
yard was like a camp. The old man, "Public Enemy No. 1,"
caught up with the new president that evening—he was close-
shaven (eyelashes seemed the only hair he had) and he wore
hunting boots—and began talking to him:

"You don't know me yet. I'm a straightforward person,
I've known poverty and I'm always dragging up the truth and
sticking it under people's noses, like Comrade Litvinov at
Geneva. What's good's good, but if a fellow tries to get away
on a dirty wagon I don't allow it. And that's why they call me
'Public Enemy No. 1.' Do you know Lavrusha?"

"What Lavrusha?"

"The tractor driver. I'm a widower and I've got two
daughters—I've no sons." The old man stopped smiling and
his eyes looked thoughtful and gentle and his voice suddenly

grew more gentle too. "My young girls aren't married. I've been thinking. A woman's lot now—you know yourself how things are: there's no need for her to sit under a cow milking all day. My girls can do more than a man—so they're well fed, well shod and clothed and everything's in order. And besides, a girl now, for instance, can be richer than a man and won't be lost even if she stays unmarried and that means . . . she's free. . . ."

The close-cropped man in high boots looked attentively at "Public Enemy No. 1." They were standing as they talked. He was busy and in a hurry.

"Well?" he asked. "And what's the tractor driver got to do with it?"

"Well, as I was saying, a girl's free. I don't argue; my daughters have more money than I do and I'm not going to start arguing. The tractor driver has fallen for my Aganka, he can't take his eyes off her, they work together in the fields, they've just got in now and he brought her some water to wash with. . . . I can't say anything against it—I don't want to give offence. But still, in the old days they got married, all in order, and had a wedding feast. . . . But now she won't let him lay a finger on her, she earns no less than he does, they'll live like that a month or two. . . . She won't die of hunger, of course, and won't even lose anything by it if he's no good. But all the same, it's not right or comfortable and it makes one ashamed. . . . What'll happen if Aganka lives six months with him, then comes home, then goes off with another? In the old days they were ashamed of what people would say. . . ."

"You should complain to the Komsomol," the other replied.

"What's that?"

"You know how it is in towns, in factories: if a man or a girl plays around and acts in an antisocial way, they have to go before a tribunal. Suppose a fellow goes with a girl, gets her with child and then leaves her. She lodges a complaint with the Komsomol cell or the president of the Women's Organization. He has to stand trial. They report his case in the wall-newspaper. If he's acted like a rotter he gets such a time of it he doesn't dare show his face. And he can't get out

of it. He gets told off so well that he thinks twice before getting disillusioned for nothing!"

"Then this is a matter for the Komsomol?"

"Yes."

The president pranced off in his boots to further his own
affairs and left the old man standing. "Public Enemy No. 1"
went onto the porch, then into the cattleyard, then into the
garage, and then finally came out again on the porch. The
yard, the porch and the garage were all falling asleep before
the new day. Over the river in the low-lying fields they had
begun plowing a day later and you could hear the voices
coming over the water, as if people were talking side by side
in forty different places. As always in spring the dogs howled
and the earth smelled strong.

Lavrenty and Aganka woke before dawn. As he refueled
the tractor, Lavrenty thought about crystallization and its
phenomena.

"Suppose you throw some cooking salt into some water.
The salt dissolves and disappears in the clear water. You add
more salt. That dissolves. You add still more. And suddenly
in the water crystals are formed. They have definite shapes.
They continue to grow very quickly until all the salt in the
water has turned to crystals. The chemical process of crystallization begins when the solution of water has reached the
saturation point." This extract just came into his mind. And
suddenly he began to think jokingly about himself, his friends
and their work in terms of the soil, and the thoughts came to
him in textbook words: "The salt of revolutionary proletarian
traditions which has been permeating the peasantry for fifteen
years now, tonight has reached in the understanding of
Lavrenty Panfelov the saturation point of proletarian crystallization." Lavrenty thought of himself in the third person because he saw his name in print on the wall-newspaper, in
which he intended to write an article on the proletarian
crystallization of the peasant consciousness. Lavrenty shouted
into the depths of the garage:

"Agasha! Come on! It's time to go!" and his voice sounded
happy.

They rode off in the dark as before when the cocks were

crowing all over the land. A thin slice of moon appeared in the sky, which in the old days had only come on the third day of Easter; a light frost hardened the ground, but the earth smelled only of spring. Aganka sat beside Lavrenty again. On the bridge they met "Public Enemy No. 1." He stopped the tractor.

"Lavrushka, are you a member of the Komsomol or not?" he asked severely. "All right then, mind what you do! And you, Aganka, I insist that you join the Komsomol. You hear what your father says! Join at once, because I won't stand for any disillusionment! . . ."

1933

The
Birth of a Man

There was a telephone call from Moscow. A public prosecutor, by name Antonova, would be arriving and would stay in the house for about ten days or two weeks. She arrived in the evening. The automobile turned off the tarmac and onto the gravel, then passed through the forest in complete darkness. The windows of the house seemed to spring out of a desert, a solitude of dense trees. The house was old, left over from the days of the provincial landowners and furnished in their style. She was led upstairs to a corner room and told that supper would be ready in twenty minutes and that afterward she might like to go for a walk. She could have a bath at ten and at eleven the electric current was turned off. She was given a smile and left alone. She laid out her things. A gong sounded from the depths of the house. Downstairs, in the empty rooms adjoining the sitting room, there came the sound of billiard balls. The hostess met her and led her through the sitting room and the library into a vaulted room that was almost in darkness.

"In the days of the landowners the Masons held their meetings in this room and this was a Masonic lodge."

There were very few people in the house and these had already made friends with each other. After supper her fellow guests came up to her, introduced themselves, pressed her hand and said:

"There's a tradition here that each newcomer must read a paper on his subject. You will have to tell us about prosecution under the Soviet."

She answered, "Very well."

The billiard balls began to click again. She went out for a walk. The night was very dark and everything seemed like a solitude and a dense forest. Owls screeched in the park. From the empty gloom beyond the park came a wind, and it began to rain gently. No sound came from the house, not even of billiard balls clicking. In the empty library next to the sitting room the reading lamps burned unwanted on the little tables. She began to examine the books and picked out a few to read. Upstairs in her own room the two ancient corner windows leaned on the darkness. She laid out some writing paper, envelopes, notebook, and moved the armchair over to the stove. Out of the empty gloom the wind drove the rain against the window. The books were old like the house, and they smelled of rot. There was a knock at the door; her bath was ready. The towels were laid out. The glass reflected a face which was completely absorbed in itself. Downstairs in the bathroom the woman examined in the mirror with great attention, with absorption, almost sadly, at the same time happily, her body and her new belly. For a moment her pupils contracted, the woman smiled and stroked her belly, which was alive and endearing. Then clumsily and carefully she began to lower herself into the water. She had not settled down to sleep by eleven and a candle burned on her bedside table. And for a long time the wind hurled the wet drops against the glass, while the pages rustled.

At eight o'clock in the morning the gong sounded in the depths of the house. Outside the window the sun shone, the sky was blue and you could see a very long way. The house was on a hill, which stood in a forest of fir trees. At the foot of the hill ran a dark-blue river. Beyond the river lay the bare autumn fields, a village, a purple wood, blue sky, open and quite ordinary. This golden autumnal ordinariness and this ordinary Russian landscape seemed perfect. In such weather in the old days the landowners, interrupting their Masonic affairs, would go hunting with borzois after foxes and wolves, moving through the footpaths. The wind had gone. A slight frost dried the ground; the fallen leaves rustled underfoot. The leafy wood was thinned out. The congealed blood of the maple trees was fading. The open air in the slight frost was more spacious than the forest. It was the time for cranes, and sure enough there were cranes flying south in melancholy triangles, gabbling. Toward evening it began to drizzle again. Again the candle burned far into the night, the pages of a book rustled, and then it grew quiet in her hand. Under her heart the child began to move.

In the dead hour just before sunset she met a fellow guest in the park. He was looking down as he walked, and was studiously picking out the places where the leaves lay thickest on the ground. He was embarrassed when he caught sight of her.

"It's odd," he said in self-defense, "but I've liked this rustling since I was a child. It calms you or it makes you brave —I don't know how to put it—like the Bolshoi Theater or a poem of Pasternak's. I can walk through the leaves by the hour."

They were silent for a moment. He introduced himself— he was Ivan Fedorovich Surovtsev, a mechanical engineer. They walked side by side through the leaves.

"Forgive me, but as far as I can judge, you are near your time," he said and again looked embarrassed.

She answered without any embarrassment, almost proudly, "Yes, in twelve days. I came here to have a rest before labor begins. They have a telephone line to town and everything is organized. I shall go straight from here, the journey is all arranged. I am going to the Clara Zetkin maternity home."

The engineer began to talk about his job—work and more work and sometimes no opportunity to visit the country even once a year, and you can forget it as you forget your childhood. And all the time the engineer was earnestly raking the dead leaves with his feet.

In the evening the rain poured down. She wrote letters and she also wrote in the empty notebook with the stamped Venetian-leather binding, which she had brought back some years ago from Turkey, from Constantinople, where she had once done some government work.

She wrote to a cousin in Saratov:

Aunt Claudia's condition is as follows. I met her at the station and took her to the Institute. She has cancer in an advanced and incurable form. She met me, started to cry, kissed me and began at once to tell me about the bleeding, the pains and the odor. Then she said, "You are a public prosecutor, you can manage anything, be sure and fix me up to live in." Aunt even told the doctors I was a public prosecutor. After the examination I was alone with the doctors. Treatment by radium rays merely alleviates the pain and might postpone death for two or three months, but death is inevitable. Aunt insisted on receiving treatment as an in-patient. The doctor said to me, "If I give her a bed, we will be depriving a man who can be cured of his chance of recovery." I told Aunt Claudia that I would not try to get her in because I consider it inadmissable to deprive a man of a bed and so of a chance to be cured. Aunt announced that she would summon the chief doctor to her house, pay him well and then he would make arrangements for her to enter the Institute. She considered me unnatural. I can understand her point of view, she lives according to the moral code by which family relationship is really a cornerstone, a defense and a support. As she sees it, I am of course quite wrong. A person living in the Middle Ages would certainly have striven to get her the best, even under completely absurd conditions, because he would have recognized their blood relationship, and even if he did not care for her he would have drained himself dry. I don't live by this code. There is no way I can help Aunt Claudia. You will answer: death, agony, your own aunt; I understand, it is painful to watch suffering. I admit that things are as they are. I would have acted the same had it been my own mother. Next month I am retiring from affairs. I never wrote to you about it: in ten days I am having a child and at present I am in a rest home before labor begins. So this month it is not even possible for me to

look after my aunt's household affairs. Write to our
other relations. . . .

She wrote to her colleague in the office for public prosecution at Moscow:

DEAR COMRADE TOMSKY,
   I left without a chance to speak to you. You will be
in charge of all the business which I had to leave unfinished. I am worried about the murder case of the
doctor from Odessa, Fränkel. Katsapov is threatened
with the supreme penalty. Look into it carefully.

Outside, the rain dripped. The wind glanced against the
windows in wet drops of rain. A dark glass reflected the table,
the books and papers lying there, a lamp, and a woman sitting
at the table. A car carried the letters into the dark. And she
began writing in the empty notebook:

   Yesterday I was shown a room in this house where
the Masons used to meet, and in the library I found
some Masonic books, left by the old landowners like
everything else in the house. I read a book dedicated to
"the Grand Master, the Masters, the Wardens and
Brethren of the most ancient and worthy brotherhood of
the Freemasons of Great Britain and Ireland," countries where, it seems, Freemasonry had its origin. It was
a book about "the salt of the earth, the light of the
world and the fire of the universe," as a certain Phila-
lethes described the Masons; they were the masters of the
"highest mysteries," a new Rosicrucian brotherhood. In
this book there are a large number of mysterious words
and innuendos and half the words are written with
capital letters: Brethren, He, Conscience, Light, Night,
Sky. Apparently all this was once very awe-inspiring and
seemed extremely intelligent. It struck me as being
nothing more than a foolish collection of senseless
words. It's all empty, dead, rubble. But all this had a
life of its own. A hundred years ago a woman may have
come to this house for solitude before a confinement.
She would have been met at the threshold with the

bread and salt of welcome, or in some similar way. Her
lawful husband would be with her. Bedraggled serfs
would have run all over the estate driving away black
cats and hens so that they would not cross her path.
The local priest must have spent a whole day indoors
so that he would not meet the lady unawares, and the
lady herself would not have been just a lady but a
princess, a countess or a baroness. Probably all the mirrors in the house were examined to make sure they
would not fall and break. The same serfs probably
hunted mice all over the house, so that the countess
would not see a mouse and there would be no birthmark
of a mouse stamped on the body of the future child.
The room where the Masonic meetings took place is a
room like any other, paneled in oak, in "Gothic style,"
as I read in the Masonic book, a dark room with
fascist swastikas, nothing out of the ordinary, a bit
dusty, and the lady will have passed the room in trepidation, for this, if you please, was inhabited by the
Reason in person, with a capital letter—the Reason of
the Masons! Demons, demonic omens, and conjura-
tions surrounded the lady on all sides, crept out of
dark corners at her, from under the bed, from the
windows, and even in the lady herself two demons must
certainly have taken up their abode—God and the devil,
registered like passports in military departments. The
lady was oppressed by these arbiters of fate. She had
no peace even in her sleep: suddenly she might dream
of a black cat. And with the lady of the house was the
master of the house—a Mason, an officer. While the
lady was pregnant he slept with the parlormaid.

Yes. It was all like that. It has all died away!

There was a knock at the door: the bath was ready. They
laid out the towels. The way to the bathroom lay past the
billiard room. All the guests were gathered in this room and
the door was open. She tried to pass the door unobserved.
Once again she could not fall asleep by eleven. Her candles
burned till after midnight. The forest, the wind and the rain
all rustled. She lay without a book, her hands under her
head, with motionless eyes.

The chauffeur had brought a briefcase containing a bottle of vodka and some books from friends in Moscow. After eleven, those who liked to drink retired to the Masonic lodge. There were three of them. They came in their dressing gowns with candles. They brought the vodka with them, together with some cucumber and salt. Not a word was spoken about Freemasonry or the place where the bottle party was being held. They had chosen the room simply because it had no windows and so the night porter could not see in and register a complaint. They drank standing up, gossiping in whispers, blissfully, boyishly.

"The public prosecutor Antonova," said one, "is a serious-minded butterfly if ever there was one, and here she is with a tummy. I heard about her in Moscow. She's as hard as nails, the daughter of a working man, a worker originally herself. She entered the Party from the Komsomol, the Party set her to study law, and she became a ferocious public prosecutor. But the main thing is she's a good-looking young woman and yet not in the least spoiled. They never even thought of her as a woman. And now suddenly she's pregnant. She passed the billiard room tonight on her way to her bath and was embarrassed."

"And who is her husband?" asked a second.

"No one knows. There is no husband."

The third drinker was the engineer and he said with some spirit:

"I don't know what kind of a public prosecutor she is. I never heard anything about her. And I don't know what her life has been like. But it's obvious that she has been unfortunate. If she had a family, someone would have brought her here. If she had a home of her own, she would never have left it at a time like this. And I draw the following conclusions. We are all members of the Party here, and we must treat her well and be attentive and friendly toward her. . . . She's lovely and she is alone. . . ."

"Shall we have another one?" asked the second drinker.

"Oh, the engineer is becoming quite lyrical."

They drank. They finished their drinks. Finally they crept quietly back to their rooms so that the stairs would not creak.

All night the rain poured, the wind howled and the forest stirred. She lay a long time with her arms under her head and her eyes motionless. The candles melted and twinkled. The night was empty of sound.

And it rained all day.

She wrote all the morning in her notebook from Constantinople.

Yes. It was all like that and it is all dead and gone now! . . .

My life has always been passed in such a way that now is perhaps the first time that I have been able to think about—how shall I put it—human instincts and my own in particular. I never had the time to think of them. And it is a fact that now for the first time I am really free, because it is a fact that I never had any spare time before. However shameful it is to admit it, even the child for whose sake I am writing this will only be mine because I never had any free time. I only began to think seriously about the child when it started to move! And this forced me to think about instinct—thoughts which led me back to my own childhood. I was ten years old when the revolution broke out and my father took a couple of shotguns to fight in the Kremlin. Our house on the Presna became the regional headquarters where nothing was talked about or done except as it affected the revolution, and we all went hungry. At twelve years old I was a member of the Komsomol and doing social work for the Party. I studied at a seven-year school, my thoughts were all taken up with study, with my courses and my work in the Komsomol, so that I had no time to read anything except the *Komsomol Gazette* and even that only in snatches, because I was always aching for sleep. In 1920 my father was killed at Perekop and, very foolishly, I took a job as nursemaid to some neighbors until I was taken on at the three-year school. I studied at Rabfac.* And again I never had a moment to spare. The Komsomol took me off working at the machines. The offices of the district Party committee became my

* An abbreviation for "Workers' Faculty."—TRANS.

flat. I devoured the *Komsomol Gazette* from cover to cover, because I had to put into action in real life all that was written down in the newspaper, which became the criterion of everything that touched my life and my affairs. And again I never had a spare moment. It is hardly necessary to write further because this sort of thing continued all through my life. I always entered heart and soul into my professional affairs—whether it was a week of mobilization for shock workers in the country, an inquiry about a drunken girl who belonged to the Komsomol, or, as now, the work in Constantinople.

It was not haphazardly that I wrote yesterday about the lady with her God, her devil and her Masons. I feel embarrassed to mention this to my future child, but I must write more about my friend B.'s dog. The child quickened in me at night and I woke up. It is impossible to express this in words. The ecstasy approaches horror: it is a simultaneous sensation of life and death, of joy approaching physical sensation, of shame approaching tears, and at the same time I wanted to leap out of bed and telephone and tell anyone how at that moment, five minutes ago, a new human life had begun to move inside me, a life which had never existed before, which could never be repeated, which was unique and would be lived in a new epoch, in a classless society, without class distinctions—a society to which I had devoted my life. This happened on the eve of a rest day. I had a telephone call, and I was told to go on important business and report to the country house of Comrade B., about twenty-five miles away, and a car was sent for me. I arrived in the morning and stayed until dinner. Comrade B. spent the time looking over the report and all the while he was irritated with the members of his household. Their bitch was due to have a litter in a few days and was exasperating the owners. They had just got settled in the house, built a sty, a cellar, a fence, planted flowers and trees, and the dog burrowed under the house, the cellar, the fence, the sty and the flower beds, each time in a new place, bent on preparing a den for her litter. They kept driving the bitch from place to place and filling in her holes, while she gazed at them with sorrowful eyes and started all over again. They shouted at her. And suddenly I got indignant at the inhumanity of human beings, very seriously indignant, without understanding where this very real anger came from—and I have not forgotten that bitch to this day. I still remember her eyes and I grow hot with anger when I think of those holes filled up again with earth.

I have not mentioned the lady and the bitch casually. From the time when I could actually feel the child I have been living in burning shame and with a physical sensation of joy. And more. My every action, every action of those about me, every line of print I read, cause me to ask the question: by what instinct is this, that, or the other action stimulated? At first I was oppressed by my awareness of these instincts which fell on me with the whole weight of all that was unintelligible to me in myself and which had so far gone unrecognized. I sat with my books and a pencil in my hand, while I studied for page after page the instincts which stimulated the actions of different people. There are a great number of instincts and they are of many different kinds, but they can be classified. I worked right through Tolstoy's *War and Peace,* beginning on the first page with the feudal discussion on international politics and Kuragin's feudal stinginess. It appears that Tolstoy operated principally through biological instincts clad in feudal dress. Feudalism left more instincts intact than capitalism. And this is what emerges and is my reason for writing all this—there are still very few socialist and communist instincts. I worked through various contemporary communist authors—it appears that these communists and their communist pages are sometimes stimulated by these decrepit, stone-bronze cavemen instincts, and so one is amazed that they should be communists. There are still very, very few communist instincts which would really stimulate communist affairs and actions. This is understandable. We are very young. We are surrounded left and right by the demons of the lady and the Masons and we do not know how to distinguish their instincts from the healthy instinct of the bitch, which Comrade B., his wife and his children were trampling underfoot. My son must live without demons and be unafraid of bitches—no, more precisely, he must be unafraid of a bitch's instincts. I am really shamed to tears by my unintelligible joy at the creation of a little man and at the same time I am not in the least ashamed to tell the world about it. I control myself at the dictates of custom and decency (also instincts), while in fact I long to tell everyone about the unintelligible and exalted condition which is called the birth of a man—both of a man and of mankind, though epochs of human development dress people up in the stone age or as feudal Freemasons!

Apart from the exceptions, friendships occur among people because subconsciously the two individuals who enter into a friendship feel not only a social but also a biological compatibility. Kretschmer's theory, which in fact was originated before Kretschmer by the Russian professor Gannushkin, is of course sound. It poured with rain for two days running, everyone stayed in, they made mutual confessions, read the news aloud, held concerts, engaged in battles of billiards. She followed the doctor's instructions and went for walks every day, in the rain, among the wet leaves, and these walks sometimes lasted five hours. Ivan Fedorovich Surovtsev, the mechanical engineer, always accompanied her. They evolved a route, along the path through the leaves downhill toward the river, and then by a field path on the river's edge to the village and back. Nature was weary in autumn, lonely and silent, and only the sound of a titmouse in the forest came to them from time to time. The village over the river melted into cottages, sties and corncribs. They walked side by side and Ivan Fedorovich talked most. He was in a lyric mood, although this seemed rather incongruous with his huge shoulders, bony forehead and rough hair style—his hair looked as prickly as a hedgehog. He joked and never finished anything he said. He spoke a great deal about mechanical engineering and about that aspect of industrialism which did not exist in Russia where new factories are being built, were creating an industry independent of Europe and America; he spoke at length about the "wisdom" of the machine, he spoke most eagerly about his visits to Germany and America, where he had completed his studies. In a jocular way he reminisced about his meetings with famous Party members, reporting their conversations, making character sketches, taking them down a little. And incidentally he gave away only a little about himself. He had been eighteen when the revolution began and was already working in a factory in Sormov. He was twenty-two when he was demobilized as a divisional commander and entered a higher technical school in Rabfac. He was twenty-four when he first read Pushkin and discovered the arts of literature, painting and music. He was twenty-nine when the Party set him the task of learning mechanical engineering and putting this industry on its legs after a visit he made to Europe for this purpose. He said in passing that he had been married twice and on both occasions without success. They took their walks in the morning and in the evening. In the evening the wet earth sank like an orphan into the gloom and seemed to descend into the loneliness of the desert. They gave no external signs of friendship. They hardly gave the impression of an incipient friendship.

The other guests were insistent, and so she gave a talk on Soviet criminological policy. Every measure taken by the Soviet power was immediately reflected in the condition of crime. By observing crime, its evolution and intensity, it was possible to see as in a distorting mirror the whole development and history of Soviet power. In 1918 there was a wave of crime when, after the nationalization of land, factories, plants and banks, some merchants, landowners, factory owners and members of the upper classes faked legal papers, antedating them to 1916 or 1915, and they sold nationalized property to foreigners including even Estonians and Finns, and people who had become naturalized in Poland and Latvia. The introduction of special police detachments and guards led to the discovery of a new criminal element—a large number of railway officials who up to this time had never been petty tradesmen. The talk was given in the smoking room after supper. When she had finished she was asked to describe a few unusual cases. She described bandits, their moral code and way of life, their "honesty," their professional affairs, and how the sternest measures were meted out to them in order to defend society, and she said she had often felt sorry that they had to be shot. She described saboteurs, their upbringing, education, manners, and how they discussed morality and honesty, and she said she felt no pity for them and had no qualms about asking for the supreme penalty.

She continued to make notes in her notebook.

. . . but the old instincts are outworn like old clothes, they no longer fit or correspond, because their basis, the recognition and social correlation of forces, is gone. I was nineteen when I first lay with a man. Formerly, a woman said of herself, "gave myself to." This expression is dead now and has no foundation. I was not conscious of being specifically a virgin or a woman, I was a person, a member of a party, a worker, and if my work demanded it I was in command over men and women alike, bearded old men and old women as well as my fellow comrades. I developed later than my girl friends. They told me about their liaisons. I understood that fundamentally it was a pleasure and it satisfied a genuine physical need. I became curious and biological urges awakened in me. I decided to have a man before this actually happened. I was studying then and was occupied with lessons and my Komsomol duties until eleven o'clock at night. I was attracted by one of my comrades, but he was very busy and we seldom met. He was the second with whom I had an affair. He began coming to see me and when I told him I was no longer a virgin the reason for our meetings became obvious to us both. The first was a colleague, about fifteen years older than I, a regional instructor. Our way home lay in the same direction, I asked him in for a moment, on a business matter, to get some literature. I had made up my mind but I spent three days warding him off. He used to come to me after eleven. I spent three days without sleeping, my thoughts covered in wool. On the third night, toward morning when it was already light, it happened. It was very repulsive. He was only with me once after that. I drove him away. And it was six months later that I told my other friend, quite casually, that I was not a virgin. He asked no questions. We did not of course speak of love. I was content with him, kept waiting for him, but he was very much occupied and came very seldom. Our meetings seemed genuine to me. I missed him.

It was all like that. But—this is what was fundamental.

I felt very ashamed for my human dignity. This is how I reasoned: when a man is a bachelor at thirty he is either a degenerate, or unfit, or has ties with one woman or many women, and this is his own private affair and in no way a matter touching society in general —whether he legalizes his affairs with women or not is a moral question. As for a woman who is unmarried at twenty or thirty, the time of woman's subjection is over, and I repeated my reasoning about the man, for in what is a woman worse than a man? How then should one bring oneself to the debasing, shaming condition which is called— Oh, it's revolting even to write it! I never thought of a child, as I took it for granted that there would not be a child. Family life with its "own," "personal" saucepans and curtains made me laugh—what clannish "own," "personal" corners and husbands could there be when the whole world was mine! The family as an economic unit is dead. To be in a stupid "psychological" dependence on a husband, as happened in the case of my friends, to be under the most stupid control of a husband and to pay attention to his "individual" peculiarities seemed to me an unnecessary yoke. In all the novels I had read and in the personal family relationships I found around me, I saw falsehood left us as a legacy by the old family system and its morality, which stinks of corruption. I did not see a single couple who were completely true to one another; the majority of them swore sexual fidelity and lied. I did not see a single pair who belonged only to each other. At best they were faithful to each other during the years they lived together, but either he or she had had other liaisons before marriage, and once this had happened it might happen again. The morality of family life is not only dead, but it stinks of decomposition. Lies, slavery and an insistence on something which no longer exists are the principal remnants of family life. I didn't want to

lie or to put myself in a false position. The need for
sexual sensations sometimes attacks one with such violence that a man may become almost a maniac; every
normal human being knows this. To live with a healthy
body seemed natural to me. Not to lie seemed natural.
Not to place oneself or another in a dependent position
also seemed natural. The second man I knew came to
see me very seldom. I told him when I got to know a
third; he seemed to take the statement as the most
normal thing in the world, but he stopped coming to
see me. I decided he had the mentality of a serf-
owner and did not torment myself. I had nothing to
feel ashamed of. Of course it was all pleasure. But one
must not forget that we were all very busy—we were
each occupied with our own affairs and all of us were
occupied with the enormous business of the revolution.
If such affairs were normal, they did not take up much
time or put everything else into the shade. The principal place in my life was occupied by communal work,
because this was a natural condition for me and I
wished it to be so, and also because I was a cog in the
great machine, and could not immediately be replaced,
because I was duty bound to my colleagues and to communism. I bore myself proudly. My sexual affairs were
my own personal concern in which I allowed no one to
meddle. They took up little room in my life. I remember how early in the revolution I was at a meeting in
the Miussky streetcar depot, where they were organiz-
ing recruits for the Komsomol—I don't now remember
for what reason—when a conductor stepped up to me
and said sternly: "I'll tell you, comrade, what our
trouble is here. We can't marry our women workers.
What could be better both for them and for us? We
live next to each other, do the same work, but we can't
marry. They've learned how to order their passengers
about on the streetcars and they know all the rules.
Some of us have married conductresses and suffer for it.
They treat their husbands like passengers—the least
thing and they whistle for the police!" I thought then
with pride that I too was a conductress, a commander,
a person! The demons who surrounded the lady and
even dwelt in her as God and devils have departed, or

more accurately they have been exorcized. The Christian virtue of "turning the other cheek," the mortification of the flesh, monasticism—that was not our kind of courage. If the lady was cramped by demons, she was also free from affairs; men worked for her and she could surrender to sex. Of the feudal slave it is hopeless to speak—she was oppressed by both demons, work, and men alike. Of course, instincts protect the human being. I saw women during the revolutionary years who were "protected" by past instincts. They did not understand when they painted their lips that they were making "chattels" of themselves, they did not suspect that in the days of socialism they were objects of barter surviving from capitalist times. Women of the class which died out during the revolution, living in the wreck of the old morality, feared to lose their lives— sex came first in the feudal tradition—and these women hastened to safeguard their right to live by sex and by sensuality. Sex, besides being a trade, became their profession. Their instincts ruined them. We, the women of the revolution, were never "chattels." We were free from all demons. My studies and my work gave me knowledge, but not sensation. Neither music, nor literature, nor art were necessary elements of my ego. My aesthetic and emotional world was very narrow; it was not, in fact, developed at all. In my naïveté I demanded of literature only political realism, agitation and description. From art I demanded manufactured pictures, photographs of life. Music seemed a waste of time. Sex and my sex life, indeed, I approached rationalistically, almost as if it were a hygienic medical undertaking. Some of my friends even made sexual feelings a matter of diversion. I realized that that was the lot of the women of a class which was dying out. I never did this. I was a public prosecutor, and it never came off with me, it was beneath me and my work. In fact, I never even thought of it. And I never thought of a child. I knew this could never happen to me. I did not have the time to spend on a child. A child was outside my experience. This was an axiom with me. I had two abortions. This was a three-day illness for which one waited one's turn. It did not arouse any special feelings.

I made my way to the hospital and warned my colleagues that I would be absent three days for an abortion. No one asked me any questions. It was all quite natural.

I guessed I was pregnant on the train for Central Asia, where I was going to make an investigation. Tashkent, Samarkand and Alma-Ata all put me to work and I did not have a single moment to myself. I woke at seven, at eight I was already at work among strangers—a public prosecutor—and at twelve I returned to my room and fell into a dead sleep. Sometimes I was in charge of inquests at night. The Central Asiatic trains are slow, and if I ever rested, if I slept off my weariness till I was in a state of mind to think about myself, it was only in trains with the wheels rattling under the carriage. In two months' time I returned to Moscow. The doctors told me it was too late for an abortion, which might now prove fatal to me. In a month's time the baby quickened. It was an explosion of instincts, instincts which I had never suspected in myself. I began to check the whole of my past life. Everything which I had done in connection with my work remained as before. But everything which had happened in my sexual experience, or which had not happened, I raked over in my memory and it took on a different emphasis. The father of my child . . . I never experienced a greater outrage against humanity! It was a casual affair, binding no one to anything, a "business," "friendly" affair during days in which sex got in my way. On returning from Asia and learning that I was to have the child, I did not telephone him. He was not a close enough friend, someone I could take into my confidence about my private life, and I needed neither moral nor financial assistance from him. He was very young, healthy and even handsome, and this was sufficient to put my mind at rest about the physical condition of my son. But when the child began to move, when I was overcome with sensations of strange happiness, I often put my hand to the telephone to lift it and speak to him. After all, it was *my* child! It was *his* child! I did not know if I had the right to keep to myself the happiness I was experiencing from him. The child was just as much an accident for me as for

him. I had known death: it is something horrible,
antagonistic to nature. I tormented myself when I saw
death, and could not eat—that is understandable and
has often been described and experienced by many during the revolution. Well, just as death is antagonistic to
human nature, and disgusting, so birth is natural, joyful
and happy—these words are too small because birth is
an enormous joy and an enormous happiness. I trans-
ferred my own sensations to the father. And I did not
know whether I had the right to conceal this happiness
from him. I wanted nothing else from him. And I telephoned him. Behind our trivial conversation I wanted
to catch his tone, find out what tone he expected of
me—whether perhaps he would guess about the child.
Of course, this was foolish and "feminine." He assumed
the tone of a lover. Then I told him I was pregnant. I
could see through the telephone wires how he became
completely confused. After a pause, he said in a
stranger's voice that he would come at once. He arrived,
greeted me in a businesslike way and stood with his legs
apart, swaying slightly throughout our short interview.
Our conversation was very brief. He asked almost angrily why I had not telephoned him for such a long
time. Three months ago an abortion could have been
performed quite harmlessly. He asked me whether I
really was pregnant and whether I had worked out
quite accurately that he was the father. He had already
telephoned a medical wizard of some sort who would
undertake to perform the abortion out of friendship. I
realized that our twofold death—my death and the
death of my child—were more convenient than the birth
of a human being. With the blood ringing in my ears,
with an intensity of loathing I had never experienced
before and never will, I said only the four words "Get
out, you beast!" In all my life no one had so insulted
and hurt me as he did then, and not only me but all
humanity—so I reasoned—in the shape of the little
being who was as yet unborn and whose father he was.
After all, his mother had given birth to him! The words
"holy," "a shrine" are antiquated, but I can find no others. I felt my body was—yes—holy, not because it was
mine but because a human being was growing there. But

I—how was I myself any better? Into what agony of shame and irremediable pain did the memory of "medical hygiene" cast me! My body was more pure, honest and wise than I—it was and still is, since it is preparing for the birth of a person. I was ashamed of my thoughts and memories. Sex is pleasure? Yes, in birth. Sex is the creation of a human being. It is not that I need material support or the support of reasoned advice, either in the clan or in the feudal manner—but I need a man, a husband, the father of my child, who will understand everything I feel, to whom alone I can describe this, whose sex will be as holy to me as mine to him. It can't be that the birth of his child is a matter of indifference to the father! The bitch tore a hole beneath all the sties to make a den for her litter. It is precisely because I have no husband, no "den," that I have come here for the last days before my labor, so that I would not be burdened with everyday cares, and not be myself a burden on anyone, and be with people who are strangers though comrades. This is more than a punishment. It is nature avenging herself. How deeply I need a close friend now—how can I explain?—a friend whose hand I could put on my belly joyfully and without shame, so that he can feel my child move and be glad with me, who will love the future child with me. I have come to this house because I am completely alone in the face of the birth of the little one moving inside me. I came to think things out, to punish myself. . . .

The weather changed. After the rain there came a wide and blue sky, golden harvest fields, the vermilion of mountain ash, autumn, silence and peace. The nights shone starry in the enormous expanse of sky. A leaf rustling underfoot could be heard many steps away.

She wrote notes to people in town.

Her first:

Katya, I feel very well, walk a lot, sleep well, take a bath every day, eat a lot of fruit, and the doctor examines me every other day. Please tell me if the little bonnets we talked about are ready. I read an advertise-

ment in the *Moscow Evening News* about a pram; have
you bought the pram yet or not? If you have, write and
tell me what it's like.

The second:

Katya, I feel very well, walk, sleep, eat fruit, take
baths, have medical examinations. It's very quiet here
and the people are very nice. I read a paper and heard
two, one about a congress of authors, another on Soviet
mechanical engineering. You don't say if the blanket was
ready. I'll need it when I leave the hospital. I left the
name of the director on a slip of paper. Don't forget
to telephone me frequently at the hospital and only
send the things the doctors allow.

The third:

Dear Comrade Yurisova, I keep interrupting you at
your work. I'm keeping Katya informed by each mail
about my health. I've read and studied all the books on
maternity and infancy which I brought with me. As for
the list of books I left in the top right-hand drawer of
my desk, if you can't buy them, please stop by at the
Lenin Library, as we agreed.

The fourth:

Dear Comrade Yurisova, you say the house painters
have started at last. I think even if it's more expensive
I ought to have my bedroom done in white oil paint.
That would be best for the baby. I'm quite calm about
the idea of the labor; I can't imagine the pain and so
don't think of it and don't feel nervous. There are still
five days to go, but I wouldn't mind if it happened
today. Everything is quite ready. I love my future son
very much! Forgive all the trouble I'm being. Katya
doesn't say anything about a nurse. . . .

After her paper on criminology under the Soviets she
had the following conversation with Ivan Fedorovich Surovtsev. It was on one of the days when the sun had returned,

in the morning, with a light frost underfoot. They were walking over the brittle leaves through the forest. He picked some "tartar earrings," the fruit of the spindle tree, and gave them to her. For himself he gathered a branch of rowan-berries and nibbled at them, grimacing. He flung the berries away.

"You were talking about the influence of our social changes on crime," he said. "Do you take into account the circumstances peculiar to our epoch? Nearly all the males of our generation were in the war and saw death. A man who has been under fire and has fired with his rifle when he was himself a target can never forget it. When a man is under fire he experiences such a sense of isolation as can be felt in no other circumstances. He brings the sense of this loneliness back into his everyday life. And a whole generation has felt this. . . ." He was silent for a moment and then he said unexpectedly, "Have you no husband?"

"No," she answered.

"You are very sweet and good, and, if you will forgive me, sympathetic," said Surovtsev, embarrassed.

They were on the outskirts of the wood. She turned back sharply over the rustling leaves. He followed her.

"I have been married twice," said Surovtsev quietly.

It was obvious that he was ready to embark on a long story. She walked on, gazing down and seeming not to listen. He grew silent. The leaves rustled underfoot.

And her labor began four days before the expected date. The first pains began at eleven o'clock, immediately after she went to bed and the electricity was switched off. She went downstairs and phoned Moscow for an automobile. No one answered her call. She phoned Comrade Yurisova and was told she was at the theater. Then she phoned the empty house again and waited a long time, but no one answered. She went to the nurse on duty and asked her to call the head of the rest home. She lived in another wing and the nurse went away to fetch her. Half-undressed, Ivan Fedorovich Surovtsev rushed downstairs and phoned Moscow. He shouted into the instrument and his voice was threatening:

"Give me the number at once, every moment is urgent, quickly!"

He called another number, spoke uninterruptedly:

"Vasily Ivanovich, a favor! . . . I've ordered my automobile, it's on the way, I need it urgently, I'm afraid of a puncture, or some hitch, I'll explain later, I beg you, send me yours, immediately! Thank you, I'll expect it! If mine gets here first, I'll send yours back en route, it will follow us. Thank you!"

"The car will be here in twenty minutes," he said to her. "Come and get dressed."

He talked and gave orders. He took her by the elbow with his left hand and put his right around her waist to help her walk.

"I won't be a moment. Just get my things. I'll be back to give you a hand."

He flung his things anyhow into a suitcase and put on his tie askew. He went into her room, picked up her case, took the books and papers off the table and laid them in the bottom of the case, opened the cupboard and the drawer in the bedside table, forgetting nothing. He bent low, put her shoes on, and laced them. He gave her her coat and tried to button it up. The head of the home and the nurse were not much use. He took both their cases. The headlights of the car threw their beam on the house from a distance. They went out onto the porch. He flung the cases to the chauffeur. He clasped her by the shoulders and pressed her head against his chest, stroking her cap.

He called to the chauffeur.

"To Moscow, to Taganka, quickly! Oh, hell!"

The chauffeur bounded off into the darkness, the car rattled through a deep puddle. He called out:

"Gently! Oh, hell! . . ."

They did not say a word to each other all the way. When he saw that she was in pain, he pressed her head to him, unreasoning, helplessly, and gently stroked her cap. In the vestibule of the maternity home, which was accustomed to everything on earth and particularly to labor, they were met by a worthy old official who gave instructions and said to Surovtsev:

"Put your wife on the seat for the present. I'll tell the

house surgeon, he'll examine her, and stay here, I'll give you her things. Give me her ticket."

She gave Surovtsev her handbag. He opened it and began fumbling through the papers. The old man went away. He came back and said dryly, "This way, please."

Surovtsev helped her to get up, embraced her and kissed her brow. She embraced him and put her head on his shoulder. She lifted her face. Her eyes were full of tears. She kissed him. The old man led her upstairs. In half an hour the old man brought out a bundle of her clothes, her handbag with documents and money, handed over her coat and said:

"I've arranged for her to go to the labor ward. You can expect a son or a daughter tomorrow. Call up or come yourself at about eleven."

Surovtsev phoned at eight o'clock in the morning. He was told to phone again in an hour. In an hour's time he was told that a son had been born, weighing nine pounds two ounces. After leaving the hospital Surovtsev went to his large, newly decorated, empty and unlived-in flat. It was already approaching three in the morning. Surovtsev woke up his old mother, gave her the suitcases and said:

"One of them has a woman's things in it. Have a look and see what has to be cleaned, washed or ironed."

He took the suitcase into his mother's room. Very soon she returned with a pile of books on maternity and child welfare, and a notebook in a Venetian binding. Surovtsev put the books on his desk. He opened the notebook, read the first lines and carefully put it away in a drawer. He made himself some coffee in the kitchen and stood waiting for it to boil. Then he sat down at the desk in his study and read the books on child welfare as he drank his coffee. Then he wrote. He did not know it was morning and had grown light. It was eight o'clock. He phoned the hospital. At eleven o'clock he was at the hospital again and handed over to a new official, a little younger than the other but just as slow and dignified, a basket of flowers and some butter, eggs, bread, biscuits, apples and pears, and he explained that all this was for Antonova. The man said, "Wait a moment," with dignity, and disappeared behind a door. At this point a bevy of nurses passed, each carrying two newborn infants. The official re-

turned after some time and brought a note. It was scrawled
on a scrap of paper with crooked letters:

> My dear, of course I went through it but I'm happy
> now. Though he's a son and not a daughter, he's just
> like me—dark! I love him. Thank you for the things.

And on the other side of the sheet in childish large letters:

> As soon as I'm put in a ward I'll write you a long
> letter about it. Please bring me some soap, toothpaste,
> a toothbrush, and my papers.
>
> Yours,
MARIA

Surovtsev came again at four o'clock. Besides the soap,
toothpaste and papers, he brought a Thermos of hot coffee.
It was his own idea. She answered with a letter:

> Thank you very, very much! I don't know where to
> put all this mountain of food! My son and I have beaten
> the record—10 pounds 5 ounces. No one else had any-
> thing so big during the night. I won't go into details
> about the labor. It's an absolutely inhuman method of
> giving birth to humanity. But the infant is there and
> makes up for everything. I shall start nursing him at
> twelve tonight. He's red with black hair. I'm not re-
> turning your Thermos as I've nothing to put the coffee
> into. I've a thousand desires—to lie on my side, to sit
> up, to sing. I adore the infant though he's still ugly and
> comic and has only been alive for seven hours and
> thirty-five minutes! I want to get home and to see you!
> They don't let you go till the ninth day. Such an age! . . .

Surovtsev came home, and again he made himself some
coffee. He drank a whole saucepanful, sat down to his desk
to write and fell asleep. Sleepily he moved over to the couch
and slept till five in the morning. At five he sat down to
write. He was constantly rewriting, spoiling many sheets of
paper and then doing them over again:

COMRADE ANTONOVA, my dear friend,

One cannot tell everything about one's life at one go, and probably it can never be told, since to describe it all one has to relive it. And besides, much in life and often the most important things cannot be realized through words nor be expressed by words. So much I have lived through! When I look back it seems like a thousand years! And each one of us when he looks back seems a patriarch. All last night—you must forgive me for this—I sat reading your books on the rearing of children. Why I love you and why your son seems to me like my own I cannot explain in words. Two things, two states seemed terrible to me in my life. One I mentioned to you when we were talking—loneliness. How can I explain it? I'm a communist, that is a collectivist, obviously, but as soon as I'm left alone between four walls or even in a wood with dead leaves underfoot, I feel loneliness and my isolation terrifies me. I feel afraid without people around me, though I know that a man sometimes needs to be alone and realizes himself fully alone. One should not feel loneliness when with a woman because with a woman, something arises which gives a man the sense of immortality. When I was with a woman I still felt my isolation because I did not feel honesty. And dishonesty is the second state of which I have been afraid all my life: the feeling of dishonesty when together with a woman, and from there—loneliness. I was married twice. My first wife was a comrade, a member of the Party: we fought together in the civil war. My second wife was a remnant of the past, a musician, ingratiating as a kitten. The first turned out to be more masculine, more of a Red Army man, than myself, and the other I was constantly discovering in bed with various poets. Neither the one nor the other wanted children, and both were ill. I was lonely with them and had the sense of dishonesty. Dishonesty was the basis of our family life: the first was biologically dishonest by refusing children and the second was in addition dishonest as regards fidelity in family life. I don't wish to whitewash myself—I have only realized this just now. As far as I myself was concerned, my relations with my first wife were those which my second bore toward me,

and with my second wife I was in the position of my
first. That is all. I observed you and saw myself as I am.
A child! Both my wives always had abortions.

My proposals to you are concrete. You live alone.
My mother, an excellent old lady, lives with me. I have
a room for the nursery which gets all the sun. My
mother will help you. I will take upon myself all the
cares of everyday life. We are both communists. I have
no children. I am quite alone. Don't accuse me of inso-
lence but I love your son as much as I love you, his
mother. I can only repeat that I cannot now express
all my feelings in words. You never spoke to me about
yourself—I only saw and felt you. For this reason I
think that I am not mistaken and so I turn to you with
this request.

Yours,
IVAN SUROVTSEV

Ivan Fedorovich put this letter into an envelope and
sealed it, having copied it without a single correction at nine
o'clock in the morning. He set out for the hospital. He took
with him soap, a toothbrush, a fountain pen and the letter.
He gave the official the soap, the paste, the paper and
some food, but the letter remained unopened in his pocket
for three days. It was only on the fourth day that he brought
it, still unopened, and entrusted it to the official to be handed
over to Comrade Antonova. During these three days Ivan
Fedorovich turned his flat upside down. Meanwhile Comrade
Antonova wrote the following letter on paper he had brought
for her:

They took me to the home at night. There was no
time for anything. To begin with, there was only the
night and the first masculine hands caressing me in a
human way, then the white circles of signposts, each crying "Quickly, quickly!" Somewhere far away in the past
there was the old house, the corner room, the rustle of
the forest. Now there was only one word, "quickly," a
feeling of embarrassment in front of the chauffeur, a
desire to enter the large door which would open without

a moment's delay and over it in heavy letters there were the words MATERNITY WARD.

Then everything was very simple, no one realizing that life was being divided into two halves which might never meet until the end. Yes, the division of a person into two individualities, two destinies, two people, one of which—myself—must overcome death.

A young man of some sort, a doctor, who didn't care, who didn't realize that he was watching the defeat of death, immortality, the birth of a man, took my pulse and examined me. A young girl of some sort filled in a form and began heating water. Actually they were not "some sort of," because one remembers them down to the last details, to the minutest particulars, to the tone of voice. You remember everything—how else! Because you don't think about it or feel it, it is outside you, far off, strange and cold. You hear only your own "I," which is dividing, you hear how outside you, something hidden from everyone and everything grows minute by minute, something which is just about to happen, which you can't describe, but which fills the whole world with itself—the actual feeling of a being about to be born, unknown even to me, though I love and will continue to love him all my life, and he will take my place.

There was not much pain. It began in the labor ward. Nine women lay screaming on nine beds. Nine women had come with their joys, sorrows, thoughts, their past and their whole lives. And each gave birth to another person that night, of another epoch, a new generation.

Long ago in my childhood (now it seems as if it happened in childhood), in my diary and notebook, I, like everyone else, dreamed of a person, in the days when I was still capable of falling in love, of a comrade and a man. I had many comrades. I almost entirely escaped that girlish period when this person is sought, found and personified by a certain profile, a certain name, written in large capitals. I never went through a time which other girls experience when this person is blotted out and diaries show the phrase: "There is no such person and the most senseless occupation in the world is to think that one can find him." I never sought such

a "person." I had friends. Such a "person" passed as
a fragmentary image through my life; my meetings and
my work and the fragments were lost. None of this
seemed strange, though in my childhood I too had such
pages in my diary about a "person" which remained
only half thought out and bore the stamp of inexperi-
ence. It must be a bad thing that I had scarcely any
adolescence. I thought of all this in my tossings and
turnings on the metal springs of the bed, and about the
indifference of the nurse who examined us one by one. I
wanted to come to grips with my pain and fear, quite
alone. It dragged at my back downward and mounted to
my heart. Like a wave, the pain grew big, rolled over
and suddenly retreated, only to return with increased
strength, catch hold of me and convulse me. And a kind
of twisted useless phrase, the remnant of intense feeling,
crawled into consciousness, out of the bedpan, the
vomit, the convulsions of myself and my neighbors—"in
the pangs of labor"—and it stuck in the brain, rever-
berating like the noise of a train, breaking off in the
middle of a letter, when the brain lost consciousness for
a while, and then a convulsion, a tossing "in the pangs,
in the pangs" and then, without words, in two sounds,
"Oh! Oh, oh, oh!" and to myself, "Steady! Steady!" The
night seemed unending. I did not see the coming of
dawn. In the morning light, the pain felt worse and I
felt more ashamed of the pain, at my helplessness in
this large public room. The beds were emptying, the
women were taken out more and more frequently and
nearly everyone was gone, and it seemed as if I were
alone in the whole world and it was frightening and
awkward to cry out alone—then my neck swelled, my
jaws clenched, my whole body bore downward, my
hands seized the bed, it became terrifying to madness,
to stupefaction. I called, "Nurse!" And I could not
restrain myself from screaming till someone came,
pushed the clothes back, looked, and I heard the calm
words: "Well done! It's all right, the little head is
showing now, mama, I can see the black hair!" And
suddenly I grew calm and suddenly understood that it
was now and only now that strength was needed and
self-confidence. I lay down on the stretcher and saw

the ceiling of the corridor retreating into the dark-blue
wall, the hospital sheet on my chest, the tall clumsy
tables of the labor room, and then I said quite calmly
and collectedly to the midwife: "The most important
thing is for the child to be all right!" And from that
point I no longer remember pain, I felt it only as
something necessary to help the child push out that silly
hairy little head, without hurrying, without listening to
what went on around, controlling by will power the
beginning of the climax of the spasms, gathering all
my strength and breathing full, so that it would be
calmer for the child. And suddenly it pulled down with
such force that it seemed as if it would throw me clean
off the operating table, tear me to shreds. The pulse beat
in my forehead, my heart beat, everything turned into
a convulsed mass—then it pulled down lightly, the belly
relaxed, and through closed eyes, clenched teeth, a cry
broke out, bold and healthy; and I saw a small,
wrinkled, red bundle, still tied to me, still retaining
the stains of my blood and body. And my first idea was
that out of the most inhuman a human being was born,
the man with a capital letter not to be found in children's books, and now felt concretely as mine—and a
Man. If the father could see this! If fathers could have
this experience! . . .

And then, when I understood the extent of birth, or
perhaps earlier, when it hurt and was terrifying, or
later, when women cried out overloud—having managed
the physical side, I couldn't manage my nerves; my head
throbbed, my pulse leaped, my eyes grew dry—then at
night, in the unending cries of women, the sense of time
was lost, and also the idea of one's own self, and it
seemed as if all this was I, yesterday, today and tomorrow, always it was I in labor, crying out: it was all
repeated, it is repeated and will continue from age to
age through the whole history of man. And this inhuman cry—neither cry nor wail, nor shriek, nor bellow
—the pain and the fear, and the newborn infants, all
alike, all crying: it seemed to me that all this was I.
I nursed all these crying infant boys, girls, dark and fair,
and couldn't get away, couldn't manage, had not

enough strength. At night my eyes grew dry and the bed was soaked in milk. And the idea of woman rose differently, as of a human being giving birth to human beings, and the feeling of injustice arose: why does death shake people and not birth, why is war an important social fact, and the birth of man, of humanity, a physiological act little deserving of attention or, in the opinion of an idiot, "the physiological tragedy of woman!"

And one thing more. Through our life, our manners and our epoch, the feudal conception of birth, blood and roots is vanquished and lost. I fought against them. Under the feudal system the woman came to the husband and was accepted into the family. I did not do that. I did not have a family which might in its roots give me the means to live. And apparently my race is not continuing but beginning—be-gin-ning. It is enclosed by a very narrow and restricted circle, by my son, who does not even have a father; but this race has an advantage, it does not look back but forward! . . .

Ivan Fedorovich Surovtsev sent his letter to Comrade Antonova. They went together to the registry office, to register the birth of the child, to give him the legal status of a Soviet citizen of the future classless society. They waited their turn in the line. Surovtsev read the notices. The registry office consisted of two offices and a waiting room. In one room they registered marriages and births, and in the other divorces and deaths. One night at home, after nursing the infant, Comrade Antonova looked through her notebooks. She tore out of the book in the Venetian binding everything she had written in the rest home, and burned these pages. And then she copied out what she had written in the hospital on the paper Surovtsev had brought her, into the book with the Venetian binding.

1933

ABOUT THE AUTHOR

BORIS ANDREYEVICH VOGAU, best known by the pseudonym Boris Pilnyak, was born in 1894, arrested in 1928, and is said to have died in a Russian concentration camp in 1942. He wrote numerous stories of the civil war and the era of militant communism. Pilnyak was unquestionably the most prominent literary figure in early post-revolutionary Russian fiction. His novel *The Naked Year* is regarded as the first major work of fiction depicting this period.

ABOUT THE TRANSLATOR

BEATRICE SCOTT is an Englishwoman with many translations from the Russian to her credit: Gogol's *Stories from St. Petersburg,* Dostoevsky's *Three Tales,* Tolstoy's *Kreutzer Sonata,* and, recently, Paustovsky's "The Telegram."